A MIND OF HER OWN!

It wasn't proper for a 25-year-old "spinster"
to reject the proposal of a highly eligible
young man. But lovely Violet Carpenter knew
that Henry Martin was not the man for her.
Living as she did in the small town of Ladykirk,
her chances of finding the love she desired
seemed very dim indeed.

Threatened by financial pressures, Violet decides
to take in overnight guests, and to seek a publisher
for a book of poems she has written. As she
opens herself to a new, exciting and ever-changing
world, she discovers that the nightingale,
a golden heirloom, is true to its legendary promise:
to sing for a true and lasting love.

"Humor and realism . . . genuine vitality.
A pleasant, nostalgic and accurate record of the
early 20th Century." *Best Sellers*

Avon Books by Agnes Sligh Turnbull

THE ROLLING YEARS

THE BISHOP'S MANTLE

THE KING'S ORCHARD

THE DAY MUST DAWN

GOLDEN JOURNEY

REMEMBER THE END

Crazy Chris

AGNES SLIGH TURNBULL

THE NIGHTINGALE

AVON
PUBLISHERS OF
DISCUS • CAMELOT • BARD

AVON BOOKS
A division of
The Hearst Corporation
959 Eighth Avenue
New York, New York 10019

First Printing, October, 1966
Third Printing, January, 1970

Printed in the U.S.A.

CHAPTER ONE

IT WAS an old town. Old maples along the main street, old lilac bushes in the back yards, old black stables along the alleys and old men chewing their quids contemplatively on the store steps. Of course there were old women too. Miss Sally Parr, who went to market with her basket every morning in a stiff starched sunbonnet in summer and a folded plaid shawl in winter, was, everyone agreed, ninety if she was a day. Much older was Becky Slade, the erstwhile seamstress, whose tongue had always been as sharp as her shears and more unregenerate. "I think the Lord's just plain forgot me," she was wont to say, "and as far as I'm concerned it's all right. I'm in no hurry."

But in spite of all this, the age of the town did not rest upon it like a melancholic blanket, as is the case with many old villages. Rather the years seemed to have enfolded it with a gentle mellowness by means of which the obstreperousness of each new generation as it came along was calmed and tamed.

One of the oldest houses there was an imposing gray stone which stood in an acre of land on one of the back streets of the village. It had been built by the first Squire Carpenter when stones and labor were cheap, so it rose now, solid, spacious and dignified from a wide, iron-fenced lawn. A white frame cornice, white window shutters and a porch with slender pillars, added much later, gave a softened, almost feminine touch to the otherwise austere architecture. At the far side, using most of the extra acreage, was an apple orchard, in recent years rather unkempt-looking except as just now, when the spring blossoms transfigured it.

The Carpenters had been important people in Ladykirk ever since the days when the first collection of houses had afforded a stopping place for the stage coaches between Fort Ligonier and Fort Pitt. There had been the Squires, father and son, then Eli, who had followed the trade his name indicated and become a fine builder of other people's houses. His son, Silas, however, had taken to books from his infancy, had gone to college by dint of family economy, even traveled a little on his first earnings, and finally, after his parents' death, established himself in the stone house with a city girl for a wife, and himself a teacher in the Mitford Academy for Young Ladies three miles away. With his horse and buggy he had driven the distance daily through all weathers and over all roads, maintaining a practically unbroken record of punctuality through the years, just as he had held his silly young students to a high level of excellence in their English and Latin. Everyone said he began to fail in health after his wife died. Even though he adored his daughter, Violet, who was left to him, the mainspring of his life seemed broken. He went on more slowly for five more years and then he, too, joined the majority on the sloping hill behind the town.

Now on this particular May morning, with the world breathing out sunshine and fragrance, the last of the Carpenter line came slowly down the stairway of the old house. She was a slight thing with gray eyes and a dimpled chin; two braids of brown hair were wound softly round her head, coronet fashion, with small irrepressible curls escaping above the ears. Her lips were full and sweetly shaped for laughter but they were not smiling now. They were, indeed, very grave as she reached the foot of the stairs and glanced briefly in the large mirror above the hatrack as though bidding herself good morning. She opened the front door, drew in deeply the blossom-scented air, stood for a minute listening to the doves' muted calling from the big oaks along the creek bank which edged the town just beyond the Green, and then walked slowly through the hall to the dining room.

This would have been an appealing spot to anyone who appreciated the marriage of comfort and beauty. It ran the width of the house behind the square parlor and the hall, and had always served both as an eating and a living room. At the end facing the orchard a great bowed, deepseated window afforded space for the dining table. The marble-topped sideboard with a deer's head crowning it stood at one side, and a tall polished cupboard with wide doors upon the other. Beyond in the main part of the room was a solid wall of books, a secretary which Eli,

6

the carpenter, had once made with his craftsman's skill, a full-length horsehair sofa opposite the fireplace, and a shorter one beneath the east window, an Empire reading table with a hanging lamp above it matching the one above the dining table, several sloping-backed rockers with carved arms and rose upholstering and two easy chairs designated in the furniture stores of that period as a "gentleman's" and a "lady's." Above the mantel hung a portrait of the first Squire Carpenter done probably by some itinerant artist, glad to exchange his talent for a fortnight or so of comfortable living. The likeness had evidently been excellent, for the picture had been handed down with care from father to son. The last of the line now stood for a moment, thoughtfully regarding it.

There was no doubt but that she—due to the strange processes of inheritance—resembled this far-away ancestor. The wavy hair, the wide-set gray eyes, the shape of the lips, the strong cleft chin, had all come down to her along with the house itself. As she watched the steady gaze of the portrait she felt she knew what his advice to her would be upon this day of decision. Even though the Carpenter name died out with her, the blood line must be carried on. She sighed, walked over to the swinging door which led to the kitchen and pushed it open.

"Good morning, Katie," she said.

The words were proper from mistress to servant, but the tone and the smile that went with them held the affection of equality.

Katie looked up from the stove.

"Oh, you're here," she said. "Well, sit you down and I'll bring your porridge."

"But Katie, how often do I have to tell you I don't *want* porridge! Just an egg, please!"

Katie went calmly on, ladling the oatmeal into a dish.

"Fiddlesticks!" she said. "How can anyone keep their strength up on one egg for breakfast! You'll eat what's set before you. Who's to look after you if I don't? Unless . . . ," She paused and her black eyes peered sharply at the girl . . . "unless you've come to your senses. . . ."

Violet turned quickly, letting the door close behind her. She walked to the table and seated herself, feeling the morning breeze as it brought the delicate weight of apple-blossom fragrance through the open window. She looked

7

at the cloudy drifts of white across the trees and felt a trembling within her.

"The beauty of it!" she whispered to herself. "The utter, aching beauty of it! If I could only catch it in words."

She laid a small paper and a pencil beside her plate as Katie set down the porridge.

"Well," the latter announced, as she dropped into a chair opposite her young charge, "I'll sit a minute and hear what you have to say. How can I get on with my work till I know? Are you going to have him or ain't you?"

Violet swallowed a spoonful of porridge with difficulty. "I don't know."

"You don't *know!* Well, it's tonight he's coming for his final answer, ain't it? And it don't take too much surmisin' to ken that he's tired of goin' on like this. You can't keep a man dangling forever, while you blow hot an' blow cold. He's been after you since you were in pigtails. And what's the matter with him that you can't make up your mind? Answer me that!"

"It's hard to explain, Katie."

"Well, I should think as much! Here's a good lookin', well-set-up, healthy young man, with a big hardware store at his back—the best business in town next to the General —and you comin' on for twenty-five this summer. You ought to be married and have some bairns already. And still you dinna ken!" In times of emotional stress Katie's language partook broadly of her native land.

Violet looked sadly into her porridge dish and said nothing. Katie got up, carefully shut the door between the dining room and the hall and came back, visibly moved. She leaned over the table and dropped her voice to a whisper.

"You've no mother to talk to you so I have to," she said. "Is it the . . . the *sleepin'* business that you canna thole?"

For a moment the eyes of the young virgin and the old one met in a look of half fright that the unspeakable had been voiced. A flush rose in Violet's cheeks until they were crimson. She answered slowly.

"No, I'm sort of ashamed to say it, but it's not that so much as the getting-awake part. I just don't see how I could stand Henry the first thing in the morning! Just now, for instance, suppose we were . . . married and eating

8

breakfast here together." Her voice became graver still. "I doubt if he would even *look* at the apple blossoms!"

"Apple blossoms!" Katie all but shrieked. "And what in the name of the Brownie of Bodsbeck have they got to do with it? Here you've got a chance of a nice young man that any other girl in town would jump at and you blether away about. . . . Ach, I'll bring you in the rest of your breakfast."

When she returned with it she laid a hand for a moment on the girl's shoulder. Her sharp eyes were misty.

"Mind," she said, "I don't want to fash you, but as I've often told you, it's a lonely clothesline that doesn't have a man's shirt on it! I know you've got to decide for yourself, but I worry about you. Here we are, us two in this big house and me getting no younger. . . ."

"Don't, Katie! I can't bear to hear you say that."

"Well, it's God's truth and we maun face it. If anything happened to me—well, I'd like to see you settled with a husband to look after you. And provide for you too. We haven't much between us and you stubborn as a mule about usin' any of my savings. You don't want to go on teachin' young ones till you're an old maid. You know how glad you were to get shed of school last week when it stopped. Now if you married Henry he could just hang up his hat here and we'd be . . ." She drew a long sigh from the heart. "Ah well, between the two of you be it, but just mind an' not be like the girl that wouldna' hae the walkers, and the riders rode by!"

She returned to the kitchen but she had chosen her last words better than she knew. She had effectively summed up all the reasons why the answer to Henry Martin's question should this evening be answered in the affirmative. Violet drank her coffee but soon put the rest of the breakfast aside. It choked her. She sat with her head in her hands for a long moment, then smoothed out the paper beside her plate and picked up the pencil. She looked again at the orchard, at the snow of bloom, at the faint green leaves, at the dark twisted trunks that sturdily bore their springtime burden of beauty. She watched, her gray eyes full of light, and then slowly set down two more lines upon the paper.

It was a long morning. When Violet finished her own share of the housework she went up to her room, copied her new verses on her father's old typewriter, and added the sheet to those already in the manila folder on her own desk. She was tempted to read them all over but she fought down the impulse. Today she must be practical; she must consider the facts of her life without ornamentation. She was too prone, she knew, to gloss them over with the patina of her natural optimism.

There was first of all the alarming fact that she had very little money. Her wage as primary teacher in the town's small school had seemed sufficient before when she could use it for extras while her father took care of the regular expenses of the home. Now all was changed. Her father's salary had ceased of course with him, and the money in his bank account had proved to be perilously low. He had apologized for this with bitter tears shortly before his death. His quivering voice told how he had once been so sure that he was going to double, even treble, his life's savings in corn. The Golden Investment Company and the conversations he had had with their representative when he came out to explain about "buying on a margin" had all convinced him that he had a chance at last to provide handsomely for his family. It was, he told her brokenly, to have been the great surprise for her mother on her fiftieth birthday.

He had invested two thousand dollars at first. In three months it had doubled, according to their report. The market, they said, was rising and he should invest more at once. He had sent two more. Next time they suggested wheat. He had sent two more thousand. This, too, had doubled in a remarkably short time, they wrote him. The letters that had come were full of market terms which he did not understand but he could grasp the important thing. After a quiet lifetime on a meager salary he was making money at last. He had invested again still more with the same good results. Then had come an urgent letter stating the the market had dropped suddenly and that since he had been buying on a margin he must send money at once to protect what he had already purchased, just, they assured him, "until the market stabilized." This was a routine matter, nothing to give him concern, but they must have funds immediately to *carry* him. He had done as they asked, for the first time feeling a small shadow cross his shining sky.

There had been three more letters such as this, each more urgent than the last. He had kept on, sending more money, bolstering his hopes that each time would be the last. He had tried to read the stock reports in the papers, but while he could enjoy Virgil and Xenophon in the original he could make neither head nor tail of the statistics on the financial page. Worst of all he could find little mention of either *corn* or *wheat*. Then it was he who had sent the urgent letters. He had reached the end of his savings; he could send no more money; they must do something; they must "carry" him, as they called it, until the market went up again as it had done before. His last letter, a mingling of threat and prostrate entreaty, came back to him finally marked: *No longer at this address.*

He had gone then in despair to Joe Huntley, an old friend and lawyer at the County seat, and told him all the story. Joe had wrinkled his forehead and in silence stroked his nose with a knobby forefinger. The man before him recognized the familiar signs. His case, then, was hopeless. Joe had finally explained how such companies as The Golden Investment operated. While he would do his best he feared it would be impossible to track the men down. By this time they would have split their gains and gone their separate ways, dropping out of sight completely. A little later they would meet, perhaps in Chicago, have some new stationery printed with a new company name and start operating again, drawing their money from a few victims innocent of all knowledge of the stock market. For a short time they would be safe until someone became suspicious. When this happened they would once again disappear and move on.

Violet had tried to comfort her father in his deep misery as he told her all this. She understood, which in itself was much. She knew that his wide gray eyes were those of a dreamer, even as her own. The strong bones of his face represented integrity, and the conscientiousness of a lifetime, but the eyes. . . . Even though young herself she had the gift of insight. She knew it was these gentle, visionary eyes that had caused him often on a winter's night to look up from his book and stare into the fire, then remark that he believed he would go down to his workshop in the cellar for a while. Her mother, that gay spirit who had made bright the place of their habitation,

11

would get up at these times from her "lady's" chair and pace the floor.

"I'm afraid it's another invention," she would say. "Oh, if only one of them would be a success for him."

But they never had been. They were rather evenly spaced over the years: the fancy can opener, the game in a wooden box with a piston and tiny balls, the new style of "blower" for the fireplace and a half dozen others. Each was conceived with delight, and completed with optimism. Then came the letters to and from the patent attorney, the payment of the fee, the hope deferred, and the final disappointment.

Violet thought of all this as she heard her father's anguished confession about the investments in *corn* and *wheat*. She threw her strong young arms about his weak shoulders and drew him to her.

"Oh Daddy, the money means nothing at all. You've been the best father a girl ever had. Nothing matters but how much you've always loved me and how much I love you! That's all I'll ever need!" She put her round cheek against his sunken one and their tears met.

Afterwards in the depths of her grief she was glad to remember the light that had come then into his eyes—the last light of all, as it proved.

But now, pushing all this aside, she must try to think sensibly of her position. Her salary would provide food for her and Katie and she could stretch it to cover clothes as well; but where was the money to come from to keep up the house? Even now the trim needed fresh paint badly and so did the stable, which, like the house, had been built upon spacious lines when a strong owner could maintain it. Within the stable was still another source of expense. This was Prince, the horse. Violet smiled even as she sighed in thinking of him. Next to Katie herself Prince stood *in loco familias* to her. She would never sell him, no matter what exigencies arose, so that was that. But there *was* the orchard. It was inanimate. The trees would not know her perfidy if she let Billy Wade cut them down—or would they? She and her father had toyed with a delicate fancy concerning the sentient quality of vegetation, which they found in the works of a new young French writer named Maurice Maeterlinck. The dear old apple trees! In her childhood summers she had played

12

among them and sat upon their low broad arms to read her first books. Each fall through the years the three of them had shared the pleasant task of the apple picking and the packing of the largest and soundest in barrels for winter use. Then had come the fun of stirring the apple butter as it bubbled in the big copper kettle over which Katie presided in the back yard, and last of all, when the days had grown more spicy, came the cider making with the small hand press, while her father beamed contentment over the kindly fruits of the earth and quoted concerning "the gentle apple's winey juice."

There was never any sale for apples. Each thrifty villager had his own tree. There was, however, a delightful sense of *largesse* as the outer fringe of the poor and the shiftless came with their baskets and gleaned the last pickings after the Carpenters themselves had taken all they could use.

Now Billy Wade, who might be considered the town's one realtor, wanted to buy the orchard, cut the trees down and build two new houses for sale upon the site. What he would pay for it would be enough to help Violet and Katie to live for several years to come. The only reason Katie had not urged this course was that she knew nothing yet about it. With a sigh too deep for a young girl's heart Violet got up from her desk and came downstairs, this time to the parlor where she would that evening entertain Henry Martin. There was one point she wished to check. She moved to the marble-topped table between the front windows and lifted the round rose-covered china shade from the lamp, setting it down carefully. She then raised the bowl and shook it gently. As she had surmised, there was barely a gurgle of oil within it when it should have been full! In spite of her general sobriety of feeling, Violet laughed aloud, the sound making the old parlor come alive. The unfilled lamp would be Katie's way of helping on the romance. When the two young people were talking over their most important subject that evening, the lamp would suddenly grow dim and gutter out, leaving them in darkness. And Katie would be quite right in her assumption of what the effect of this would be upon Henry! He would at once gather the girl beside him in his arms and ply her with kisses.

Violet dropped down in a chair and thought upon this

13

particular phase of her problem. Henry had never kissed her until recent months because she had not permitted it. She had then decided that she must make this test before she made up her mind about the future. She had found that she liked being held in his arms; that she didn't even *dis*like the kisses (except that there was always the faint odor of *Sen-Sens* about them, since every young man then felt that these breath purifiers were essential to his desirability as a suitor). But each time after Henry had gone and she sat alone, considering, her heart spoke in honesty to her. She liked the feel of Henry's arms because they were strong and she was lonely and sad. If she married him she knew she could tolerate the dimly discerned physical intimacies attendant upon such a union, but oh, toleration was such a long, long way from rapture, wasn't it?

Violet thought of the day years ago when she had come in unexpectedly upon her father and mother and found them standing with arms entwined while they kissed. The young girl watching had felt utter amazement. She had felt the love of her parents for each other as she had felt the quiet security of their love for her. She had never dreamed that there could be between a man and a woman this passionate need for each other, as she had seen it that day on their faces; and this new conception had colored her first budding dreams of love.

The laughter had left her face now and she brooded again. She was strongly tempted to marry Henry, even without the rapture and the passion. She had always liked him. He was cheerful and good-natured, albeit, she knew, rather stubborn; he had no commerce with books, but after all she could not demand a husband with her father's taste in literature, and he *was* familiar and dependable. She so wanted to marry and have children and feel safe and loved and cared for again. She pictured her life with him as it would be, from the Sunday they made their "appearance" at church (she in her new wedding-trip clothes) to the passing years with their various cares and pleasures. They would, of course, join the Reading Circle, a select club to which only married couples were admitted; she would become active in the Women's Missionary Society, another important organization for the more mature; Henry would become an Elder in the church in due

14

time, like his father and her own, and doubtless a member of the School Board and the Town Council; the small honors and the respect which the village accorded their prominent families would be theirs. The big hardware store would continue to prosper as it had during two generations, and in the now empty rooms upstairs there would gradually be . . .

"Come on," Katie called. "Your dinner's ready."

Violet picked up the lamp and carried it out to the kitchen table.

"This needs filling," she stated briefly.

Katie made no reply to that but set the dishes on the dining table with more emphasis than was necessary, then lingered.

"I pressed your last summer's voile," she said. "I thought you might as well wear it tonight. It's warm enough and pink becomes you."

She eyed her charge keenly to discern her reaction.

"Thanks, Katie. I guess that will be all right," she said with a smile.

Katie's countenance changed. Her plump, rosy face became suffused with a pleasure she tried to hide.

"There's plenty of flag lilies in the garden if you'd want a bunch for the parlor," she threw over her shoulder as she retreated.

Violet's ideas of decoration were different. She went out later to the orchard and cut a great armful of the blooming boughs. She brought from an upper kitchen shelf a large glass bowl which had once held a hideous collection of wax flowers. She arranged the apple blossoms in this and carried it to the parlor where she set it on the grand piano which her mother had brought with her to the stone house as a bride. Violet stood off to admire the effect. It was lovely! Indeed, she thought, the whole room was, in an old-fashioned sort of way. There were a few other parlors in town much like it except for the pictures on the walls. These prints her father had brought back with him from his one unforgettable trip abroad. One was the Magdalen Tower at Oxford and the other was "The Blessed Damozel." The girl looking at this latter now felt a quick kinship with its subject. *She* had been wedded to a man in some respects uncongenial apparently and yet she had loved him! So, it just might be . . .

15

Katie appeared in the doorway. "Why don't you have a little lie-down," she said earnestly. "A wee nap would freshen you up. I heard you prowling around last night till all hours. Get away with you now, and have some beauty sleep."

Violet laughed. "I'm not tired, Katie. I was just thinking I would take a walk up to the Lyalls'. I have a music book I want to give to Faith."

"Well, don't let her be puttin' high-flown ideas in your head. I always thought she turned John Harvey down because she was too uppity. An' look at him now, in that big house on the farm, with an *autta* even, married to Seena Harris, an' Faith could have been in her shoes as easy as spittin' if she'd been sensible. I know, for I've watched John lookin' at her in the choir on Sundays. It was her he wanted. . . ."

"Katie, what about making some ginger cookies? The kind Henry likes?"

"They're made now. Ready to put in the oven. I'll be gettin' back to them. Oh, an' if you're goin' up the street, take the poker with you an' leave it at the blacksmith shop. Tell Joe Williams to make a good straight job of it. He may just do it while you're off to the Lyalls'. I doubt if he'll charge anything but take a dime with you just in case."

Violet walked slowly along the worn flagstones, a book of anthems in one hand and the kitchen poker in the other. She liked the errand to the blacksmith's. From childhood on the mighty fire of the forge in the cavernous twilight of the big shop had fascinated her. Mr. Williams, he of the heavy arms and the leather apron, had been a boyhood friend of her father's, and their talk, to which she had often listened, held the comfortable, easy equality of reminiscence. ("Do you mind the day we set a tack on the chair when the County superintendent was comin' to visit the school?" "Do you remember the time we jumped a sled at recess and rode on clear to Denville?") Besides, her father had always considered Mr. Williams a homespun philosopher, and respected his practical wisdom.

She was nearing the corner where she would turn into Main Street, a spot they had always playfully dubbed "Scylla and Charybdis" in the family because it was so difficult to get through. If Mrs. Hummel did not appear for a chat on the one side, Mrs. Dunn called out from the other. Village etiquette demanded that civil and sometimes lengthy greetings be returned, and if one was in a hurry it was most annoying. Now, although Violet quickened her steps, counting upon the fact that Mrs. Hummel, beating a strip of rag carpet on the clothesline, could not see her, it was to no avail.

"Well, Vi'let," a penetrating voice called out, "what are you in such a hurry for? Now if it was what they call *wedding haste* it would be something like! When are you and Henry going to wind things up? That's what everyone wants to know." She had approached the rose hedge and leaned against it, pushing back the bandanna that encircled her head. "You and Katie all your lone in that big house and Henry such a nice young man. He's got no bad habits. He don't drink or smoke or chew."

Violet laughed in spite of herself. "I should hope he doesn't *chew*," she said.

Mrs. Hummel's tone became immediately defensive.

"Well, while I admit it's a dirty habit and nobody hates to clean a spittoon worse than I do, I will say this. When a man comes home sort of cranky and ornery, if you just give him a good plug of *Five Brothers* and set him down in a rocking chair, he'll turn meek as a lamb. That is, of course, if he's a chewing man to start with like my Ben. . . . Why, wasn't that John Harvey's autta just passed down? It went so fast I could hardly see it. Looked like his hired man at the wheel. Do you spose anything's the matter?"

"Probably Bill's just learned to drive and he wants to show off. Good-bye, Mrs. Hummel, I really must go on."

"You're always in a hurry, just like your father. . . ."

Violet waved her hand as a friendly terminus and rounded the corner. She could have gone the back way to the Lyalls' and escaped Mrs. Hummel but the blacksmith shop was on Main Street, a circumstance which no one in town thought unusual. It was flanked, indeed, by two very pleasant frame houses, but those who lived therein were apparently by long association oblivious to the rich odors of horse and hot iron which drifted on the neighboring air, and, like old Squire Hendrick, felt that "the sounds of industry could never annoy." Just now, Violet saw, there were several men standing on the sidewalk outside the smithy, looking anxiously down the street. Mr. Williams himself being one. Her heart beat faster. There must be something wrong, then.

As soon as she was near enough the blacksmith himself called out to her.

"We've just got bad word, Vi'let. My wife heard it over the phone. John Harvey's been gored by his new bull but we don't know how serious. We just seen Bill drive down in the autta like Jehu. We spose for Doctor Faraday."

Lem Hartman, a farmer, spoke up. "And it's my opinion Doc ought to get himself an autta. They're the things for speed and in his business he needs it. Might make the difference between life and death sometimes. The farmers are even beginnin' to get them now an' they're comin' through town thick as flies."

Mr. Williams spat furiously. "All this talk of auttas," he said. "They're all very well, mebbe, for pleasure ridin' now an' then but it's the horse for steady service. There will still be horses, mind you standin' waitin' their turn to get shod in this here shop when all the auttas will be in the junk heap."

"Here he comes back and Doc with him," Lem said, starting into the street. He ran toward the car.

"Is he bad?" he shouted as the car passed.

"Bad enough," Doctor Faraday called in reply.

They could see now that Harris, the miller, and his wife, Seena's parents, were in the back seat. All eyes followed the retreating car in its cloud of dust.

"Must be goin' twenty-five mile an hour!" Lem said wonderingly. Then a gravity settled upon them all.

"It's bad, that, to be gored by a bull. You mind Cy Thompson? He never come to afterwards at all."

"But there's been others that's lived. That hired man on the Hunt farm, he got over it."

"Yep. While there's life there's hope. Well, we'll get word before long. Poor chap! Just gettin' started for himself the last two years, and now this happenin'."

"What's that you've got, Vi'let? Goin' out to hit somebody on the head?" Mr. Williams tried heavily to introduce a jocular note.

"It's our kitchen poker. Katie wondered if you would straighten it. I'm going on up to the Lyalls' and I thought

18

if you weren't too busy, perhaps you could do it while I'm gone."

"Sure, sure." Mr. Williams took it and eyed it with professional interest. "I'll have it ready for you. Katie's got a heavy hand when it comes to pokers. You'll get news at the Lyalls'. They'd call the Reverend right away—if John was bad. You can tell us then when you get back."

Violet walked on up the street, where the blue of the Maytime sky was adumbrated through the young maple leaves. How quickly the physical sunshine of a day could be changed by the shadows on the heart! Poor John Harvey! With his bride of a year and his new auto and the big family farm for his own. Oh, a fatality just *couldn't be!* She was glad she was on her way to the Lyalls', and especially to Faith for she knew Katie had been right. John had been fond of Faith. How much she had cared Violet did not know, for Faith had never confided this even to her closest friend.

She had reached the manse now, which stood well back from the street, its somewhat rambling proportions showing whitely against the pine tree and the waking green of the honeysuckle vine. She opened the gate and took the path which led around to the back porch, which was the family's summer sitting room. Before she reached it she heard sobbing and as she came to the steps Faith threw herself into her friend's arms.

"Oh, Vi," she cried, her whole body trembling, "I'm so glad you've come. Father and Mother left a little while ago, and I'm all alone. I feel as if I couldn't bear this!"

"Is he worse? Is it so bad?"

Faith drew back, her tear-flushed face raised to Violet's.

"He's . . . *dead*," she said. "Before the doctor even got there. And oh, I feel as though I had killed him!" The hard sobbing began again.

"Why Faith! You mustn't say such a thing! How could you possibly have anything to do with it? Don't cry so. Let's sit down here on the steps, Oh, it's all so terrible, so ghastly! Poor John. And poor Seena!"

"And poor *me*. Can't you pity me a little when I caused it all?"

Violet drew the girl's shaking body down beside her and held her close. Her own face was white from the tragic news and the shock of Faith's wild words,

19

"Tell me," she said quietly, "what you are talking about. How could you have done anything to prevent this?"

"By . . . by *marrying* him," Faith said between shuddering breaths. "He asked me two years ago and I refused him. I never told anyone but Mother and Father for it seemed hardly fair to John. Then before that year was out he married Seena Harris, but oh, Vi, he hasn't been happy with her."

"How can you be sure of that?"

"He told me himself. You know my brother Jeremy's farm is just next to the Harvey's and once I was there and I walked out to see the young lambs and John was ploughing in the next field and he saw me and came over. He told me Seena didn't keep the house nice and that she was often cross with him. And"—Faith's voice broke completely—"she was the one that urged him to buy the bull because her uncle up at the Four Corners had it for sale and needed the money. John didn't want it. He told me so. He said there were enough on the farms around, and he thought they were dangerous to own. And then he said, 'But I suppose I'll get it like everything else, to keep the peace.' So you see how it was."

Violet put Faith's head against her own shoulder and gently smoothed the soft hair. She had no words to combat the sorrow beside her.

"Decisions are so dreadful to make," Faith burst out, as though to release a long-pent burden. "When John asked me I was sure I was right to say no. You understand, Vi, what my music means to me. Well, he never liked anything except 'In the Shade of the Old Apple Tree,' and songs like that. I felt we were utterly uncongenial and just at first I was a little proud of refusing him."

As she paused Violet's heart beat thunderously within her.

"Then as time went on," Faith said, "I began to wonder if I had been wise. When I saw Seena driving past with him in the new auto with her long veil flying—this seems petty of me but I suppose I wouldn't be human if I hadn't pictured myself in her place. But, oh, of course it really wasn't so much the auto and the other things Seena got, the worst was at bedtime when I would kneel down by the window to say my prayers and the night would be so beautiful, maybe with moonlight, and I would think how

20

there might be no one ever to love me. And I'd feel how quiet and still the old town was and lonely, sort of. And I'd see myself getting older year by year and just going on and on like so many other women here. . . . Oh, Vi, am I dreadful? You *do* understand, don't you?"

It was Violet's throat now that was choked. "Yes," she managed to whisper. "Yes, I understand."

Faith's eyes were dry at last, but her face was utterly stricken.

"I'd have had a good life with John if I had just taken it. Maybe what he had to offer would have been enough. And now it's too late for me and everything's over for him."

They spoke very little after that, only sat close, looking off past the bee boxes along the fence, over the flowering fruit trees in the back garden to the blue hills beyond the creek. The bright warmth of the afternoon sun faded suddenly, just as Mr. and Mrs. Lyall drove past toward the stable. Mary Lyall got out of the buggy and came slowly up to the porch. The usual happy serenity of her countenance was overcast by distress. Her eyes too were reddened.

"Oh, Violet," she said, "I'm so glad you've been here with Faith. David and I had to leave so suddenly I had no time to think of her until we were on the way. I mean," she added in embarrassment, "this is such a frightful shock to all of us. We did what we could out there now and we'll go back tonight. Jeremy and Peggy came right over and they will help. And of course the Harrises are there. Seena is clear beside herself. The doctor gave her something to quiet her and we got her to bed. The worst of all was having to call up John's father and mother. They're out in Ohio, visiting. David had to break the news and he said it was one of the very hardest things he's had to do in all the years."

Mary sighed deeply as at the remembrance of many vicarious sorrows.

"I must go on in now and start the supper. We all need something to strengthen us." She looked keenly at her daughter and then turned to Violet. "Can't you stay?" she asked. "It would do us good and you could keep Faith company while we're back at the Harvey's this evening. I can call Katie and explain."

21

Violet colored, wishing for the thousandth time that she did not blush so easily. "Thank you so much, Mrs. Lyall, but I'm afraid I'll have to go home. I'll see you tomorrow, though," she added to Faith, and then bent swiftly and kissed her. And she made her way around the house and back to the street she feared her unusual gesture of affection might have revealed Faith's secret too clearly. But of course Mrs. Lyall knew the facts and would surmise the rest.

As she walked slowly again beneath the spreading maples Violet knew that a certainty was growing within her. All that the afternoon had brought—the tragedy which had taken John's life and the pitiful anguish of her friend's regret—all this had added immeasurable weight to her own slow-growing decision. She knew what Faith meant by the still loneliness of the moonlight nights! Of what avail would be the beauty of them if the longings they engendered could never be fulfilled? Always up to this time she could enjoy the transport of the pale radiance upon the garden flowers or upon the snow-covered roads; she could dream upon the stars in the wine-dark midnight because love was attendant upon her wish, there, ready, waiting only for her heart's consent.

But she knew—how could one help knowing?—the women of the village, the unpossessed, in whose lives year had succeeded year while their tender hopes had sickened and died and been buried. How could she have forgotten this as she considered her own problem? A sudden warmth, different from any she had ever known, welled up within her. Dear Henry, who loved her and would marry her and forever save her from the loneliness of which she had been thinking. It was her silly, over-romantic heart that had confused her. Now at last she was seeing clearly.

The relief of the decision arrived at brought with it a swift composite blur of certain material felicities which would result from it. She would have a diamond ring and a nice one. Not as large perhaps as that of Lucy Lyall, Faith's younger sister, who had married Ninian Ross, the coal magnate's son; but it would be larger than most in Ladykirk for Henry was very proud and after all there was money in the hardware business. Their wedding trip might even be to Atlantic City! Henry had hinted once of that. She would buy herself some really nice clothes, for now her teaching money would not have to be saved to live upon. And oh, bliss supreme, she wouldn't have to teach again at all!

As she neared the blacksmith shop, however, the burden of the day's calamity fell again upon her, outweighing all other thoughts. When she entered the wide door she saw Lem Hartman and two other farmers sitting dejectedly on a bench, with Mr. Williams himself, strangely idle, beside the forge.

"I spose you've heard by now," he greeted Violet. "My wife got it over the phone. I guess everybody on the line was listenin' in today. Oh, it's a terrible business, this! John was such a good, steady young man. Never a word again' him by anybody. A sad thing an' no mistake. The Reverend phoned John's mother and father out in Ohio. My wife just listened in till he got them an' then the line was bad so she hung up to let them hear better. Are the Lyalls still out at the farm?"

"They've just come back but they'll be going out again tonight," Violet told him. "The Harrises are there, and Jeremy Lyall and Peggy went right over."

"How's Seena takin' it?" Lem asked.

"Very hard."

"And well she may. A good husband and a good farm just gone from her in an hour, you might say. Was the farm in John's name, think you?" he asked, turning to Mr. Williams. "That'll make a difference to Seena."

"I'm not sure. My wife did see the Harveys goin' in to the Squire's one day before they left for Ohio, and we thought that might be to make their wills, since they were goin' off on the trip and not being so young any more. Ah, well, it's a warning to us all. Death can come like a thief in the night and none knoweth the day nor the hour. But I don't see why he ever bought the bull in the first place. There's plenty round to serve all the cows he's got."

"Is the poker ready, Mr. Williams?" Violet asked hastily.

"Yes, yes. It's fine now an' you tell Katie to keep it that way. Tell her to hold it up when she pokes the fire an' not press down so hard on the end of it."

"Is there any charge?"

"No, Vi'let! I'd do more than straighten a poker for your father's daughter! Just look in betimes when you're passing. That's all the pay I want."

As Violet went on toward the corner she knew that already the tragic news had spread through the town. There were small groups on the sidewalks here and there, and there were women talking over back fences. Both Mrs. Hummel and Mrs. Dunn were out in their respective yards calling across to each other and waiting for her when she came in sight.

"I told you," Mrs. Hummel began, "whenever I saw the autta going down that fast, I knew something was wrong. Vi'let here can tell you that I said there must be something wrong, didn't I, Vi'let?"

"Yes, you did," Violet answered, feeling she must somehow break through and get away.

"What we can't find out was whether it was *instant* or whether he lived for a while. Did you hear, Vi'let?" Mrs. Hummel probed.

"I heard it was instant," Mrs. Dunn put in. "They were sayin' down at the store that he never breathed nor moved after. They said Bill found him just layin' there dead in the field. That's what *I* heard."

"He wasn't living when the doctor got there, but I think he did . . . Oh, please excuse me, I can't talk about it any more," Violet said brokenly. "I've got to get home."

She could hear the voices behind her, still exploring every phase of the accident. So it would be from one end of the town to the other. Nothing else would be talked of for days. There would be constant repetition of each minute detail, each fact and individual surmise about past, present and future possibilities in the lives of the Harvey family; but because of this uninterrupted flow of conversation in kitchens, store, Post Office and barbershop, the members of the tightly-knit little community would experience a catharsis of the emotions, a release from the shock, and the very real sadness of their hearts, and would be able eventually to do as they had done so often before —weave the tragedy into the communal fabric of village experience and go on about the usual business of living.

Violet went along the garden walk and in at the back door. She dreaded meeting Katie for now it would all have to be gone over again. However, her recently-made decision would have a sustaining effect as she looked into Katie's black eyes.

"I've got the news already," the latter said at once as

Violet entered. "And a sadder thing I've never heard in my life. Mary Jackson's just been in and she says she heard down street that Seena's *expecting*. It's high time, of course, them being married a year, but I doubt it myself for Mrs. Harris's tongue wags at both ends and you can be sure she'd have spread it about her daughter if it was true. It might be better for Seena now if she had a bairn to think of, but on the other hand it's a bad business to bring up a child without a father. Did you hear anything about this up at the Lyalls'?"

"No, of course not," Violet answered with some asperity. "But oh, Katie, isn't it dreadful about John? Why do such terrible things have to happen?"

"It's not for us to question the doings of the Almighty. I've brewed some tea. Sit you down here an' have a cup. You're white as a sheet. I wish this hadn't come just to-day. But maybe for you it's a good thing it did, if it had to hap at all. It'll maybe make you think again how it's a lonely clothesline that hasn't got a man's shirt on it, as the sayin' goes. Just mind that when you're answerin' Henry. Sup up your tea now an' get some color in your cheeks."

"All right, Katie, I'll try to do as you say."

Katie stopped suddenly and looked keenly at her young mistress.

"Did you mean more by that than the *tea?*" she demanded.

Violet smiled faintly. "I might," she said, "but I'll tell you more tomorrow."

That night as she dressed in front of her tall bureau in the golden lamplight Violet made a discovery. If she had been a vain girl she would have made it long before; but aside from seeing that her hair was tidy, her dress as becoming as might be and the whole effect one of general prettiness, she had never pondered too much upon her looks. Now, suddenly and with a feeling almost of guilt, she knew that she was very lovely to look upon. She stood there staring at her image in surprise, as though it were that of a stranger. Her gray eyes were wide and shining. Something of the doubt, the sorrow and then the decision of the day, had given them new depth. She had brushed her hair until it curled upon her shoulders, then fastened it in a low "figure eight" on her neck. It waved softly from the parting, making a frame for the pure oval

25

of her face. She studied her nose, lips, rounded cheeks and dimpled chin, and realized that they were more than physical features, that in some mysterious way they together achieved beauty. This she might once admit and then try forever to forget since the thought savored of unbecoming pride. She hastily took a small chamois skin from the drawer of her dresser, shook some talcum upon it, dabbed her forehead, nose and chin, then blew out the lamp and went downstairs. What she did not know about herself was that there lay upon her a certain eagerness as that of a bird poised for flight, a sort of breathless expectancy as though she were waiting for the bells of the world to ring.

Katie had already lighted the lamp on the parlor table and Violet stood in the doorway surveying the room with the apple blossoms dominating it. She was glad she had cut so many. Since it was too cool as yet to sit on the porch and also since that would be too open to kindly, prying eyes, it was good to have the springtime inside, when she and Henry exchanged their private vows and made their plans. She walked on back to the kitchen to show herself in the pink voile. Katie sat in her big wooden rocker with Simon, the cat, curled on her shoulder like a fur boa. Her Bible was open on her knee as she always read her evening chapter here before going upstairs. Now, she removed her "near" glasses and looked upon the young girl before her, trying hard to cover the shameless adoration in her old eyes.

"It looks very nice," she said primly. "The pink suits you. An' just mind now what I've always told you. 'It's a lonely . . .'"

"I know, Katie, you needn't repeat it. 'It's a lonely clothesline that doesn't have a man's shirt on it!'"

"Well, so it is. I put a pitcher of milk on the dining-room table and a plate of cookies. They turned out pretty well, if I do say it. There! That's likely him now! I hear a step on the walk."

Violet turned quickly and walked through to the front door. Henry Martin stood there, his ruddy cheeks freshly shaven, his blond hair brushed until the faint curl in it lay flat, his shoulders broad and square in his best striped suit, his feet ashine in new patent-leather shoes. Violet thought she had never before seen him look so handsome.

26

"Come in," she said with quick warmth. "Let me have your hat."

Once in the parlor Henry stared at the bowl of orchard bloom upon the piano.

"Why, I could have brought you some flowers," he said, "if I'd known you hadn't any. My mother had a whole bed of lemon lilies out and lots of flags."

"But we have, too," Violet said. "Plenty of them. It's just that I like these better. Don't you think they're lovely?"

"I guess so. It's just that I never thought of apple blossoms as *flowers* somehow."

"Just as incipient apples?"

"Insippy—what? There you go with your big words. Mind, I just talk plain English," Henry laughed.

Violet tried to join him, and then as they sat down opposite each other their countenances fell and they began to speak of John Harvey and the sad events of the day. Like the rest of the town they lingered upon each detail, recounting, conjecturing, accepting or rejecting various new surmises which Henry had heard spoken in the store. They continued, indeed, beyond all normal interest as though by this postponing discussion of their own crucial problem.

At last Henry began nervously to cross and recross his legs and to clear his throat every few seconds.

"Come on over here beside me," he said, moving over on the sofa. "After all what's done is done and we can't bring John back by talking about him. Come on over. It's time we talked about ourselves."

Violet got up, slender and palely pink like the blossoms, and sat down shyly at one end of the sofa. Henry moved nearer, placing an experimental arm along the carved wood of the back.

"Well, don't keep so far away. You know what I've come for tonight. I've been after you this long time to give me an answer. We can't go on forever like this. I want to get married and I think you do too, if you'd just let yourself go and make up your mind." He cleared his throat again. "How about it, Vi? The answer's *yes*, isn't it?"

She sat, interlacing her fingers, a great seriousness falling upon her face.

"Before I give you an answer, Henry, there's something I have to tell you."

27

"There is?"

"Yes. I have to make a confession and I'm afraid to. I've kept putting it off for I couldn't bear to—to hear what you might say. But I can't marry you without telling you. You have to know about it. It wouldn't be right of me to wait till you found out—later."

The color flamed in her cheeks as it always did when she was nervous or excited. She looked up beseechingly at Henry. He had removed his arm and his face looked suddenly pale. A hard male wariness crept into his eyes. He seemed to swallow with difficulty.

"Well," he said thickly, "let's have it."

"It's hard somehow for me to speak of it. But please, Henry, try to understand. I write poetry. I always have and I know I always will. I even have enough now, I think, to make a little book if I could get any publisher to take it. I don't suppose I can, yet awhile, but I'll always be trying, and thinking about it and working on it. You see I'll be writing poetry all my life, and I thought you ought to know. . . ."

Henry stared at her for a long moment, then he threw back his head and laughed strangely.

"Good God," he said, when he could speak, using a profane word for the first time in her presence, "why didn't you tell me this in the first place instead of scaring the wits out of me, making me think . . . making me think . . ."

"Think what, Henry?"

"Well, for heaven's sake, what would you expect? Here you start saying you have to make a confession and you've been putting it off but you couldn't marry me without telling me—what would *any* man think?"

Violet rose and moved over to the piano. It was she now who was pale and Henry whose face was aflame. He went on, his speech growing more and more involved as he defended his private thoughts.

"How was I to know what you were talking about? I thought—well, there was the time just after your mother died when your father took you to New York to visit those cousins and—well, everybody here got the idea they lived pretty fast, and I never knew who you'd met there or anything. You were always kind of quiet about that trip. So when you started in now with this confession business— well you can see how it sounded. *Poetry!*" He laughed

28

again. "Gosh, I don't care how much poetry you write as long as you don't expect me to read any of it. Come on back, Vi. Let's sit here now and settle things. . . ."

When she did not move he rose and stood anxiously before her.

"Everything's all right, isn't it? You know I love you. And by the way, I haven't had a kiss yet tonight."

With a quick step forward he had her in his arms, his lips on hers. All his desire was in his grasp and for a small breathing time Violet rested upon the warm young strength encircling her. Then she freed herself gently and moved out of his reach.

"I'm sorry, Henry, so *terribly* sorry, but I can't marry you."

After all the pondering, the doubts, the hopes and the so-recently-made decision, the final answer came out as simply as that.

"I can't marry you," she repeated while he watched her face in a stunned silence. "We wouldn't be happy. We are too different. As long as we were just going together it didn't matter too much, but marriage is so serious. I . . . I really thought I could, Henry, but I find I can't."

Henry came alive then. He caught her hands in a tight grip.

"You don't know what you're talking about! Why wouldn't we be happy? I'll do anything for you. I can get you just about everything you'd want." He hesitated. "You're not . . . it isn't what I said about . . . well, about what I thought just now . . . that's not the trouble, is it?"

"Not entirely," Violet said, her eyes downcast. "But my mind is now made up. I'm so very, *very* sorry to disappoint you but I can't say yes."

"I don't believe it!" he burst out. "After the way we've gone together for years, then for you to throw me over now—is that a nice trick? The whole town will know you turned me down and how's that going to make me feel?"

As she stood silent, beside the apple blossoms, his face showed his hunger.

"You can't mean this is final, Vi. Please say it isn't. I'll wait longer if you want me to."

"It's final, Henry. I'm ashamed that I couldn't make up my mind before. But I have now. You'll have to believe me."

He turned sharply toward the hall and got his hat, then stood in the doorway.

"I don't think you know what you're doing," he said, "and some day you'll regret this. But it will be too late then," he added ominously, and left.

Violet did not move as his steps sounded on the porch and along the walk. Then there was no sound at all as the night stillness of the old town engulfed her. Strangely enough the one thought that rose from her benumbed heart was how she should tell Katie! She went out through the hall and opened the living-room door. There Katie stood, like one of her embattled Covenanter ancestors, her eyes blazing and her fists clenched.

"He insulted you, that's what he did," she burst out. "The gall of him! Imaginin' things like that about *you!* I could have brained him with my poker, so I could! It just goes to show what men are always thinkin' about, that's what it does. Ugh! Men!"

"Katie, you've been eavesdropping. How could you?"

"Well, I just had to hear with my own ears whether you were takin' him or not. And a good job you didn't!" she flamed. "Thinkin' things like that about *you!* And I always thought butter wouldn't melt in his mouth. We'll have none of his ilk in this house, I'll tell you that."

As Violet did not speak, Katie's voice softened. "We've had about all we can take for one day. I'm going to put the cat out and go on upstairs. An' see you get to bed soon. You look as though you'd been drawn through a knothole an' no wonder. But just mind this, dearie. You're well shed of Henry Martin an' there's no call to worry. Get yourself a good sleep an' tomorrow's a new day."

"What about the lonely clothesline, Katie?" Violet asked with a faint smile.

Katie had started for the door but she looked darkly over her shoulder.

"Let him hang his shirts on his own clothesline," she said, and disappeared.

Violet sank down in her mother's chair as though life had been drained out of her. The emotional stresses of the day had, indeed, left her weak. As though to postpone thought she listened to Katie's familiar movements in the next room. Simon, the cat, when not on someone's knee or shoulder of an evening, enjoyed the warmth of the upper air on top of the tall kitchen cupboard, from whence it was difficult to dislodge him. Violet listened now as Katie began to wheedle.

"Come, Simon. Kitty, kitty, kitty. Come now. Be a good cat an' you'll be the mair thought on! Pussy, pussy, pussy. Kitty, kitty, kitty. Come on down now."

Katie always as a matter of principle tried persuasion first, as though to give Simon a chance to exercise his better nature. This proving useless, as now, she practiced subterfuge. Violet could hear a tin dipper drawn raspingly around the edge of a crock as though to skim cream. Simon never failed to accept this delusion as reality. There was an immediate soft thud upon the floor and then low mutterings from Katie as she picked him up, as she always did, and carried him to the door.

"Get away with you," she could be heard to say. "Get on out now an' catch a rat the way the Lord made you!"

The kitchen door closed, there were footsteps on the back stairs, a few movements above, and then silence.

In spite of her alternating rage and feigned cheerfulness, Violet knew that Katie must be bitterly disappointed that her child's future was not safely assured tonight. As to her own feelings? She, too, felt a great emptiness which was like pain. It was not regret at her decision for she could have done no other wise. But there was within her an overwhelming sense of loss and disappointment. It was as though with plain food set before her she had risked starvation in the hope of more delicate fare. No! She repudiated the thought quickly. This was not a true parallel. There was an essential integrity of the heart involved, which had to be respected.

She sat very still for a long time feeling a loneliness greater than she had ever felt before, then she rose slowly and went to a certain spot in the bookshelves. She drew out three volumes and reached for a small worn leather box which lay behind them. Beneath it rested a thick square yellowed envelope. After a moment's hesitation she picked it up too, and returned with both to her chair. The letter, addressed to her mother, had always been kept beneath the box, but she had not seen it or even thought of it for many years; now, as though impelled by a vague memory, she opened it and slowly read the contents.

My dear niece (it began in a clear but apparently aged handwriting):

As you must know you are very dear to me. I wish at your marriage I could settle a fortune upon you, but unfortunately I have now very little of this world's goods. I do, however, have one treasure which I am sending as a wedding present. I am giving it to you not only because it is a rather rare possession, but because to me it has sentimental significance. From your letter I feel you are truly in love with your young man, and I know from experience that when real love enters the heart it is as though a nightingale sings. So I send you my little bird, with the love of your

great-uncle,

Alexander Harrington

The date was September 15, 1882.

She sat very still sensing the full meaning of the words. Then she opened the leather box and from its faded satin cushioning removed a smaller one made of tortoise shell and the key that wound it. She turned this carefully, then pressed the spring on the side. Suddenly, incredibly, the golden filigree oval on the top of the box rose and a tiny feathered bird appeared and burst into song. The small throat throbbed, the little wings fluttered, as the music that had once bemused Keats fell upon the ear. Then, when the brief ecstasy was over, the bird disappeared as suddenly as it had risen, the filigree oval fell into place and only a small black box remained in the hand.

Violet pressed the spring again and once more listened to the delicate miracle. She had been familiar with it from childhood; indeed, there were few people in the village who had not at one time or another shared the wonder of the treasure. But tonight she was hearing it for the first time to the accompaniment of the words of the letter. It was like a message from another world.

She carefully replaced the square envelope beneath the box on the shelf and set the three books on guard in front, as usual. She blew out the two hanging lamps, and walked through the hall to the open front door, where she stood looking into the springtime darkness. Keats' ode to the golden-voiced bird was running through her mind. It had been one of her father's favorites. *Tender is the night,* she quoted to herself, *And haply the Queen-Moon is on her throne*. There was, indeed, a three-quarter moon showing to the south above the creek where veils of mist made brides of the tall oak trees. The old town slept. No sounds drifted back from Main Street. But strangely, this silence now did not seem lonely, even as the darkness rested not heavily but lightly, almost transparently, upon the young leaves and the freshly reborn earth. Violet lifted her face to the fragrant air and spoke into the night as though taking a vow.

"I'll wait," she said softly, "I'll wait for the nightingale."

CHAPTER TWO

WITH the incredible elasticity of youth Violet slept soundly that night and rose late in the morning, refreshed. The sun was bright, a sweet air was moving and the doves were calling in languishing notes from the creek bank. It was, as Katie had predicted, a new day and a fair one. Violet brushed her hair slowly, looking into the mirror as she did so, watching with interest the girl she had only discovered the night before. She would pray earnestly each day to be delivered from vanity, but surely it could not be wrong to feel thankful that she had certain physical attributes which might be attractive to a man. She held her thoughts firmly to a consideration of her face even though within her heart she knew shyly that she had other forms of beauty which nature had bestowed upon her. This realization was new and startling, but it carried with it a certain reassurance, even as does money in the bank.

It was Katie who looked the worse for the night. Her eyes were bloodshot from lack of sleep and the lines of her face were sharpened.

"Well," she announced as Violet appeared, "I'm glad to see you look in pretty good fettle and dressed for church. We're late, for I didn't want to rouse you till I had to. I'm ready too. Only have to throw off my apron."

She sat down opposite Violet and dropped her voice.

"I had an idea last night, or towards morning. A way we might make a bit of money. I'll tell you on a weekday."

"Katie!" Violet exclaimed. "You can't rouse my curiosity like this and not satisfy it. Tell me this minute!"

" 'Sunday fraught
    Comes to naught,' "

Katie quoted sententiously. "I'll say nothing more today. Well, at least not till after church tonight. Hurry, now, with your breakfast. There's the first bell ringing."

Usually on a Sunday there was a gentle animation evident in the congregation before the service began. It was considered in Ladykirk a delightful thing to go to church! People donned their best apparel and repaired to the house of the Lord with a pleased expectancy. There was always the assured meetings between town and country friends; there was the worldly satisfaction of having some place to go (in a village where formal social contacts were few) mingled with the spiritual one of having their souls fed when they got there.

Today the members entered quietly. Even the feet of the young men, which usually sounded vigorously upon the wide stairs leading up to the sanctuary, made a subdued sound, for the tragedy of John Harvey lay upon them all. Faith Lyall looked pale as she took her place at the organ. The anthem planned for could not be given for Seena's strong, if slightly off-key, soprano had been necessary to it. Now Seena was moving, half drugged, amidst the ruins of her new life and Faith must try with eyes not quite clear to play a voluntary while the collection was being received. Violet seated herself as usual in the choir, trying to avoid looking at the Martin pew where Henry sat, straight, grim and, it must be admitted, handsome, between his father and his mother. At last Mr. Lyall walked slowly up the aisle to the pulpit in his long ministerial coat and the congregation rose to sing the doxology.

When it came time for the announcements, the stillness was absolute. "The funeral service for Mr. John Harvey will be held at his late home on Tuesday afternoon at two o'clock," Mr. Lyall said with slow, sad emphasis. Then, as though a tension had been released, there were slight movements in the congregation, a baby cried, the Elders taking up the offering started down the aisles in their stiff, squeaking Sunday shoes, with their woven baskets in

34

their hands, and Faith began to play a nocturne on the organ, striking a wrong key now and then, which was unusual for her.

When the service was over many groups gathered in the churchyard, mostly of the farm people, who had had no opportunity before to talk over the sad event face to face with their neighbors. Violet and Faith walked slowly along together, noting these, knowing the words being spoken, but saying nothing to each other. At the corner Faith broke the silence.

"I'd like to come down this afternoon if it's all right."

"Oh, do come," Violet urged. "I have something special to tell you."

Faith looked up, startled.

"Henry?" she asked.

"Yes, but not what you think."

It was almost as though a relief showed in Faith's eyes. "About three?"

"Yes. We'll go up to the orchard where we'll be quite alone," Violet said as they parted.

While Katie's presence in the home was both precious and indispensable, there were some disadvantages connected with it. Her knees and elbows were afflicted with rheumatism to the extent that it was now necessary to get help to beat the carpets and wash down the woodwork at the semi-annual housecleanings; but her hearing was in no wise impaired by the years. Indeed it was so keen and her subtlety so great that she seemed to know every word spoken in the house. Violet had often wondered with an inner amusement if Katie did not somehow manage to eavesdrop at her very prayers! One thing, however, was certain. The secrets of the family were safe with her. She would have been torn asunder rather than reveal what she felt was unbecoming or disloyal.

All the same, Violet was relieved that afternoon to guide Faith up the stone steps in the wall which separated the lawn from the slightly higher ground of the orchard. They kept on until they found a soft grassy spot under a tree, and there Violet spread the cushions and the girls sat down, their faces as tender and young as the bloom above them.

"If you hadn't come today I would have gone up," Violet began. "There was something I felt I must tell you

35

at once. I thought it might help you, might make you feel a little better perhaps."

Violet's face flushed as usual in her embarrassment, but she went on.

"I'm like you. I don't think it's ladylike for a girl to tell that she's refused a man's offering of marriage. But this is different. I have to confide in you and I know you'll never speak of it to anyone."

"Oh, never!" said Faith earnestly.

"Well, Henry asked me some time ago to marry him and he was to come last night for his final answer. My mind wasn't entirely made up until I left you yesterday. Then I knew that I would say *yes*. I felt, all at once, so sure of myself. I even thought of many things I feel ashamed of now—the ring and my trousseau and the wedding trip and how our lives would be, well, rather important in the town, and how I wouldn't have to teach again and . . . everything."

"And what happened?" Faith asked breathlessly.

"I got dressed in my pink voile and I felt all excited and happy. And after he got here I still thought I was sure for a little while. But then . . ." She stopped. Even to Faith she could not confess all the conversation of the night before. "When it came to saying *yes*, I found I couldn't say it."

"And so it's all over between you?"

"All over. And Faith, I'm telling you this because it may ease your heart . . . about John. I know now just how you felt. And you couldn't have married him. You would never have been happy, and sooner or later he would have found it out and that might have been worse for him than being married to Seena. Don't you see? And it's not your fault in any way about what happened. You couldn't help doing what you did. Just as I couldn't help refusing Henry."

Faith's eyes were filled with amazement and then with a vast relief.

"Oh, Vi!" she cried, "you don't know what a burden this lifts from me! Nothing anyone could merely *say* in the way of advice helped me at all. Father and Mother tried and it was no use. But now, for you to have had the very same experience and understand so perfectly, oh . . ."

36

I don't believe I'll feel guilty any more. I think I can sleep tonight. For the first time I can even pity Seena."

"Poor Seena!" Violet said. "And yet I have a feeling that after the first shock she won't—oh, maybe I shouldn't say it . . ."

"Feel too badly," Faith finished.

"Of course we don't know her the way we know each other. It's been only three years since they came to town. But I think she may be the kind to remarry before long. She's so lively and all the men seem to admire her."

"But she wasn't very nice to John. He told me so."

"John was easy-going and would give in to her, whether it was right or not. Now with you or me the kinder a husband would be to us the more we would love him and try to make him happy, but Seena may be different. My father used to say women were like horses. You had to use a tight rein on some and a slack rein on others. He always smiled at my mother and said, 'I use a very loose rein, myself,' and she would make a little face at him and say, 'You'd just better, sir!' Then they would both laugh. They were so happy together," Violet ended with a sigh.

"And so are my mother and father. I don't believe I ever thought about it much when I was younger, but now since I've been grown I notice things. Last week I was passing the parlor door and I saw my father put his hand on Mother's hair as he went by her chair and she drew it down and laid her cheek against it. They didn't say a word and I slipped on past. It was such a little thing, not dramatic at all, and yet it made me think of all that lay behind it. Vi, do you wonder what real love will be like when it comes? *If* it comes," she amended.

Violet looked off through the trees as though seeing a far-off land.

"Yes," she said. "Of course I've thought of it. I tried to put all such dreaming out of my mind when I was persuading myself that I could marry Henry. Now, I don't need to. Oh, Faith, I've always wanted love to come like a great rushing torrent sweeping me on with it. You know those lines from *Water Babies*, 'The flood-gates are open, away to the sea!' That's the way I would want it to be. The flood-gates of my heart wide open. . . ."

She paused, remembering the nightingale. "Or like mu-

37

sic, suddenly filling the whole air so that I would hear nothing else but the beauty and the wonder of it!"

A light covered her face as she spoke.

"I've thought of that too," Faith said softly, "only I can't say it as poetically as you can." She paused, considering. "I believe, though, that there is another way love can come. Quietly, sort of like daylight. Just coming slowly and gently but so surely you couldn't mistake it. I think I'd rather have it come that way to me than . . . the other. Of course," she added, "I wouldn't really care which, just so it came."

"You're pretty poetic yourself," Violet said. She moved her cushion a little nearer to her friend and leaned close as though someone might be listening from the treetop.

"I have something else I'd like to tell you. No one ever knew but Father and Mother, but I felt I had to explain to Henry last night because it's so much a part of me. I hope you'll keep this a secret too, for I feel a little shy about it."

"Of course I will, Vi!"

"For a good many years I've been writing poems. At first Father merely encouraged me to keep on, but later he began to say that they were—that they weren't too bad."

"Oh, Vi, you're so modest. Tell me the truth. Did he really think they were good?"

"Well, yes, he did. He was guarded of course in his praise even then for he didn't want me to have any exalted ideas about them, but he kept going over and over them those last months, and he said when I had written a few more I should send them all to a publisher."

"Vi, not . . . *a book!*"

"I don't think it's likely, yet. But I do mean to send them off soon and see what happens. After all, I have to make the try some time. It may be years before I have anything accepted. Maybe I never will have, but I know I'll keep on writing as long as I live. I can't help it! It's just in me."

"What did Henry say about it?"

"That it would be all right for me to write poems if he didn't have to read them."

Faith drew in her breath sharply and made no answer to that. Then she cried out in eager enthusiasm, "I'm so glad you told me your secret, Vi, and I'll keep it, you may

38

be sure. But we can talk about it together and it will be something new and exciting to think of. I can't tell you how proud I am of you! I must go now, but I feel so much better than when I came. Thanks, Vi, for everything!"

They walked together to the iron gate and stood for a moment leaning upon it.

"Faith," Violet said hesitantly, "will you come out of church with me tonight? You know, this will be the first time Henry hasn't seen me home. Everybody will notice of course and guess that we've broken up. It's sort of a miserable business."

"I know just how you feel! It *is* nice to have someone step up and take your arm, especially on dark nights. That was one thing I missed after . . . after John. But we'll come out together and walk straight along, not looking left or right. After a week or two it won't be so hard. And you can always count on me, Vi, for anything."

"I'm glad I have you;" Violet said as they parted.

Katie kept entirely to the kitchen during supper. For one reason, Violet supposed, she did not wish to be pressed further to reveal her plan, and for another she was busy scolding Simon, who had not appeared that day until afternoon and then with a slit in one velvet ear. In spite of her darker musings Violet laughed to herself as she heard Katie's concluding remarks to the cat.

"With a nice home like you've got an' good care too, to go stravagin' off with dirty old Toms that ain't your equals! And on the Sabbath day! Shame on you. Sit still now till I wipe off that ear."

Night church went its peaceful way as the soft spring air drifted through the opened windows. Violet kept her eyes from straying until the sermon began, then she allowed herself to look at the back seats where most of the young men sat at the evening service. One glance told her that Henry was not there! So he had been sensitive, too, about appearances. Would he never come again or would he only wait until the news of their severed relations had become common knowledge in the town? This, indeed, would not take long. Katie had said at dinner that Henry had gone home the night before by way of the alley.

"And," she had added, "if even just Mary Jackson and

39

Mrs. Hummel saw him go it would be plenty to spread the news. For him to be seen comin', all dressed up as slick as if the cats had licked him an' then leave *at nine* an' go home down the alley! Well, it wouldn't take long for them to put two an' two together. Ach, well, it's no disgrace to you, that's sure, so let them talk!"

When the last hymn and the benediction were over Faith and Violet walked along the aisle together, down the stairs and out between the lines of waiting young men, who would each, either with assurance or awkward hesitancy, depending upon the degree of the friendship, step up as the young lady of his choice appeared to squire her home. The two girls, arms linked and heads high, looked straight ahead, each drawing a breath of relief as they gained the outer walk. At the Carpenter gate they paused before Faith went on home.

"Have you ever thought," she said in a low voice, "that there really aren't any young men left that either you or I would be . . . well, interested in? That's the trouble with a little town. There aren't quite enough people in it."

"I know. The older boys who went to college have all married girls from a distance. And whether we would be interested in them or not, the others here are already going with someone. Did you see Jack Forbes tonight with the girl from the Four Points? I believe it's serious with them."

"Mother is urging me to stay in the city next winter, in a boarding house, maybe, instead of going in once a week for my music lessons. I know she feels that I might—meet someone. But I hate the idea. It seems so calculating. I'd be more self-conscious than ever. When my sister Lucy and Ninian have some young man out from the city and invite me up to meet him I never act naturally. Just because I *want* to seem attractive I get all tongue-tied and flustered. I haven't cared too much for any of them anyway so it hasn't mattered—so far."

"We're only twenty-four," Violet said. "And we each have a big interest to occupy our minds outside of getting married. That's more than most girls have. Besides," she added, looking up through the evening sky at the moon, "'on such a night as this,' I feel that anything could happen. Let's not worry. Oh, Faith, what about the service on

Tuesday? There ought to be some special music, don't you think?"

"Yes," Faith agreed slowly. "We've got to do it even if it's hard. They have a piano, I know. If you and Mrs. Dilling would sing, I'll get two of the men from the choir to make a quartette. What do you think would be the best hymn to use? 'Some day the silver cord will break'?"

"No," Violet said with a sharp catch in her breath. "I couldn't get through that."

"Oh, it's hard for you, Vi, no matter what you sing! Maybe I could find someone else."

"I'll be all right if the song isn't too harrowing. After all, it's no time to think of my own sorrow. What about 'There is a land of pure delight'?"

"Perfect, and it's so familiar. I'll play it in good time. You're sure you can, Vi?"

"Yes, I want to. It's the least I can do. And the words will seem appropriate now that it's spring. If the others agree, we won't need to practice together beforehand for we all know the tune so well."

"Then we'll consider it settled and I'll take the hymn-books out along with me. Good night, Vi. It's been a strange week-end, hasn't it?"

"Very, very strange. Good night, Faith."

When she reached the porch Violet found Katie awaiting her.

"I've just been thinkin'," the latter began, "there's some even now that considers the Sabbath over by sundown, so I don't think there will be any sin of it if I tell you the idea that came to me last night. You see when Mary Jackson was in yesterday talking about John Harvey, she just happened to mention she'd been down at the hotel and that Mrs. Rayburn had said she was takin' no more people for just over night. By the week, she said, or the month like city folks come sometimes, but no more *transhens* she called them. One-nighters, that is."

"Why?" Violet asked.

"The sheets. She said she didn't mind changin' a bed once a week but to have to keep washin' sheets that had only been slep' on once she said was too much. An' Mary Jackson says there's signs up now all along the highway, *Tourists Accommodated*. She says some tumbledown-look-

41

in' farmhouses even have a sign up since the auttas are comin' through so thick."

Katie paused for breath, then went on. "An' what just come to me was this. Here we are, our two lone, in this big house. Three nice bedrooms idle upstairs an' me always likin' a good big white wash on the line, why couldn't *we* take the transhens?"

"Katie," Violet began dubiously, "I don't think I like the idea of strangers in the house."

"Nor do I, but neither do I like to have to stop an' think twice before I put an extra pinch of tea in the teapot! An' that's what it may come to! Now, I'll show you how I've got it planned out. We'll tell Mrs. Rayburn to send all the one-nighters up here, and then we can get a sign made and put it up down at the corner with a hand on it pointin' up this way. I've seen them like that. An' we'd put *Tourists Accommodated* on it. That sounds genteel. Not like a boarding house or anything."

"What would tourists pay?"

"Well, we'd have to check on that. I've heard tell, though, that it's a dollar for one person and a dollar and a half for a couple. That's just for the bed, mind you. Breakfast's more. An' I'd see to it fine they ate their breakfast before they left. I'd have a good smell of coffee an' bacon meetin' their noses when they came downstairs. Well, what do you think? There's no easier way to make a bit extra money, is there?"

"I suppose not," Violet said slowly. "If you want, we could try it. It would be simple enough to stop if we find it doesn't work out. But, *strangers*," she added. "There's no telling who might come. A criminal, even."

"Tut!" said Katie. "What would a criminal be doin' here? But I've got one thing all worked out. If a couple comes we've no call to worry. But if a lone man ever comes, I'll sleep in the big chair in your room. Put it across the door an' keep me poker beside me! There'll no harm come to you when I'm here, I'll tell you that."

Violet laughed. "I wasn't thinking of being abducted," she said, "or seduced. I just meant that it seems odd to have people you don't know sleeping under your roof. The only strangers we've ever entertained all through the years have been returned missionaries. And," she added with a twinkle, "I guess we were reasonably safe with them. But we can try your plan, Katie, and see what happens. It should, as you say, bring in a little money and it may even add some interest to the 'quiet level of our days,' as Daddy used to call it."

"Good then!" Katie stood up and shook out her full black skirt. "I think we'll do nothing about it till after Tuesday." (Katie pronounced it "Chuseday.") "Then we'll start. We'll ask Joe Hicks to make the sign an' put it up for us, an' I'll speak to Mrs. Rayburn myself. Well, I'll be gettin' back to the kitchen an' see to Simon's ear. He sits on the stool like a gentleman while I bathe it. A knowin' beast he is, an' no mistake."

In a moment she was back. "I declare it fair scunners me the way people in this town know your business before you know it yourself. Mary Jackson walked out of church with me an' the minute we were on the front walk she says, 'So she turned him down last night,' she says. An' I says, 'Who turned who down?' An' she says, 'You can't fool me. I saw Henry go up at eight dressed to the nines and in an hour go hurryin' *down the alley*, his face red as a turkey wattle. An' tonight he's not at church. The first time he's missed I do think since he was sixteen an' had the mumps. I thought the match was as good as made. What ailed her at him, anyway?' she says."

"And what did you tell her?" Violet asked breathlessly.

"I just said, 'Curiosity killed the cat, an' how did you like the sermon?' An' she shut right up. Well, at least we can hold our whisht an' let them go on surmisin' if they want. But how could she see what color his face was? At nine o'clock at night? If she brings it up again I'll ask her, mind. Well, I'll say good night the now."

On Monday morning the good ladies of Ladykirk washed their clothes. This was a rite as fixed and unalterable as the church services themselves. On every clothesline in the town (excepting of course those which belonged to the outer fringe of respectability) there hung upon this day the snowy fruits of soapy suds and rinsing blue. The only variation was in the hours when these billowing clouds first made their appearance. There was keen rivalry here. Mrs. Hummel and Mrs. Dunn had actually, as everyone agreed, carried this too far. When Mrs. Dunn had risen one spring morning at six o'clock to see Mrs. Hummel's wash already blowing in the breeze, she had first felt mortal anger, and then a sense of relief in giving up the struggle. When she took a cherry pie over later to her neighbor, Mrs. Hummel had been so touched by the Christian charity thus evinced that she, too, had decided to avoid all contest in the future. It was a common sight from then on to see the two women hanging their clothes out at the same hour, calling across in friendly fashion as they did so.

The Monday wash was the occasion of gossip in connection with its quality as well as its timing. Poor Amanda Hicks, as kind and likable a little soul as ever was born but no housekeeper, always came in for the brunt of this criticism. Her sheets had a yellow look. It was even whispered, though never really substantiated, that she ran some of her colored clothes through with the white! She had no knack at hanging the straight pieces up properly either, and as to Joe's union suits! Old Becky Slade, who lived in a two-room ell off the Hicks's house, said (behind her skinny hand) that when the wind filled these garments "they showed his shape something awful."

Everyone was unanimous in one opinion, however, and that was that Katie's wash was the whitest in the town. It was, in the words of the hymn, "whiter than snow." When asked for the reason for this Katie put her questioners off somewhat testily.

"Plenty good soap an' hot water, an' don't skimp on your rinses. That's all I know, I'm sure. When I was a girl back in Scotland we bleached the linens on the hedge rows. Here we've got none of them, more's the pity, but we've got plenty sun which we didn't always have there."

Although Katie would vouchsafe no more advice it was generally felt that she must have some magic formula. For look, everyone said, at Violet's shirtwaists! There was about them a peculiar purity of whiteness that those of the other girls did not have, however hard their mothers tried to achieve it.

"A few drops of ammonia, could it be?" one woman would ask another.

"Two blue rinses instead of one, think you?"

"You don't suppose she'd put indigo in her *suds!*"

But the mystery, if there was one, remained unsolved.

On this Monday Katie finished her washing by ten o'clock and sat down in the kitchen rocker to have a cup of tea. Violet was shining lamp chimneys at the table and smiled at the older woman as she worked.

"What's become of Mrs. Jackson?" she asked.

"Just what I was thinkin'. She's always over as soon as she gets her clothes on the line an' if she beats me she's terrible set up. It may be I turned her off too short last night, but I was a little miffed. Sh . . . here she comes now!"

Mary Jackson was a tall thin woman of fifty with bleached blue eyes and a rather extensive nose. She had a good smile, however, and while no one could scent news as quickly or tell it as pungently as she, no one in the town was a kinder neighbor. She lived in the next house beyond the orchard and a friendly, well-worn path ran beneath the trees. William, her husband, whose character was partially evidenced by the fact that he had never been nicknamed, was, like many other men in the village, employed at the coal mine two and a half miles from town. It came about therefore that he, amongst his fellow workers, was able to collect all the information that his wife with her feminine contacts missed. Mary came up the back steps now as Violet got another cup from the cupboard and set a plate of ginger cookies on the kitchen table, remembering with an odd pang that they had been baked for Henry.

"Such a morning!" Mary began. "The phone never stopped ringing. I thought I wouldn't get my last tubful hung up till dinnertime. I did find out a thing or two more though about the Harveys. Seena's *not* expecting. That come straight, for someone asked her mother right out. It's a funny thing to me, too, that nothing like that's happened in over a year an' Seena a big bloomin' girl an' John so strong an' hearty."

She lowered her voice. "William did hear something in the barbershop Saturday night. It seems John was always closemouthed on the subject, as he naturally would be, but once he let slip something to Bill Horner that sort of made him think Seena might have been a bit cold an' stand-offish with him. And, as the old saying goes, you don't get in a family way just by havin' a pair of pants hangin' on the bedpost. Oh, well, it's all over an' past now an' the truth of it will never be known. Thanks, Vi'let, I will have a cookie. But," she went on, "there's something about that Seena that's always baffled me."

"How so?" asked Katie.

"Well, she's always sort of makin' up to the men. An' there's hardly a one of them that doesn't give her a good eye when he gets a chance. Yet there's a high-headedness about her too, as if she'd have her own way, come hell or high water. She mebbe just wanted to prove she could get a man and then just *tantalized* him, sort of. I spose of course you'll be goin' to the funeral tomorrow?"

"Yes," said Katie. "It'll be a big one, I doubt."

"The farm's still in the old folks' name, I heard on the phone this morning. That means Seena will only get her third if they sell. I spose they'll háve to. An' I didn't mean to talk against Seena. Poor girl! She's in trouble heavy enough now. I just was merely wonderin'. A body can't help that."

Violet picked up two lamps and excused herself. They were both for the parlor so when she had placed them where they belonged she dropped down before the piano and opened a hymnbook. When she had found the place she struck a chord and began to sing softly in preparation for the morrow's service.

"There is a land of pure delight, where saints immortal reign;
Eternal day excludes the night, and pleasures banish pain;
There everlasting spring abides and ever blooming flowers;
Death like a narrow sea divides that heavenly land from ours."

Her voice, while not unusual, was fresh and sweet and trained at the Mitford Academy for Young Ladies where she had received her education. The old words of Isaac Watts reached the two women in the kitchen and the flow of gossip stopped.

"It's a sad providence," said Mary Jackson, sighing.

"Aye, it is, that," said Katie.

When Violet finished the hymn she leaned forward, her elbows on the piano, her head in her hands. Where *was* this land of pure delight of which she had been singing? This place of eternal spring and perpetual day? Was there indeed such a heavenly country? Since the death of her mother and then of her father, the terrible fact of mortality had cut into her soul like a knife thrust, and in the still darkness of the nights she had often looked up into the starry sky and felt a questioning stir within her. Now there was the sudden taking off of John Harvey. In less than an

46

hour of time he had gone from his normal routine in this world to another, but where? *Where?* A poem had been growing in her mind these last months. In it she was saying what she could not speak to another human soul, but it would ease her mind to write it. She would call it "Oh, Paradise!"

The next day was fair and all Ladykirk noted the fact with relief. A wet day for a funeral added sorrow to sorrow. Katie had dinner ready at noon, then when it was finished Violet repaired to the stable to hitch Prince to the buggy before she dressed. She had a piece of apple rolled in sugar for him, and she stroked the smooth, white star on his nose while he ate it. When the tidbit was gone he rubbed his head against her arm affectionately for there was a fine *rapport* between them. In a few moments she had the bridle on him and the harness buckled into place. He went willingly to the buggy shed, backed delicately between the shafts and, once secured in them, stood still as Violet got into the buggy and grasped the reins. She drove around to the front of the house, wound the lines around the whip handle as she dismounted, then fastened Prince to the hitching block with the bridle rein and went in to dress. Her gray lawn and navy hat, she thought. While many older women, like Katie, would wear black, it was not necessary for the younger ones to do so.

They set forth at last with Violet driving. Once out of the town the wide rolling farm fields fell away from either side of the road in all the loveliness of spring, the brown of the plowed ground dark and rich between the changing greens of the young grain. Far to the east, ahead of them, was the misty, undulating fairy-blue of the mountain ridges. Violet drank in the beauty like a draught of wine as she rode in silence beside Katie.

Although it was only one-thirty when they reached the farm there were many people there before them. One of the men led Prince away to tie him beside other horses at the orchard fence, and Violet and Katie passed through the groups of men standing in the front yard and into the house, now well filled with women. Faith Lyall spoke huskily to Violet in the hall.

"I forgot," she whispered, "that *he* would be in the parlor. I'm afraid I can't use the piano there. Could you sing without it?"

"Of course," Violet said. "We'll stand out here, beside the stairs. We can be heard through all the house better this way."

"Father would like you to sing just after the opening prayer," Faith said. "I'll tell Mrs. Dilling and the men."

When the big clock on the sitting-room mantel struck the hour, Mr. Lyall took his place by the front door and a hush fell upon the crowded rooms and upon the men in the yard, broken only by occasional heavy sobbing from above. That would be Seena. A few minutes later it was time for the quartette. The four stood close, softly feeling for the key, Minnie Dilling with her fine contralto, the tenor and bass untrained, but each having an instinctive feeling for harmony. Then out of the silence the voices rose unaccompanied and so richly blent that many there caught their breath at the sound of them.

There is a land of pure delight . . .

Even Seena's loud sobbing ceased as the music filled the house.

Sweet fields beyond the swelling flood
Stand dressed in living green.

As Violet sang the words she looked through the open door to the stretches of new wheat beyond the front lawn. Would there truly be fields for John, the farmer, where he had gone? Would they, could they, be lovelier than these?

When Mr. Lyall's words of comfort were over at last and everyone had joined in singing the Twenty-Third Psalm, there was the benediction, and then the slow, heavy feet of the young men as they bore him who had been their friend out of his house forever. Henry Martin, his face set, was one of these. There was a stir in the rooms above and Seena came down the stairs on her father's arm. Her black dress fitted tightly over the voluptuous curves of her bosom and a thick black veil fell over her face. At the door something strange happened. With a quick gesture she flung the widow's pall back over her head, and with her features uncovered walked through the lines of men standing with their hats against their breasts.

48

"And don't tell me," Katie said as they were driving home, "that there was a man there who didn't take a good look at her. You could see them gapin'. But it was a hussy-like trick to put up her veil just as if she wanted to show herself. At a time like this!"

"Those crepe veils are very heavy and hot," Violet said. "She maybe just wanted to get her breath."

"She could have stood it till she got in the carriage! No, you can't excuse it. There's something brazen about that girl. I'll say it even if she is in trouble. An' I heard before the service started that some wonder if the Harveys are goin' to have a sale. Farm, stock, house an' everything. It would be the biggest one ever held in these parts. And now as for us," Katie's tones changed to an anticipatory complacence, "we'll get right to work tomorrow gettin' ready for the transhens. I may even go down an' see Mrs. Rayburn the night."

The report from the hotelkeeper's wife, as Violet heard it later, was that she would be greatly relieved to have somebody else take over the "one-nighters." Each week there were from one to six of these, including couples.

"So you see," Katie reckoned excitedly, "we can a'most count on twenty or twenty-five dollars a month! An' no trouble at all!"

Violet did not entirely share Katie's enthusiasm, but conceded that the plan was well worth a trial and entered into the preparations necessary to it, from Katie's point of view. While the house had undergone its regular spring cleaning in March, Katie insisted that everything (except lifting the carpets) should now be repeated.

"Them two spare rooms where we'll put the transhens ought to have the woodwork all washed down. I let them go this spring. I wish I was up to what I used to be."

"I'll do it, Katie, if you think it's got to be done."

"You'll do no such thing. Mebbe fall off the stepladder an' break your neck an' the blame be on my own conscience. We'll get Mag Parks for a day or so. She's glad enough now she's alone to have fifty cents an' three good meals. We can stand that. I'll send word with one of the children that live back her way. What do you think?"

"A good idea," Violet said, smiling unconsciously, for Mag was one of the town's characters and had afforded much amusement to the family over the years.

Tall, gaunt, strong as a horse even now, she had through the years supported old Jake, her husband, a lazy, shiftless, tobacco-drenched creature whose one gift to the world was an apparently endless succession of progeny, all of whom grew up unfortunately in his own likeness. One of Mag's most famous remarks had been made to Violet's mother when she once remonstrated delicately with her about the size of her family. Mag had bridled at once.

"If you'd read your Bible, Mrs. Carpenter, you'd see plain the Lord says we're put here to multiply an' replenish the earth. Well, as I see it, them as can *oughta,* an' them as can't, better keep quiet about it."

And she had continued her prolific way.

But once after old Jake's death, as she sat in their kitchen having a cup of tea between the laying of carpets, she had looked dreamily off into space and said, apropos of nothing, "Twelve childer I had to that man an' I never could abide the sight of him no way!"

"You just see to the sign," Katie was continuing, "an' Mag an' I'll take care of the cleaning. I think I'll get a whole flitch of bacon to have in the house for breakfasts. If we have that an' plenty eggs an' coffee on hand we can't go wrong."

When Violet went up to see Joe Hicks about making the sign she had a warm welcome. Little Amanda, eager, kindly and pretty in her somewhat washed-out fashion, took her through the garden to Joe's carpenter shop on the alley. Old Becky Slade called from her back window so Violet knew she would have to stop there before she could get away.

"Here's Vi'let, Joe," Amanda said at the door. "They're going to take night-lodgers and she wants a sign made."

"Well, now," said Joe. "I call that real sensible of you with all them upstairs rooms goin' to waste as you might say. An' these here machines raisin' the dust more every day. It's sort of nice to watch them passin' by, though. Makes the old town livelier. Now, Miss Vi'let, you just tell me what you want."

Violet explained in detail, carefully writing out the words *Tourists Accommodated* on a bit of paper for which Amanda had run back to the house.

"And we thought, Joe, if you would have the sign hanging from an iron arm it could be seen from both

50

sides. You could fasten it to the big maple at the corner and have a sort of hand pointing up our way. Couldn't you?"

"Sure, sure," said Joe. "I can fix it all right. Now what colors will I make it? Black letters on yellow background mebbe? That would show up."

"Fine," said Violet, trying to sound enthusiastic. She still had grave misgivings about the whole venture. "Katie is very eager to get everything ready by next week. Could you do this soon, Joe?"

"Sure, sure! I ain't so busy just now. I'll fix it up for you right away."

"And . . . could you tell me about what it will cost?" Joe spat, winked at Amanda and pulled a long face. " 'Bout a hundred dollars."

"Joe, you're a caution," said Amanda with tender pride at his humor. "Now tell her, honest."

Joe grinned, well pleased with himself. "Tell you what I'll do, Miss Vi'let. I'll fix 'er up an' then later when you're gettin' rich off your roomers I'll stop round an' present my bill. O.K.?"

"Fine," said Violet, again noting the worshipful glance Amanda bestowed upon her husband. Everyone said they were conspicuously happy except for one shadow. They had no children.

She had no chance to escape Becky, who was waiting at her door when Violet came out.

"Well now, I call this nice," the old woman began, as though Violet had come with no other purpose than to visit her. "Sit down here and let me look at you. I declare you get prettier all the time. What's this I hear though, about you giving Henry Martin the gate?"

As Violet merely blushed Becky went on, "I'm ninety-four and been a virgin all my life, but it's not the way the Lord made us. I was too persnicketty when I was young. You wouldn't think it but I was awful pretty then. I had my chances an' I turned them down. But any one of them would have been better than livin' my life the way I've done. So you just take my advice. Wait, I've got something to show you!"

She went to a chest, drew out a quilt and spread it for Violet's view. The girl exclaimed in delight.

"Why, Miss Becky, that's the most beautiful thing I've ever seen!"

"I'll bet it is," said Becky. "There's none can beat me at quilts if I do say it. It's the Wedding Ring pattern and I made it for you!"

"For *me?*" Violet echoed, astonished.

"Yes. I like you. Everybody does. You ain't proud an' you can always take time to be nice to the old. I liked your father an' mother too. Well, this is to be yours when you get married."

"Oh, I *love* it," said Violet. "How can I ever thank you?"

"Well," old Becky cackled, "you haven't got it yet! I want this to go on a marriage bed, and not on an old maid's like my own. So you just mind that, an' think it over."

Violet did think it over all the way down the street with the result that her face was sober as she entered the house. Katie's, however, was beaming. She had told Mary Jackson of the great plan and Mary heartily approved, even adding that, if anybody ever came that they didn't like the looks of, Katie had only to ring the big "teacher's bell" now on the kitchen shelf and William would be right over. The news now would soon be through the town, which in this case was pleasantly stimulating. Furthermore Katie had given a small boy two flour sacks (redeemable at the General Store for candy) and dispatched him with a message to Mag Parks. She had sent back word she could come the next day.

Like many projects in life which are motivated by a sound purpose and pressed forward with unflagging zeal, the preparations for the "transhens" proceeded without a hitch. By Saturday of that very week, the sign was up on the maple tree at the corner (in the opinion of all quite a masterpiece of Joe's skill) to strike the eyes of those who came along Main Street, especially from the east; Mrs. Rayburn at the other end of town was alerted to send all travelers entering it from the west who might stop at the hotel, on up to the Carpenter home. A small board with only the single chastened word *Tourists* was fastened to the iron fence next to the gate. This hurt Violet's pride but she accepted it as necessary. The house was immaculate, the beds freshly made up, and Katie in such a state of nervous excitement that Violet feared for her.

"You know what I've decided?" she told the older woman on Sunday evening as they sat on the porch after church. "If we get some tourists and make a little extra money we're going to have Mag come one day a week to do the heavier work. As you say, it's only fifty cents and her meals. It would save you and help her. I mean this," she added, trying to sound like the mistress of the house.

"Well, well," Katie answered, in a meek voice for her. "We'll see."

As a matter of fact Katie ached all over. The extra exertions of the week had stirred up the rheumatism in both elbows and knees. After all, she thought, it would be a comfort to have Mag sometimes. It was a big house to care for and no mistake. And the stable work was heavy and took a lot of Violet's time. She was determined to do that and Katie was glad enough. She never got used to getting too close to a horse. "Them as owns a cow has to stand nearest the tail," the old saying went, and she supposed it was the same with a horse. Violet, now, had no fears at all. She brushed and curried Prince till his coat shone like satin, just the way her father had done. And of course she was nimble to climb up to the hay mow. . . . She did most of the gardening, too.

"Well, " Katie said at last, preparing stiffly to rise, "I doubt we'll get no transhens the night."

And just at that moment there was the sound of an auto driving slowly along the street. With a gulp and a rattle it stopped before the gate and the passengers in it peered through the dusk at the sign. There was a man in the front seat in a sort of uniform with a cap and goggles now pushed up on his forehead, and there were two people in the back: a man in a long coat and checked cap, and a woman in a duster and a veil. The man now got out and came up the walk to the porch. Violet rose to meet him as he raised his hat.

"I beg your pardon, but could my wife and I have a room here for the night?"

"Of course," Violet answered.

"There is one other thing. My chauffeur. Could you put him up, too?"

"The hall bedroom," Katie said quickly. "The bed's all made in case of an overflow."

53

"Fine," said the man. "We're very tired and would like to get settled at once if we may."

He helped the woman out carefully and she leaned upon him as they came up the walk.

"I'll go ahead and make a light," Violet said, "and then you can come right along."

She felt a little thrill of excitement as she ran up the stairs and lighted the lamp on the side table (upon which she had placed a vase of yellow lilies, just in case) and the smaller one on the bureau. Then she hurried back to the hall and spoke over the banister railing. The man and woman came up slowly, the chauffeur following with their bags. They stepped inside the room and surveyed it with apparent satisfaction.

"Oh, it's so peaceful here," the woman said. "I'm sure we'll rest well."

"I'll bring a pitcher of hot water, and some cold too," Violet said eagerly. "Is there anything else you would care for?"

"Not a thing," the man said.

When she took the water up, after showing the chauffeur to his room, she knew the woman had been crying.

"Well," Katie said when she heard it, "they've mebbe been on a sad errand somewhere. You can't tell. That shoffer looks a civil chap, an' since the man and his wife are here too I guess I can sleep in my own room. Well, who'd 'a thought it would all happen so quick? I'll be down early an' have the bacon on the way in good time. I must say they look to me as if they had money. I've a notion to charge them fifty cents apiece for breakfast!"

"Oh, Katie!"

"Well, I'll try them on that. If they turn the word I'll come down to thirty-five. Now you just let me run this end of it."

Violet sat up late in her room that night. Old Becky Slade and her Wedding Ring quilt had given her an idea for a poem. As she sat, though, with the night air blowing sweetly in at the window, her thoughts wandered to the strangers in the spare room. They had come from the unknown; they would return to it. Would all the strangers who slept under her roof in the weeks to come bring an indefinable atmosphere of joy or sorrow to the old walls?

A foolish thought, she finally decided, and concentrated again upon her poem.

The guests stayed for breakfast as Katie had surmised. There were hot biscuits and homemade jelly along with the bacon and eggs. Even the woman's face looked less pale after her second cup of coffee. When the man asked for the bill, Katie, who had been serving the chauffeur in the kitchen, with one ear cocked for this moment, appeared and took charge.

"I thought I'd say four dollars for everything."

"Four dollars?" the man questioned. "For breakfast too?"

Katie's iron will weakened. "If you think it ain't too much."

The man smiled as he drew a five-dollar bill from his wallet and handed it to her. "It is certainly not too much. The extra is for yourself. And thank you," he added to Violet, "for your hospitality."

The woman did more. She shook hands. "That lovely room," she said, "and the quiet. It was just what we needed. Good-bye, my dear."

There was a rattle of the cranking, a gurgle and a sputter out in front, and in a few minutes they were gone.

Katie sank down on a chair quite overcome.

"Five dollars! Just for that! I'm goin' to keep the transhen money in the big blue sugar bowl in the kitchen cupboard. When we get enough we can bank it. Well, it does look as if the Lord is favorin' us!"

There came then several other couples in quick succession. First a pair of young things, evidently bride and groom, who arrived in a buggy, the horse spending the night in the empty stall beside Prince. They sat late on the porch looking at the moon. Violet, above, could hear the soft murmurs and the long silences before they crept up the stairs to their room and closed the door.

She lay awake quite a while that night.

The next couple were elderly and condescending to a degree. "Stuck up, they were," Katie pronounced, "an' glad I was to see the backsides of them. Their money's good as anybody's though."

There were two school teachers in a buggy, off for a little vacation and delighted with their night and breakfast there; there was a middle-aged, nondescript couple bound for their son's in Ohio, in their first car.

Then came a week in which there were no "transhens" at all. Katie was calm for Mrs. Rayburn had prepared her for the irregularities of tourist travel. She counted the money in the sugar bowl often and gloated upon it.

"Fourteen dollars an' seventy cents," she would say. "An' a round fifteen it would be if I'd charged them school teachers fifty cents apiece for breakfast. But I hadn't the heart to say more than thirty-five. They looked sort of pinched-lookin' to me. Well, we started them off with a good meal, that's sure. Now this week I'll catch up on me sheets an' I don't mind if I do have Mag for a day. The garden's goin' to keep you busy."

As a matter of fact even while she worked in the flower and the vegetable beds, Violet's mind was ardently engaged upon her own personal project. She had finished the Wedding-Ring-quilt poem, which she called "The Spinster Speaks," and was working over and, polishing "Oh, Paradise," which she had decided should be the last one. In the book? She tried to put the expression out of her mind. It was too much even to dream of a book. But neither, her father had told her, must she discount her own talent and its possibilities.

"Don't overestimate your gift," he had often said, "but don't belittle it either. Try to have a certain modest confidence in yourself. Send the poems out and see what happens."

So, as soon as she had recopied one or two of them, she was going to do just that. Her father had suggested several possible publishers. She shivered a little inwardly, as she weeded the nasturtiums in the hot sun. Even the thought of her poems being read in the office of a great publishing house gave her a near nervous chill. Then, once sent, how could she eat and sleep and *thole it,* as Katie would say, until an answer came? Her father had told her that if the manuscript came back, as it probably would, she must waste no time in regret but send it somewhere else at once. If he were only here, Violet thought, he and her mother, to share the disappointments and the possible joys! She was so alone when it came to this!

In the late afternoon of May twenty-first, a date they were always to remember, Violet carried to the Post Office a large brown manila envelope, addressed to:

Poetry Editor
Haversham & Hill, Publishers
179 Fifth Avenue, New York City

Mr. Gordon, the postmaster, eyed it with interest as he weighed it upon the scales.

"First class, eh? Must be doing a lot of writing to these people. *Publishers!* You been making up some little stories or something?"

"Maybe a little something. It will probably come back to me soon. Meanwhile, shall we just keep it as our secret?" She smiled engagingly at Mr. Gordon, who at once became a flattered ally.

"Right, Miss Violet, mum's the word and the best of luck."

She felt at once a strange emptiness, and an acute uneasiness as she walked slowly back up the street. For several years the writing of the poems had been her solace, her refuge. She had poured her deepest thoughts and emotions into them. She wondered now if they were too revealing, if through them her inner self stood forth indecently naked. She had never thought of this as she had sat in her quiet room all those hours creating them, writing them down, copying them on the typewriter. It was only now, when they were gone from her on their way into alien hands, that she had this disturbing sense of having offered her very heart for sale in the market place!

She tried to throw off the thought as a foolish result of tension, reminded herself sharply that poems must have the life blood of the author in them or they were worthless, also that they were made to be read by the many if possible and not to lie a life away on a desk. She had worked for years toward the great moment of this day when she would send them out to test their validity. Now, how utterly childish of her to repent of it and wish them back or to feel bereft without them. She fastened her attention upon the sky, which was a strange color. The afternoon had been unseasonably hot and heavy. Now a pale orange light filled the north and east, with the west and south dark and glowering. It looked like the brewing of a storm. She hurried along, giving friendly but brief greetings to the various women fanning themselves on their front porches. When she got home the air was suddenly thick with thunder and Katie was rushing about, putting down the windows. All at once the rain came, lashing, driving, beating, with sharp lightning and the cracks of detonation adding to the fury.

"My, that's a bad one," Katie said, putting her feet up on the chair opposite her as she always did in a thunder storm. She had never become used to these American phenomena. "Get your feet off the floor," she adjured Violet. "You don't need to take chances. If lightning hits it runs right along the bottom. An' keep away from the fireplace. Oh, I hope there will be no barn struck the night!"

The violent electrical storm spent itself but the rain continued in increasing downpour. Violet had just finished her supper when there was the sound of steps on the front porch and the ring of the bell. She jumped, startled, and ran through the hall, opening the door cautiously because of the rain. A man stood there, his cap now off showing iron-gray hair above a ruddy face. He was dripping wet and spoke apologetically.

"I had just found I couldn't go any farther when I saw your sign. Could you possibly give me a room tonight? If I can get inside without ruining your rugs and furniture," he added ruefully.

"Oh, of course," Violet began just as Katie appeared with an armful of newspapers.

"You can walk on these," she said briskly as she spread them, "an' come right back to the kitchen till you get dried out a bit. An' get the door shut before the wet blows in any more."

The man did as he was bidden, stepping carefully on his improvised highway until he and his bag were safe on the kitchen linoleum. Here he looked about him with apparent pleasure. The big lamp on the table was lighted due to the early dusk of the rain, the range glowed, Simon lay curled on the mat before it, the old wooden rocking chair looked inviting and the good smells of cooking hung in the air.

"What a cozy place for a man to come into out of a storm," he said. "My name is Smith and I am certainly grateful to you for giving me a night's shelter. It had come to the point that I couldn't see the road before me, and my machine was acting up too. I put my raincoat over the engine. That's why I'm so wet," he explained.

Katie was taking delighted charge of the situation.

"I'll open the oven door and we'll put your coat in front of it. Ooh—ee, your shirt's wringin' wet an' your shoes as well. We'll leave you here to change if you want. Just don't step on Simon there. He's on the mat an' he won't move for anybody. Have you had your supper?"

"No, I haven't," Mr. Smith confessed.

"We've got fried ham an' apple sauce left from our own an' I could fry you a couple of eggs. Could you make a meal on that?"

"Could I!" said the man, beaming. "I can't think of anything in the world better!"

In a few minutes he opened the living-room door.

"I certainly feel more comfortable now," he told them, smiling. "And I do appreciate your kindness. I'll use a dining-room chair if I may, for I'm still damp in spots. The wrong ones for sitting down," he laughed.

When Katie set his meal before him, he turned to Violet.

"Won't you join me, Miss . . . ?"

"Carpenter."

"Perhaps you'll have a cup of tea at least, to be companionable?"

She sat down opposite him and he began to chat easily about the problems of automobile driving, and then turned to a consideration of the old furniture in the room.

Violet felt a lift of the heart as the conversation progressed. He spoke like a man of culture, having what her father would have called "a secure grip on the English language." It was pleasant to talk with someone other than Katie as she drank her tea.

"Please forgive me if I admire your possessions. That old sideboard with the marble slab and the deer's head on top is such a fine old piece! Very early Victorian, wouldn't you say?"

"I suppose so," Violet answered. "It's just always been here and I haven't given it much thought. You're interested in antiques?"

"Very much so. I might say it's a hobby. That Empire table is beautiful, too. As a rule I don't care too much for Empire pieces but that has a great deal of charm."

When he had finished Violet struck a match to the grate fire, always kept laid, for a chill had descended along with the rain. In the soft glow they grew more and more friendly. She called his attention to the portrait of Great-great-grandfather Carpenter, which he studied with care; she showed him the desk which the real carpenter had once made, and at length, cheered and excited a little by the presence of the congenial stranger, she moved toward the bookshelves.

"Since you are so fond of old and unusual things I'm going to show you our most precious heirloom."

She lifted out the three volumes that concealed the treasure, then the leather case itself. She had now the breathless feeling she always had before listening to the nightingale. Under the man's astonished eyes she pressed the spring on the tortoise-shell box and the bird sprang up, its melody filling the room.

Mr. Smith stood speechless. Violet could have asked for no more appreciative response. His face looked awed and almost incredulous, as though he couldn't quite believe the testimony of his senses. When the song was finished he seemed unable to find the right words.

"That's the most beautiful, the most amazing thing I've ever seen!" he said at last.

"Isn't it?" Violet agreed eagerly. "I'll play it once more." She pressed the spring and again the miracle happened.

When the nightingale in its box had finally been put back in its usual place behind the books, Mr. Smith seemed rather quiet. In a short time he said that he was very tired and if he might be excused he would go on up to his room. Katie, with a look at Violet implying that it would be more becoming if she herself showed him to his bedchamber, got a pitcher of hot water and a box of matches and led the way up the stairs. The man spoke courteously to Violet before he followed.

"Good night, Miss Carpenter, and thank you for everything. I think Providence certainly brought me here tonight."

When Katie came down she was complacent. "A proper gentleman, that, if ever I saw one. I'll press his coat through a cloth before I go to bed. I'd have asked him to take his pants off for me, too, but it wouldn't have sounded ladylike. I'm sure we've nothing to fear from him but I'm settin' the teacher's bell in your room just to be sure."

"Katie, how silly of you!"

"Well, if I'm any judge yon's a fine man but only

the Lord knoweth the heart. You've always got to allow for mistakes."

"In other words, 'a man can smile and smile and be a villain still,' " Violet laughed.

"Where'd you hear that? You sound like your father."

"It's Shakespeare," Violet said. "I'm sure Mr. Smith's no villain, but if it makes you feel any better I'll keep the bell beside me. If I once rang it, the whole street would be roused, let alone you."

But the old house remained quiet all night, and both Katie and Violet, wearied from different causes, slept well. Mr. Smith was up in the morning almost as soon as Katie. He seemed very eager to get an early start away. In fact it developed that he had not planned to wait for breakfast. At Katie's evident disappointment, however, he allowed himself to be urged, but, as they recalled later, he ate with haste and was soon ready to ask for his bill.

"I'd thought two-fifty," said Katie. "Last night's supper was sort of warmed over."

"Oh, that's too little," he said. "You even pressed my coat!" Like their first tourist, he took out a five-dollar bill and put it into Katie's hand, then turned to Violet.

"I will never forget your hospitality," he said. "The pleasant acquaintance as well as the meals and the comfortable room. Thank you for taking in a stranger out of the storm."

They heard then from the front a prolonged cranking, strange gulps and chugs and rattles, with the final sound of moving wheels. As the others before him, so Mr. Smith had now departed into the unknown.

Katie brought the blue sugar bowl and counted the money again.

"Near twenty dollars," she said. "Plenty to pay the store bill and some over. I tell you it's just like *findin'* money, this. Mag's comin' the day after tomorrow an' we'll do up some extra sheets an' summer blankets. Nobody will think it queer me washin' again the middle of the week on account of the transhens. Well, he was a nice man an' no mistake. I hope we get plenty more like him."

The next day was the Annual Missionary Tea, and since the young ladies were to serve, Violet and Faith Lyall found themselves together. There was little time for conversation while the refreshments were being passed, but when all was over and the cups and saucers washed and put back in the church cupboards the two girls sauntered slowly along the walk together and Violet told her friend her big news.

"I actually mailed them, yesterday, Faith!"

"Oh, Vi, you didn't really! I'm so excited! When do you suppose you'll hear anything?"

"That's just what worries me so. I've no idea whether it will be a week or a month or *three* months. It's really dreadful to be so uncertain. I'm nervous as a witch already."

"You must keep very calm," Faith declared, "and think of other things. If there was only something big and definite to take your mind off this. Any more tourists?"

"Oh, yes, and such a nice one!" Violet's face was alight as she told of their last-night's guest.

"What age was he?" Faith asked.

"Oh, fifty or fifty-five perhaps."

Faith sighed. "If he had only been young, Vi! You never know what could happen."

Then, because they were young themselves, they laughed together and Violet came on into the house as Mrs. Lyall overtook her daughter. Katie had already changed her dress and was busy in the kitchen.

"A nice tea," she said judicially, "though whoever made the ham sandwiches cut it pretty thin. My piece of cake was good though. Marble with white icing. And I thought our cookies stood up about as well as any. Oh, Mary Jackson was over. She said Joe Hicks had been here. She saw him goin' out the kitchen door when she got home. Bein' a Methodist he wouldn't know about the Tea an' I spose he just sat a while here waitin' for us to come in. It would be about his bill for the signs, I doubt. You'd better run up tomorrow an' pay him, Vi'let. It's not right to keep him out of his money when it's comin' in so fast to us."

Violet's state of inner tension continued the next day. When would the poems get to the editor's desk? How soon would he read them? What, oh what would he think of them when he did? She tried to busy herself with the small duties of the household. It was strange, though, not to be slipping off to her room to work on her book, as she was unable to resist calling it. By afternoon, when Mag was ironing sheets in the kitchen and Katie had gone across for a cup of tea with Mary Jackson, Violet hitched up Prince, deciding to stop first at the Hicks's and pay Joe, then pick up Faith and take a drive through the country to calm her nerves. But nothing worked out as planned. Joe was away somewhere, had been gone all day according to old Becky Slade, and Amanda was out in the country visiting her mother. No one was home at the Lyall's either, and Violet remembered only then that this was the day for Faith's music lesson in the city.

She headed Prince out the "low" road to Westburg and drove slowly along, thinking her own thoughts. She loved this road. The smell of the woods on either side was fresh now from the recent rain and from the new growth of May. There was the languorous sweetness of the May apples and the mixture of faint scents from the trilliums and skyrockets, the mosses and upspringing ferns. It was a fragrance impossible to describe. Or was it? A line of verse came to her mind as though dropped from the sky. As she grasped it her lips parted in a smile of wonder. Why, of course! This was her panacea; this was the cure for the tension and suspense. She would go on to another poem! No matter what the editor said about the others, there would always be a new one stirring in her mind. As it was now. "The Woods in Spring." Too ordinary a title, of course, but that would be the theme. A hard one, indeed. How could one with words bring forth the reality of the young leaves, the white of the dogwood, the strange rose of the Judas trees, the perfume which was more to the soul than the senses, the delicate withdrawal of the quiet, shadowed grove itself? But one must try and never give up.

When she came to a spot in the road wide enough, she turned Prince around and drove slowly back. She stopped at the Gill farm for a gallon of buttermilk to give some reason in Katie's eyes for the drive, and after the trip with Mrs. Gill to and from the cool springhouse, she unreined Prince at the watering trough and let him drink and nuzzle in its clear, moss-lined depths.

All evening she was filled with the new elation. She stayed late on the front porch allowing the nebulous poem to take shape in her mind, searching for words and phrases, brooding tenderly over the first full sentences. Once again there was the enchanting sense of struggling creation with the possibility of ultimate beauty to lure her on. A desire began to grow upon her as she sat watching the waning moon. She wanted to hear the nightingale again now, tonight, to bathe herself, lave herself in the sweetness pouring from the tiny throat. It would be like an earnest of fulfillment to come.

She shut the front door and locked it, then walked to the living room and moved eagerly toward the bookshelf upon which lay the precious box. She took down the three guarding volumes as usual, then began wildly to toss more and more books from their places, letting them fall to the floor behind her as they would. When only empty spaces confronted her she gave a cry that rang through the house. The nightingale was gone!

CHAPTER THREE

VIOLET's midnight cry, which roused Katie and brought her down the back stairs at a dangerous speed, was heard also by Mary and William Jackson as they neared the house, returning from an evening with the latter's brother Andrew, who lived down by the bridge. They hurried on along the street, over the porch, and William knocked sharply upon the front door. Katie opened it.

"What's wrong?" he asked.

"We thought we heard a scream," Mary added anxiously.

"Aye, did you?" Katie said. "Come on in an' we'll tell you. Vi'let here looks like she'd go off in a faint any minute an' no wonder. The shock of it! An' us treatin' him so well an' him seemin' a gentleman from his toes up. But none but the Lord knoweth the heart."

"What is it?" William burst out. "Have you a lodger tonight? Did he do you harm? I'll see to him. Just tell me what's the matter."

"Sit you down an' I'll make a cup of tea to fettle us all. Vi'let, tell them, an' don't just look at them. It's the bird. It's the nightingale that's gone! An' I even stood up pressin' his coat that night an' would have done his pants too if I could have got them off him. Oh, I could near brain him with me poker if I just had holt of him. Tell them, Vi'let, while I get the kettle on."

Violet drew a deep breath while the tears overflowed at last.

"I'll tell you all we know," she said. "I'm so glad you're here. Maybe you can advise me what to do." She motioned them to chairs and then told them briefly about Mr. Smith's stay with them.

"I remember now he was very quiet after he listened to the bird, and went off at once to bed. He was in a hurry to leave the next morning, too, but Katie kept him for breakfast. He seemed *so* nice. That was only three nights ago and now when I came to get the bird—I just suddenly felt I'd like to hear it—it's gone."

"You're sure you've looked well?"

"I put it back that night exactly where we've always kept it and it's simply not there. As you can see I've turned out nearly the whole bookshelf."

"Looks bad," said William.

"There must be ways to catch him!" Mary cried. "Oh, what a miserable, wicked trick to come sneakin' down the stairs in the dead of night while you and Katie were asleep an' steal that bird! Why, the whole town's goin' to take this to heart, mind you. Nearly everybody's seen it an' heard it an' brought all their visitors over the years for you to show it to them. An' all the school children too! You've been so good lettin' them . . ."

"Now see here," William broke in with solemn, masculine importance, "we've got to find how to go about tracin' this fellah. His name was Smith, you say?"

"Yes."

"Didn't give his first name?"

"No."

"You ought to keep a book an' make everybody sign. Like a hotel. Where did he come from?"

"We don't know."

"Well, where was he headin' for?"

"He didn't say."

"Jupiter Peter! This is goin' to be tough. You know, Vi'let, you ought to go up to the Squire's in the morning early. This'll be likely up to the law, though I'll do what I can. Did he start off up town or down toward the bridge?"

"I don't even know that," Violet said mournfully. "He came in the pouring rain after dark, and before he left in the morning he insisted on paying five dollars, and Katie and I were so excited over that that we didn't look out when he started."

"Jupiter Peter!" William said again, the strength of his language betraying the depth of his emotion. "This may take a lawyer or a detective or something. Who's that friend of your father's at the county seat?"

"Mr. Huntley. I think I'll go to see him, but I'll talk to Squire Hendrick first, tomorrow morning. Oh, it all looks hopeless to me."

"Tut, tut, nothing's hopeless," Katie put in as she entered with the tea. "A deed like yon one did will come to light. I did think when I woke once that night that I heard like a stair creakin'. But I just turned over an' paid no attention. I tell you it's taught me a lesson. Here's your tea, Mary, an' William, help yourself to the cookies."

"I can't, Katie. I'm full as a tick. You know how Andrew's wife always stuffs us."

"Go 'long with you. Better belly burst than good food lost. Here you are, Vi'let. The thing that's just struck me is the money we've made. I've been keepin' it in the big blue sugar bowl in the kitchen. The one we never use. Now that's goin' to be dangerous. We'll have to bank it."

"Will you keep on takin' tourists?" Mary asked eagerly.

Violet hesitated but Katie was ready. "We'll have to consider about it. But just because Mr. Smith was a thief we've no call to think ill of everybody. It's an easy way of makin' money an' no mistake." She leaned forward. "The next one that comes, I'll make sure. I'll sit in the upper hall all night where I can see the door of the room."

"I tell you it ain't safe. Two lone women like you takin' in people off the road. *Men!*" William licked his lips. "I can't say it no plainer but *things could happen.*"

"What I can't figure out is how I came to miss seein' this Mr. Smith drive off," Mary repined. "Even when I'm doin' the dishes I usually run to the front once in a while to see—to see—well, you know, to see if there's anything to see. An' to think this time I missed it! Just when I could have been of use to you."

After every detail had been rehearsed again, William spoke. "Well Vi'let, it's pretty late an' you look as if you could use some sleep. You go up to the Squire's in the morning. I'll find out if any of the men might have seen a car—'bout what time was it he left?"

"Seven-thirty to the minute for I noticed the clock. I heard him stirrin' early an' I had breakfast on the table by seven," Katie said.

"An' I'll spread the word as well as I can," Mary added with relish. "The more that knows it the better. Somebody might have seen something. I'll be over in the morning an' hear what the Squire has to say. An' don't worry too much, Vi'let. It might be worse."

"I don't see how it could be," Violet answered, "but thanks to you both. I'm glad you came in."

A terrible exhaustion had fallen upon the girl. She did not wait while Katie blew out the lamps, ejected Simon (who had managed to insinuate himself in the door when the Jacksons entered) and locked up with extra care. She climbed the stairs slowly, undressed with seemingly numb fingers and got into bed. But she could not sleep; this new weight of loss lay too heavily upon her heart; she felt desolated. Her mother and her father gone, and now the nightingale which had been a romantic treasure of joy through the years, and to her recently, in some mysterious way, an earnest of love yet to come. To be deprived of a rare and valuable heirloom was sad enough, but the ache in her heart was most of all for the lost beauty and the lost symbol of hope.

As she lay in her loneliness she thought of Henry. He too was gone. But even if he were still now on the old footing she could not have shared this inner sorrow with him. She remembered her recoil when she had first shown the treasure to him a few years ago. For some reason he had not seen it as a child. He had watched then as the tiny wings fluttered and the song poured forth.

"Huh!" he had said when the miracle was ended. "That's cute. Wonder how it works? Say, I'll bet your folks could get a pretty penny for that if you wanted to sell it."

"We don't," Violet had said shortly, and put the box back behind the books without allowing the bird to sing again.

No, all she was feeling at the moment only emphasized her wisdom in breaking with Henry. But oh, how could

67

she indefinitely eat the bitter bread of solitude? There was a sore, surprised hurt also in her heart, as that of a child who, all innocent and trusting, has received an undeserved blow. They had tried to be so kind to Mr. Smith. They had given him their best hospitality, and he had repaid it with this criminal offense!

The birds were waking when she finally fell asleep.

The next morning Katie was brisk and decisive. She had made hot biscuits to tempt Violet's appetite and she sat with her to see that she ate them and to give her views on the whole matter.

"I called up the Squire to be sure he'd be in when you go. I just said we've been robbed, thinkin' to let you tell the details yourself an' blest if Mary Jackson hadn't rung them up an hour before an' told the whole thing. Before noon it'll be all over the town, an' the county too. This is once, though, that Mary's blether won't hurt. The more that knows it the better. Eat another biscuit, now, with some quince honey. It'll do you good."

Violet smiled. "I believe you think food can cure anything, Katie."

"Well, they say meat an' mass never hindered anybody. An' its my opinion you ought to go into Harrisville this very afternoon an' see Mr. Huntley. If he thinks you need one of them detective fellahs he'll know how to get a one for you. I'll drive in with you. This thing has made me nervous about you bein' alone on the road even."

"I doubt if anyone would steal me," Violet smiled. "Or Prince. I'll go along now to Squire Hendrick's and see if he has any ideas."

The Hendrick house at the upper end of Main Street was a large white frame one, trimmed with an airy and delectable "gingerbread" scrollwork at the eaves and below the front-porch roof. This had been so designed to delight the Squire's young bride many years ago. After her death in the first bloom of her wifehood the Squire had settled into a bachelor existence with his sister, Miss Annie, to keep house for him. Since he was good-looking in a homespun way, kindly and, according to village standards, of comfortable means, derived not from judicial business but from a rich farm which he owned, there had hardly been a spinster in the town over the years who had not made tentative overtures to gain his interest. But the Squire had eyed them all with shrewd and distant appraisal, and continued his way unmoved. He had loved once and once only, and the pattern of his heart and his life was set.

He was waiting in his office now, his swivel chair tipped back, his spittoon in comfortable reach of his excellent aim. It was clear from the start that he did not consider Violet's loss overwhelming.

"So your lodger run off with your bird, eh? Better that than money. Mary Jackson was saying you had quite a few dollars in the kitchen that wasn't touched at all. Count your mercies, child."

"But Squire Hendrick, the bird was a very rare possession. It was more than merely valuable. It was *precious* to me. I have to do everything possible to try to get it back."

"I know. I know. Pretty little thing. Your father showed it to me once. All I mean is you may just have to kind of accept this. Mary Jackson says you don't know anything about this man except that his name's *Smith*."

"That's all," Violet said in a choked voice.

"You don't know where he come from or where he went. By this time he's likely far enough. Three days since he was at your house?"

"Four today."

"Well, Vi'let, I'd like to help you. But my common sense tells me the best thing you can do is just to forget the whole thing. There's no use tryin' to find him when you've nothing to go on. It's like huntin' in a dark cellar for a black cat that ain't there."

"That's all . . . all you can say, Squire?"

"That's it as I see it. Now just don't fret yourself about this. Pretty little thing it was but don't get too worked up. There's bigger troubles in life."

He stood up. "Always glad to see you, Vi'let. I still miss your father. Him and me had many a good crack. Well, come in again if there's anything I can do."

Violet went home the back way to avoid the certain interruptions she would encounter by this time along Main Street. She found Mary Jackson in the kitchen with Katie, imparting the news as she now had it. Bill Hawkins at the General Store had noticed a car going down street toward the bridge a few minutes past seven-thirty. He knew the time for he was just opening up. But Mr. Williams, the blacksmith, had also seen a car just then going up street and on out the Pike. So the two reports canceled each other.

"The thing is," Mary kept repeating, "which of them cars was Mr. Smith's? The east-bound one or the west-bound. I doubt we'll ever know. It's a mystery an' no mistake. But the whole town's takin' this hard. I haven't seen everybody so stirred up for years. One thing people are sayin' is that you folks oughtn't to take in any more strangers."

"Tut," said Katie, a gleam of cupidity in her eye. "That's our business."

"But as William said last night, it ain't safe to have *men* here. You never know. You've had a thief an' you might have a . . . Well, Violet's a young girl an' even you, Katie . . ."

"Even me, what? I guess I'm no temptation."

"You're a *woman*," Mary pursued.

"An' I'd like to see one of them try to prove that!" Katie returned with spirit. "What did the Squire have to say, Vi'let?"

"Nothing. He thinks it's absolutely hopeless. He says we've nothing to go on."

"He's a briggle," Katie said. "We can go on faith till we have something better, can't we? Let's get a bit early dinner an' go into Harrisville to see Mr. Huntley. The Squire's all right for a spite fence or a come-by-chance bairn but this is *robbery*, and it needs a lawyer."

"I'll bring you over a slice of ham ready-cooked," Mary said, "an' some light cakes we had left from yesterday. Oh, I'd like to do *something* for you. I don't know when anything's been really stolen out of a house before. It gives you a queer feeling, sort of."

When they set off at last with Katie driving because she insisted Violet was too nervous, their progress down Main Street was slow. At the Post Office, which was also the drug store, Mr. Gordon, who was standing in the doorway, came running toward the buggy.

"Any wind of him yet?" he asked anxiously.

"Nary a thing," said Katie. "We're on our way to see Mr. Huntley."

"And a good job, too. He knows his business. I'm certainly upset over this, Violet. I mind the time years ago when my wife was sick your mother brought the bird over

70

to play it for her. She always said that's what gave her the first turn for the better. She'd been sort of low in her spirits before. Well, good luck to you!"

Mrs. Wilson, the schoolmaster's wife, was crossing the street a little farther down and stopped to speak to them.

"I just heard about the nightingale! Oh, Violet, I am so distressed! I've never told a soul this before but now I'll tell you and Katie. My Louise met Richard first at the big Fanshaw reunion five years ago. You know a lot of city people were there. He asked to come out later on a Saturday to see her. Well, they were both sort of shy and when he got here they just sat and had nothing to say to each other. I saw things were going badly and I said to Louise, 'Why don't you take Richard up to the Carpenter's and let him hear the nightingale?' She jumped right up and they left and when they got back they were talking away a mile a minute. He kept right on coming after that till they were married. But I often think about that first day. If he'd been bored and not really gotten to know Louise . . . well, you can't tell. Such little things turn the tide at the beginning."

At the General Store, where Main Street started its descent toward the covered bridge, three men sat sunning themselves on the wide wooden steps. With one accord they rose as they recognized Prince and came into the street. They were Kim Hart, a farmer who was doubtless waiting for his wife to finish her shopping inside, Harvey Bostig, who was just getting over an attack of pleurisy, and old Nappie Newton, whose days were always given over to uninterrupted leisure. His pants now presented a long expanse of greasy patina, his ragged shirt was well spattered with tobacco juice and his suspenders spliced with twine. He was the first to reach the buggy.

"Vi'let, you know what I was just sayin' before we seen you come along? I says, If I could get my sights on that fellah that done it I'd shoot him down like a rabbit, I says."

"Oh, Mr. Newton, don't talk like that," Violet demurred.

"I think we'll stop one short of murder," Katie said dryly, "but we are goin' in to Harrisville to get the law on him. If we can ever get started," she added.

"Sure," Kim Hart said. "We don't want to hold you up. Just anxious to know if you'd heard anything. Stand back. Nappie, let them get on their way."

71

But Nappie still clutched the buggy frame.

"I just have to say this about that there bird. I'd heard tell of it for years an' never expected to lay eyes on it. Then one day when I'd a few drinks inside me I went up to your house, Vi'let, an' I says to your pap, I says, 'Any reason why I can't hear this nightingale bird like everybody else in town?' An' he says, 'None at all, come right in.' An' damme if he didn't get it out an' show me. Wonderfullest thing ever happened to me, I guess. Well, get along now, an' good luck to you!"

As the buggy started once more Katie took the whip from its stock.

"There's Andrew Jackson's wife out on her porch. If she stops us, we might as well go back home."

As they neared the bottom of the hill Katie laid a sharp stroke on Prince's broad and unsuspecting back. He sprang forward in surprise, straining the harness, and the buggy had clattered halfway across the bridge before his ears rose to a normal position and he allowed himself to be reined in.

"Poor Prince!" Violet said, "he's not used to that kind of treatment."

"I had to get past Millie Jackson," Katie said grimly. "Now we can jog along."

Violet watched the undulating fields as they fell away sweetly in the Maytime sun. The greens, the browns, the budded woods, the little rippling freshets, the sheep with their young lambs, the plowmen at their furrows—all these made up the beauty that filled the eye. She wondered, as farm succeeded farm, whether her poems had yet reached the great house of Haversham & Hill! In four days they must be there. But when would they ever be read? And by whom? Would they come swiftly back to her in the envelope she had enclosed for that sad but highly probable contingency? Of course she knew them all by heart. To keep her mind now from her loss as Prince drew the buggy over the hilly miles, she began to repeat some of them to herself.

When she came to "Imagined Love" a soft rose crept into her cheeks. This was the poem she still wished she had omitted from her manuscript. She was ashamed of the way she had poured out her heart in it. The words, she feared, were too revealing. She recalled the advice her father had once given her. "You must see beauty steadily and unfalteringly, if you are going to be a poet. You must never turn aside from it even though it brings a kind of divine pain. And above everything, you must be honest and unafraid in interpreting human emotions."

Well, she had tried to do just that. She sighed as she thought of her father. With her more mature perceptiveness heightened by the shock of sorrow, she realized that, like him, she led a dual life. There was the world of the village she loved. Within its dear, familiar and undemanding milieu she shared its joys and sorrows, its comedy and drama. Into this small, bounded and cohesive aggregate of souls she had been born and of it she would always be a part.

But even as she trod the uneven flagstones of Main Street—(Good morning, Mrs. Abbey, is your rheumatism better? . . . Good morning, Mrs. Vail. How's your garden doing? . . . Yes, our lettuce is well up, too. Hello, Mr. Gordon. It *is* warm for May, isn't it?) even as she lived and moved and had her corporal being in Ladykirk, she dwelt also in another world, remote, vital, in a sense intransigent, where her mind had commerce with the immortal and her own inner thoughts pursued their hidden way.

Even so, she said again to herself, she should have kept that one poem out of the book, if book it would ever be.

The golden dome of the courthouse in the widespreading county-seat town finally came into clear view, and in a little while Prince's shoes were clattering over the brick pavements. When they entered Mr. Huntley's office Katie for once held back, cowed by professional eminence, and allowed Violet to take the lead. Mr. Huntley smiled with pleasure.

"Why, Miss Violet, what a nice surprise! I haven't seen you for so long. Not since . . ." He stopped for they both knew the sad day from which he was reckoning the time.

"And, Katie, how are you?" he asked hastily.

"I can't complain," Katie replied.

He went on speaking to Violet, his aging glance taking in the girl's young loveliness as he offered the chairs.

"You're looking wonderfully well, my dear. I hope no trouble brings you here."

Violet leaned forward, her eyes eager, anxious, luminous.

"Oh, but we *are* in trouble, Mr. Huntley. Did you ever over the years see and hear the nightingale which was a wedding gift to my mother?"

"Once. And I never forgot it. Incredibly beautiful thing!"

"It's gone, Mr. Huntley. It was stolen!"

She told him all the story while he began to rub one side of his nose with a long forefinger, even as he had done when Violet's father had sat there confessing his investments in *wheat* and *corn*.

"There must be some way to recover it. Oh, Mr. Huntley, tell me there's something you can do!"

He was silent for a long moment and then he spoke gently.

"I would do anything in the world to help you, my child, but you've given me an almost impossible problem. A detective would be of no use for we don't know where this Mr. Smith is—east or west. The only thing I can think of to do . . ."

"Yes?" Violet prompted.

"I will have a notice of the loss put in the Pittsburgh and the Philadelphia papers. Maybe even in Chicago and New York. Then I know a policeman in Pittsburgh who for various reasons keeps in touch with the pawnshops— I'll alert him. But beyond that, I really wouldn't know what to do. You say he seemed interested in antiques?"

"Oh, very much so."

"H'm. Well, I'm afraid then he wanted this for his own pleasure, and not to sell. Which makes it even worse for us. But I'll do what I *can* do, Violet, even though it doesn't sound very promising. You can count on me for that."

"Will . . . will it be very expensive?" Violet asked falteringly.

Mr. Huntley looked at her. He was thinking what a pity it was that this girl with her beauty and her fine mind was being wasted in a little village like Ladykirk. She would either teach school all her life or marry some one there who . . .

"If you'd like a bit on account, as it were," Katie spoke up, feeling in her large, shabby reticule, "I've got some here. The lodger money. I thought after the robbery we oughtn't to keep it in the house."

"No," Mr. Huntley stopped her firmly. "Nothing now,

74

thank you. Let's see if we get any results. But in any case there will be very little charge."

Violet rose and held out her hand.

"I feel so much better just knowing that *you* know," she said. "And I'll keep on hoping."

"Right," said Mr. Huntley. "I've lived too long and seen too many strange things happen to believe anything is ever hopeless. My motto always is, Hope, but don't *expect*. Blessed are they that expect nothing for they shall never be disappointed."

Violet laughed and shook hands again. "I'll do that," she said, "and thank you so much. You could call me up if ever . . . if there should be . . ."

"Don't worry. I'll keep in touch with you, if for nothing else than to hear the sound of your voice. How's that for a pretty speech from an old man?"

"It's delightful," Violet said. "I'm afraid I could develop a taste for pretty speeches."

"You should," said Mr. Huntley, "for you merit them. And while you're hoping why not hope this Smith man will have an attack of conscience and bring the bird back?"

"Well," Katie burst out, "now that's sensible, that! It's something we can put in our prayers, and not be ashamed of. The way I've been prayin' these last four days—wishin' ill on that man—I wasn't sure the Lord would pay much heed to me."

They left Mr. Huntley chuckling, and took their way down the wooden stairs, reeking with dust and ancient cigar smoke, to the street. The banking took but a few minutes and then, to lighten their spirits further, they stopped in an ice-cream parlor and ate some of the confection (five cent dishes!) at one of the marble-topped tables. Thus fortified they found Prince and jogged back between the smiling fields, now touched with the early gold of sunset.

When they got home Faith Lyall was waiting on the porch. Katie volunteered to put Prince in his stall, so the two girls sat down on the swing together.

"It seems incredible," Faith kept repeating, "but we never heard about it until this afternoon! Oh, my dear, this is dreadful! Have you any clue at all?"

"None whatever," Violet answered sadly. "We've just been in Harrisville to see Mr. Huntley. He'll try putting

75

some ads in the *Lost* sections of the papers of various cities, but he isn't encouraging."

"And to think," Faith said, "that I was wishing from what you told me of Mr. Smith that he had been young and single and maybe, well . . ."

Violet laughed, which broke some of the tension within her. "We mustn't ever let our imaginations run away with us," she said. "Because of all we've talked over in confidence we mustn't be silly. Just now I feel far removed from romance. In fact I feel very, very depressed over life in general. Simon!" she broke in as the cat crossed the porch and vaulted to her knee. "You know you don't like to swing. He'll make us stop," she added.

Simon composed himself comfortably, only the faint switching of his tail revealing that he was not entirely content. When the girls continued to swing gently he raised his head, looked into Violet's face and uttered a faint mew, then settled again as though sure this appeal would be sufficient. When the swing did not stop, he reared up on his forefeet and gave an ominous growl.

"Oh," Faith laughed, "let's stop and see what he does."

"He'll lie down and stay there!" Violet said. "He's a domineering creature, but we love him anyway."

Simon sensed the sudden cessation of motion, gave a small sound of satisfaction, fell into a round ball and was instantly asleep.

"There, you see?" Violet said. "We spoil him terribly but it's fun. I hope nothing happens to him," she added. "I'm growing more and more aware of how alone I am. Katie and Simon and I against the world," she added with a faint smile.

"Let's talk of other things," Faith said. "There really is some news about Seena. The Harveys were in last night to see Father and they told him they had deeded the farm over to John just before they went to Ohio. They thought it would please him and of course they were sure he would always be here to look after them if they needed anything."

"But Seena will only get her third now, won't she?"

"That's the pity of it. Evidently she got round John right away to make a will and he left the farm to her. And you can see how he would do that. She was his wife. He has no brothers or sisters and naturally he would expect to

76

outlive his parents. But isn't it tragic for them? They told Father that Seena doesn't even seem to want them to go out there at all. And Vi, she's staying at the farm *alone*."

"She's brave," Violet said. "I wouldn't do it. It must be two miles to the nearest neighbor."

"It's a little less than that over the hill to the O'Dell's but of course they wouldn't have a phone. Jake O'Dell always helped John at harvest and busy times so now since Bill, the hired hand, has left he comes over every day and does the farm work and Seena gives him his dinner at noon."

The girls were silent a moment.

"But she stays there all alone at night?"

"I hope so," Faith returned and then they both laughed shamefacedly.

"That was dreadful of me, but Jake is a big, good-looking fellow and he must be twenty-one by now. I don't think Seena is being very—well, *discreet*."

"I can't understand her. But then no one does. However, no matter what we may think of her, she's near our own age and she's had trouble and I believe it would be our duty to drive out some day and call on her. What do you think?"

Faith agreed at once.

"I'm ashamed I've never thought of that myself. But it would be a kind thing to do. Let's try to go soon. It might take your mind off your loss for a little. I suppose you haven't . . . I mean of course it's too soon to hear anything yet about your book?"

"Oh, heavens, yes!" said Violet, trying to give an impression of great casualness. "It may be weeks, months indeed, before I have any word."

When Faith rose to go she said, "Father and Mother sent their sympathy. They both loved the bird."

All that evening and for days to come there was a steady stream of callers at the Carpenter house. There was, of course, the impelling motive of curiosity to relieve while all the details of Mr. Smith's visit were recounted again and again. Here Katie shone. She told of the storm, the sudden ringing of the bell, the newspapers on the floor, the hanging of his coat before the kitchen oven, his care in not stepping upon Simon, his general genteelness, which events had proved concealed a black heart. The town listened, questioned, exclaimed and went home to tell it all over themselves with zest and with the drama of unconscious exaggeration. Before long the picture of the silent house and of Mr. Smith stealing downstairs in the darkness at perhaps two in the morning, feeling in the shelves for the nightingale and then furtively creeping back to his room with his prize was vividly fixed in every mind.

But along with the curiosity of the townspeople Violet was aware of the ever-increasing examples of the feeling of personal loss. So, in spite of the fact that she fell into bed each night wearied from the day's endless conversations, she had a small sensation of comfort. She smiled ruefully to herself as she recalled what her father had always called the Village Equation:

$$1 \text{ (Burden)} \div 500 = 1/500$$

There was truly a certain sharing of the distress in the warm, absorbed interest of all the people in Ladykirk. Her mother, city-bred, had never grown entirely reconciled to the fact that her every movement was noted and discussed.

"I *hate* to be the subject of conversation," she had often remarked.

But her husband had consoled her. "Don't feel that way," he said. "It's a kindly curiosity. I like it. I feel surrounded not only by the love of my family but by the affectionate interest of all the town."

"I could get along with less of it," her mother had always insisted.

But as Violet lay lonely in her bed, as the soft scented darkness of the spring night encompassed her, she like her father was eased by the general sympathy.

On a certain June morning when the pink cabbage roses were in bloom along the garden wall and the red Jacqueminot by the front walk, Violet came down the kitchen steps dressed in a pink checked gingham dress, cotton gloves to save her hands and a white sunbonnet thrust upon her by Katie, who lived in mortal fear that her charge might become tanned by the sun. Inside, Katie and Mag Parks were doing a large ironing. It had been decided after much consideration that the practice of taking tourists would continue, with one difference: there would now be received only *couples* and *women*. No "lone men," as Katie described them, would be taken in. And, as

78

though once again Providence was supporting their plan, there had been already two couples and one nervous woman who was timid about driving alone in her buggy after dark. Because of the continued source of income Mag Parks was still coming once a week to help with the heavier work. She, of all the town, however, would not discuss the loss of the nightingale. She had often over the years begged to hear it to "cheer her up." Now, she only shook her head lugubriously when it was mentioned and heaved a long sigh.

As Violet proceeded with her weeding her thoughts were far away from Ladykirk. They were in fact centered upon the offices of Haversham & Hill, Publishers, which, while she could not actually envisage them were still a vivid reality in her mind. So lost was she in her private contemplation that she did not see the slight form of Amanda Hicks approaching along the walk and across the garden. When she spoke Violet jumped to her feet.

"I didn't mean to startle you," Amanda said. "You must have been dreamin' about a young man from the scared way you bounced up. Well, I've brought you a present for your hope chest."

"Why, what do you mean?" Violet asked, eying the big flat package Amanda was carrying.

"It's from Becky Slade. You know! The Weddin' Ring quilt she promised you. She's been worryin' ever since you were in to see her that day. She says she wanted to keep it till you got married but what if she'd die sudden an' somebody else got hold of it. I told her I'd watch out for it but she couldn't rest till I brought it down to you. So here it is, an' it's a dandy."

"Oh, I know it! Really, I couldn't be more pleased, and thanks so much for bringing it. I'll go up soon to see Miss Becky but do tell her when you get back that I'm simply delighted and I'll treasure it all my life!"

Amanda looked each way and then lowered her voice.

"She said to tell you she wanted there to be *four* legs under it and not just two. She's a caution!"

Violet colored and laughed. "Come on in and we'll show it to Katie and Mag Parks," she said.

When it was spread out in all its beauty over the living-room sofa, Katie exclaimed rapturously. "Aye, that's a fine one, that! Look at the colorin' an' those stitches! As if piecin' it wasn't enough she's quilted it all herself, too, hasn't she?"

"Every inch," said Amanda proudly, "an' never a pair of glasses on her nose. She's got second sight now, I guess. Well, I'll be tickled to tell her how you all like it." Her glance moved to Mag who as yet had said nothing. She now, for some curious reason, wiped her eyes.

"It's a nice quilt," she said, "but it's what's under it that counts. I hope you get a good man, Vi'let. A poor fist I made of it when I married Parks. Of course it was a have-to at the time or I'd never have took him. Then once it was done I just had to keep goin'. Twelve childer one after the other an' me nearly pullin' the bed post to pieces with every one of them! An' now where are they? Scattered an' gone an' no good to me. I've had a hard life, Vi'let. I want you always to mind that. I've had a hard life."

And with tears still oozing she retreated to the kitchen.

"She's not well, I doubt," said Katie. "I'll go make her a cup of tea to fettle her."

When Amanda had gone her pleased way, Violet carried her new treasure up to her room and laid it out upon the bed. There was, indeed, tender significance in the circling symbols of love. Wedding rings! Would she ever wear one? Somehow the quilt sent into her heart a delicate warmth of expectancy. Not the same compelling assurance which the nightingale had brought after she had read Great-uncle Alex's letter; but rather a soft affluence of girlish hopes and dreams. She smoothed her gift gently, admiring the pinks and blues and pale yellows which made up its pattern. Old Becky could so easily have chosen garish reds and greens. Probably as she worked she was thinking in terms of the budding colors of her own faraway youth.

"Vi'let!" Katie called from the foot of the stairs. "You're wanted. Billy Wade's here to see you."

Violet's heart suddenly beat hard.

"It's about the orchard, he says," Katie added, her tone managing to convery infinite reproach that she had known nothing of this before.

"I'll be right down," Violet responded, and then stood very tense and still for a second while she collected herself. I'll promise nothing yet, she thought.

Billy was short and stout with a bald head and a pair of shrewd eyes.

"Well, Miss Vi'let, I was just drivin' past an' I thought I'd stop an' see you." He wiped his perspiring face. "Is it hot enough for you?"

Violet was long used to this familiar salutation and accepted it for what it was: a friendly comment on the weather rather than a personal question.

"It is warm today," she agreed and waited.

"That orchard of yours there is sure goin' downhill," he said as his trial opening.

"In which way?"

"Oh, them trees are old. Look at that one next the wall. It's gone. A lot of other ones don't look too healthy to me."

"We had a good crop last year."

"Could be, but apples are cheap. You could buy all you'd ever use. I don't see why you want to hang on to that orchard. Wouldn't you rather see two nice new houses there than them old trees?"

"Well, no," Violet said, "as it happens I wouldn't."

Billy shook his head. "Women sure are funny," he remarked. "Course if you ain't interested in the *money* . . ."

"But I am," Violet said honestly, "only I can't decide to sell just yet, Mr. Wade. Could you give me a little more time?"

Billy scratched his head and considered.

"That field above the parsonage may be for sale later. It an' your orchard are about the only good spots left in town for building so I can't hold myself up too long. Tell you what I'll do. Spose I give you two more months to think it over, then I've got to know. O.K.?"

"That would only bring it into September!"

"Well, the fifteenth or twentieth mebbe. I couldn't wait any longer than that for I'd want to get the frames up before the cold weather. What do you say?"

Violet spoke very slowly. "All right, Mr. Wade. We will have the apples picked by then and I'll give you an answer."

"Good," said Billy. "Just think how much more the money would mean to you than them old trees. Well, so long, Miss Vi'let. I got to be movin'."

He left with an air of assurance and Violet turned to face Katie, her black eyes full of resentment.

"An' what's this all about? What's been goin' on behind

my back? If Billy Wade wants to pick the apples on the shares you might have told me!"

"It's not that, Katie, and I was afraid to tell you before. He wants to buy the orchard."

Katie sat down limply on a chair. "To *buy* it! *Our orchard!* Oh Vi'let, you didn't . . ."

Violet shook her head. She knew of what Katie was thinking: the golden autumn days when the fruit was gathered, the barrels packed and stored for winter use, the apple butter made and the cider pressed! By her white face Violet knew now how much this had always meant to Katie.

"I have till late September to decide. We do need the money, of course," she said.

"We don't need it that bad! We've got the transhens money, haven't we?"

"There may not be much during the winter."

"There'll be some. Mr. Rayburn says so. And there are little ways we can be savin' more. For one thing it's rideeculous havin' Mag Parks, an' me perfectly able."

"Listen, Katie. We are keeping Mag Parks on, and that's the end of that. But about the orchard. It would break my heart to sell it and now I know you feel the same. Let's forget all about it for the time being and see how things work out. If we keep on making enough on the tourists to pay our store bills, maybe we can take a chance. Next school year I think I could save what we'd need to paint the stable and the house trim. That has to be done. Of course you know a good deal of last year's salary went . . ."

"Hush, child," Katie said gently. "I know."

"So," Violet went on, trying to sound cheerful, "I think somehow we can beat Billy Wade yet!"

Katie rose and shook a stern finger. "And I'll tell you one thing, Miss. I'll use every penny of me own savings before I see that property sold! It's for you an' your children after you an' we're goin' to keep it!"

Violet's face broke up in sudden laughter. "I'm all ready for marriage," she said. "I've got a quilt and an apple orchard."

"And I must say you could worse prepared," Katie returned with spirit, as she left for the kitchen.

Violet walked around the house to the garden to resume her weeding. As she carefully eliminated the chickweed from the pinks and petunias her thoughts were entirely upon the conversations just ended and not at all, as before, upon the publishers to whom she had entrusted her precious manila envelope. And this was odd, in a way, for at that very moment a conference was going on in one of the central offices of the house of Haversham & Hill relating to the poems of a certain Violet Carpenter whose address was simply *Ladykirk*, a town small enough apparently to need no street or number to designate her dwelling.

CHAPTER FOUR

ONE of the greatest marvels in life, Violet was thinking as she woke up on Thursday, was the resilience of the human spirit. Here, for example, was she, orphaned, bereft of those nearest and dearest to her, and now so lately saddened by the loss of her chief material treasure, and yet at this moment acutely conscious of the delicious early breeze as it blew the curtains, of the scent of roses and the brightness of the new day. Moreover the thought of various small pleasures lying just ahead had power to move her with pleasure. There must be, she decided as she sprang out of bed, a vital and inextinguishable spark of happiness deep in every human heart.

She stretched her arms above her head in healthy abandon, not knowing as she stood there in her thin white nightgown, with her hair falling upon her shoulders and her sensitive face full of light, that she herself represented a beautiful adjunct to the June morning.

At breakfast she told Katie of the plans she and Faith had completed the night before when she had been up at the Lyalls'. This afternoon they were going to drive out to call upon Seena. On hearing this Katie grunted.

"I don't hold with that one, mind you. She's a hussy an' mark my words she'll be married again afore the year's out. But duty is duty an' I spose you ought to go."

The next piece of news she received with approval. Faith's younger sister, Lucy, was married to Ninian Ross, son of the man who owned "the works," as the mines three miles away were coloquially known. Ninian was learning the coal business from the ground up, as he always said with a twinkle, and as assistant superintendent was housed with his young wife in a very spacious frame dewlling on the edge of the woods just back of the Patch. Their romance a few years ago had been, with its somewhat Cinderella quality, one of the sweetest morsels ever rolled upon the town tongue. Lucy had always been a favorite with everyone and Ninian had quickly made himself adaptable to village life. Katie was his slave because each time he came to the house, Simon, who was haughtily discriminating, at once jumped up on his knee and was well received.

Now, Violet was saying, Lucy and Ninian had decided to have a picnic in their woods on Saturday afternoon, and she had promised to take a veal loaf, one of Katie's specialties, and a cake. Would that be agreeable?

Katie, trying hard to cover her pride, conceded that she would try to find time to make the loaf.

"Oh, I love Lucy's parties," Violet went on. "There are always some of Ninian's city friends there. It seems an odd thing to say of any picnic but there's really a sort of *intellectual* quality at theirs."

This being entirely too much for Katie she left for the kitchen while Violet pursued her own thoughts. It would be pleasant to be again in a group where there would be clever young people, college-bred and socially experienced. Thanks to her own home training she never felt ill at ease with them, only appreciative.

Faith was to do the driving today, so at two she drew rein at the door and Violet stepped into the buggy. When they reached the farm lane they saw a car parked in the barnyard. Faith drove on in and tied the horse to the end of the corncrib, then they looked about them, wondering what to do next, for they saw a sunbonnet lying, as though tossed there, by the barn door.

Suddenly two figures emerged from the barn, Seena, wearing her usual enigmatic smile, and a strange young man, looking rather flushed and embarrassed as he saw the girls. Seena stopped, eying them with a glance less than welcoming, and then came slowly toward them.

"Hello," she said briefly.

"We came to call," Faith began, "but if you're busy . . ."

84

Seena paused for a second as though thinking it over.

"It's a man who wants to buy the farm," she said. "I've just been showing him round, but he's seen it about all, now. Would you girls mind waiting on the front porch till I'm through?"

"Are you sure you want us to stay? We can easily come again," Violet said.

"No, just wait. I'm lonesome. I'm glad to see anybody. I won't be too long." And she turned back to the man.

The girls made their way around the house and sat down on the wide porch steps.

"You would think she would have introduced him," Faith said.

"He has a pleasant face, though he looks rather shy. I hope some nice people do buy the farm. It's always been in good hands."

Suddenly the girls heard steps at the back of the house, coming on through. "Seena! Seena!" a man's voice called eagerly. In a few minutes young O'Dell opened the screen door on the porch, then fell back, overcome with surprise as he saw the girls.

"I . . . I just come in to get a drink," he stammered. "I got awful dry up there in the field. It's . . . it's warm today."

"How are you, Jake," Faith said. "Mrs. Harvey is showing a man round the farm. He's thinking of buying it. We're waiting until he's finished."

The boy looked stricken. He had a big frame topped by an open ingenuous face and a shock of blond hair showing under his straw hat, which he had evidently not thought of removing.

"Buyin' it," he repeated. "This man's buyin' it *so soon?*"

"We don't know. At the moment he's just looking around."

The boy stood for a second, as though he had received a blow.

"I gotta get back to the field," he mumbled. "I just come down to get a drink." And he disappeared.

Faith felt a wave of pity as, with her quick perceptiveness, she read a story between his few words.

"I hope Seena is not playing with that boy. He seems nice."

"Oh, he is," Faith said quickly. "We were talking about

85

him just last night. Father's been after the O'Dells for years to come to church, but they're a pretty careless lot, all except this young Jake. Father thinks he's got good stuff in him. If . . . if nothing goes wrong," she added.

They were speaking in low tones and Faith now leaned nearer.

"You know Father's so tolerant and judicial. Always seeing both sides. He said we should not blame Seena too much because nature made her in such a way that every man liked to look at her. Then he added, 'I mean every average man,' and Mother said, 'Good. That lets you out then,' and we all laughed."

"She *is* pretty," Violet said. "Like a big red rose."

"A very full-blown one," Faith said tartly. "Oh, I don't mean to sound spiteful but I can't forgive her for the way she treated John."

A car rolled past and on down the lane with the strange man driving. The girls drew quickly apart as Seena came on the porch.

"I'm sorry I was so long," she said, "but I think I've sold the farm. At least he likes the house and the barn and the way the land lies. He said he'd come back next week, but I have a feeling he'll buy."

She stood still, looking off across the wheat field. "It's a good farm," she added in a dull voice.

"What will you do, Seena, when you've sold it?" Violet asked gently.

"Go on home, I guess, and live with the folks. What else could I do? I wish I could teach like you girls, or do something. Oh well . . . Come on in the house. I baked fresh gingerbread today."

They sat in the big sitting room trying hard to make conversation while the mantel clock ticked heavily.

"What is this man's name, Seena, or don't you want to tell?" Violet said after some time.

"I don't care," said Seena. "It's no secret. It's a queer name. Halifax. Robert Halifax from over in Indiana County. He said he'd been renting up till now but he'd saved up and also he inherited some money lately and was now ready to buy. He saw the notice I put in the papers and he came right over. That's all I know about him."

"Is he . . ." Faith began, "I mean does he have a family?"

86

Seena shrugged. "Search me," she said, "but he *acted* like a married man."

As though realizing that her words had been revealing Seena blushed until the rose extended to her throat. The girls took note of her collar, which lay apart widely over the fullness beneath, and hastily began together to say they must go.

"Well, thanks for coming," Seena said, calmly enough. "I'll be in to choir practice next week, Faith. Jake says he'll drive me."

Violet looked her straight in the eye.

"He seems a nice boy, Seena, a good boy."

Seena shrugged. "He's all right. I have to have somebody farm till I get the place off my hands."

She walked with them to the buggy and before they drove off she spoke with a certain crispness.

"I hear there's talk going round about me being mean to the Harveys. That's not so. This place is mine. It's legal. What do they want me to do? Tear up the will? I can't have them out here to stay. He's not able to farm. That's why he turned it over to John. And when she comes she just sits and cries all day and it drives me crazy. When I sell the farm I'm going to give them some of the money. I don't have to but I will. So you can just say that, when the tongues start wagging."

"We certainly will," Faith said heartily, "and I'm glad, Seena, you're going to share the money with the Harveys. That is truly kind of you and I know they will appreciate it."

The good-byes were said and the buggy moved on along the lane; as it turned into the main road, Violet looked back. Seena was standing where they had left her, her face now raised and laughing, but she was not alone. The O'Dell boy stood beside her.

The girls talked seriously all the way home. Like most young people brought up in a country village they were at once unsophisticated, and yet wise beyond their years in the mysteries of human relations. Their hearts were pure, their language inhibited by custom, but their minds were completely aware of the significance of all they had seen that day. When they had reached the edge of town they had agreed upon a conclusion. Seena would tempt any man with all her physical powers—which were great—but she would go no further than design and intent, stopping short of any overt act, thus leaving a victim like young Jake crazed with longing and desire. The girls did not of course express their thought in exactly these words but by means of delicate circumlocutions they made their meaning clear to each other.

At the manse gate Violet got out of the buggy.

"I want to go down for the mail, Faith, and the little walk will do me good. Thanks so much for the ride. I'm glad we went, even though we are disturbed by what we saw. At least it helps to know about a situation."

"I'll tell Mother how we feel and she can talk to Father. He might be able to say something to Jake, though it's touchy business. Oh, about Saturday! I almost forgot to tell you."

The faces of both girls brightened as they spoke of the picnic.

"I had supposed you and I would drive together but Howie Gordon says he'll take their new surrey and we can go with him and Kitty."

"That's fine!"

"Vi, you know Lucy invited Henry. She couldn't very well help doing so for he's always been in the crowd. Will you mind?"

"Of course not. We have to keep on meeting, in a little place like this. Oh, I'm looking forward to the party. The first real one this summer, isn't it?"

"Yes, and if the weather is good it should be a nice one."

They spoke then earnestly of the relative merits of devil's food, sunshine yellow, and white cake, deciding at last which one of them would take which variety; then, conscious of the humor in their concern, laughed and bade each other good-bye.

Violet walked slowly down the street under the freshly leaved maples, beside the front gardens bright with roses, until she reached the Post Office. Mr. Gordon smiled as she approached the small window. He slipped a letter under the wire mesh.

"Think you've got an answer," he said in a stage whisper, smiling broadly.

Violet took the envelope in her hand and turned pale.

"It may not mean a thing," she managed to say. "Please don't . . ."

"Mum's still the word," he said. "Just let me know the news when you can."

Violet walked home dazedly, uncertain whether to hurry and at all costs put an end to suspense, or to delay and allow herself longer to hope. As a matter of fact, however, all elation had left her. That the letter should have come so soon was, she felt, an evidence of the book's rejection. She pictured with a sinking heart what the printed slip inside would probably say.

Your manuscript, which is being returned to you under separate cover, has been carefully considered. We regret that we do not feel we can make a place for it on our list at the present time. Thanking you for your kindness in submitting it to us, we remain, etc.

She reached the house, went up on the porch and sat down in the swing. All was quiet inside and nothing stirred on the street. A faint southern breeze blew through the orchard; that was all. She was entirely alone, unless perhaps her father's spirit could penetrate ethereal space and be with her in this portentous moment. She sat, fingering the envelope which bore the chaste script of Haversham & Hill in the corner; then, because she hated cowardice, she ripped the seal and drew out a typewritten page. It was a personal letter! Scarcely breathing, she read the lines.

Dear Miss Carpenter: I wish to acknowledge the receipt of your manuscript and to inform you that it has already been read with very real interest by Mr. Giles, our editor-in-chief, and by myself. Unfortunately we cannot as of this moment assure you of our acceptance and offer you a contract. However, I felt you would be glad to know that we intend to give it further consideration both by ourselves and by several expert readers. May we beg your patience if this takes a little time?

Meanwhile, would you care to let us know something about yourself? Just as we like to know personal details about our regular authors, so we are interested in those who we feel may be potential ones.

I may add that Mr. Giles feels that your poems, includ-

*ing the more romantic ones, have a rare quality. Like him,
I hold that opinion. Indeed, I congratulate you upon what
I feel is the beginning of a real career, whether this
first book is publishable in its present form or not.*

*Hoping to hear from you and thanking you for your
courtesy in submitting the manuscript to us, I am*

Very truly yours,

Philip Haversham, Associate Editor.

Violet leaned weakly back against the swing, filled with
ecstasy. No lesser word could describe the unspeakable
joy and relief that flooded through her veins. They had
liked her poems, these two editors; they felt she had
talent and would some day write a publishable book even
if the present one was not wholly satisfactory to them.
After being prepared for the despair of an impersonal
rejection the warmth and encouragement of this letter
overwhelmed her. Here were praise and hope held out to
her by a friendly hand. She wondered whether an outright
acceptance could have made her much happier. She read
the letter again slowly. She pictured these two men,
elderly, bearded perhaps, austere-looking from their long
use of critical power in reading, weighing and pronouncing
upon the written word. Most young writers would naturally
feel timid in their presence. But *she* knew that behind their
Jovian aspect they were not only wise but kind.

She went slowly through the house, one dark clutching
ache in her happy heart. Her mother would not turn with
bright anticipation from her reading! Her father would not
look up with eager eyes from filling his pipe! She went
into the kitchen where Katie was mixing ingredients for
the meat loaf.

"I got a letter from the publishers, where I sent my
poems."

"Well, and what do they have to say?"

"They like them but they won't be sure for a while
whether they can print them in book form or not."

"Huh!" said Katie. "Keepin' their distance, are they?
You can't ever trust strangers. Look at the time I ordered
that suit from the National Dress Company in New York.
Sent the measurements and the money an' all, an' the thing
never touched me any place."

"This is slightly different, Katie. This is a fine, reputable publishing house."

"Well, well, you can see what comes of it but when you've got a good job teachin' school, why are you worryin' about tryin' to write books? Just now I'm in trouble enough with this meat loaf."

"What's wrong?"

"My recipe calls for one-half veal, quarter pork and a quarter beef, an' I could swear that Bill Seilers forgot the pork and put in extra beef. He was talkin' about his potatoes. He says he'll have new ones by the Fourth of July as big as a hen egg. He's a blather! But if he left out the pork it will make a difference in the taste. I'd hate for anything to go wrong with this for the picnic."

"It won't," Violet assured her. "If you made it all of breadcrumbs it would still be good. You have such a knack with it. I'm going to bake my cake in the morning so it will be nice and fresh."

She left Katie muttering to herself. In the living room she paused and with a gentle hand touched the back of the "gentleman's" and then the "lady's" chair before she went up to her own room where, in a pleasant glow, she read all the poems over from her notebook. Once or twice she paused at a line and looked off through the window. Could she actually have written this? Had she really this insight, this felicity of expression? At the end, however, she laughed, a soft, sweet chuckle. She knew that if the printed rejection slip had come all the contents of the notebook would now seem to her like vapid and inane maunderings. Was every author influenced so by outer opinion? Did they, chameleonlike, take their emotional coloration from the praise or dispraise of others? Or would it be possible for some to say strongly within themselves, *My work is true, it is valid, it has beauty,* no matter what criticism had fallen upon it? Well, at the moment she did not have to apply this test. Someone else was doing that for her.

She closed the desk and, filled with the joy of the thought that always within her, as part of her very being, the creative springs would well up, she moved over to the clothespress to decide what she would wear to the picnic.

The next day was one of June's fairest—warm, balmy and filled with soft airs. In her first half-waking Violet was oppressed with a heavy dream. In it her father and mother were weeping with her over the loss of the nightingale and then, all at once, they left her alone, frightened and lost. When she woke her heart was beating stiflingly and there were tears on her cheeks. Then she saw the brightness of the morning, and recollection brought back *the letter* and the coming events of this Saturday. She jumped up quickly and began to dress, repeating aloud, to exorcise the darkness of the dream, a favorite quotation of her father's which he had once made her write down when, as a very young girl, she had been dejected over some trifling mishap.

"Each day is a little life. Fill its hours
with gladness if you can; with courage if you can't."

Everything went well. The cake was perfect; so, from all appearances, was the veal loaf. They were both packed in the big flat market basket after lunch, the cake in a tin container and the meat in a crock covered over with rhubarb leaves. A glass, fork and spoon, together with one of the older linen napkins, were tucked in the side with a snowy tea towel over all.

The era, or even the idea, of clothes *pour le sport* had not yet struck Ladykirk, so Violet wore her second-best sprigged voile and her last summer's wide hat, trimmed with roses. Katie, who out of principle was chary of praise, was moved to remark, "You look very well, and nicely got up, I must say. Don't forget to take a cushion. I don't want you to get grass stains on that dress."

At three-thirty the surrey stopped at the door and Violet, with basket and cushion, was handed into her place by Howie Gordon in a tall white collar and pepper-and-salt suit, while Kitty Kinkaid, whom he had been "going with" now for a year, held the reins. Faith was already in the back seat, so in a moment, amidst young and pointless laughter, they drove off, round the corner and down Main Street, where many eyes took in the equipage as it passed. In front of the hardware store a saddled horse was tied.

"I guess Henry's going to ride out," Howie remarked with a flicker of his eye toward the back seat. "I haven't heard who all else is going today. How about it, Faith?"

"Well, of course, Jeremy and Peggy. They're driving over the back road since it's nearer than through town.

Then there will be the Superintendent's two girls, Bess and Jane Hardwick, and three of Ninian's friends from the city whose names I don't know. They're coming out in an auto. I guess that's all."

"That'll make a nice crowd. A picnic's better when it's *not* too big."

Howie and Kitty settled to a low-toned conversation and the girls in the back seat were free to regard each other. Faith was looking unusually pretty in a pale-blue lawn and leghorn hat. Her face was delicately flushed and her normally thoughtful eyes were bright.

"What do you think?" she said. "Jeremy was in last night and he says that this Robert Halifax we saw out at Seena's is really buying the farm. He went over yesterday to talk to Jeremy for he had heard somehow of him and knew he could give him some facts about the productiveness of the fields and all that. Jeremy says he's a very nice fellow and a real gentleman. The oddest thing is that he thought first of going into the ministry, just as Jeremy did, and then, he said, something always drew him back to the land."

"What a coincidence!" Violet said. "And how nice for Jeremy to have a congenial neighbor. There aren't too many of the farmers round him that he can really talk with about anything but cows and corn. What about this man's family?"

"He isn't married," Faith said briefly, her cheeks coloring a little more. Then she leaned closer to Violet.

"You know I hate myself sometimes. I almost wish we had never talked so freely to each other. I'm embarrassed even before you. What difference does it make whether this new man is married or single? And yet," she added honestly, "it does a little."

"Of course," Violet agreed, trying to be casual. "There aren't too many young people around here. It will be nice to have an addition. How old do you suppose he is?"

"Thirty-two, Jeremy says, but young-looking for that, wouldn't you say?"

"Very. What about Seena?" she added half under her breath.

Faith shook her head. "She'll try, I imagine, but I don't believe it will be any use. Mr. Halifax told Jeremy he did not intend to go back there *alone*. That sort of tells the tale!"

93

"What does your father think about Jake?"

"He's worried. He doesn't know quite how to approach it without assuming more than he should. It's a *very* delicate situation. I'm not sure he'll do anything except try again to get Jake to come to church."

There was a small pause and then Violet turned to her friend.

"I've a little piece of news myself. I'm dying to tell you if you'll be sure not to make too much of it!"

"Your book!"

"Now listen. There's nothing definite yet, but I had a letter saying they were interested enough to give it further consideration. That's all. No promise that they will ever publish it. However, they do like it a little."

"Oh Vi, how could you be so long telling me? Even this is wonderful, isn't it? Aren't you pleased?"

"Of course I am. It may be silly but I'm simply thrilled to get a real letter at all. And it *did* contain some praise. So if I wear a fatuous grin today you'll know why, even if . . ."

"Well," Howie said, raising his voice as he urged the horse up the last little hill to the house, "here we are!"

It was a charming spot, even though the smoke from the long snaking lines of coke ovens tinged the air with carbon when the wind blew in the wrong direction. The view of the Patch and the gaunt tipple and washer was screened from the house by a grove of oaks. There was a wide front porch and a pleasantly spacious look about the place since this had been originally the home of the Superintendent, who now lived in a larger and more modern dwelling on the other side of the works. Howie guided the horse up the drive and on to the rear of the house where voices and shouts of laughter indicated that activity was going on there. An auto was parked in front of the barn, and under a maple tree three young men, one with a large apron around his waist, were contending for a chance to turn the handle of the big ice-cream freezer. A tub of ice stood near by, and a bag of coarse salt completed the usual equipment for making the confection at home.

"Hey, you," the young man with the apron was saying to one of the others, "it's not time yet to take the lid off, Ninian said. Besides, we don't know how. We might get

94

salt in it. Take a turn at the grinder. The stuff's getting heavy."

They all looked up as the newcomers got out of the surrey and Ninian and Lucy came running out from the kitchen. The latter threw herself at once in her sister's arms. Marriage had not changed the quick young impulsiveness which had always been part of her nature. It had added, however, a sort of vibrant beauty to her girlish prettiness. Her curls now were caught up high on her head with a pink ribbon, and the cotton dress she wore, while simple, had an undeniable air of quality about it. Ninian was a tall young fellow with the social ease of manner that came from his formal upbringing and a charm that was all his own. A growing touch of maturity now sat well upon him. He greeted his guests warmly and began to introduce them to the three young men under the maple, who proved to be Don Wilson, big and blonde, Dick Travers, fair and stocky, and Mike Dorsey, swarthy and slight. Howie lifted the baskets from the car and demanded to know what was to be done with them.

"Just leave them there for the moment," Lucy said. "We're going into the woods when everyone gets here. Oh, aren't we lucky in the weather! There's just one disappointment. Jeremy and Peggy can't come! She . . . she isn't feeling well," Lucy added in a low tone to Faith and Violet. "You know why. Lucky Peggy!"

There was the sound of horse's hoofs and Henry rode by, tied his horse to a ring at the side of the barn and walked over to join the group. Violet's heart skipped a beat as she watched him, not from deep emotion certainly, but from the affection of long association. This was the first party in years to which Henry had not brought her.

"Hello," he said now, giving a sweeping glance around. "How are you, Ninian? Lucy, you look fine. This fellah doesn't beat you, then?"

At the words Lucy looked up at her young husband, and a smile of such naked tenderness was exchanged between them that Violet caught her breath at the beauty of it. Ninian went on with the banter.

"Oh, I'm the one who has to look out! The rolling pin, you know! Come on over, Henry, and meet these chumps who think they're making ice cream."

In a few more minutes Bess and Jane Hardwick drove up in their buggy and were graciously handed out and their horse led away by the various young men. They were nice-looking girls and pleasant enough but since they had always maintained a slight air of aloofness toward Ladykirk village were still considered alien.

There was a sudden flurry over the ice-cream freezer as Ninian pushed away the salty ice and carefully lifted the lid.

"By Jove, I believe it's done," he said. "Come on, Faith, you're the expert at this. Isn't it stiff enough now?"

Faith went over to peer at the white mass.

"It looks perfect!" she pronounced. "Bring a plate to put the fan on, Lucy, and some spoons so we can all sample it. Workmen's hire, you know," she said to the three young men who were hovering over it.

"I never knew before how ice cream was made," Mike said. "I'm entranced with the whole idea. Consumer produces the consumed. Interesting economics, that. You mean we can all pitch in and taste it now?" he asked Lucy incredulously as she proffered him a spoon.

"Of course," she said. "That's half the fun. Hurry, everybody, before it melts. Just one spoonful apiece."

When each one had dipped, savored and pronounced the result excellent, Faith lifted out the fan and laid it on a plate, then she and Ninian together packed the contents down, put on the lid, stuffing the handle hole carefully with wads of waxed paper, covered it all over with more ice and a burlap bag and it was ready.

"Now then," Ninian called out jubilantly, "we're set to go. We'll take turns carrying the freezer for its heavy. Henry, would you and Don take the first lap? Down the path to the run. You know the way. Howie, will you take the lemonade? It's in the big milk can on the back porch. Can you carry the lighter baskets, girls? All right, everybody, just grab something and heave to!"

In a few minutes, laden with their burdens of delicacies, they were all on their way through the outer edge of the woods and on down the sloping path to the little stream that wound through the glade at the foot. There was much screaming and laughter as the boys once all but dropped the freezer as it changed hands, and Bess Hardwick tripped on a stone and upset her box of rolls.

But without serious misadventure they all reached the level stretch beside the run and relaxed in the pleasant shade. Ninian arrived last, his arms filled with blankets, cushions and a basket of dishes. Soon the quiet spot had taken on the air of sylvan habitation. The blankets were spread out, cushions set against tree trunks, and a checked tablecloth arranged for the feast.

"I don't know about the rest of you, but I'm hungry right now. We didn't have much lunch," Ninian remarked.

There was a loud approving chorus from the boys, so without further delay the girls began to unpack the baskets. There was the veal loaf and fried chicken; potato salad, hard boiled eggs colored in beet juice; cucumber pickles, rolls, jam, and the two cakes, white and devil's food, a tempting array, with the lemonade and ice-cream receptacles nearby.

"Sup . . . per!" yelled Ninian at the top of his voice when all was ready, to signal the boys who had wandered off a little into the woods.

It was a gay meal. They were all young, healthy and hungry, with the titillating consciousness of the presence of the opposite sexes to accentuate the flavors of the food. The June sunshine sifted through the leaves above them, the descant of the little stream rose over their voices, and the air that touched their faces was delicately fragrant of the woods. When Don Wilson had finished his third dish of ice cream he leaned back in utter repletion.

"I've never eaten as much food before in my life!" he said.

"Nor so many ants," Mike added, brushing one away from his piece of cake. "But don't get me wrong. Even a few pismires could not spoil the delights of this feast. As a matter of fact this is not only the best picnic I've ever attended but the *only* really bona fide one in a bosky glen beside a rippling brook, etc. I wish to express my thanks to our host and hostess and toast them in lemonade. To Ninian and Lucy," he said, raising his glass. "May they continue to have picnics and always invite me!"

When the laughter subsided, Don Wilson said, keeping a sober face, "You know this raises the whole question of marriage for us bachelors. It was always just an academic one for me till Ninian here took the plunge, and after seeing him reasonably content . . ."

"Hey," Ninian interrupted, "there's a prize understatement for you!"

"Well, as I say, seeing him in his present state of grace has made me wonder whether marriage might not be a good thing for all of us."

"Steady there," Mike adjured. "Go slow, you. You know the song that's going the rounds now." In a strong, clear tenor he began to sing:

> "You can't do this and you can't do that
> When you're married!
> You can't go here and you can't go there
> When you're married!
> There's only one place that I know,
> Where wifie'll tell you you may go,
> And that's the place where they don't have snow,—
> When you're mar—r—ried!"

There were loud guffaws from the boys and lightly shocked laughter from the girls. Lucy alone was puzzled.

"I don't know just what that means," she said. "There are so *many* places where they don't have snow."

Ninian took her hand. "I think the particular place the song refers to is spelled with four letters and is a word we should leave for the use of the preachers. Come to think of it, though, I've never heard your father mention it."

Lucy's face suddenly became enlightened. She laughed.

"Oh, that!" she said. "Oh, Mike, I don't think that's nice at all. As if any wife would ever tell her husband . . . why, how *awful!*" she ended.

The boys laughed again but Violet detected a gentleness in their mirth.

"You're right, Lucy," Mike said. "I withdraw my song and its dark implication. Later when we're not so stuffed we must sing some real love ditties to make up. What about a quiet game now until we're able to get to our feet again?"

"Right," said Ninian. "What shall it be? Let's make it simple. For some reason what passes for my brain seems a bit dulled."

They settled for a few rounds of "Buzz" and then packed

98

"My Grandfather's Trunk" until Dick Travers put in a hornet's nest, and then the lid was closed with laughter.

"I'll tell you what we'll do now," Ninian exclaimed, getting up and helping Lucy to her feet. "My wife and I will tidy things up here while the rest of you go explore the woods. We've had the underbrush cleared and there are plenty of paths. Run along now like good children. When you get back we fellahs will pitch some quoits while the girls sit and admire us."

With an amazing ease and speed the other young people paired off. Mike came at once to Violet's side, Don went to Faith, and Henry and Dick got together with the Hardwick girls. Howie and Kitty had already started, and in a few minutes they were all scattered along the various paths entering the deep woods.

"This is the first time I've been out at Ninian's," Mike began, "and it's certainly a nice experience. Have you always lived around here?"

"I was born in Ladykirk. So were Faith and Lucy. Their father is our minister, you know."

"Yes. A fine man, Ninian says. I've never been very close to the clergy myself, I'm afraid, but I gather he's a little different from the common run. Quite a student, too. By the way, I've just had a thought. That's my auto you may have noticed beside the barn."

"Oh, I did!" Violet said with enthusiasm.

Mike grinned. "I got it for good behavior. Well, if Don and I drove out some Sunday, would you and Miss Faith, perhaps, care to go for a ride in it?"

"Oh, we'd love to," Violet returned, "but not on Sunday."

"Why ever not?" Mike asked in surprise.

"You see in Ladykirk no one, least of all the minister's daughter, would go for a pleasure drive on the *Sabbath!*"

He looked at her with interest. "I think this needs more elucidation."

"Well, it's really quite simple. Everyone goes to church twice on that day and some even three or four times if you count Sunday School and Young People's Meeting. In between they just stay home and relax."

"Egad, I think they'd need to!"

Violet laughed. "I agree," she said. "During the intervening hours now in summer they sit on their porches

99

or under a shade tree and read religious literature."

"Not even the Sunday papers?"

"Oh, heavens, no! There's not such a contaminating influence in the town. There was an attempt once to introduce it, but the men bringing in the papers to sell were stopped by a committee at the far end of the covered bridge, and that was that. In other words you get no news in Ladykirk on the Sabbath." Then her eyes turned mischievous. "Of course local items are different. They are transmitted as usual by word of mouth *every* day of the week."

Mike threw back his head and laughed. "But this is amazing. I've got to see this place for myself. And incidentally I'd like to see you again. One thing surprises me. You're in all this and not really of it. How come you can be so objective?"

Violet looked suddenly serious. "I didn't mean to poke fun at my town. It's only that I can't help appraising it from two points of view. It's worth seeing, though—if you care to come out."

"What about a Saturday? They are not sacrosanct, are they?"

"Saturday would be fine and I'm sure Faith would be as thrilled as I am. I may as well make a clean breast of my provincialism and be done with it. I've never been in an auto!"

"Wonderful!" said Mike. "Now mine will have the honor of your first ride. I'm busy next week but what about the one after that?"

"That would suit me. You'll speak to Faith?"

"Of course. Or Don will. I'll talk to him when we go back."

There was a long halloo from Ninian, and the strollers all turned about, except Howie and Kitty. They could be seen close to a big beech tree where Howie was engraving their joint initials inside a heart!

The boys played quoits for an hour while the girls watched them and visited, and then they all sang, the girls sitting primly on the cushions, the boys lounging against the trees. They sang "Row, Row, Row Your Boat," and "In the Shade of the Old Apple Tree," and then wandered into the older fields of sentiment as the moon rose.

They had just done "Juanita" with fine effect when Howie sprang up.

"Gosh," he said. "Look, it's beginning to get dark. We've got to start. If my horse sees an auto with the lights on she cuts up like anything. I hate to hurry you, girls, but we really must go."

There was a hurried picking-up of baskets and paraphernalia and they all climbed the path together. Then came hasty, but hearty good-byes all around, Mike managing to tell Violet that she would hear from him about the drive, and then the surrey departed with fluttering farewells from the girls trailing after it until it was out of sight at the foot of the hill. Howie concentrated on his horse, keeping a sharp lookout ahead, Kitty leaned near him to talk in low tones, and Faith and Violet behind discussed the party with relish. It seemed that Mike during the quoits game had managed to consult Don about the trip to Ladykirk and he, in turn, had asked Faith if she was agreeable. It was pleasant and a little exciting, they kept saying now to each other, to have this in the offing, and the young men were nice and full of fun. Would they be likely to stay to supper, and if so, should it be served at Violet's or at the manse, they wondered.

Suddenly Howie gave a quick exclamation. Over the hill in front of them gleamed two large red eyes. The horse had seen them too and was slowing his pace.

"I think I'll get out," Howie said anxiously, "and try to hold him by the bridle. And you'd better all get out, too, girls, for I can't tell what he may do. Give me the lap spread, Kitty."

The girls climbed out quickly, mounting the small bank beside the road. The great red eyes came nearer at what seemed an alarming pace. Howie put the spread over the horse's head and gripped the bridle tightly but the animal shivered in terror. The sound of the auto was now upon them and all Howie's strength upon the rein was to no avail. The horse gave a mighty spring forward, shook off the blinding spread and tore away with Howie clinging to the bridle.

"Oh," Kitty screamed. "He'll be killed! Let go, Howie! *Let go!*"

All at once they saw Howie thrown aside as the horse increased its speed, the surrey rattling and careening behind it. The girls ran as fast as they could until they came upon Howie lying entirely too still at the side of the road. Kitty, in tears, knelt beside him.

"He's dead!" she gasped.

"No, he's breathing. You can see it. But he's hurt. He's struck his head. Oh, if only someone would come along. Let's lift him up a little, Kitty, and see if he won't come to," Violet suggested anxiously.

When Howie's head was raised his eyes fluttered and then opened.

"W . . . where's the horse?" he muttered.

"It's all right. Just lean against me and rest. Oh . . . listen!"

There was a sound of quick hoofbeats and in a few seconds Henry appeared, riding through the gathering dusk. Forgetting everything but their need, Violet ran toward him and breathlessly told him what had happened. He dismounted at once and with his hand at the bridle walked quickly back with her to the little group by the roadside. Howie was sitting up now, rubbing his head.

"Gee, am I glad to see you, Henry. I was thrown and must have got a good crack. I'm worried about the horse and surrey. Will you try to . . ."

"Now don't get excited! You sit right still and I'll ride on as fast as I can to catch up with the horse. It's sure to go home. I can hitch mine to the surrey and drive back for you all. Are you sure you're all right?"

"Sure. Just a little dizzy. I'm worried about the surrey. It's new, you know. Well, go ahead as fast as you can, and thanks, Henry."

Henry's glance swept Violet's and took in the other girls.

"You'll be all right here, won't you? I'll be back as soon as I can."

Without waiting for a reply he jumped on the horse and galloped off.

The moon rose higher but a cloud soon covered the brightness so the darkness gradually became complete. The group on the bank sat close. Howie talked a little but seemed glad to rest his head against Kitty's shoulder and keep his eyes closed. The other girls could see enough to know that from time to time Kitty pressed her lips to his forehead. It was evidently serious, then, between the two. Faith whispered once to Violet: "Isn't it sad this had to happen after such a lovely afternoon?"

"Yes. I think all will end well, though."

"How lucky Henry came! I thought he couldn't be far behind us. There's one thing about him. He is dependable!"

"Oh, very," Violet agreed, and spoke no further.

As a matter of fact she was clutching again to her heart the warmth of the letter's message. Here in the quiet darkness she was free to experience once more her own inner delight. If only Howie was not seriously injured and the precious surrey saved intact she would be glad for this hour on the edge of the fields, isolated from her usual surroundings.

A large tree spread its branches above them and a faint and unfamiliar fragrance disseminated itself in the light breeze.

> *I cannot see what flowers are at my feet*
> *Nor what soft incense hangs upon the boughs. . . .*

The words rose to her mind as she drew long breaths of the June air, a captive to the gentle thralldom of her own thoughts and of the country night.

There was a great quiet along the road; no other autos came by; not even a buggy passed as time moved slowly on. At last, when the girls were growing very anxious they heard the sound of wheels coming from the direction of the village. They came nearer and finally a lantern light showed from the dashboard of a carriage. It was Henry, drawing up to the side of the bank and calling out as he did so, "Everything all right?"

They roused Howie, whose head felt much clearer after his sleep, and helped him to the road, where Kitty and Faith on either side of him got into the back seat while Henry watched his horses. He explained then that he had overtaken the other horse with the surrey at the bridge, and kept close to it until it was safely in the Gordon's driveway. One shaft of the surrey was broken when it struck the side of the bridge, but he added comfortingly to Howie, "There's not a scratch on it anywhere else and a shaft's easily mended."

There was nothing for Violet to do but get into the front

seat beside Henry. It was awkward but inevitable at the moment.

"I got this rig from the livery," Henry went on. "I thought after what happened I'd better bring horses that are pretty well auto-broken, and of course we couldn't all come in our buggy. It sure is a dark night. I've been glad of the lantern."

As the carriage moved on there was little conversation except Kitty's tender solicitous questions and Howie's low replies. At last Henry addressed a rather crisp remark to Violet.

"So I hear one of your tourists made off with your nightingale."

"Yes," Violet answered. "I've been very broken up about it. I loved that little bird. Then I had a great shock about this Mr. Smith. He seemed such a gentleman. It really has rather shaken my faith in human nature."

"You can't tell about strangers. There's all kinds of people traveling the roads now since autos have come in. Everyone's saying you folks ought to stop this tourist business."

"We have changed our . . . our policy." In the darkness Violet smiled over the pretentious word though she knew Henry would see no humor in it. "We're just taking couples and women," she added.

"Well, that's a little better, I suppose."

And then there seemed nothing more to say and the carriage rolled on in silence.

When they reached the village and drew up to the Gordon's house, there was a light on the porch and Howie's father and mother were waiting anxiously at the gate.

"I'm really all right," Howie kept repeating as he got out stiffly and went toward them. "I just got a crack on the head when I fell and it sort of made me feel funny for a while. But I had a sleep while we were waiting for Henry and now I'm fine. Come on, Kitty, we'll go in and tell the folks all about it and then I'll walk you up home. Thanks a million, Henry, and I'll settle for the team. Good night, girls. Sorry I gave you a scare."

Henry drove on straight up Main Street and Violet felt a qualm. He was going to take Faith home first then, just as he would have done if . . .

104

Faith got out at the manse gate, Henry assisting her while Violet held the reins.

"I'm sure Mrs. Gordon will take care of our baskets. We can get them Monday. Well, thanks so much, Henry, for everything, and I'll see you tomorrow, Vi."

The good-byes were said and Henry climbed in, turned the carriage and started down street again. Violet tried now to make light conversation until they reached the Carpenter house, then Henry reined the horses but made no move to get out.

"Well, seems like old times to be bringing you home," he said.

"Yes," Violet answered nervously, "yes, it does. It was a nice picnic, wasn't it?"

"Yep. It was all right. What about those city fellahs? They seemed a little fresh to me. Are they wanting to come out?"

"Well, yes, they did mention it to Faith and me, that they might come and give us a ride in Mike's auto."

"Dangerous!" pronounced Henry. "I guess I could afford an auto as well as the next one, but I'm not taking chances. Give me a good horse any day for safety."

"Like tonight," Violet said.

Henry had the grace to laugh with her. "I guess this wasn't the best time to make that remark," he admitted, "but you know what I mean. And it was an auto that started all the trouble. And Vi, there's something else. It's over between us and I'm letting it rest there. I'm not one to burn my fingers twice. But you know I'll always be watching what you do. I mean I'll be interested. Don't be taken in by these city chaps when you don't know anything about them."

"I won't, Henry, and you're kind to care."

"Well, of course I care," said Henry. "You were my girl for a good while."

"I'm so glad we can go on being friends . . . that you're not angry with me. I really should go in now. Katie will be worried since it's so late."

But Henry made no move to get out. Neither did he attempt any expression of affection. Instead, after an appreciable pause, he said, "Heard what Seena's going to do?"

105

Violet felt a sense of shock. Could Henry be among those who liked to look upon her?

"Yes, as it happens, I do. Faith and I were out to see her just the other day. She thinks she's sold the farm to a Mr. Halifax from over in Indiana County and when she does she's coming back to town to live with her folks."

"Well, the Mill house is big enough, that's sure, but it's hard for a girl, after she's been married and . . . and all, and had her own place, to come back home. . . . How did she seem when you were out?"

There was a faint curtness in Violet's tone. "Just as usual. I didn't notice any difference. And Henry, I really must go on in now. Katie will be nearly crazy."

Without more words Henry wound the lines around the whip stock, jumped out and in a second was helping Violet to alight.

"Don't leave the horses to come up to the door. We don't want any more runaways. And thank you so much, Henry, for everything!"

"That's all right. It's been good to see you. Do you suppose she'll have a sale, or what?"

"I really wouldn't know," Violet answered briefly. "Good night."

She walked up to the porch, an assortment of emotions stirring within her, then she heard a breathy sound as she reached the steps. It came from Katie, sobbing, on the swing behind the vines with Simon on her lap. She tried hard to cover up her lack of fortitude with a disciplinary tone.

"Well, it's about time you got back! Scarin' a body out of their wits. Wasn't that Henry's voice? Don't tell me you've made it up with him! Sit down and give account of yourself. It must be midnight!"

"I'm so sorry you were worried, Katie, but I couldn't help it. I'll tell everything that happened, then you'll understand."

With Katie's prompting and from long experience Violet gave the story of the picnic and its aftermath to the last detail. At least she thought she had overlooked nothing until she had risen wearily and started to go into the house. Then Katie's voice rose in a last and touching question.

"What about the veal loaf? Was it any good?"

Violet turned back. "How could I have forgotten to speak of it?" she said. "It was simply delicious! I've never known you to make a better one. And, Katie, there was fried chicken too—Howie's mother had sent it, and two of the city young men kept passing it by for the veal loaf. They said they had never tasted anything like it and wanted to know the name of it. So there! Wasn't that a compliment?"

"Well, well," Katie returned, trying hard to sound casual, "there's no accountin' for tastes. Now go along an' get some sleep. Get away with you, Simon! Get away! . . . Oh, well, if you want to lie on the swing there's no harm to it, I guess."

The next afternoon, when the lethargic Sabbath calm had settled upon the village, Violet sat down on the front porch with a tablet and pencil. Not that she intended to write the actual letter of reply to Mr. Haversham on this day, but she wanted to jot down a few preliminary notes. What sort of things should she tell him? What could she say of her life and surroundings that could conceivably be of interest to him? Also, while a carefully prepared outline for the letter would be helpful, might it also make it sound contrived and lacking in spontaneity?

As she sat pondering, there was the sound of an auto coming up the back street. She watched its approach with surprise. Could it be tourists coming here at this hour? A man in heavy goggles was driving with a woman beside him swathed in a chiffon veil, the ends of which floated behind her. Violet put down her pad and pencil and stood up to see more clearly. The auto did, indeed, stop before their gate. The man dismounted, helped the woman to alight and then, as they started up the walk, he removed his goggles. With a scream Violet ran down the steps to meet them and in her precipitous haste all but fell until the man caught her.

"Mr. Smith!" she cried. "Oh, Mr. Smith, somehow I *knew* you'd come back!"

The man, amazed and embarrassed, looked down into her ecstatic face, while the countenance of the woman beside him showed an even greater astonishment.

"This is my wife, Miss Carpenter. I hadn't expected to be along this way again so soon but another errand presented itself, so . . ."

107

"Oh, come in," Violet said, her face still radiant. "Nothing matters now but that you came back. You doubtless meant to all along, but you can see how awful the suspense was to me. Indeed, your coming"—here she laughed gaily—"is really an answer to prayer. When I went to see our lawyer about it . . ."

"Your *lawyer*," Mr. Smith echoed, looking really alarmed.

"Yes. You must excuse me for that but you see I had to take whatever steps I could. The last thing he said to me was that you might really begin to feel sorry and come back, so you see . . ."

Mr. Smith all at once, after a glance at his wife's face, took charge of the conversation.

"Miss Carpenter," he said firmly, "you are evidently speaking of something which we know nothing about and you must explain fully the mystery to us. It is pleasant to see you again and thank you once more for the kindly shelter you gave me on that wet night. But my real reason for stopping now was that my wife might see and hear the nightingale."

All color drained from Violet's face. She looked from one to the other, stricken.

"The . . . the nightingale," she echoed.

"Yes," he went on. "I've talked so much about it to my wife, I was determined that she must see it too—if you will be so kind as to show it again," he added.

Violet looked dazed.

"Then . . . you didn't take it?" she brought out painfully.

For a moment Mr. Smith could not speak and then there was justified anger in his voice.

"*Take* it!" he said. "You mean you thought I had . . . you thought I was a *thief!*"

His wife laid a gentle hand on his arm and spoke for the first time.

"Tell us, my dear, exactly what happened."

"The night Mr. Smith was here I showed him the bird. He seemed impressed but was very quiet after and went at once upstairs. He left early the next morning. Two nights later I was feeling rather sad and I wanted to hear the nightingale. I went to the shelves where it's been kept for nearly thirty years and it was gone. We had had no

108

tourists here in between. Can't you see how it looked to me? You must try to put yourselves in my place."

"I can," Mrs. Smith said. "I can see it all. A perfect stranger coming in out of the night, leaving the next morning, and after that your finding your treasure gone. Yes, I can see just why you thought as you did. You needn't apologize. But tell her, Jeffrey, who you are and what you do."

"I'm a professor at Langton College in Ohio. I am making trips this summer to see prospective students. I assure you"—and here he smiled—"I am an honest man. But leaving me out for the moment I'm so terribly distressed over your loss. You had a priceless treasure there and I'm truly sorry for you and for your disappointment now that I don't have it in my pocket."

Violet's face had changed again. The first pale, stricken look had passed and the color had returned, also a certain light to her eyes and a smile to her lips.

"There is a funny side to this, isn't there, when I really catch my breath from the first surprise and then the shock? You must have been amazed when I all but knocked you down in my excitement. But though you can't give me back the bird you really have given me something else that's precious. You've restored my general faith in humanity. You see, Mrs. Smith, Katie and I liked your husband *so* much that it was very painful to . . . to think ill of him. Come on up now to the porch where we can talk in comfort. It seemed as though we had to say all this at once but I'm sorry to have kept you standing."

When they were seated it was but natural that all the facts and the emotional details should be gone over again for the Smiths' sympathetic ears. Then Violet went to tell the news to Katie, who came back to the porch to speak to the guests.

"Aye an' didn't I say you were a gentleman from the toes up? An' I'm pleased to meet you, Ma'am. It's a good job you come when you did for we've been tryin' to get the law on you. I'll just be bringin' out a bit lemonade for I doubt you're dry after drivin' in this dust."

With which rather confusing speech Katie returned to the kitchen.

When the guests had been refreshed and they rose to

109

leave, a new note of tenderness entered the conversation.

"There is another reason for our stopping today, my dear," Mrs. Smith began, "of which we haven't told you. You see we lost our only daughter a few years ago and my husband said you reminded him of her, especially when you were looking down at the nightingale. That's why he went up to his room so abruptly that night he was here. I, too, see the resemblance, so it makes me feel very close to you. May we come again?"

"Oh, *please* do!" Violet said, her heart in her voice. "I feel the bond, too, for I've lost my parents." She walked with them to the gate where Mrs. Smith kissed her and Mr. Smith held her hand warmly in his own.

"You must stop in whenever you are passing through," Violet went on. "Not as tourists but as my guests. It will give me so very much pleasure. You'll promise?"

"And I hope you'll find your treasure. God bless you, my dear," Mr. Smith said. Then he cranked the car, there was a shivering rattle and they moved off with fond good-byes.

Violet came slowly along the walk and up on the porch where Katie was collecting the glasses.

"They're so nice," she said, "and I feel now we are real friends. Oh, the burden it's lifted from my heart to know Mr. Smith didn't take the bird! I could hardly bear the thought of that."

"Aye," Katie answered, "I didn't like it myself for he seemed a good sort of chap. But," she added, fixing her shrewd black eyes on the girl before her, "I think there's something you're forgettin'."

"Why, what's that?" Violet asked.

"Well," said Katie, "it's this. If Mr. Smith didn't steal the nightingale, *who did?*"

CHAPTER FIVE

AND a dark cloud, at the beginning no bigger than a man's hand, began to settle upon Ladykirk. It had its first issuance (as she thought) from the lips of Mary Jackson when she came over for the second time on Monday just as old Mag Parks was preparing to leave after the day's laundry. She and Katie had done a big washing and completed the ironing too and Katie was stacking the clean clothes on the kitchen table with complacence.

"As white as the driven snow," she remarked to Mary, "if I do say it as shouldn't."

She got Mag's money from the blue sugar bowl, which was now used only as a receptacle for silver. Mag took it with a lugubrious sigh.

"If things had just stood as they was before that Smith man come back!" she said heavily.

"That's just what I've been thinkin' all day," Mary Jackson agreed. "When we believed the thief was a stranger it was all easier to bear, somehow. Now when it's brought down to the town itself—oh, it's a blacker thing for certain."

"Aye, is it," said Katie. "Good-bye, Mag, and I'll see you next Monday. Oh, an' here's a bit ham for your supper. . . . She feels it too," she added to Mary, as Mag made her ponderous way down the back steps. "She always admired the bird."

"Who didn't?" said Mary, as she hitched her chair nearer. "There's something on my mind I feel I've got to speak of to you an' Vi'let. It just hit me this afternoon an' it nearly staggered me. You knew Joe an' Amanda Hicks had their tenth wedding anniversary two weeks ago?"

"Oh yes," said Katie, dropping conversationally into the rocking chair.

"An' you mind I told you then about *the ring*."

"Aye," said Katie, "you an' about twenty others. Who wouldn't know that when Amanda's been showin' it to everybody she meets. Poor little soul! She's over the moon about it. She's never had much so she can't help bletherin' a bit about this. A real diamond they tell me, though a smallish one."

Mary leaned nearer. "An' what beats everyone is *where did Joe get the money for it!* It's not as if he was a carpenter like the Wallace boys. Buildin' houses an' barns an' big jobs where there's real profit. He's just worked under them or done repairs and such."

"That's right," said Katie thoughtfully. "He's always done the little futy things, like makin' our sign for instance. We'd never have bothered the Wallace boys for the like of that. Joe's a nice chap but a bit slack in the twist. Not much get-up in him."

"So," said Mary, leaning nearer, "how come he had enough money to buy Amanda a diamond ring?"

Katie eyed her shrewdly.

"What are you drivin' at? Lookin' a hole through me like that. What's it got to do with me an' Violet?"

"It's got this to do with you an' it takes me all my time to say it. It was *Joe Hicks* I saw comin' out of your kitchen that day you an' Vi'let were at the Missionary Tea. He'd been in here all by himself for dear knows how long. An' it was just two days after that you found the nightingale was gone. It was thinkin' of the diamond ring that made this hit me an hour ago an' the two things just seemed to fit, though I hate like anything to say it for I've always liked Joe. . . ."

"Fiddlesticks!" Katie exploded. "That's wicked even to think of! Joe's as honest as the daylight. I never heard such a blether. Why Joe wouldn't steal a ten-penny nail. He's . . . he's . . ." She stopped, her black eyes narrowed in concentration. "But where *would* he get the money for the diamond ring?" she finished slowly.

"That's it," said Mary. "If he took the nightingale, an' sold it somehow . . ."

"Ach, I still don't believe it. What would possess him to do such a thing? It's rideeculous!"

"They say a man'll do anything for a woman. An' you know how Joe is about Amanda. The men always sort of laugh about him bein' so *soft* over her and them married now ten years. It's mebbe because they've no children. And yet," Mary, herself childless, added wistfully, "it don't affect every man that way. Well, anyhow, there are the facts. You can make what you like of them. I've got to go now an' start the supper."

When Katie told Violet later of Mary's supposition the girl laughed at first and then showed real annoyance.

"I never heard anything so absurd, and I hope Mary doesn't go spreading that tale around. Poor little Joe! He's about as likely to steal as to commit murder. However he got the money for the ring I'm sure it didn't come in any way from us. Oh Katie, our problem will be unbearable if one person after another falls under suspicion. I'd almost rather *never* find the nightingale than have that happen."

But the small dark cloud gathered and grew and took to itself form and definition. The relation between the diamond ring and Joe Hicks's having been alone in the Carpenter house the day of the Tea, so shortly before the theft of the bird was discovered, had occurred not only to Mary Jackson but to Mrs. Hummel at the corner as well. The latter, having a boil under her cheek which many cups of sassafras brew failed to alleviate, had not attended the church function that day, but had gone into her back yard as the afternoon advanced, ostensibly to pull some rhubarb but actually to watch from behind the syringa bush as the other ladies came down the walk and note who had been there. From this vantage point she had looked across the gardens and seen Joe Hicks come out of the Carpenter's kitchen. She knew Katie and Violet were both at the Tea—in fact she saw them returning later at slightly different times—but the juxtaposition of these events did not then impress her. No one locked their doors in the daytime. Joe had likely walked in and called to see if anyone was home. He was maybe going to make another "Tourists" sign for them to put down by the bridge, she surmised. There were those who thought this ought to be done.

Even when she heard about Amanda's diamond she still did not, as she later expressed it, "put two and two together." But when the word ran like wildfire through the town that Mr. Smith was innocent of the theft of the bird, she pondered deeply with knitted brows as she hung her wash on the line, and then went hastily across to Mrs. Dunn, who had finished a trifle earlier. After long and repetitious discussion they had agreed that it looked suspicious for Joe, and a pity too for he had always been well liked. But if what they thought was true it would explain about the diamond ring over which everyone was still puzzling. They further decided that they wouldn't mention their sudden mistrust to anyone except their husbands for the time being.

"It would be awful to spread a story like this about Joe if there was no truth in it," Mrs. Hummel said virtuously. "At the same time it looks bad to me, and I may just stop in this evening at Mary Jackson's. She's promised me some yellow tomato plants. I could feel her out to see if she knows anything."

After three days everyone knew. In kitchens, in gardens, in the General Store, the Post Office and the barbershop —everywhere in fact but in Joe Hicks's little carpenter's shack on the upper alley—there were spoken not only the original facts but others even more damning to support them. For the corporate memory of a small village defies every rule of fallibility, so subtly, so variously and so surely are past events, large and small, recovered from the limbo of temporary forgetfulness and brought forth to form a pattern.

It was remembered now by several Main Street citizens that they had seen Joe Hicks pass down toward the bridge on the morning after the Tea, and that he carried under his arm a smallish square box carefully wrapped in brown paper and tied with cord. As the rumors spread the station agent added to them by saying Joe had on that day bought a ticket for Pittsburgh and he had seemed nervous and embarrassed.

"I mind," said Mr. Clee, "that I said to him, 'Going to the big city, Joe?' and he seemed kind of short with me and said, 'That's what the ticket says, ain't it?' I thought at the time it didn't sound like Joe. He's always as pleasant as a basket of chips."

Three other townsmen also recalled Joe's attitude that morning as they all waited for the branch train. One of them had said to him, quite naturally according to village standards, "And where might you be off to, Joe?" and had received a somewhat muffled reply to the effect that this was his own business. By the time the evidence was all in, it amounted to this: On that morning (the one after he had been alone in the Carpenter house) Joe had left for the city with a small boxlike package under his arm and had been nervous, red in the face and "short," as Mr. Clee expressed it, whenever anyone spoke to him about his reason for making the trip. He had even passed down the coach aisle and refused to sit with Homer Berger when he motioned Joe to a place beside him. All these trifles, vaguely noted at the time and forgotten, were now recalled, put through the crucible of endless discussion and accepted for truth. A week after his trip to the city, Joe presented his wife with a diamond ring.

114

Katie, her work, as she lamented, suffering greatly, heard all this in the kitchen, where Mary Jackson, Mrs. Hummel and Mrs. Dunn came each day with the latest reports. Mary had been obliged to concede to Mrs. Hummel the prestige of being the first to connect the initial facts, but there remained so much of vibrant interest to hear, examine and pass upon judicially that there was small room for regret on this point. The one absorbing question that at last became paramount in everyone's mind was, *What was Violet going to do about it?*

Lost for the most part in her own private world, Violet emerged as Katie presented to her each new shadow of the dark cloud settling in general upon the town and in particular upon Joe Hicks.

"Katie," she exclaimed one day in real distress, "please don't tell me any more of this. I am perfectly sure Joe never took the bird. It grieves me to think he is under suspicion."

"Well, what did he go in to Pittsburgh for that day? What was he carryin' in the little box? Why did he turn as red as a turkey wattle when anyone spoke to him, civil-like an' all? An' where did the money come from for the diamond? Can you answer them questions?"

"No, of course I can't."

"Well, ain't you goin' to face him with them an' see what he's got to say for himself?"

"I certainly am not. I think this is all purely circumstantial evidence and when the right time comes it can be explained."

"An' you ain't goin' to charge him with it?"

"Katie, how could I? Joe's a decent man. It was bad enough to think Mr. Smith was guilty but it's even worse to think a thing like that about Joe Hicks. Oh, what wracks me most is that anything as lovely as the nightingale should bring trouble like this! Do you suppose Joe's heard the talk?"

"Well, it seems he never knew a thing of it till yesterday, for somehow Becky Slade hadn't got holt of it till then. Nobody in to see her, I spose. But Mrs. Hummel stopped to sort of sound her out and she almost had a conniption. Seems Joe's been awful kind to her. She said she was goin' to tell him the whole thing an' get him to sue for slander. But who would he sue? I says to Mary Jackson.

115

She says now she's just as glad she can say Mrs. Hummel was the first to start it. Well, what'll I tell them you're goin' to do then? They're all askin'."

"Tell them I'm going to do nothing, and I want this wicked talk about Joe *stopped!*"

Katie gave a small snort. "You can stop the sun shinin' mebbe, but you'll never stop tongues from clackin'. It would be easy just to say, *Among them be it,* if we weren't so tied up with it all ourselves."

"I think I'll go up to my room and finish some writing. If anyone comes and asks for me you can just say I'm busy."

"Highty-tighty," said Katie. "That would sound stuck up for sure. I hope that letter from the editor man hasn't turned your head!"

Violet suddenly put her arms around the old woman and laid her head on her shoulder as she used to when a child.

"I just feel I can't face anybody today, Katie. I'm worried about this whole thing, and I keep thinking if only Father and Mother were here they would know how to cope with it. I miss them so!"

"I know! I know! Get on away to your room then, and have a bit of peace. I'll see to the callers. If I *have* to," she added staunchly, "I'll say you've got a headache." Katie had a tremendous regard for the truth.

Violet kissed her cheek. "You won't be stretching your conscience if you do say so—for I have."

Once in her room Violet drew a long breath, half a sigh, and half relief, and sat down at her desk. Her reply to the "editor man," as Katie called him, was not quite finished. She meant to write the ending now. As a matter of fact she had written several letters which finally, in *very* small bits, ended in the waste basket. She found the task harder than she had anticipated. Finally, a few days ago, a sudden thought had brought her help. This Philip Haversham, evidently of the publishing-house family, would certainly be elderly, maybe much older than her father. Why not then pretend she was writing as though to a man like her father himself? Freely, simply and without inhibition. After this decision, the words fairly fell from her pen.

Now, after an hour's addition and revision, the letter was completed. It was quite long, so she copied it on the

116

typewriter. She read it over rather hastily for she feared if she perused it with a calmly critical eye she would not send it at all. Just after she put it in the envelope she remembered an omission and drew the pages out again. At the end, in her own handwriting, she appended this postscript:

I forgot to mention one thing, though, unlike Katie, I'm not at all embarrassed to tell you. I'm nearly twenty-five years old. My dearest friend, Faith Lyall, our minister's daughter, is a little older, and sometimes, in view of the large number of spinsters in our village, we wonder about our future. However, a young man from the city is coming out next Saturday with a friend to give us a ride in his auto and a new young bachelor has just bought the nicest farm in the countryside, so who knows what might happen!

After she had sealed the envelope she regretted the postscript. It sounded entirely too intimate and too frivolous. But her father would have smiled over such a girlish confession, and surely Mr. Haversham would know she meant him to take it humorously.

Dear Mr. Haversham (her reply read): *It is impossible to tell you what happiness your letter brought me! To have received even the most formal crumb of commendation for my poems would have elated me; but to have actual praise given with real friendliness—oh, you can't imagine what this means to me! I have read your letter so often and bedewed it so many times with a joyous tear that it looks now a bit blurred. However, I know it by heart, so complete illegibility would not matter.*
As to your question about myself and the way I live, how good of you to care about all that. I'll try to tell you as briefly as I can. I am sadly alone as far as family goes. My father died a year ago, my mother five years earlier. I still live in the big old house which was built by my great-grandfather, whom, I believe, I somewhat resemble, as I consider his portrait. The only other human occupant is Katie—and how shall I describe her? She came originally from Scotland and has never lost what she calls "the twist to her tongue." She had lived in my moth-

er's family in the city and came here with her when she first came as a bride. I don't know exactly how old she is now for she is terribly sensitive on the subject and has long since eschewed birthdays. Indeed she shows anger at their mention. She is short and stout with Highland black eyes and cheeks like Winesap apples. I love her devotedly and I know she would lay down her life for me at a moment's notice. But she does often drive me to distraction by making me wear rubbers when there is nothing wetter than dew on the grass, for example.

She, in turn, is tyrranized over by a tiger-striped cat named Simon, the most overbearing and truculent animal I'm sure that was ever poured into fur. But we are both quite dangerously fond of him, that is, if anything happened to him we would feel actually bereft, Katie in particular. Each night before she goes up to bed she sits in the armchair in the kitchen and reads her daily chapter from the Bible with Simon sometimes curled like a boa around her neck. This rite Katie will never omit though often at the end of a washday I have found them both sound asleep in the middle of Exodus or Deuteronomy!

Above our yard proper and separated from it by a low stone wall there is an apple orchard. A man here wants to buy it and I am having a bad inner struggle over the matter. If it comes to a final choice between apple blossoms and bread and butter I may be forced to choose the latter but I'll hold out as long as I can. Oh, the utter beauty of that orchard in spring! The sight of it in bloom is like a dream but the fragrance is, I think, the most delicately ravishing in the world. Oh, yes, for the moment I forgot that one of my poems is about that.

We have a garden, flowers near the house, vegetables near the stable where dwells Prince, my father's horse, a black, gentle creature with a white star on his nose.

As to the town itself. Oh, the dear, funny little town! I don't know how I can give you the feel of it. Everyone stoutly maintains that the population is five hundred, even though knowing this may be a slight exaggeration. The main street is in summer a dusty thoroughfare where the horses scatter white clouds as they plop-plop along it. In winter, when there is usually snow, the farmers come in, in big sleds with strings of bells chiming around the work horses' vast tummies.

118

There are, even here, social castes, *as it were, but the essential joys and sorrows, drama and comedy, are shared by all. We drink of the same cup, we villagers.*

The town, to me, is loveliest on a summer evening. You can hardly imagine the peace and quiet of it! Last night I went into the garden to watch the fireflies, clouds of them twinkling gold as they flew. I wonder if you ever caught one in a jar when you were a little boy! Then I walked around the house under the serenity of a full moon. There is a creek, faintly vocal, flowing between high banks back of our street which was once called The Green. My father said that in his boyhood anyone walking at night on The Green had to tread carefully in order not to step upon a sleeping cow! Oh, we have progressed far since then! We have walks of a sort now, though we do have to use oil lanterns on dark nights to be sure of our footing. There are oaks along the creek bank which in the morning are filled with cooing doves.

This is a very long screed and I still may not have given you much idea of what you so kindly wished to know. Of course I hope you may at length decide to publish my poems. But even if you cannot, I will take heart of grace from your letter and keep on writing.

With my thanks again, I am

Sincerely yours,
Violet Carpenter

A squarish, mellow-looking envelope was in Violet's mail a few days later. It had a Pittsburgh postmark so she knew it must be from Mike. The note was very correct, with only what might be described as a slight quirk at the corners, like a smile. He trusted that it would be convenient for him to come out on the Saturday designated bringing Don with him. They would try to arrive in the early afternoon and then if it was agreeable to her and Miss Faith they would drive over to Westburg and have dinner. He had checked and found there was a hotel of sorts there, and that even if red tablecloths were used they were likely to be clean. The fact that he had phoned to the proprietor for a reservation had thrown that poor gentleman into a state of surprise verging upon apoplexy. He hoped he would be recovered sufficiently to serve them when they got there. He (Mike) was looking forward with pleasure to seeing her again and trusted the weather would be favorable. Perhaps having a minister's daughter along would propitiate the elements. And he remained very truly hers.

As soon as she had read the note, Violet caught up a sunbonnet and hurried up the back way to the manse. Because of party-line conditions it was not wise to discuss private matters over the telephone. She found Faith on the back porch with a letter from Don still in her hand, so the girls sat together to discuss the two missives and the prospect described in each. Their cheeks were flushed, their eyes were bright; life all at once seemed vastly exciting.

"And dinner at a hotel!" Faith kept repeating. "Did Henry ever take you anywhere *for dinner?*"

"Never," said Violet. "I don't believe he ever thought of such a thing. Of course we went all around the countryside to strawberry festivals, and in winter to church suppers, but never to a hotel like this. Oh Faith, whatever shall we wear? I do hope we won't seem too . . . too . . ."

"Provincial?" Faith supplied.

"Yes. After all, we can hold up our end of things on a mental level, I think, but all the little extra chit-chat that city girls must know—we may fall short of that. For instance, that song Mike sang at the picnic was completely new to me and you said it was to you too."

The girls looked soberly over the garden to the hills beyond, weighing their limitations. Then Faith spoke encouragingly.

"Don't let's worry. Father always says if you let a man talk about himself he'll have a good time. We can do that. Anyway, while I *like* Don and I'm thrilled over the drive and the dinner, I don't believe . . . I mean I don't think he's just the type I would ever . . ."

"I feel the same," said Violet. "That is, at the moment, anyway. Oh, let's just enjoy ourselves and pretend that young men take us out to dinner every night of the week!"

But after an animated discussion of clothes, the cloud that hung over the village fell suddenly again upon them. Faith said her parents felt as Violet did, that Joe Hicks could surely not have been the thief. But they also agreed that the evidence was rather overwhelming and that a man of Joe's shy and colorless personality would find refutation difficult.

"Father can't very well go to talk to him about it since he does not belong to our church, but perhaps his own minister will. Meanwhile Father says he's going to go out of his way to be friendly with Joe and maybe try to scare up a little work for him. But *the ring!* Amanda rushed out to show it to Mother one day when she was passing—before the rumors started. The poor little soul was so happy. Quite transfigured, Mother said. It's all too bad. And a mystery too," she added.

"I believe I'll stop and see Becky Slade on my way back," Violet said. "I won't insult Joe by going to see him about it, but I can get any message across to him through Becky."

As they stood later, talking at the gate, Faith, evidently a little self-conscious, said, "Oh, Seena's farm is really sold. Jeremy called up last night and told us. He likes this Mr. Halifax—Bob, he calls him—very much. There's to be a sale of some of the stock and some of the household goods too in a couple of weeks. That seems so sad. It just emphasizes the thought that 'the places that knew us will know us no more,' don't you think?"

"Yes, a sale is always depressing to me. But when this one comes I think we ought to be there, for Seena's sake. I wonder how things are going with her anyway. I keep thinking about that poor Jake. He could get desperate, you know, one way or another. It does seem as though Ladykirk can always stir up more drama than its size would warrant."

"I know," Faith agreed. "We've always said that just when we think the town has run the whole gamut of human events it comes up with a completely new one."

"And we're so close to them all, that's the trouble. Oh, well, let's concentrate on the pleasant things right now. And I think you're right about wearing our best hats on the drive since the boys have already seen our other ones, at the picnic."

Violet pursued her way thoughtfully down the street until she reached the tiny ell off Joe Hicks's modest house, where lived Becky Slade, still sharp-tongued and lively at ninety-three. When Violet tapped on the door the

121

old woman looked up from her quilt patches and haled her eagerly in.

"You're just the person I want to see. I won't deny I'm in a state about this thing that has set the town by the ears. It's the wickedest lie I've ever heard an' if you've come here to talk again' Joe you can just get on home."

"But I haven't, Miss Becky. I'm as troubled as you are. I don't for a minute believe Joe took the bird. I stopped because I thought maybe you could let him know that. I'm ashamed even to speak to him directly about it. Could you tell him?"

"I certainly could," said Becky with fervor, "an' I'm glad you have some sense. I kind of tried to break the news about it to Amanda. yesterday before supper after Mrs. Hummel had been here. Amanda just laughed at it. But then Joe come in an' he'd got wind of it down-street. He was white as a ghost an' there was no more laughin' I can tell you. I watched them out of the kitchen window in the evening. They just sat on the bench in the back yard, their arms round each other an' then *they went up awful early to bed.* Oh, it's a cruel thing an' them both so happy over the ring." Becky looked sharply at Violet as though daring her to speak a question concerning the diamond. But she made no comment.

"They've been kind to me," Becky went on. "I feel like they belong to me since I've got neither chick nor child of my own. I'll stand up for Joe till my last breath, but oh, I'm feared this will break him. Joe can't fight back like most men. He ain't made that way."

Becky hitched her chair nearer. "There's just one thing bothers me," she said in a half whisper, "an' since you feel like me I can tell you. But don't you dare breathe it even to Katie."

"I won't," Violet pledged soberly.

"Well, it's this. When I was there yesterday talkin' it all over with them, I says, 'Joe,' I says, 'can't you just say right out what took you up to the city an' stop the gossipin' right there?'" Becky swallowed painfully. "An' he turned red just like Mr. Clee told an' he says, 'I'm tellin' nothin' to nobody,' he says. An' Amanda looked scared to death, as if she never knew he'd even *been* to the city. She was out at her mother's at the time. Well, I

122

still believe Joe an' always will, but this bothers me, sort of."

"Don't worry," Violet said, though she felt troubled herself by this latest disclosure, "and please tell Joe what I asked you to. The truth always comes out, no matter what!"

Becky sighed. "I know," she agreed, "but sometimes it gets bedraggled along the way. I'm glad you stopped in, Vi'let. I wish your father was here. He'd make short shrift of the story. He always liked Joe."

"I keep thinking that, Miss Becky. But cheer up, now! This is bound to come out right."

She walked slowly home, a heaviness in her heart. There was no end for her to the pain of it all. If it could finally be proved that Joe did not take the nightingale, then, once again, who did? Would the dark cloud of suspicion rise only to settle again? Oh, her beautiful treasure! Lost to her, and the cause of trouble and distrust among her neighbors!

And the week passed. The bloom of the cabbage roses was over now; the currants were turning red at the foot of the garden; the vegetables were well up in their beds; a languid summer warmth began to settle upon the town in the afternoons—and the talk about Joe Hicks continued. It was counted unto him for evil that now he scarcely left his little carpenter's shack on the alley behind his house. Amanda, her face all but concealed in a large sunbonnet, scurried downstreet to the Post Office or the store and home again "like the dogs were after her," as Mary Jackson put it. Violet knew that the consensus of village opinion was that she herself should take some action. This, in spite of passing questions in her own mind, she could not do. Neither, as Katie suggested, could she bring this latest suspicion to the attention of Mr. Huntley. She had called him up at once after the visit of Mr. and Mrs. Smith. He had seemed relieved, insisted that the ads in the papers had been of such short duration that there would be no charge to her, and told her comfortingly that now he felt sure the bird would ultimately be returned, since it was evidently a village problem.

She did go up one evening to Squire Hendricks, hoping against hope that the shades of darkness would protect her from prying eyes. It would be the final condemnation of poor Joe if the word went round: *Violet's been to the Squire's.* So she went quietly up the back street and in by the side door. She liked the Squire; she trusted his judgment; and he had been a close friend of her father's.

"Well, Vi'let," he began, after first taking the precaution to draw the blinds, "you don't need to tell me the story over again. I've had about twenty versions of it already."

"And what do you think?" she asked anxiously.

"It's a bad one, confound me if it isn't! Do you believe it?"

"No."

"Neither do I, though I've kept my mouth shut. I've been wrong plenty of times. Now the way I feel about Joe is that he's likely as innocent as I am, and the fact that he looks more like a scared rabbit than a thief ought to help him now. Howsomever, I've often found that these little meek-lookin' men are often stubborn as the devil on the inside. I'll bet it's that way with Joe. If he's done nothing wrong he don't see any reason to explain an' in a way I don't blame him."

"Everybody has been pressing me to go to him and ask him myself. I can't do that, Mr. Hendricks."

"No, no. You just sit tight a while. I'll tell you, Vi'let, a rule I've followed all my time as Squire. When people come to me kickin' up a big dust over something, you know what I do? I just wait *till the dust settles.* Now, let's do that about Joe. I'll keep my eyes an' my ears open an' if I find anything you ought to know, I'll tell you. How's that?"

"Oh, that's a wonderful relief!" she said. "That's just the way I felt, myself, and now you've bolstered me up."

"Don't go," the Squire said as she made as if to rise. "Can't we have a little dish of chat? Nobody's likely to come about a shot-gun wedding or a spite fence tonight, so I'm pretty free. Fact of the matter is I've been wanting to ask you something. Report says you and Henry have broke up. That so?"

"Yes."

"H'm. Your doing, I take it?"

"Yes."

"Well, guess you must have had your reasons. I've been wondering about Henry lately. Seen him riding out the

124

Pike a coupla times about dusk. I spose he'd hardly be goin' out to see the young widder. Not *this* soon."

"Seena?" The word sprang from her lips. "Oh, surely that couldn't be!"

"No, I guess not. Only when a young fellah starts off like that in early evening he's usually headed for some place in particular. You knew Seena had sold the farm?"

"Yes. To a Mr. Halifax."

"Nice chap. I like his get-up. He's been in to see me about some papers. I guess Seena's goin' to have a sale before long."

"Oh, that's it," Violet cried out. "That could be what Henry was seeing about, if he really went to Seena's. The hardware store might be buying some things before the sale!"

"Could be," said the Squire, "only you'd think daytime would be best for lookin' at machinery. I'll tell you, Vi'let, I'm glad you broke up with Henry though he's a nice young fellah at that. No bad habits or anything. It's just that . . . well, I feel like your father. He was talkin' to me once about you two. 'I won't put a straw in her way,' says he, 'if she really loves him, but I'm not happy about it,' he says. 'Vi'let's worth somebody much, much finer in the grain.' That's the way he put it an' I knew what he meant."

"Why, he never said a word like that to me," Violet exclaimed. "Oh, I'm glad you told me. I've never regretted my decision, but still there have been moments . . ."

"I know," said the Squire. "Evenings can be pretty lonely. But cheer up! You're young yet. Somebody's sure to come along." The old man's wise eyes brooded upon the delicate beauty of the girl before him. " 'Much, much finer in the grain,' that's what he said."

As Violet went cautiously out the side door again and made her way down the dark street she had much to think of. Disturbingly much. The Squire had talked a little more about Seena. While his remarks were guarded she felt he had his own anxiety in regard to young Jake and that he had very much wanted to know whether *she* knew anything about Henry's evening trips out the Pike. Oh, what a tangled web of emotions Seena had managed to draw around her. And Violet, because Henry had professed to love her and asked her to marry him, felt herself to some

125

extent embroiled in it. Even a little sullied by it. The more she thought of the Squire's words the more certain she was that Henry *was* going out to see Seena. But surely he must have some pretext. It could not be just a man-and-woman errand this short time after John's death. That was a horrible thought. Knowing Seena, however, she could imagine that some plausible excuse for the trips had been invented. And all at once she felt a great and almost maternal pity for Henry. Another fly seduced!

But as she lay in bed later, too busy in mind to go to sleep at once, she felt that the role of fly in the spider's web did not exactly fit Henry. He was too strong and stubborn and dominant. Suddenly she recalled the conversation she and Faith had once in regard to Seena's nature. Perhaps they had been right. Perhaps what Seena needed and even unconsciously craved was male dominance, and was determined now to have it where she thought it might be found. But even if this were true, was it not still *poor Henry?*

On the morning of the Saturday when the young men were to arrive from the city Violet received a letter with the publisher's script in the corner. She fingered the envelope in the Post Office under Mr. Howard's inquiring gaze but there was no word spoken by either. She scarcely believed the testimony of her eyes! She had supposed that Mr. Haversham, having received the answers to his questions, would not write again until he was prepared to give a final report upon her poems. She had never dreamed of an immediate reply.

She hurried up the back street to avoid conversational delays, and, having reached the house, went directly to her room. She sat down, a little breathless, to see what the letter might contain.

Dear Miss Carpenter (she read), *It is difficult, in my turn, to explain to you what pleasure your letter gave me. I've been a city man all my life, with my summers, during the time I was growing up and during vacations later, spent at the seashore. I know boats and fishing but I've never seen a golden cloud of fireflies over a garden on a summer evening—nor caught one in a jar! As I read your description of your home and of the town, the rasping rattle of trolley cars outside my window and the stale hot air—when there is a breeze at all—seemed to disappear. I was transported to another world, a beautiful and peaceful one. I have no right to ask this and I must make it clear that I am not writing now in any editorial capacity, just as a man "long in city pent," as Mr. Keats would say —but would you be gracious enough to tell me more of your village and your way of life generally? This is a rather impulsive request but I hope you will feel like granting it.*

> *Very truly yours,*
> *Philip Haversham*

Violet read this for the second time and then laid the letter carefully in a pigeonhole of her desk, her cheeks a little flushed. So he had actually *liked* her letter, over which she had had so many qualms! And now he wanted her to write again. She pictured him as she thought he would be: tall and thin, with a rather ascetic, certainly a scholarly face and perhaps a gray mustache like her father's. He must be either a bachelor or a widower since he spoke of being lonely, and most important of all to her, he evidently loved poetry. She thought of him as she ate her lunch and later as she dressed for the drive in her last summer's pink voile and this year's wide leghorn hat circled with roses. His letter sounded as though he might be thinking of a real correspondence! This idea was odd but strangely pleasant. For it would be nice, writing to him, easily, freely, about all the town doings and even of her own thoughts on many matters about which now, she had no one to whom she could voice them. Some subtle quality in his letter made her feel she could confide in him. And what a relief to her heart this would be! "It will do me good to write to him," she said aloud, "a great deal of good!"

So, when the front doorbell rang she hurried down the stairs to greet Mike with a high color and shining eyes, which he had no way of knowing were not caused by his presence. Indeed he looked at her a moment in silence without speaking.

"Hello," Violet said, "is . . . is anything wrong?"

"Quite the contrary," he said, smiling. "Here we are, the day is fine, and the machine seems to be on its best behavior. You don't feel nervous about it, do you?"

"No, only pleased! I'll run and tell Katie we're leaving. I'll only be a minute."

Katie came back along to the porch, looked Mike over critically and gave advice about returning before it was too late, then watched with interest as he helped Violet into a duster he had brought along and himself tied a wide chiffon veil over her hat.

"You'll really need these," he said, "for it's awfully dusty! I have some for Miss Faith too. Good-bye, Katie," he called to her anxious countenance. "I'll take good care of her."

Faith and Don sat in the back seat and Violet could hear as they drove along that the conversation was not going well. She exerted herself to the utmost, trying by a turn of the head to include the other pair in her remarks. But Faith's answers were jerky and her laughter nervous. In the large picnic group this self-consciousness of which she had once spoken had not been noticeable. Mike finally gave Violet a humorous glance.

"You're supposed to be my girl for the afternoon, so how about concentrating on me and leaving those other two to get on as best they can? You're not obligated to entertain them, you know."

Violet laughed. *"Touché,"* she said. "I'll give you my whole attention. First of all, I love the auto! It's incredible. How fast are we really going?"

"Twenty-five or a little better," he said proudly, "but that was really just to show off. I'll slow down now. It's more exciting than a horse though, isn't it?"

Violet considered. "Oh yes, exciting. But as compared with Prince—our horse—you see I brush him and stroke his nose. He nuzzles against me and eats bits of sugared apple from my hand, so while he's less exciting he's more, well, shall we say, affectionate!"

Mike laughed but she thought she felt in it a shade of disappointment which she hastened to dispel.

"But don't think I don't like the auto! I've never been so thrilled in my life! To ride along like this with the landscape flying past—and my veil blowing in the breeze —oh it's lovely, and exhilarating! And," she added, "it makes me feel so . . . so sophisticated."

This time Mike only smiled but he seemed satisfied.

"I'm glad you're enjoying it. And it's all right to *feel*
128

sophisticated if you just don't act so. I've seen enough of that and I like a change."

There seemed to be many silences in the back seat in spite of Faith's efforts, but Violet found it was not difficult to keep a light conversation going with Mike. When she asked him what he had been doing since they met before he made a grimace.

"Working in my father's factory," he said, "and I hate it like murder."

"What kind of a factory?"

"That's it. I'm ashamed to say it. Pickles. My great-grandfather came from Germany and had a delicatessen store. He made pickles himself in a barrel. They got to be quite famous so *his* son started a little factory which grew into a big one. Then my father took over and now it's really a large concern. Since I'm the next son I'm naturally expected to go into the business and I hate every da . . . darned pickle."

Mike's voice was so unhappy that Violet did not laugh though she felt like it. Then all at once she gave an exclamation. "You aren't . . . why of course you must be . . . *Dorsey's Pickles.* We use the little sweet ones all the time and I've often noticed the name on the label. They're delicious, you know. You must try to feel proud of your product and not ashamed of it. What would you like to do if you don't go into the business?"

"That's the funny thing. It's not as though I hankered after the law or medicine or any profession. I'd like to *make* things, build things. What I'd do in a minute if I could would be to apprentice myself to a regular carpenter till I learned the trade. Get the practical experience. I did have engineering in college. Then later on of course I would expect to do big things—bridges, skyscrapers! A far cry from pickles," he added bitterly.

"Well," Violet answered reasonably, "if this is what you really want to do, why not do it? Make the break right now. Your father would understand, wouldn't he?"

"Never. And I don't have the courage to do it against his opposition. He'd likely cut off my allowance, and the plain fact is I like money. I like a lot of it. This doesn't show me up in a very good light but at least I'm being honest. I'll probably stick with the pickles."

"My grandfather was a carpenter, a real one," Violet

said. "He built some of the best houses in Ladykirk. There must be a great deal of satisfaction in that. Sound, beautiful work that will stand long after the builder is gone! Not a bad kind of immortality, is it?"

He gave her a quick glance but did not answer, and they rode on in silence. A little later Don called from the back seat, "Hey, watch your signs! Isn't that Westburg you can see from here?"

It was, indeed, and in another half hour they had caught up with the red and brown roofs and the slender spire that showed from the hill, and were driving slowly along the town's main street. The hotel, while modest enough according to urban standards, was imposing to the two girls who had never before partaken of its hospitality. It was exciting to be handed down from the auto before a group of small boys who watched the "horseless carriage" with avid interest. The proprietor himself received them unctuously, and after they had all divested themselves of their dusters and sat for a little while on the front porch, the cynosure of all passing eyes, they were ushered to the dining room and a round table near the window. The cloth was not red-checked but spotlessly white, and it developed they were to have a regular "course" dinner.

Violet watched Faith keenly. She was so pretty in her quiet way with her gray eyes and high blonde pompadour, but she was shy and uncomfortably self-conscious. Violet tried constantly to draw her into the conversation, and finally introduced the subject of music, hoping to give her friend a chance to display her knowledge, but the effort fell flat. Don, big, hearty and faintly boisterous, kept up a generally inane raillery in which Mike joined. Violet tried to enter into it though ineptly, she felt, but Faith seemed helpless. One thing saved the occasion from complete failure. The food was excellent; both young men ate with prodigious appetites and commented eloquently upon its fine quality and their surprise at finding it so. But neither, Violet noted, said, "We must come here again."

By the time dessert arrived Faith's cheeks were an embarrassed red, and Violet herself felt wearied with the strain. She rallied as best she could to try for a few moments of normal talk before they left and had to admit that Don could speak with real intelligence when he cared to, but he soon dropped into his former light, teasing manner.

On the way back it was Don who kept raising his voice to reach the front seat, and Mike who was silent. Violet felt annoyed. "He needn't show so plainly that he is bored," she thought, with a sidewise glance at her companion. "Oh, let's sing," she said, looking back at Faith and Don.

So from that point on their voices blended on the night air with only small lapses between songs.

"And that," Violet thought, "takes care of *that*."

When they reached the manse, Faith thanked Mike for the drive, said good night to Violet, and she and Don went through the white gate and on up to the house. The leave-taking there was very brief, however. They could hear Faith's low voice and Don's hearty "wonderful time, really." Then he started, whistling, back down the walk.

"Miss Faith is quite different from Ninian's Lucy, isn't she?" Mike observed.

Violet's tone was slightly crisp. "Different, but just as nice," she said.

"No doubt," Mike answered.

When they reached the Carpenter house Violet divested herself of the duster and veil, leaving them in the car as Faith had done, then Mike escorted her to the porch, his guiding hand firmly upon her bare arm. They climbed the steps, and when they were behind the honeysuckle vine, now sweet upon the air, he spoke.

"Miss Violet—or may I drop the *Miss*?—I would like to come back sometime soon, *alone*. May I?"

"You want to come back?" Violet said incredulously, the words slipping out without volition.

"I've just asked to."

"Of . . . course . . . if you really wish."

"I do wish it. Very much. I'm busy next Saturday. Would two weeks from today be convenient for you?"

"Yes, I think so. Yes."

"I'll bring a picnic basket and maybe we can find a pleasant spot in the woods somewhere. I enjoyed the one we had at Ninian and Lucy's so much I'd like another."

"Would Don not like to come too?" Violet asked eagerly, "and bring Faith?"

"I don't believe so," Mike answered, a smile in his

131

voice. "But if you would rather, we could go back to Westburg for dinner. Think it over."

"I will," Violet said, "but if we picnic I'll bring the food. Katie and I love to pack baskets."

"That's awfully kind," he said, "but it would seem rather like inviting myself to dinner. However, we can settle that later. I can count on coming out in two weeks, then?"

"If you really want to."

This time Mike laughed aloud. "You must allow me the privilege of knowing my own mind," he said.

Violet laughed then too, and held out her hand.

"Thank you so much for today!" she said.

"Thank *you*," he rejoined.

There were two toots from the horn when he was back in the car and then the noise of its driving away.

Violet sank down on the swing behind the vine and drew a long breath. "And I thought he was *bored*," she said to herself in amazement.

She sat on for a long time thinking it over. How could she tell Faith that Mike wanted to come back but Don did not? It had seemed so ideal to go out with the boys together, to plan for it, to talk it all over. Now it would be different. Should she, she wondered, for Faith's sake, write to Mike and tell him not to come? No, she decided, that would not be fair to anyone, least of all to Faith. But her heart felt sore for her friend. As to her own feelings she scarcely knew what to think. In a way, Mike was attractive, but he was still a stranger. It was pleasant, however, to have a young man interested in her if only temporarily, and it would be nice to look forward to another drive, thus diverting her mind somewhat from all the troubled complexities which had lately sprung up around her. Seena and young Jake *and Henry!* Poor Joe Hicks with his weight of suspicion upon him and Amanda with the joy of her little diamond shattered. And then, the lost nightingale itself! How incredible that this had all happened since the coming of the first apple blossoms in the orchard!

She sighed and then started back to the kitchen to give Katie the news.

"I heard you come," the latter said. "Well, I'm glad you're back all in one piece. I don't hold with them new-fangled machines at all. It's temptin' Providence to go

132

in them. How were your young men?"

"Very polite and nice. And the dinner was excellent."

"Humph," said Katie, "you can't tell me hotel cookin' can come up to a home table!"

"Oh," Violet amended hastily, "that goes without saying. It couldn't compare to *yours* for instance, but for a hotel it was good."

"Now, now," Katie said, "you needn't go bletherin' about me. I was just waitin' to hear how you made out. Get along with you, Simon. He's warm on my shoulder these nights, but he likes to lie there, poor beast. The top of the cupboard's too hot for him now June's in. Well, we'd better be off to bed for tomorrow's the Sabbath!"

Once in her room Violet undressed slowly and then sat on the edge of the bed brushing her hair. When she had finished she went over to the desk, drew from its pigeonhole the letter from Philip Haversham and standing there, all white and lovely, read it again. Indeed she read it over three times before she finally blew out the lamp.

CHAPTER SIX

ONE thing in connection with Ladykirk which Violet's father had often remarked upon was that rarely were two topics of consuming interest discussed at the same time. It was as though each new matter of moment as it came along must be given full stage. So, as the problems of Seena began to loom larger in the popular mind, conversation centered upon them and lapsed from those of Joe Hicks.

As a matter of fact there was not much more to be said about Joe. All the old reports had been threshed over by everyone in town and there were no new ones. Joe still, looking like a hunted rabbit, avoided everyone's eyes and seemed to be trying to find jobs in the country. Amanda no longer displayed her little diamond and ceased from the neighborly visits which had always been her great joy. One thing was noted in connection with the couple and the information passed along for what it was worth. Each evening, when darkness had barely fallen, the lights suddenly went out in the Hick's downstairs, a lamp shone briefly in the bedroom and then it, too, was extinguished.

"Poor things," old Becky Slade, the ninety-three-year-old virgin, said to herself as she watched this nightly phenomenon, "they mebbe just don't know any other way to find comfort in their trouble."

All the news in connection with Seena and the farm was now discussed with avidity. Those who had met Robert Halifax had been favorably impressed; it was definite that Seena would come back to live with her parents in the Mɪⁱ house; and the forthcoming sale of household goods and some of the stock and farm machinery would doubtless be an event of major importance in the countryside. Since the Harveys had divided the furniture with John before he married Seena it was not considered unreasonable of her now to sell her share for what she could get. When asked if she didn't want to save some in case she should ever remarry she had said flatly that if she ever married again it would be to someone who could buy her new furniture and she hated this old stuff anyhow.

One morning Violet was called to the telephone and found it was Seena on the wire.

"You've heard about the sale?" she asked.

"Oh, yes. Faith and I are planning to go to it. I know you'll have a big crowd. Is there anything I can do to help you?"

"Well, that's why I called. I've decided to give everybody a lunch."

"Oh, Seena, you couldn't!"

"Yes, I could. Dave Wright is going to auctioneer and he says it's often done now. You put a couple of sandwiches and some cookies in a paper poke for each one, you see? I've got it all thought out. I've got plenty of smoked hams. I'll bake two or three, and the bread and cookies won't be any trouble. I'd rather be working hard than not. I can get a hundred pokes from the store. That ought to be enough."

"Not if the word gets round that you're giving a free lunch," Violet said, "and it's probably round already."

Seena laughed. "I spose I should have driven in to talk to you but I have a lot to do. Mother's coming out the day before and we'll have everything ready. What I wanted to ask you was, would you and Faith care to come out early the day of the sale and the four of us would make the sandwiches and put them in the pokes? Would you?"

"Why, of course! I'll be glad to and I know Faith will, too."

"Could you speak to her? I know how it was with John about her. Do you think she'd do it?"

"I'm sure of it. I'll go right up and see her now. I'm glad you asked us, Seena. When should we get there that morning? Six? Seven?"

"Seven would be fine. They're selling the stock and the machinery in the forenoon, so you won't miss anything. I've an idea Bob Halifax will buy a good deal, but he says he wants to keep some of his own cows and horses. Well, thanks, Violet."

Violet had not talked with Faith since the Saturday's drive. On Sunday there had been no chance for conversation after church and Faith had made no move to get in touch since. This silence could not go on, so, feeling that her errand was in a sense a godsend, Violet went up to the manse. She could hear Faith at the piano when she got there so she walked around to the back, where Mr. Lyall was working over his bees whose boxes stood along the garden wall. When he noticed her, he looked up, smiling.

"Oh, Violet, it's nice to see you. Don't come too close, though you're one person I remember who isn't afraid of my interesting friends here. This hive is getting ready to swarm so I'm making preparations, and very glad to do it, too. You know the rhyme:

> "*A swarm of bees in June*
> *Is worth a silver spoon!*"

Violet quoted back:

> "*And a swarm in July*
> *Isn't worth a fly.*"

"Ah, I see you've been properly brought up!" Mr. Lyall laughed. "I can't leave this business, I'm afraid. Could you go on in? Mary's out but you'll find Faith." He lowered

135

his voice slightly. "Nothing new about the nightingale?"

"Nothing. I'm trying to forget it for a little."

"That's wise. I have a firm conviction it will finally turn up, so don't despair."

"Thanks, Mr. Lyall. I'll keep hoping."

She went on over the back porch and into the hall, calling as she did so. The sounds of the piano stopped and Faith emerged from the parlor.

"Oh, Vi, I *am* glad to see you. Maybe we'd better sit in here on account of the bees. I like being round them ordinarily but I wouldn't care to have them swarm and settle on my arm as they did once with Father. What a sight! He sat down and never moved until his whole side was covered with them. Then we held the new box and very gently he brushed them all off into it. They're very drowsy and stupid after they settle, you know."

"Was he hurt?"

"Not one sting! He has a wonderful knack with them and I think they feel it. Well, Vi, any news?"

"Yes, a little. I had a call from Seena and she wants us to help her the day of the sale."

Faith listened carefully as the plan was outlined and then gave a cry.

"Oh, if the whole thing weren't so sad, wouldn't this be *fun?*"

"That's just what I thought as I was coming up. Well, no matter how we feel on the inside ourselves it's likely to be a lively time. While we can't call it fun exactly, I don't think it will be wrong to enjoy what we can. I imagine everyone from the whole countryside will be there."

"Jeremy will be helping, too, I'm sure, though Peggy can't do much just now. We'd better take our own aprons, don't you think? Our best ones. Do you think white or colored?"

When they had settled all the details pertaining to the sale, Faith spoke hesitantly as she folded and refolded a plait in her skirt.

"Did . . . did Mike say anything to you about coming out again?"

"Yes."

"I suppose you guessed that Don didn't. And Vi, I did feel so disappointed at the time. It's not that I like Don so much, for I don't. He and I have nothing in com-

136

mon. Never could have. But I feel so ashamed that I can't be even a little interesting and attractive to a man. I freeze up. I can't think of anything to say. I tried to get Don to talk about himself and even that didn't work. It must have been the way I asked the questions. I feel so *humiliated!* And I'd hoped we would have other good times this summer, the four of us. It would have been so nice to have something to *do* now and then. Little ripples in the stagnant pond. And now, I've spoiled it all."

Faith's blond head suddenly dropped to the arm of her chair and her shoulders shook with sobs. Violet was overcome with tenderness and pity. She moved closer.

"Don't, Faith! Oh, please don't feel so badly. You're pretty and sweet and gifted and you just haven't met the right man yet."

"I never will," came in muffled tones from the chair. "I'll just get older and older and keep on giving music lessons the rest of my life!" Finally she lifted her head. "What about Mike? Do you really like him?"

"He's nice, but . . . that's all. I was so amazed he wanted to come back that I couldn't think of any good excuse for saying no. I believe he enjoys getting into the country. Faith, please don't worry about things."

Faith dried her eyes and smiled. "Heavens, I don't know what's gotten into me. I'm a very happy girl. I *love* my music. Even if I kept on with it indefinitely I'd have a good life. I think John's death stirred me up. And then the other night I felt like such a *ninny* that I was ashamed. Don't pay any attention to what I said." Her eyes became mischievous. "I'll tell you what I'll do. I'll concentrate on Squire Hendrick. I can talk to him by the hour and he told Father once that I was *very* entertaining. So you see I do have a way with some men!"

The conversation ended in laughter and final arrangements for the trip to Seena's the next week. They would leave at six-thirty, which should get them there on the stroke of seven. Violet would drive. They said their goodbyes brightly enough, but as Violet walked home she was disturbed about her friend. This shyness of hers where men were concerned could get worse instead of better. All she needed was confidence in her own feminine powers, but how could that be acquired? Was it a native gift or could it be cultivated? Poor Faith! She was so

137

lovable, so dear, when you really knew her. And it was not as though no man had ever found her desirable. John Harvey had asked her to marry him, and once a few years ago Faith had confessed to her, half in amusement and half in fright, that the famous man with whom she had been studying piano in the city had suddenly whispered that if she would only allow him to give her experience he could make a great artist of her! Of course she had changed teachers at once; but the episode, instead of giving her new assurance of her own charms, had rather made her slightly distrustful of mankind in general. Oh, by what strange, devious and unexpected routes did girls and men arrive at their own true loves—if they ever arrived at all!

When she got home Katie had a small piece of news as a result of Mary Jackson's morning call.

"It seems Henry's been goin' out to Seena's every few evenings for a week or more to help her take inventory of the house goods. She called up an' asked him, so his mother says. An' whether she's made sheep's eyes at him when he's been there nobody knows but himself, an' her. What do you think of it?"

"Henry would be a logical person to take inventory when he's used to doing it at the store," Violet said reasonably.

"Well, there's one thing. I doubt any woman will catch Henry by the coattails unless he wants to be caught. But that hussy will try, belike. I wouldn't put anything past her."

"Now, Katie, don't be too hard on Seena. She's going through a bad time."

"With a wanderin' eye all the while," Katie summed it up. "Till she gets what she wants no man is safe. That's my opeenion."

Violet walked away, vaguely agreeing with Katie, but with something more important on her mind. How long should she wait before answering Mr. Haversham's letter? Since he had replied to hers almost at once it would seem perfectly proper for her to write again soon and she found herself pleasantly eager to do so. Late that evening she seated herself at her desk.

Dear Mr. Haversham (she began):

It seemed amazing to me at first that you should care to hear more about our little town. And yet in a sense I understand. I was once some years ago in New York with my father and he kept quoting those lines from Matthew Arnold:

'. . . this strange disease of modern life with its sick hurry,' etc. We were happy then to get back home. So with this in mind I'll try my best to tell you more about our slow-paced village.

Perhaps I should begin with its physical setting. The town lies in a farming community so that we need only leave our long main street at either end to be surrounded by rolling fields. In the spring there is the beauty of the brown plowed furrows and the living green of the new wheat (adjective by Isaac Watts); in high summer, the tawny gold of the ripe harvest and the long waves of shimmering silver in the tall, uncut hay as the wind passes over it. In autumn—oh, I don't know which season I love the most! One of my greatest pleasures is to harness Prince to the buggy and drive slowly and aimlessly around the country roads. I should say, too, that from the tops of the many hills one can look off to the east and see the long, blue, undulating line of the real mountain ridges.

In the town proper Main Street runs from Cobb's Hill on the east in a gently sloping fashion for nearly a mile down to the long covered wooden bridge over the creek. (Pronounced "crick" here.) At the left of the bridge is the old mill which for long years has ground the farmers' grain. A lovely, fragrant, dusty place it is! Townspeople go there often to get bran to make brown bread or muffins. I always like this errand. The dam spans the creek just above the mill and an impressive sheet of water tumbles over it. Just at the spot where the creek happens to be deepest and the water strongest stands a rather remarkable physical feature called Miller's Rock. It is an enormous stone on the very edge of the bank; the largest they say in this end of the state. It is a dangerous and tempting object for small boys and each one is well warned about it in his childhood. One or two over the years have not heeded and have tragically fallen or jumped off into the "deep hole" below. The lads who grow up into very strong swimmers sometimes dive off the rock as a proud test of their skill, but even for them it is precarious.

It is truly a pretty sight, though: the weathered mill, the dam, and the great rock, with the covered bridge just below.

The village goes its way emotionally in a strange mixture of serenity and excitement. You could walk down Main Street on most summer afternoons and see the good house-wives languidly fanning themselves with palm-leaf fans, as they rest from their labors on front porches—which incidentally stick out into the sidewalk as though afraid of missing something—and feel they were as apathetic as the horses standing in patient rows at their hitching posts farther down in front of the stores. But let one woman suddenly come along with a piece of real news—which she may perhaps have heard over the party-line phone— and ripples of strong feeling spread quickly through the town. For everything that happens anywhere happens here. All except murder and suicide. As far as I know we've never had a murder and the only suicide was one, "Pappy" Hawkes, away back in my grandfather's day— a terrible old reprobate, according to verbal legend. He got hold of some poison and took it, leaving a brief note stating, 'It ain't no more fun livin'.' But everything else happens—including theft, as I happen now rather bitterly to know.

Here Violet stopped and stared for a long time out the window. Then she set down the whole story of the lost nightingale.

But with small and great sorrows, or even tragedies, there is still here a certain peace (she wrote at the end). *It comes perhaps because we are all close to the earth and elemental things. And no matter what tension the days may bring, the nights are always still. Just now waves of honeysuckle fragrance rise from the porch vine and give a beautiful and haunting substance to the darkness.*

I apologize for the length of this letter but I've enjoyed writing it. If you care to reply (she hesitated and then bravely finished the sentence) *I shall be glad to hear from you. Your life must be so filled with interest and excitement.*

I wonder, she thought to herself as she addressed the

envelope, this time not to the publishing house but to the street and number he had given her—*I wonder how old he really is!*

The day of the sale was fair. Roused by the alarm clock Violet rose, dressed and breakfasted promptly, and at a few minutes past six was going down the garden walk to the stable. There had been a heavy dew during the night and now the delicate symmetries of the spider webs sparkled on the grass. The madonna and tiger lilies were all blooming along the orchard wall, and around the stable itself great clumps of hollyhocks were in urgent bud. All the garden was brightly verdant and the big old pear tree was like green air as she passed beneath it. What grace the morning held, she thought, wishing she had written of this to Mr. Haversham—telling him not only of the peacefulness of the nights but also of the tender waking of the village mornings. She stood, drawing deep breaths of the freshness, listening. There was only a faint sound of Mr. Williams' anvil, since he always began work at the crack of dawn, and the muted rumble of wheels on Main Street which quickly died away. The normal sounds of habitation began either earlier or later. This time between six and six-thirty was usually almost hushed.

She harnessed Prince expertly to the buggy, telling him affectionately all his good points as she did so; then, waving to Katie, who was driving out to the sale later with Mary Jackson, she went on to the manse where Faith was waiting at the gate. The latter looked happily alert this morning as though no tear had ever risen to her eyes or girlish uneasiness to her mind. They talked as they rode along of the excitement attendant upon a sale, of Seena, of Henry, of Mr. Halifax and of Jake.

The latter came toward their buggy as the girls drove into the barnyard. He looked thinner than when they had seen him, almost gaunt in his cheap best suit. His eyes were red as if he had not slept for many nights, and they burned with an inner fire.

Seena had heard the sound of wheels and came running out. No matter what questions rose to mind about her general characteristics, there could be no mistake about her beauty. Her lips were scarlet, her cheeks pink, her skin white, her hair glossy dark. Violet and Faith in girlish slimness gave only a hint of their bodily attrac-

141

tions, but Seena's full breasts and curving hips made her every movement voluptuous.

"You're here in fine time," she greeted them. "Jake, put Violet's horse in the barn, will you?" She gave him a side-wise look and a smile. "Just see they don't auction him off!" Jake laughed too loudly as his eyes devoured her. "Come on in, girls," Seena went on. "We're going to be busy, I tell you. I got a hundred and twenty pokes to make sure. Mother says I'm crazy to do this but the auctioneer says it does bring the people. I guess he's spread the word round, sort of. This way the folks can come in the morning and stay right through. That makes a difference."

She led the way to the big kitchen where Mrs. Harris, the miller's wife, was covering a long extension table with papers and white oil cloth. Great mounds of cut bread and sliced ham upon the doughtry and smaller kitchen tables were quickly now transferred to the long one. Jake brought up from the springhouse crocks of butter which Seena had churned only yesterday, the girls donned their aprons and the work began. They were all efficient and soon the task was organized. Mrs. Harris spread the bread, Faith put the ham between the slices, Violet put the sandwiches in the bags, Seena added the cookies on top and Jake put the pokes in a barrel on the back porch.

"I thought we'd make coffee outdoors in the big apple-butter kettle," Seena said, "for them as want a hot drink, and I've plenty of milk and buttermilk in the springhouse for the others. The problem is cups. I've got a good many and Henry said he'd bring some tin ones from the store. Oh, here he comes now," she added, glancing out the window. "And Bob Halifax behind him! And Jeremy!" Her voice kept rising. "He's just legged it across the fields, I guess, if Peggy isn't up to coming."

It was evident that any sad thoughts Seena might have been presumed to have in connection with the sale were drowned completely in the excitements, small and large, attendant upon the occasion. Her eyes sparkled and her cheeks took on a deeper rose as she went out to the porch to greet the young men, with Jake close behind her.

"You girls haven't met Mr. Halifax yet, have you?" she said as they all came in. "This is Violet Carpenter and this is Faith Lyall, Jeremy's sister. Meet Mr. Halifax," she added.

There was an exchange of greetings between Violet and the young stranger, and then he turned toward Faith. She was wearing a white apron with a pinafore top, which made her look like a little girl. Her blonde hair was soft about her face as she looked up shyly to acknowledge the introduction. And then Violet saw something which the others, busily talking, did not see. She saw that Faith's eyes and those of Mr. Halifax clung for an instant as they met and that their lips stammered a little on the conventional words. In a second it was over. Faith was busy again at her task and Mr. Halifax was following Henry and Jeremy into the other rooms to help set the furniture out into the yard. But the moment had been there and Violet, with her quick and unerring perception, had seen it. The words her father often quoted, smilingly, rose to her mind:

"Who ever loved who loved not at first sight."

So said Shakespeare, or was it Marlowe? Violet went on putting the sandwiches into bags with an astonished feeling of both pleasure and pain in her heart.

The first big barrel was finally full and a new one started. Dave Wright, the auctioneer, tall, lanky and richly profane, with a big quid of "Five Brothers" in one cheek, arrived and entered the kitchen with the assurance of a man who has command of the day.

"Well, well! Here's where the work's goin' on an' no mistake. Mrs. Harvey, them sandwiches look good enough to eat an' I'll have one with your permission, just to try them out." He spat his tobacco expertly into the coal bucket. "Um . . . um! Yep. They're damned good! I've spread the word about the lunch so I think we'll have a big crowd. More bidders, more money," he added. "Small turnout, you have to let things go for what you can get. More people, you can bid 'em up till you get a good price. You goin' to sell *all* the household furniture?" he asked.

"Every stick," Seena said briefly.

"H'm," he said, moving toward the sitting-room door where the young men were working, "you got some nice old pieces here. Well, I guess you know your own business."

143

"I guess I do," Seena replied crisply, but the next instant flashed him a smile.

"No offense meant," Wright said hastily, looking with bold enjoyment at Seena. "Which one in there's Halifax?" he asked.

Hearing his name the new owner came into the kitchen and shook hands with the auctioneer.

"Thought we might go out to the barn an' have a look round while the folks is gatherin'," the latter said. "I hear you'd like to buy some of the machinery. Mebbe if it's all right with Mrs. Harvey here, we could come to a deal before the sale."

"I'd rather everything was auctioned," Seena said decidedly.

"O.K." Wright agreed, "but it won't do no harm to have a look round."

The man went out and Seena paused a moment looking after them.

"I've heard you have to watch Dave Wright," she said. "They say he's likely to knock things down low to people he likes. I hope he doesn't play that trick here."

"I don't think he would," Violet said. "He gets his commission on the whole amount sold, doesn't he? So, he'd only be cheating himself to do it."

"Why, I guess you're right. I never thought of that. Henry's going to keep accounts while the sale's on, and I guess we can trust him, anyhow!"

"I should think so," Violet answered a bit coolly.

Jeremy and Henry with help from Jake had set the furniture from the sitting-room out on the grassy lawn and were beginning now on the parlor. It was a sorry sight, Violet thought, to see the faithful, inanimate friends of two generations now deserted, left naked to prying eyes and covetous bargaining of strange new owners. A sad spectacle! She watched through the door as a marble-topped table, a horsehair rocker and a tall desk which she knew had been John's, were added to the rest; she sighed deeply and went on with her work.

It was nearly nine o'clock and the lane now was all but choked with buggies and riders. The horses were tied at the long fence at the side of the barn and the men walked about, shrewdly eyeing the machinery set forth on display or entering the barn to have an appraising look at the cows and horses. The women, greatly in the minority, made their way toward the house and set about examining the furniture on the lawn, or, in the case of some, went to the kitchen door to speak to the workers there.

"My, Seena, you surely have a big heart to feed all these people!" one farmer's wife observed as she watched the preparations.

"Well, if you must know," Seena replied, "I'm not doing this for charity. I'm trying to get a good crowd for the sale."

The woman, somewhat abashed, retreated to the lawn, saying over her shoulder, "Well, it looks as if you're getting it!"

And so it did. Still they came: buggies, buckboards, spring wagons, farm wagons, all rolling and rattling up the lane. When Henry came into the kitchen with a ledger under his arm he spoke to Seena.

"I guess I'll have to get on toward the barn now. Dave's about ready to start. Say, could we take that doughtry out? I'll need something to write on and Dave likes a table or something to stand behind. Maybe Jake here would help me carry it."

"Sure," Seena said, "take it if you want it. And Henry, mind you keep the accounts straight for me."

She looked up at him, not as she looked at other men. There was in the glance no coquetry; it was rather an expression of appeal. But Henry's face was set like flint. His look was not anger such as he had shown, Violet thought, when she had refused to marry him. It was cold as stone.

"Well, I'll certainly expect to do that," he answered her. Then, laying his ledger on the doughtry, he took one end and Jake the other and, easing it through the door, they started toward the barn.

It was only a few minutes until the sound of a hand bell, vigorously shaken, rang out. Then came Dave Wright's voice, loud, strident, practiced, and a bit ragged about the edges.

"Sale's about to begin! Sale's about to begin. Come on! Get as close as you can. First thing we're goin' to auction off is this fine *harrow*. Look at it. Practically good as new. Here's your chance, men. Who'll make a bid? Come on, now, speak up. What-am-I-bid? What-am-I-bid? *Ten dollars?* Oh, now, we're not *givin'* things away here! This is
145

a *sale*. Come on. Come on! . . . Well, all right, since it's just a starter. *Ten* dollars I'm bid, go the five, go the five. *Fifteen* dollars I'm bid, go the five, go the five . . . that's better . . . man in gray in back row. *Twenty* dollars I'm bid! Twenty go the five, go the five, go the five! Twenty go the five! *Twenty-five* I'm bid. Man in second row there. *Twenty*-five I'm bid, go the five, go the five, go the five, to the five . . . make it thirty . . . go the five . . . make it thirty . . . go the five . . . make it thirty . . . make it thirty . . . going, *going* and *sold* to the gentleman there in the brown shirt—Get his name, Henry—Sold for twenty-five dollars!"

Dave's wooden mallet came down hard and final on top of the doughtry and then he started to harangue his crowd.

"Now, that was a bargain because it was the first sale, but I'm tellin' you right now you're goin' to have to bid up from now on. This here's good stuff and has to bring a fair price. Get your tails behind you now, and look at this *reaper*. Like new. Not many as good round here. Look it over now and make a bid. Who'll start it at twenty-five? . . ."

In the kitchen the women settled into work again after listening to the first sale. The shrill tone and steady rhythm of Dave Wright's voice became a fixed background for their own conversation. Only Seena seemed able to hear the words even as she talked.

"There!" she said. "Bob Halifax has bought the reaper! Jake! Jake, where are you? Listen. I want you to take the two biggest buckets and bring water up from the spring. Then light the fire under the copper kettle for I'll have to be starting the coffee. I always think the spring water makes the best coffee," she added to the others. "This pump gets rusty sometimes. I've got the coffee sewed up in bags like they always do at the church suppers. Hope I have enough."

Katie and Mary Jackson arrived just then and several other conveyances filled with town women drew up to the crowded barnyard. A constant stir of small noises, men's voices, horses' whinnying, the sharp yapping of a half dozen boys who had no business there at all but who ran and milled about in high excitement—all blurred together below the shrill, steady descant of the auctioneer's chant, with occasional loud bursts of laughter at his sallies. The thrill of vitality, present in any crowd, was accentuated here by the pleasure of the bidding gamble and the social contacts for those who knew the solitude of lonely farmhouses.

The fire already laid under the huge kettle was lighted and soon roared brightly. The two barrels of sandwiches were now on the porch and the workers mingled with the other women under the trees. Seena, with Jake to help her, set all the available cups, together with the three dozen tin ones Henry had brought from the store, on the rough board table near the kettle.

"There won't be enough for everybody," she said, "so they'll just have to pass them around. I won't put the cream and sugar out till the last minute on account of the flies."

By eleven-thirty the great caldron of coffee was boiling hard and the rich, pungent fragrance was spreading out on the air. Seena started toward the barn saying she would check with Dave Wright as to when he wanted to stop for lunch.

"Want me to ask him, Seena?" Jake called.

"You stay and tend the fire," she said. "I want to see how things are going." She settled her red-and-white-checked gingham dress, smoothed her hair and threw a smile at Jake, casually including the group of women who sat about on the chairs which were waiting to be sold, or on papers and cushions they had brought with them. There was a subtle exchange of glances among them as they watched Seena's swaying, retreating figure, but her mother's presence prevented any comment.

Faith and Violet had volunteered to dip out the coffee as Seena wanted to supervise the distribution of the sandwiches. They sat now, resting, near the table, and Jeremy, who was interested only in the purchase of the big mantel clock, which would not be put up for sale till afternoon, came over and dropped down on the grass beside them. He was a broad-shouldered young chap with a tanned face and a pair of merry eyes. They had all been friends since childhood so they settled now for an easy chat.

"How's Peggy?" Faith asked quietly.

"Happy as a lark, but not feeling too well," he said. "I didn't think this was the best place for her and I didn't
147

like to leave her alone so I went over early this morning and brought Lucy to spend the day. Ninian will come for supper and take her home. I think the girls are going to *sew*," he added, a bashful pride in his voice.

"How nice! I want to come out soon and help too."

"And say," Jeremy went on, "what do you think? Mr. Ross has told Ninian that by next year he'll move Mr. Hardwick to another mine and let Ninian be full superintendent. Isn't that great? Ninian's taken to the business like a duck to water. He gets on with the miners too. I tell him he has a personal interest in every separate lump of coal. Gee, it's good to like your job."

"You've never regretted farming, have you, Jeremy?" Violet asked.

"Me? Well, I should say not. I know it was a blow to Father when I didn't go on to school but the land's in my blood somehow. Throw-back, I guess. Bob Halifax says it's the same with him and he did go two years to college. It'll be fine having him for a neighbor. He's going to keep young Jake on with him if he'll stay. In my opinion," Jeremy lowered his voice, "the sooner the present set-up is busted the better. Oh, here, I guess they're coming!"

Seena was leading the way back, laughing up in the faces of the men beside her, calling back to the crowd behind, tossing sallies to Dave Wright! Violet and Faith sprang up and collected the long tin dippers they were to use for the coffee; Mrs. Harris and Jake went to the sandwich barrels; Seena hurried to set the big pitcher of cream and the sugar bowl on the wooden table and the lunch began.

The men at first stood about hesitantly until the women were served, and then with much loud laughter and jesting they lined up and received their pokes of food.

"There's coffee here as you can see," Seena called above the racket, "and for those that want a cold drink there's buttermilk and sweet milk in the springhouse and a dozen glasses. You can just rinse them out and pass them round."

A group of twenty-five or so at once left for the sloping path that led down the hill to the springhouse while the others stood or sat about waiting their turn for coffee. Within the great kettle the dark brown liquid boiled furiously over the fire.

"Watch out! It's very hot!" the girls kept warning as they

148

filled the cups which Jeremy and Bob Halifax were passing out.

Dave Wright was in high feather as he leaned against a tree and devoured his food.

"Kind of sale I like," he said, his voice carrying as usual. "Good stuff and good fair prices. Everybody satisfied including the auctioneer! Last sale I cried I was ashamed even to be seen at it. Now this here one I'm proud to cry. And a picnic for everybody into the bargain! Hey, Mrs. Harvey, what about the bull? I didn't see him anywhere."

A sudden silence like a wind moved over the crowd. For this instant John Harvey, amongst his erstwhile possessions, was held in remembrance.

"I sold him. Private," Seena answered in the hush.

And at that moment the accident happened. Two of the young boys who had been roistering about were chasing each other regardless of scattered admonitions. One of them lurched as he passed Faith, striking her arm as it held a dipper of coffee. The boiling liquid was poured over her bare left arm, leaving it scarlet from elbow to wrist. Faith did not cry out but plenty of others did. Violet, Jeremy and Bob Halifax were at her side at once. It was Katie who called, "Get the soda, quick!"

Seena ran for it and under Katie's supervision a moist plaster was made and put upon the poor burning flesh.

"It's a bad one," Jeremy kept saying. "Move back a little, you folks. Don't crowd in on her. Here's a chair, Faith. How are you holding up?"

Faith tried to smile but her face was white with the pain and her eyes filled a little in spite of her efforts at self control. Voices were raised high, contending over remedies.

"Apple butter," a woman kept calling. "I tell you if you'd spread apple butter over it . . ."

"Tar," a man shouted. "Soak a cloth in tar and put it on. It'll take the heat right out."

"I'll drive her home at once," Violet said quietly to Jeremy.

"No," he answered. "I'd feel better to take her myself. She ought to go right to the doctor. Will you lend me your rig, Bob? I walked over."

"Yes, yes," Bob cried. "Anything! Oh, I feel dreadful about this. I'll go get the buggy."

149

Violet and Peggy walked with Faith to the lane, Seena and young Jake following.

"I'm sorry this happened to spoil things for you, Seena," Faith managed tremulously.

"Oh, that's all right. A couple of men are dipping coffee. I hope you get this fixed up soon. Thanks for making the sandwiches."

"Oh, Violet," Jeremy said, "if I'm not back will you bid on the mantel clock for me? Peggy wants it. Five dollars would be my limit, but I think it will go for less."

It was Bob Halifax who helped Faith into the buggy, put the duster over her knees and spread a fresh white handkerchief for her arm to rest on.

"To think that this happened on my own place!" he said. "May I stop in this evening and find out how you are?"

And Faith, with no trace of embarrassment, smiled into his grave, concerned face. "Of course!" she said, and the buggy drove off.

Violet and young Halifax walked back from the lane together.

"I'm afraid she'll have a very sore arm," he said. "There's nothing worse than a bad scald."

"The hardest thing for her will be stopping her music for a while. She plays the piano—beautifully," Violet added, in praise of her friend.

"She does? I like music but I've never learned to play anything—except a mouth organ," he added whimsically. "Well, I guess the sale's about to start again."

Dave Wright was wiping his lips on the back of his hand, and then mopping his brow and balding head with a red bandana. He took a quick look around to satisfy himself that the crowd had finished their lunch and then rang his hand bell vigorously and led the way back to the barn where two cows were yet to be sold. Violet helped Seena clear up the debris of crumpled bags while Mrs. Harris, with Katie's help, washed the cups and the glasses which Jake brought up from the springhouse, while they discussed dry burns, wet burns, sales, auctioneers and the general providences of God.

"It's hard to understand," Mrs. Harris sighed, "this that's happened to Seena. John Harvey was such a good young man, no bad habits, and kind too. And now to

150

think it's all over as if it never had been at all. She'll be home again in her old room just the same, but the thing is will she be contented now after having her own place and . . . and everything. That's what I wonder."

"Aye," said Katie, "it'll be a big jolt for her. Life's full of mysteries, so it is, and we have to take what comes without repinin'. Well," she added with a side glance at Mrs. Harris, "Seena's a good-lookin' girl with plenty spirit. She might a bit later on . . ."

The other woman nodded. "Yes, it's likely."

Jake suddenly appeared in the doorway.

"Where's Seena?" he asked breathlessly.

"I don't know," Mrs. Harris answered in a cold voice. "Why don't you go on out among the men? There's nothing more for you to do here."

When Jake's bloodshot eyes had disappeared, she added to Katie, "I've told Seena well of it, mind. She'll have trouble with that boy yet. You can see he's clear crazy over her and she wouldn't wipe her feet on him."

"He looks wild-lookin', that one," Katie agreed.

When the last of the stock was disposed of there was a thinning out of the crowd. Wagons, buggies and riders passed down the lane, and the men who were left joined the women in the yard where the furniture was put up, piece by piece, for sale. It was three o'clock before the mantel clock was knocked down for two dollars to Violet. She put it in the kitchen for Jeremy to claim and pay for when he got there, after first explaining to Henry that she had not bid it in for herself. She thought Henry looked tired and strained. She was weary herself and anxious to hear some news of Faith so she told Katie she was leaving, said good-bye to Seena and asked Jake to get Prince out of the barn. The boy hurried to comply and then hitched the horse with quick, skillful fingers to the buggy. Violet watched him with a tug of sympathy at her heart.

"That's fine, Jake! Thank you very much. I heard Mr. Halifax wants you to stay on here and help him. That will be a good job for you."

Jake's face darkened. "I don't know what I'm goin' to do." Then more loudly, "Haven't made up my mind yet."

As Violet drove along between the familiar fields her thoughts dwelt upon the subtle overtones of the day. The event had been more than just a sale, interesting as that always was. She and Faith had driven out that morning happily eager for the simple excitations that might await them. But something momentous had happened there. She was sure of it. And here was the mystery of the inter-weaving threads of fate. Would that sudden, first, startled clinging of the eyes which she had caught between Bob Halifax and Faith ever have taken place if he had not seen her in the white pinafore *in his own kitchen?* Would Faith ever have been able to look up at him later with a smile free from even a trace of self-consciousness if it had not been for the accident, the pain of which wracked her even as the thought of it made his face anxious and tender?

So perhaps the sale had had a necessary place in the destiny of two people! She could be wrong, but a per-ceptive certainty grew within her. Poor Faith, indeed! She had been pitying her friend from the pinnacle of her own feminine assurance. It would, she felt, be poor Faith no longer, but rather *poor Violet.*

She drew rein at the manse, tied Prince to the hitching post and hurried up the walk. Jeremy was just coming down the steps, with Mr. Lyall bidding him good-bye at the front door.

"Oh, Vi," Jeremy said, "I'll hurry back now and let Father and Mother give you the news. I'll call up tonight, Dad!"

"It's a very nasty burn," Mr. Lyall said as they sat down on the porch. "Faith was quite shaken when she got home so we had Dr. Faraday come up. He treated the arm and then gave her a mild sedative. He says if she sleeps a couple of hours she'll wake up feeling better with much of the first pain gone. The thing will bear watching, though, he says. Oh, here's Mary."

Mrs. Lyall came out, her gentle countenance a little distraught.

"What a thing to happen!" she exclaimed. "It's really pretty bad. The only good thing I can see about it is that she'll have to take a vacation from her music, which I've been urging anyway. She has seemed so intense about it this summer, just when she could be relaxing a little. You must come up often, Vi, and keep her company for she won't know what to do with herself."

"There is still such a thing as a rocking chair and a

152

good book," Mr. Lyall put in mildly, and they all laughed.

"Tell us about the sale. How did you get on with the sandwiches?"

Violet gave the details as entertainingly as she could and then rose to go.

"Mr. Halifax was there, of course. I heard him say he would drop by tonight to see how Faith was. He was terribly upset about the accident. He seemed to feel responsible because it happened on his property," she added smiling.

Mrs. Lyall's eyes brightened with quick interest. "Oh, I'm glad you told me—I mean about his coming in. I'll stir up a cake. We haven't a bit in the house at the moment."

"Now, Mary!" Mr. Lyall said, his eyes twinkling humorously at her.

"Well," she defended herself, "I never knew a young man who couldn't eat a piece of fresh cake. And I'm sure Faith will be able to come down after supper. She's sleeping now."

Mr. Lyall walked with Violet to the buggy and untied Prince.

"How did Jake seem?" he asked quietly.

"He looks strange, I thought, but he may have just been excited. Jeremy told us that Mr. Halifax means to keep him on if he'll stay."

"Good!" said Mr. Lyall. "That may solve everything. Young Halifax is a nice fellow and he'll be good for Jake. Well, that relieves my mind a great deal."

As Violet drove down Main Street to get the mail before going home she wondered why she did not feel unreservedly happy over Faith's subtle but, she felt, sure promise of romance. The weight on her own heart was certainly not jealousy, but the old one of loneliness. She had never before pictured what her life would be like if Faith fell in love and married, while she was left *sur la branche*.

When she reached the Post Office Mr. Gordon, whose sharp eyes missed nothing on the street, waved to her and then came out to the buggy with a letter in his hand.

"This is all, today," he said, "but it seems lately you get your share. Well," he added cryptically, "you're only young once."

The letter did not bear the name of the publishing house

in the corner but it did have a New York postmark, which Mr. Gordon had doubtless noted. Violet thanked him, laid the envelope on the seat beside her and turned Prince's head toward the alley. When he was safely in his stall and the feed in his manger box she walked again through the garden, the letter in her hand. The late afternoon sun was now slanting on the flowers and grass. The freshness of the morning was gone but a full-flavored and mellow warmth brought out the fragrance of the lilies along the wall. The morning, she thought, woke the spirit; the afternoon, the senses.

Katie was not home yet. She had expected to be late. "You know Mary Jackson!" she had said that morning. "She'll never leave till the last dog's shot!" So Violet went through the quiet house to the porch to read what Mr. Haversham had to say. The pages were written in a firm small hand, and there were a good many of them.

Dear Miss Carpenter:

Once again I can't express my pleasure in your letter. I feel now as though I know your little town intimately from Cobb's Hill down to Miller's Rock! I've pictured the Mill, itself, the dam, the covered bridge and the rolling fields beyond. You have, indeed, as you wished given me the feel of the village. And I like it. Your request, however, to tell you of my own work strikes me at an unfortunate time for tonight I am feeling rather low and ashamed of myself. It isn't fair to make the account of my misdeed a return for your delightful letter but the thing is on my mind and somehow I feel you will be understanding.

One of our authors, an elderly woman, Miss A. from the Middle West who does a yearly book of Bible exposition for us came to New York for the first time two days ago to meet her publishers and see the city if someone would act as guide. Well, that job fell to me. So yesterday after she had met the various people in the offices we started on the schedule she herself had mapped out. This included a ride on top of the bus in the blistering sun all the way up Fifth Avenue and on to (you've guessed it!) Grant's Tomb, a trip to Bedloe's Island where we climbed to the top of the Statue of Liberty, and finally a visit to the Aquarium where she slowly and carefully examined each fish. Please count it unto me for righteousness that I tried to entertain her as the day progressed. How I tried! But while I'm sure she could give the Greek, Hebrew and Aramatic equivalent for every word in the New Testament, she hasn't one ounce of humor in her cosmos.

Today was hotter than yesterday. We spent the morning hours in Wanamaker's Emporium and in the afternoon we covered the Metropolitan Museum inch by inch!

At dinner, assuming the end was in sight I let myself go and if I do say it, was, I think, somewhat amusing. At least she smiled twice. When I said good-bye, however, she was startled. "Oh, but we have tomorrow yet!" she said. Her wish as she then stated was to go to one of the largest churches in the morning, through Chinatown in the afternoon, and then as the crown of her experience, to the Jerry McAuley Mission of which she had heard so much, at night. "I hope," she finished, "that you will be agreeable to carrying out this plan."

And then it happened. I heard myself saying, "I'll be damned if I will!"

I believe I was actually as surprised as she was. To think that I, at my age, had no more self control! She started for the elevator and I followed with all the apologies I could muster but the last I saw was her stunned face going up in the cage.

I do feel very sorry about this. She may take her books to another publisher which would be bad, but the worst thing to me is that I have hurt the poor soul just when— as I now realize—she was having a wonderful time according to her light. I've probably ruined her trip. I stopped on the way back and ordered her a dozen roses and splashed a bit of my life's blood on the card, but I doubt if it does any good!

Forgive me for telling you all this but you asked about my work and for two days it has run thus. Selah!

Katie got home at this point and all the details of the sale were carefully gone over. Once in the midst of her supper Violet laughed out loud. Katie stuck her head in the door.

"What struck you?" she asked.

"Nothing," said Violet meekly.

"For my part I saw nothing today to laugh about."

"Nor did I."

"Humph!" Katie said, "you take a queer way of showin' it," and withdrew to the kitchen.

Violet read the letter over before she went to bed, and then lay thinking about it before she slept.

It had its funny side. In spite of herself she laughed again. Yet she sympathized completely both with poor old Miss A. and with Mr. Haversham. He was a *nice* person, she thought. Clever, warmly human, with a fine sense of humor and *kind*. She felt as though he and she had now advanced to terms of real friendship. How revealing letters could be! If they had met in person two or three times they would not know each other as well as they did now. As strangers their conversation would have been conventional and inhibited. As it was . . .

One phrase of his she pondered over. *At my age,* he had said. That seemed to imply a good many years. She had placed him first at sixty, but there was a certain vitality in his letters that seemed to indicate he must be younger. Fifty, perhaps, and a bachelor. She decided to reply promptly, perhaps by tomorrow evening.

But the next morning when she walked down to the Post Office she was amazed to receive from Mr. Howard's hand another envelope exactly like the one of yesterday. The postmaster eyed her keenly and her cheeks colored under his gaze. She went up to her own room as soon as she got home, to read the new missive.

Since I bored you with the other part of my story (it ran) *I feel I must tell you its climax. In the first place the roses did the trick! She called me as soon as they were delivered (I'd given her my number so she'd feel safer) and the poor lady could hardly speak. She had never, it developed, had flowers given her in her life, and she was completely touched. We had quite a love feast over the phone, she protesting that she now realized I'd done too much already, and I with entire truth that I wanted nothing so much as to carry out the Sunday program. So we did. And here is the amazing thing that happened. The Jerry McAuley Mission was the hardest thing for me to swallow. You've probably heard of it. The place is in the slums on the edge of Chinatown and their work is among the bums and down-and-outers. When we went in, it was pretty hot and very smelly. After the usual revival service a man stood up to tell his story and ask for help. He gave his name but I would have recognized him anyway. I knew him in college! He has had a sad life, took to drink, and finally reached the gutter.*

When the meeting was over I went up to speak to him. Miss A., to whom I explained it, was beside herself with emotion. I wasn't much better and Bill was the most moved of all. I asked him to come back with me, so we dropped Miss A. at her hotel and this time the good-byes were really heartfelt. She had opened up a lot that day. When I got Bill to the apartment he had a hot bath and I rigged him out. We're near a size. Then we talked till daylight. I think he'll go straight from now on and I'll keep a finger on him and help him about finding a job. The whole thing is completely incredible, but it happened! If such an incident had come to my desk in a manuscript I would have ruled it out at once as too improbable. And yet here it is, true. The stranger life is, with its unbelievable coincidences, the more I believe in it and in Something still bigger.

I should have told you in my last how deeply touched I was by the whole beautiful and sad story of the nightingale! I grieve for you in what seems now an irreparable loss. But don't give up. If it's in the town it surely will eventually come to light. Please keep me informed about further clues. I wish I were a detective and could be helpful. What a triumph it will be when the mystery is solved!

By the way, do you happen to have a snapshot of yourself which you could spare? I would appreciate it very much.

CHAPTER SEVEN

As SOFTLY as a breath June changed to July. The sweet peas in the village gardens had reached the top of their wire or cord supports and were blooming in a luxurious rainbow of scented colors; the cherries were ripe; Mr. Gordon had won his bet and proudly displayed in the Post Office window new potatoes as big as a hen's egg on the second of the month; glasses of bright currant jelly sunned themselves on most kitchen window sills; Seena had moved back to the Mill house again; and Howie Gordon had given Kitty McNeil a diamond and they were planning an early wedding. There was no further word about the nightingale but it was reported that Joe and Amanda had now stopped going to church. Robert Halifax had been seen entering the manse on two occasions, once on the evening of the sale and again later in the week, but it was assumed he had some business with Mr. Lyall.

"It'll likely be about liftin' his letter from the Indiana church to put in here," Katie remarked after hearing this bit of news from Mary Jackson.

"Probably," Violet had responded absently.

Faith's arm, while still sore, was healing rapidly, and Violet on her calls had noticed that her eyes were unusually bright, though no explanation was suggested for the shine.

On the day before Mike was to have come out for his second visit, he called up on the telephone to say he had been in a bit of an accident and that his car would be laid up a week for repairs. Could they set another date? As soon as was convenient to her, he added.

Violet had talked to Ninian one night and with some embarrassment had asked if he thought a picnic à deux in the woods would be proper. Ninian's wise young eyes had smiled at her.

"Mike's a perfect gentleman, if that's what is worrying you. But he does go with a pretty fast crowd. The one I used to go round with myself before I met Lucy. They're always getting into scrapes. But Mike's essentially a nice fellow."

"We're only the most casual friends," Violet hastened to say.

"Oh, naturally," Ninian agreed and smiled again.

So Violet had written Mike a neat little note suggesting that since he liked picnics and since they were the chief form of social diversion in Ladykirk's summer, perhaps he would care to come out on the Fourth for the annual Union Church affair in Beecham's woods. Though this might sound provincial enough it really was fun, she added, as their own crowd of young people got together for the early supper and the grove itself was a pleasant spot. Also their group always came back to her home afterwards for the evening. Ninian and Lucy would, of course, be there. Would he care to come?

Mike would, though intimating mildly in his return letter that he had hoped for a little visit with her alone. But, he wrote, he would be glad to get away from the city on the Fourth and he would bring a load of fireworks with him to help enliven the evening. This latter information sent Violet excitedly to the telephone to tell Faith first of all, and then, with her help, to remind the rest of the young people that they were expected at the Carpenter's as usual after the picnic with the lure of fireworks into the bargain.

"Would you mind telling Mr. Halifax?" Violet asked Faith. "I think this would be a nice way for him to get acquainted."

Faith's voice sounded as though she were trying hard to be casual. "Yes, it would. I'll ask Jeremy to call him and tell him the plans. Jeremy and Peggy are bringing him with them to the picnic. Peggy's feeling fine now so she intends to come. It's simply thrilling about the fireworks! Oh, Violet, things have such a . . . a strange way of working out, haven't they?"

Violet murmured an answer to this rather cryptic remark, but her thoughts were not upon either Mr. Halifax or Mike as Faith evidently supposed. For something else had happened as it were between June and July—something subtle and unseen by the Argos-eyed villagers. Mr. Gordon of course would be aware of the fact that there was now a steady exchange of letters between Ladykirk and New York, but even he could not discern the changes within them.

Violet had looked through the snapshots in her album and had finally selected one of herself which Faith had taken the previous summer. It showed her standing in the garden in front of the low wall, her face lifted and laughing and a recalcitrant curl blowing across her forehead. She was wearing the pink voile with the open lace-trimmed neck which Katie had urged upon her on the evening of Henry's last visit, and she was holding a flower-trimmed hat in her hand for she and Faith had just been to a tea.

159

The picture was indeed that of an extremely pretty girl, with bright eyes, a sweet smile and a dimpled chin. Violet judged it critically, then, her heart beating faster than usual, she put it inside the envelope which contained her reply to the letter in which Mr. Haversham had written of his experience in entertaining the woman author.

She wrote him of her complete understanding of what he had been through during those hot and boring three days, for his *Miss A.* had a counterpart in Ladykirk. This was a Miss Hastings who, while she did not write Biblical exposition herself, taught the Women's Bible Class on Sundays with a volume of *Peloubet* glued to her hand. She was President of the local W.C.T.U. also, and was an estimable, righteous and thoroughly uninteresting woman who would probably go to the stake if need be for her faith but who couldn't see a joke if it was under her nose. Violet said that she herself was always irritated by what her father had called "sanctimonious stupidity" and yet she felt there was something truly pathetic about both Miss A. and Miss Hastings, wasn't there? So, with a completely unconscious tenderness she went on to praise Mr. Haversham for his kindness and patience, and thrilled with him over the strange and touching climax at the Jerry McAuley Mission. It was into this letter that she dropped the picture.

And it was in the return missive that the subtle change began to take place, for the so-called "complimentary close," which heretofore had read "Very truly yours, Philip Haversham," now said "Faithfully yours, Philip H." And only two letters later the signature had become simply "Philip."

At the other end of the line, as a small red spot grew upon each of the writer's cheeks, a corresponding mutation had been effected: "Violet Carpenter" to "Violet C." to "Violet."

The morning of the Fourth dawned with the usual sporadic bangs of firecrackers set off by small boys, but also with a sharp electrical storm. A wave of apprehension swept the town, for the annual Union picnic was an outstanding social landmark in the community and rain would ruin the looked-for pleasure. There were those who admitted that they always prayed earnestly for fair weather for this occasion, though Mr. Lyall, the Presbyterian min-

160

ister, had been known to state gently that he felt the disposition of the elements had best be left to the discretion of the Almighty without human suggestion. On this day, however, whether because of the prayers of the faithful or Providential good fortune, the skies cleared by nine o'clock, and by noon a hot sun beat upon the town, the surrounding roads, and Beecham's woods itself, where the thickness of the shade had prevented most of the moisture from reaching the ferny ground beneath. So, all was suddenly well and the basket-packing continued with happy assurance.

In the Carpenter home Katie was in high feather. Any picnic, even a small one, was to her a culinary challenge but the big Union one brought out all her native powers. So on the kitchen table now were arrayed fried chicken, the famous veal loaf, crocks of potato salad under cool rhubarb leaves, eggs, pickled beets, cherry pie and two kinds of cake, not to speak of buttered rolls and fresh jam. With Violet's help two baskets were filled—the larger for Violet and Mike, the smaller for Katie, who would join some of the older folk for supper.

Mike arrived promptly at two-thirty, very smart in a light linen suit. As she greeted him Violet dropped her eyes a little beneath the ardor in his own.

"I'm certainly glad to be here," he said. "About the fireworks, I have several boxes of them and I'd rather not take them along to the picnic. Some small vandals might get into them. Could I bring them into the house?"

"They won't blow up?" Katie asked anxiously from the background.

"No," Mike laughed. "As a matter of fact they have to be very carefully lighted or they won't go off at all. Ninian knows how. I thought he might help me tonight. Could I bring them in?"

"Of course," Violet said. "What about the pantry, Katie?"

"I don't hold with gunpowder, mind," said Katie, "but if you're sure it's safe, fetch them along."

There were four large boxes! Violet exclaimed over them in delight.

"Oh Mike, this *is* good of you! It will be such a treat for everybody. We never see fireworks except the two or

161

three rockets Mr. Gordon always puts off in front of the Post Office. Why this will be an evening to remember!"

"I'm sure it will," agreed Mike.

When they reached Beecham's woods the activity was already in full swing. Women were staking out their claims under the trees by spreading colored table cloths and setting their baskets upon them. Men were removing coats and collars and drifting toward the amusement area in the adjoining field where baseball, quoit games and the various races were getting under way. Ninian and Lucy, Jeremy and Peggy, Faith and Bob Halifax were already waiting within the first deep shade and now hurried to meet Mike and Violet. There were the necessary introductions, and then, the young men bearing the baskets, they made their way to the far edge of the grove where the girls pre-empted a special place year after year.

"You boys run along now," Lucy said with a delightfully matronish air. "We girls have to arrange things and set out the supper. Heavens, what a lot of food there must be! We'll call you when it's time to eat—and when everybody's here," she added.

"Come on, fellahs," said Ninian. "They want to gossip and we'll keep out of the way. I'm setting up the ice cream later on," he called back. "I see Billy Kinkaid's here with his freezers."

"Drunk as a lord, too," Jeremy said. "Look how he's tipping his hat to every woman that passes. The more whiskey he has in him the politer he grows."

"I wish it affected me that way," Mike said with a grin, and then as the others laughed he glanced hastily over his shoulder to be sure his remark had not carried to the girls.

In a few minutes Howie and Kitty arrived and there were excited congratulations and examination of the new ring before Howie went on to join the men; then the girls sat in a close circle and admired it all over again.

"I thought we'd be married in September but Howie wants it the last week in August if I can get ready by then. There really isn't any reason for a long engagement since Howie has his job in the store and he thinks he can rent the Scudder house across the creek. Oh girls, I'm so happy I don't know what to do!"

"It's so wonderful being married," Lucy exclaimed impulsively, "when you're truly in love!"

Kitty lowered her voice. "You know the time I was sure I really loved Howie was that night when he was thrown out of the carriage on the way home from your house, Lucy, and he lay there without moving. I *knew* then. I felt if he was dead I didn't want to live either. Oh, there's something Howie said to speak to you about. That's Henry. He's always been with us before. . . ." Her voice trailed off as she looked at Violet in embarrassment.

"Of course we should ask him if he comes," Violet said promptly. "We must keep a look-out for him."

"And then," Peggy said hesitantly, "there's Seena. What about her? She and John were with us last year."

There was a barely perceptible pause before Lucy broke it. "I think we should ask her too. Do you suppose she'd join us?"

Faith's voice was faintly cool. "I rather think she would."

"I'll watch out for Henry then," Kitty said, "and Peggy, why don't you speak to Seena? I think we'd feel better to have them both—as usual."

When the sun began to slant across the trees and rich shadows dappled the ground beneath, the men were all hailed from the playing field and, red-faced and jovial, gathered in their respective groups. The ten young people settled with much laughter and badinage around the amazingly laden table cloths and with healthy zest fell upon the food. They had seated themselves almost automatically by couples so that after all the others were paired off it left Faith, with a pretty color in her cheeks, next to Mr. Halifax, and Henry and Seena, whether they would have wished it or not, together at the end. Seena's color was high as usual and her black hair as glossy in the afternoon light as a bird's wing. Her eyes seemed to pass from one young man to the other, dwelling most upon Mike and upon Robert Halifax, with the bold and luring look which seemed to be second nature to her. Violet, watching, studying her, noted again that she dropped her eyes in speaking to Henry, who in his turn scarcely answered her. While he joined occasionally in general laughter he was very quiet during the meal.

Suddenly, as she glanced about the grove, Violet gave an exclamation.

"Oh, Mr. Halifax, there's Jake! You see? Over there near the road. He's just wandering about all alone!"

Young Halifax jumped to his feet.

"That's too bad!" he said, real worry in his tone. "I asked him about the picnic and he said he had never come to any of them. He was almost surly about it. But he must have wanted to, all the same. Do you suppose I could take some supper over to him?"

In a minute a plate was heaped high and Mr. Halifax hurried with it through the woods. They could see him overtake Jake, who seemed at first to turn away but who finally accepted the offering and sank down with it under a tree.

"Poor kid!" Halifax said as he rejoined the others. "He ought to feel better when he gets on the outside of all that. He hasn't been eating too well lately. My cooking, I guess."

"It's pathetic," Violet said, "to be all alone at a picnic. I'm sure he wouldn't have eaten with us though, even if we had asked him. He seems so shy."

"Oh, he's just a nuisance," Seena burst out. "I wish, Bob," (using his name with ease) "that you'd stop him from coming into town every few nights. There's no sense in his being a pest!"

"I can speak to him," Halifax said slowly, "but I'm not sure how much good it will do. He's a first-rate worker but aside from conversation about the farm I can't seem to get next to him at all. He's an odd boy."

"He certainly is," Seena exclaimed. "I've decided he's a little off in the upper story."

"Ice cream!" Ninian called suddenly from the other end of the group, rising with feigned difficulty. "Tell me your flavors, everybody. Lucy has some bowls here to put it in. As far as I can see Billy Kinkaid is in one of his most generous moods! Come on now. How many for vanilla?"

There were groans from the young men and delicate disclaimers from the girls. Mike voiced the general feeling.

"Have a heart, Nin," he said. "After that supper topped off with cake and cherry pie, how dare you suggest ice cream!"

Ninian laughed. "I'll tell you what. I'll get Billy to

pack a small freezer for us and we'll take it in to Violet's and have it after the fireworks. Agreed?"

"And we have plenty of cake left to go with it," Lucy said.

"If, in a few hours time, I'll be ready for more food," Mike protested, "it will be because there's something *in the air* here!"

"Oh, there is," Ninian laughed. "When I get a chance I'll tell you about all the men and women in this town who are bustling around between eighty and ninety. You'd better move out," he added slyly.

"I'll consider it," Mike answered, giving him a shove. "Here, let me go along and help order the ice cream. As a matter of fact I'd like to buy it myself."

They set off, wrangling cheerfully, and the rest turned in to clear up the remains of the feast. Though she looked all about, Violet could see no further sign of Jake. He had evidently just glimpsed Paradise and then set off on his solitary way. Poor lad! she thought again. She felt a special invitation for the evening was now due both to Seena and Henry so she went over to where they were standing in a strange silence.

"The others are coming back to our house and I hope you'll come, Seena, and you, Henry. Mike brought out four big boxes of fireworks so it really will be a lovely sight, I imagine. You'll come?"

Seena spoke quickly. "Why of course. I've never seen many fireworks. And Mother says I have to get out and mingle again with young people. I can't just sit around the house. I'd go crazy. I'm glad you asked me, Violet."

"And you'll come, Henry?"

He nodded. "Thanks," he said briefly.

"There's just one thing," Seena said. "Mother and Father were leaving early. I think they've gone already. Do you suppose I could get a ride in with . . . with anyone?"

Henry's countenance was still immobile. "I'm afraid our carriage is full."

"I'll tell you," Violet said quickly. "Wouldn't you both like to go in with us? I'm sure Mike would be glad to have you. It's fun to ride in an auto."

"I kept ours," Seena said. "I spose people have been wondering about it. What's more I'm going to learn to drive it, but it will take me a while. Yes, I'll be glad to go in with you." She glanced at Henry as she spoke and so did Violet.

"Why, yes. Thanks. That would be all right."

He's certainly not exuberant, Violet thought to herself, but then he never was. She found Mike and told him of her invitation.

"You don't mind?" she inquired a little anxiously.

"Of course I mind," he said. "This whole day has evidently been arranged with the sole purpose of keeping me from having a minute alone with you." Then at the sight of her troubled face he laughed and patted her arm gently. "I'm only teasing," he said. "How could you think I'd really mind? I'll go ⟶ now and speak to them both. Say, this Henry person. He certainly looks glum. Does he, by any chance, not like my being with you?"

"No, no! That's all over. I mean . . . I mean . . . no, of course not!" Violet floundered.

"I see," said Mike. "Well, I'll be very gentle with him."

When they all reached the Carpenter house at last, the girls sat about on the porch while the young men brought out the boxes, unpacked them, and then in a businesslike way began to set up the various pieces for use. They all lent a hand under the experienced direction of Ninian and Mike.

"Do you think it would hurt to fasten some of these to the fence?" Mike asked Violet.

"I don't see how it could. The iron is strong and it needs paint anyway."

So, when night finally fell, the front yard and the green strip beyond looked spectral from the dozens of tall pale supports sticking in the ground or tied to the fence itself. Then, while all breaths were held in suspense, Mike lighted the first tall ghost, and with a terrific explosion a thin streak of light soared through the heavens, burst into a great rainbow cluster of balls and finally ended in clouds of golden sparks. It was surpassingly beautiful, everyone said as they cheered and clapped in delight. But they settled soon into an awed and ecstatic silence as one by one the various rockets rose aloft and fell in fairy showers. Small boys soon gathered in the roadway and older people came in a crowd, lured by the unexpected entertainment.

At last there was a long pause.

166

"Well, I guess it's all over," Howie said regretfully.

"No, it isn't. Look!"

Mike and Ninian were going back and forth, checking something with great care. Then the incredible happened. A miniature Niagara Falls ran suddenly over the iron fence! There were gasps, excited cries and shouts, and when the glorious colored ripples subsided at last there was quite deafening applause from the lawn and the roadways. Mike seemed quite overcome with embarrassment.

"Gee," he said to Violet, "I never dreamed this would be such a . . . a novelty."

"Oh, it is!" Violet answered warmly. "There's never been anything like it in town before. Just think how many people you've given pleasure to tonight. How can I ever thank you?"

"It mightn't be too hard," Mike said significantly, while Violet pretended not to hear.

She did overhear Henry, however, saying to Ninian as he passed, "That must have cost some money."

"Plenty," Ninian answered. "But don't worry. He can afford it."

"He *can?*" Henry sounded as though the idea startled him.

"Yep," Ninian said briefly, and went on into the house for he and Lucy were going to help Violet serve the ice cream and cake.

The moon had risen and they all sat about in the pale light on the steps and the lawn eating the delicacies with perfectly unimpaired appetites and talking everything over. Then the young men cleared away the debris from the fireworks and by midnight they were all gathered at the gate, saying their final thanks and good-byes. Someone suddenly started to sing "The End of a Perfect Day," and in a moment everyone had joined in. It was first-rate singing for there were good voices in the group, and out of their own enjoyment of their chorusing they sang it all over again. As the final notes fell into the soft summer night there was muted clapping from the porches along the street. Then the last sound of wheels and footsteps died away with the last farewells, and Mike and Violet walked slowly back to the porch.

"Do you mind if I stay a little longer?" he asked.

"Of course not. Please do," Violet said with a trace of nervousness.

They sat down on the wooden swing, which swayed gently beneath them.

"It has been a perfect day to me," Mike began, "and I guess this is the nicest part of it right now. I do want to talk to you. You remember all that high-flown stuff I told you about wanting to build bridges and skyscrapers?"

"Yes, indeed," Violet said.

"Well, I've scrapped all that. It was only an air castle and much too late for it anyway. I never finished college. I'm no student, so I could never get enough technical training to be a real engineer. And the little jobs wouldn't appeal to me I know. So—I'm going to stick to the pickles." He gave a short laugh. "While, as I say, I'm no student I think I can become a fairly good businessman if I apply myself. My father wants me to start on a selling trip next week, so I may not be able to get out again for a short time. I do mind that," he added.

"Oh, I think you're probably very wise, Mike," Violet said, "to go into the family business. It's not every young man who has such a chance."

"That's true, and I don't feel as unhappy about it as I did once. We're expanding, too, into other kinds of foods. I suppose it's not too bad a career to cater to human appetites. Good ones, that is. Violet?"

"Yes."

"I wish I were more of a bookish person. I'm not, you know. And I can't walk through your house, let alone talk to you, without realizing that you are. Indeed I know a secret about you that scares me a little."

"What in the world?" said Violet even as she guessed uneasily what he might say.

"It's that you write poetry! Ninian told me."

"Oh," Violet exclaimed, half angrily, "how could Faith break her promise to me and tell them. . . ."

"She didn't," Mike said. "He and Lucy found it out because there was a piece of paper in a book you lent them. He said he could tell from the interlinings that the poem was one you had written yourself and he said it was so good he was amazed. So there, you see why I'm scared."

"That's terribly foolish," Violet said earnestly. "I've always liked to make verses since I was a little girl, and I still do. It's silly to think that makes me any different."

"I'm not so sure," Mike said. "It might fix a sort of gulf between us and I'd like to see a nice straight road ahead. Anyway I want to come back as soon as I can, if it's all right with you. Is it?"

"Yes," Violet said, a slight hesitation in her voice. "It's always nice to see you."

"Thanks," he said. "I appreciate that. Needless to say I come to see you, but in addition I like this old town. There's something about it and the things you all do that calms me down. I've always been a restless creature. Now that 'Perfect Day' business at the gate as they were all leaving I thought was rather lovely, but the crowd I go with would have thought it was maudlin. There is a difference out here." He paused and then said in a low tone, "I hope *I* have made a friend as the song says."

Violet reached her hand impulsively.

"Oh, you have!" she said.

He grasped it and then rose to go. "Good! That's enough for the present and probably more than I deserve. Give me a thought when I'm off selling pickles. By the way, do you like them?"

"Love them!" Violet said.

"I'll send you some. Sours to the sweet, instead of the usual way."

They laughed over this as they said good-bye. Mike turned at the gate to wave, then started his machine and was gone. Violet locked the front door and went thoughtfully up the stairs. Once again there was the turmoil of a choice in her heart. She had not known Mike long but he had already made his feeling clear. If she gave him any warmth of encouragement she felt that he would one day declare his love and offer marriage. At least her woman-heart made her sure of this. But although it was sweet to know herself desired she could not rejoice in the thought. Not now. Not as she looked at the desk where two pigeonholes were filled with the letters of Philip Haversham.

She arraigned her facts. Mike was a gentleman, as Ninian had said, and a sophisticated one. He was clever in his light, superficial way. He was fun to be with. In short, he was *nice*. And he would one day probably be a very wealthy man. Even now, apparently, he had ample means. Violet drew a long breath. She was not worldly but oh, the joy of having plenty of this world's goods! Sometimes, as she battled with herself about selling the orchard, she felt that money was the root of all good instead of evil. At least it could buy true blessings.

But having admitted all this she sighed again. With Mike, pleasant as he was, she would never feel those moods of shared insight, that intellectual excitement of mind leaping to meet mind, which were to her irresistibly attractive. These, coupled with real love, would satisfy the urgent craving of her heart. And only these. With Mike she knew she would never feel the rushing waters nor hear the nightingale sing. But should she demand so much? There were so many variants of happiness.

She prepared for bed, and in the quiet darkness settled herself to think of Mike and of all the pleasures there might be in a future marriage with him. But she could not sleep. Finally she got up, lighted the lamp, took Philip's latest letter from the pigeonhole and read it over. And then over again.

The next day Faith came down to discuss the events of the Fourth. There was a brightness on her face which Violet could not fail to note.

"I think Mr. Halifax enjoyed himself yesterday," she said, tentatively.

"Oh, I'm sure he did," Faith answered. "He said so. He seems delighted with the farm and with the . . . the community. You know I found out that he likes music! He's never had any training but he's fond of it. It's a pleasure to play for someone who enjoys it."

"He's been in to see you then?" Violet could not help saying.

"Yes, a few times. But he's just been calling on the family," Faith returned primly. "Vi, there is something I wanted to ask you. Do you think you could sing something at night church this Sunday? You know Father's trying so hard to build up the evening service, and a lot of new people are coming—more young folks from back in the country. Haven't you noticed?"

"Yes I have. It's wonderful."

"Well, you know extra music always adds so much, but I couldn't get the choir this week to prepare anything

170

more than the morning anthem, so I thought if you would sing . . ."

"Not a solo! You know I'm not good enough for that. But maybe Minnie Dilling and I could do a duet. We go pretty well together. I'll see what I can find, and get in touch with her."

"Thanks a million. I'll rehearse with you any time you want. I believe I'll play something while the offering is being taken and then have your special music after that. It would be a change and prolong that part of the service, and I know Father would be pleased over any little innovation."

They were both conscious as they talked on of a constraint between them. Faith refused to be drawn into any further conversation about Bob Halifax; Violet skilfully turned aside any questions concerning Mike. The mutual confidences they had poured out before had been concerned with the nebulous quantities of hope and anxiety and love in the abstract. When male flesh and blood came upon the scene there was a withdrawal each into her own heart.

That afternoon, as the town drowsed in the heat, Violet sat in the parlor looking through old music books to see what she could find that might answer Faith's request. Suddenly, with a rustle of starched petticoats, Katie burst into the room, her face flushed and her black eyes snapping. Her words came out in a sibilant whisper.

"Vi'let, who do you spose is at the back door askin' to see you by yourself? *Joe Hicks!* An' mebbe he's even got the bird in his pocket this minute, else why would he be comin' at all? An' if you ask me he acts guilty enough, stammerin' an' stutterin', an' I've said to Mary Jackson a dozen times, mind, where there's so much smoke there's bound to be some fire, I said, an' now . . ."

"Katie," Violet managed to interrupt the excited flow, "if he wants to see me alone, send him in here."

"In here?" Katie's sense of social shock was perhaps not so great as her disappointment over the difficulty she would now have in listening in on the conversation.

"I must say it's hardly suitable havin' him into the parlor," she muttered as she turned to go.

A great wave of elation swept over Violet until her very face colored with it! While she had stoutly maintained to all and sundry that Joe was innocent of the theft of the nightingale, she had had occasional secret misgivings in the dark hours of the night when she weighed the overwhelming evidence against him. *Could it* after all be true? Had she been wise never to mention the whole matter to him? Had her scrupulous kindness stood in the way of a possible recovery of her treasure? So she had sometimes pondered in the darkness. Now, Joe had come to see her of his own accord! Oh, it could only be to make a confession. Even if he had pawned the bird in Pittsburgh, as most people thought he had done, it might still be redeemable. Or if it had been sold outright there would be perhaps a way to trace it. Her heart leaped at the thought.

Joe suddenly appeared before her, a nondescript, timid little man, his face twitching in embarrassment.

"Come in, Joe," Violet said with eager warmth. "You wanted to talk to me?"

Joe looked behind him. "Could you shut the door, Miss Vi'let? I . . . I want to speak to you private."

Violet went at once to the folding doors which separated the parlor from the hall and drew them tightly together. "Now, we're all alone, Joe. Sit down and tell me what you want to say."

Joe sat down on the edge of a chair and for a few moments seemed to be tongue-tied.

"Don't be afraid, Joe. No matter what it is, you mustn't be embarrassed to tell me."

Joe swallowed with difficulty. "That's just it, Miss Vi'let. I've wanted to come to see you before but I've been that ashamed. I says to myself how could I ever put it in words, I says. But when it's gone on this long now with every man's hand again' me, as it were, I couldn't stand it no longer, so I just come an' no matter what you'll think of me I've got to tell you."

Violet's spirits were rising with each of her guest's labored sentences. So it *had* been Joe. Incredible, but true.

"You did right to come! Please go on."

"Well, you see the thing that's so hard is for a man to say this to a young lady. I mean I'm not sure I can put it delicate-like. An' you'll have to excuse me, Miss Vi'let, if it don't sound just . . . delicate, but I'll do my best."

He looked at her beseechingly, and as he did so Violet

172

felt her elation mysteriously ebbing within her. This was not the kind of opening she had expected.

"Of course, Joe," she said.

"Well," he went on, "it's like this. You know me an' Amanda's been married ten years an' we have no children. It's about broke Amanda's heart. She keeps up real cheerful most of the time but at night she often used to cry, an' baptism days at the church she'd pretend she had a headache or somethin' so she wouldn't have to go. Course I knew why."

He swallowed again self-consciously and went on.

"So I got to thinkin', me not bein' a big husky man like some that mebbe it was my fault somehow. Well, last May I seen an ad in the city paper about this Pittsburgh doctor who just treated *men* only. There was one thing in it that . . . well it just seemed to fit me . . . or I thought so . . . an' I says to myself I'll go to see him if it's the last thing I ever do. For Amanda's sake, you understand."

"Of course," Violet echoed again from a constricted throat.

"So I decided the last time she went to the country to visit her mother that I'd go an' never let her know. I knew I could use a little extra change so I come here one afternoon to collect for the Tourist sign. The kitchen door was open so I knocked an' then I stepped inside an' called. I set a while in the rocker holdin' Simon, an' then when nobody come I left an' the next morning I took the early train. I had a little box in the shop I always kep' my ten-penny nails in so I emptied it an' put a couple of san'wiches in it to save me goin' to a restaurant. I wrapped it up an' that's what I was carryin'. You see, Miss Vi'let?"

"Yes," Violet said in a strange voice, "I see."

"An' the funny thing was I hunted till noon tryin' to locate the address in the ad an' when I found it the doctor wasn't there at all! I was put out, I can tell you. I asked about him at a little store nearby an' the man said he'd left an' he didn't know where he'd gone. He said he didn't think he was a *real* doctor anyway. This man let me set down there in the back of the store while I et my lunch an' then I just went to the station and got the train back. An' that's the whole story, Miss Vi'let."

"But . . . but Joe," Violet exclaimed, "why didn't you tell this to people right away when you knew you were suspected?"

"How could I?" Joe said with asperity, "without givin' away what I went to the city for? You know this town. They'd never have let up suspicionin' me till they found out, an' I wasn't tellin' that to nobody."

"I suppose you're right," Violet said slowly, "but we've got to find a way now to clear your good name. I'll certainly take care of that if I can only . . . Joe, how about saying you went up to the city to see a *specialist*? That would satisfy everybody and you wouldn't need to explain further."

Joe looked at her in wonder and admiration.

"That would do the trick as slick as skinnin' a mole! An' I never would a thought of it. Danged if I would! Oh, Miss Vi'let, if you could just pass that around. *Specialist!* If I'd thought of that there word at the start what a lot of trouble it would have saved us! Still an' all . . ."

Joe suddenly leaned forward and his face became suffused with a tender light. As she watched his smile Violet realized how he could have inspired a woman's love.

"I don't begrudge a bit of the trouble, Miss Vi'let. I guess I'm even glad it all happened. I've saved up something to tell you at the end. If I can put *this* delicate-like too, me bein' a man and you a young lady. Amanda says it's a miracle just like the ones in the Bible. She says God just done it to make up to us for what happened! I'm not sayin' it ain't so but what I think is, it was mebbe like this. When the whole town seemed to be thinkin' that awful thing of me, why Amanda an' me we just drawed closer an' closer to each other . . . the closest we'd ever been. An' now . . . I hardly know how to say it but, Miss Vi'let, for the first time we got *hopes*. After ten years we got *hopes*! If you know what I mean," he added.

"Oh Joe, of course I do! And I'm *so* happy for you!"

"Happy? Why Amanda says with her diamond and now the *hopes* she don't think heaven could be any better than right here. An' then on top of that if my name gets cleared . . ."

"The ring!" Violet cried. "For the moment I'd forgotten it. That was one thing that made everyone suspect you,

174

Joe. Your getting the ring just after the nightingale disappeared."

"I done nothing of the kind," Joe said. "I had the box with the ring in it—an awful pretty little box lined with white satin!—I had it in the toe of one of my socks in the bureau drawer a month before your bird was stole, I saved for ten years for that ring! Kep' the money in a little trunk up in the attic. Amanda never knew a haet about it. When I got fifty-five dollars I went in to Harrisville an' bought it. Haven't you seen it yet, Miss Vi'let?"

"No, but I hope to soon. Why didn't you tell people about *this,* Joe? It would have helped so much."

Joe's face stiffened. "What call had I to be givin' *deetails* as though I was on my hands an' knees beggin' them to believe me? I earned that money honest, I bought the ring an' paid for it, an' I give it to my own wife. Let them think what they like, I says. I'll keep my personal dealin's to myself."

Violet had a sudden picture of Squire Kendrick as he had said out of his wisdom: *Sometimes these meek little men are stubborn as the devil.* So it had evidently been with Joe.

But now his face softened again. "That is, until we got *hopes.* Then I knew I had to get my name cleared some way."

She showed him out the front door and they parted with a warm handclasp. Violet watched him go down the walk and through the gate, his narrow shoulders held high. Poor little Joe! He had indeed been sent to Coventry by his townsmen but he would come safely home now before long.

She walked slowly through the house to the kitchen where Katie was entertaining Mary Jackson with a cup of tea. They both jumped as they saw her.

"What did he have to say?" Katie burst out.

"Did he bring back the nightingale?" Mary cried.

Violet sat down at the kitchen table. Nothing could have been better for her purpose than to have Mary Jackson here at this moment.

"No, of course he didn't bring it back because he never took it. But he did come to explain all about his trip to the city that day, and his buying the ring."

She told them then, the whole story just as Joe had told

175

it to her except for the one variation they had agreed upon. When she came to the word *specialist* both Katie and Mary broke in at once.

"Aye, that would be about his asthma, I doubt. You know Joe gets it betimes," Katie said.

Mary's long nose pointed. "An' it could have been some *male* complaint, you know. If it was, that would explain why he was sort of grouchy an' short with the men at the station. He'd be sensitive, kind of. Did he tell you, Vi'let, what his trouble was?"

Violet hesitated. "He seemed embarrassed to talk about it."

"Aye, so he would be," said Katie. "That's the way men are. They never like to admit there's anything the matter with them! Well then, what about *the ring?*"

When Violet had told them all except Joe's final precious secret, Mary had tears in her eyes.

"Oh, it's an awful thing we've done to Joe an' I was one of the first to start it. May the Lord forgive me. But we'll put it right as far as we can. I've got a gingerbread in the oven now. I always bake it slow. When it's done I'll take a big plateful up to Amanda for their supper an' I'll look at her ring an' be as friendly as I know how to her an' Joe both. An' I'll stop an' tell Mrs. Hummel an' Mrs. Dunn the truth. An' you can count on William to spread this amongst the men. Oh, I never was so ashamed of myself but I'll do all in my power to atone."

When she had gone her kindhearted and repentant way the two in the kitchen looked at each other.

"Well," said Katie, "I guess this leaves us where we started as far as the nightingale's concerned."

Violet nodded. "I'm going to take all the books out again. I know it's no use but I have to do something."

"Come along then," said Katie. "I'll help you."

But their lengthy labor was to no avail. Only the empty shelves stared back at them except for the spot where lay the yellowed envelope containing the letter of Greatuncle—*For when true love comes it is as though a nightingale sings in the heart.* The words kept repeating themselves over and over in Violet's mind as she put the books back in their places.

That night Katie came up with an idea. "Why couldn't

you put up a notice an' offer a reward?" she said excitedly. "Why didn't we think of it before? It's what Jim Peters did when his horse was stole. An' he got it back, too. You could get the Newburt boys to print the sign an' Mr. Gordon would put it up in the Post Office. Well, why not?"

"How could we pay a reward?"

"With the money from the transhens! This'll be a good month, I daresay, an' you know what we have in the bank already."

Violet considered and her eyes brightened.

"I think you're right, Katie. That's just what I'll do."

By the end of the week Joe Hicks stood justified in the eyes of the town. No one put the matter into words, but there had been many a handshake from the men as Joe once again went his accustomed way among his fellows; and there had been so many calls upon Amanda from neighbors bearing gifts of food that, as old Becky Slade put it, "it might 'a been a funeral!"

As they looked upon Amanda's face, suffused with her own inner beatitude, they set it all down naturally to Joe's reinstatement. When they learned all the secret later on, Violet kept thinking, new conversational waves concerning the Hickses, but this time those of surprise and pleasure, would sweep the village from end to end.

Violet had found an old song, a favorite of her mother's, and she and Minnie Dilling had practiced it with Faith. It was a quaint and tender little evening hymn set to the music of "Träumerei." Violet had been especially earnest about the enunciation, and they had worked hard to make sure the words would fall distinctly upon the ear.

The Sunday-night service was to Violet the most beautiful of the week. This evening, as she walked over to the church, her poet's eye watched the sunset, its golden embers now fading along the hills beyond the creek. She felt the delicate premonition of dusk in the sky, with its one early star, and the brooding Sabbath stillness which always enfolded the town. Behind the church the old and now unused graveyard slept under its myrtle and mosses, and the last twilight note of a robin came from one of the pines there.

The big upper sanctuary, devoid of ecclesiastical adornment but hallowed by a hundred years of worship, was now slowly filling as Violet took her place in the choir, from where she could view without effort the congregation before her. Henry had returned to the evening services and was now sitting near the back, gazing solemnly ahead of him. There was an encouraging number of young people, many of them couples, disposed mainly about the rear of the church while the older folk sat nearer the front. The soft air blew in through the tall, opened windows and the first crickets sounded tentatively from the grass outside.

It was as they stood for the opening hymn that Violet gave a start of surprise. She saw Mike enter, pause for a minute and then take his place in an empty pew. He stood with his gaze fixed upon her as though, like the ostrich with its head in the sand, he felt his eyes were invisible.

Oh dear, Violet thought to herself, *why did he come back tonight? Now I will be nervous over the duet!*

Her color rose and her heart beat uncomfortably as she waited. When it was time for the offering the haunting old strains of "Träumerei" fell from the organ under Faith's touch, and at the end Violet and Minnie stood up to sing the same melody, with the words falling clearly, sweetly into the silence:

> *"I lay me calmly down to sleep*
> *When darkling night comes on,*
> *And leave to God the rest:-*
> *Whether I wake to smile or weep,*
> *Or wake no more on life's fair shore,*
> *He knoweth best.*
> *Dear Father, bless in love thy child!*
> *I lay me down to sleep."*

There was a hush when they sat down and Faith moved from the organ bench to sit beside them. It continued for a long minute before Mr. Lyall rose and started his sermon.

Violet had been trying to prepare herself for the time she felt was inevitable, when Mr. Halifax would step up to Faith at the church steps and she herself would be left to walk home alone! A little thing, indeed, and yet there would be an embarrassment in it, a new reminder of things past and of old ties broken. The young men at

178

the close of the benediction always left the sanctuary at once, almost precipitously in fact, to wait below at the outer door, in the case of some merely to watch and in the case of most to approach the various young ladies as they issued forth, with a view to seeing them home. As Violet started down the aisle with Faith she saw Robert Halifax going out the door with Henry, who had evidently apprised him of village custom. Mike, unaware of it, waited at the end of his pew until the girls reached it. Faith, whose eyes and thoughts had been elsewhere before, suddenly now caught Violet's arm.

"Why, there's *Mike!*" she whispered.

"Yes, I know. I mean, I saw him come in, but I wasn't expecting him."

He came up to them and included them both in his greeting.

"I was at loose ends tonight and I remembered you had a service so I decided to come out to it. How's the arm, Miss Faith?"

"Oh, practically well, thank you."

"I enjoyed your music. Violet, I'll just pop along now if you're engaged in any way tonight." He looked at her hopefully.

"No," she said smiling, "I was just going to sit and cogitate on the porch for a while. You can join me if you wish."

"Thanks. I'll be glad to."

They were at the outer door by now, and Violet felt Faith's arm slip from her own. At the same moment she heard a low voice as Robert Halifax stepped from the shadows and they started off together. Faith turned for a muted goodnight and then they were gone. Mike commented as he and Violet reached the Carpenter gate.

"It looks as though your friend Faith and Halifax might be interested in each other."

"Yes, it does."

"Well, he seems a nice chap."

"I think they would be ideally suited."

"How do you mean?"

"Oh, congenial tastes. . . . You know."

"You think that's so important in love?"

"Why yes. Don't you?"

"That's what I'm trying to find out," he said. Then,

as they sat down he added seriously, "That was a beautiful little song you sang tonight. It seemed to affect a good many people, me included. I saw several handkerchiefs in use among the women, and your Katie had tears streaming down her cheeks."

"Oh," Violet said hastily, "as far as Katie was concerned it wasn't the song that she was crying over. It was Simon, our cat. He's been gone now for four days and nights and she's nearly crazy. I'm very upset myself."

Mike laughed. "Upset over a *cat!*" he said. "I can't imagine that."

"But he's our pet! We've had him for eight years and he's like one of the family." Violet's tone was not only earnest but injured.

"I'm sorry," Mike said quickly. "Cats have just never come into my acquaintance. But I do hope Simon turns up safely. Violet, have you any other talents I don't know about? You write poetry, you sing . . ."

"Not much."

"Oh, yes you do. You have a nice voice. Well, anything else?"

"Yes," she said mischievously. "I'm really a pretty good cook, due to Katie's instruction."

Mike drew a sigh as of relief. "Oh, now you're down on my level. I wish you were there all the time. There's something I wanted to ask you when I was here before but I hesitated. I shouldn't now, but I'm going to. Is there . . . someone else?"

There was such a long pause that Mike grew anxiously apologetic.

"It's all right for you to ask," Violet said at last, "but although I know it sounds strange, I really can't answer."

"Never mind. It's no one here, is it?"

"Oh, no," Violet said so emphatically that Mike smiled.

"O.K. Let's talk of other things."

But when he stood up to leave he reverted for a moment to what was apparently uppermost in his mind.

"There's one thing I can quite properly tell you now," he said, as he held her hand. "No matter what direction our friendship may take later on, I'll always be glad that I've known you this summer."

Then he went quickly down the walk and through the gate.

CHAPTER EIGHT

From Violet Carpenter to Philip Haversham

Dear Philip: What can I ever say to express my utter joy in the books which arrived safely on Thursday! Our branch railroad stops across the creek and all luggage, express packages and some passengers—those who, through frailty of body or the lack of a rig of their own, are unable to walk the distance over the bridge and up the hill—are conveyed in an old black "hack" driven by Josiah Hunt, one of our town characters. He appeared at our door, therefore, carrying the box, and when he had delivered it stood about as he always does at such a time, hoping to view the contents. So I opened it, with his most eager help. "Can't decide what's in it," he kept saying. "It's heavy as all get-out but when you shake it, it don't rattle." When the wrappings were finally off he peered for a moment and then drew back disgustedly, glancing at the shelves behind him. "Books! Ain't you got enough already?" "Never!" I said. "Oh, never enough, Josiah."

"Humph," he said, "I'd thought it might be fine groceries mebbe. Well, everybody to their taste as the old woman said when she kissed the cow." And he went on his somewhat deflated way. While I . . . oh I simply gloated like a miser as I took up the volumes one after the other, reading the titles, smoothing the bindings, for I love the outsides of books also, don't you? As an editor I'm sure you must. You couldn't have made a selection more to my taste. I can't bear as yet to put them in the bookshelves but have them stacked on the reading table where I can see them all together. What richness! You were far, far too generous, but I am reveling (with one l or two—I never can remember which) in them every free moment since their arrival, and of course my pleasure in them will last indefinitely.

Do you know the one I love best of all? The little volume of George Herbert's poems! I've come across selections of his of course, here and there, but for some reason this was one classic my father did not have. Now I'm reading it with the deepest delight. The ones you have marked are my favorites too! Isn't that a nice coincidence? Ever since I've been alone I've made it a habit to take a book to the table with me to sort of companion me at mealtimes. This drives Katie distracted. "Readin' a book while your food gets cold! It's rideeculous." But in some things I have to assert my independence. So now I am having Mr. Herbert with me each morning at my late breakfast after the "transhens," if any, have departed. I hope he doesn't feel hurt that it isn't dinner, but he seems to me so definitely a morning poet. Did you ever think of that?

"Sweet day, so fair, so calm, so bright."

And the lines I love best of all from "The Flower":

"I once more smell the dew and rain,
And relish versing: O my only Light,
It cannot be
That I am he
On whom Thy tempests fell all night."

Doesn't that sound like a morning mood?

So thank you again a thousand times for your kindness in sending me such a wonderful gift.

We have just been through a dreadful emotional crisis in the household. Simon, the cat whom I've mentioned before, was put out as usual last Wednesday night and did not return. He has been gone before for short intervals, but when four days and nights passed and there was no sign of him we were sure he had been killed. I was really very sad myself, but Katie, I knew, was inconsolable. She kept a stony countenance but I caught her often at the kitchen window wiping her eyes when she thought she was unobserved. Saturday night I slipped along to her room before I went to bed. The door was ajar and while she didn't hear me I could hear her. "O Lord," she was praying, "Send Simon back safe! He's a good beast an' we set such store by him. O Lord, if you'll just send him safe back I'll read two chapters in me Bible every night for the rest of my life!"

182

I can smile a little over this now but at the time I saw no humor in it. I've been getting up early to be down in the kitchen when Katie opens the back door, for this had become an act of the most extreme suspense and tension as hope and fear mingled. This morning as Katie with unsteady fingers turned the lock and flung the door open, there, under our eyes, sat Simon, smirking on the top step! Every other time he has been away, even overnight, he has come back with a torn ear or a bloody paw or tufts torn from his tail. But this time every hair of him was in place with what I might term a sleek elegance while his inscrutable green eyes looked up at us as if to say, "You could never guess where I've been this time!" And we certainly can't.

Katie grabbed him up in her arms and he touched her cheek with a paw as he does when in a gracious mood. Then she gave him all the cream in the house and opened a box of sardines, while I hastened to turn my back for fear my weakness would betray me. I had been so upset over the loss of Simon, but most of all over Katie's distress, that the sudden relief left me rather shaken. Katie, with her usual eagle eye, saw my condition and spoke loftily. "Tut! Tut! It's rideeculous to get so worked up over a cat. I knew all the time he'd come back when he got ready. Get along with you now while I make your breakfast." I could hear her lecturing him severely while I was eating.

How silly of me to write you all this! But I have told you before that life in our household is made up of small, inconsequential episodes. Of course in the town proper anything can happen. Do elevate my mind, however, when you answer, by telling me of your own important doings. And by the way, may I ask you a rather impertinent question? How old are you? I began by placing you in your sixties because I thought all editors were Olympians, but I've been scaling you down quite a bit. Am I right? And also, would you have a snapshot of yourself you would care to send me, in exchange for mine?

Sincerely,

Violet

From Philip Haversham to Violet Carpenter

Dear Violet: I loved your letter as I do all of them and I must say that your so-called quiet episodes have a way of seeming very dramatic to me. I was in a state of high nervous tension over Simon's disappearance as I read, and certainly now rejoice with you in his safe, and smug, return. As to Katie, she has become so real to me that I'm sure I should recognize her if I met her on Broadway! Rideeculous, as she would say, but true. I might add that somehow I didn't find her prayer amusing, either!

I'm so happy that I hit the mark at all with the book selections, and that they are giving you pleasure. George Herbert has always been a great favorite of mine and it pleases me that he is breakfasting with you. And yet it makes me quite envious, too. Breakfast can be such a charming meal under the right conditions!

Now to answer your questions. I am far from being an Olympian in either age or wisdom. I should have made this clear sooner. I came to the company right from college twelve years ago, my name, I suppose, helping me get the job since the house was founded by some sort of collateral ancestor—if that's the way to put it. I was boy-of-all-work at first until I finally became really acquainted with Mr. Giles, our editor-in-chief. I've admired him tremendously from the first, for he has discriminating literary judgment and mellow taste. While we disagree slightly occasionally we really get on together and I'm proud to be his associate.

I don't believe I've ever told you about our conference over your manuscript, have I? It came first to my desk and I took it back to my apartment to read that night. I began with a sort of duty-to-be-done attitude for we have had a great deal of very ordinary verse submitted to us this last year. And then—I can't describe to you my utter absorption. When I had read "Love Imagined" I put down the paper and stood for a long time at the window, thinking. Even after I went to bed I got up and read the poems all through again.

The next day I gave them to Giles and asked him to consider them soon, which he did. When we came to discussing them he said that he felt an unusual talent was shown in them but that he wanted several expert opinions *from readers before a decision was reached. He especially liked the small-town ballads scattered through the book. He chuckled over "The Spinster Speaks," with its "any man is better than none" motif, though he admitted that it caught the heart a bit too, as did the others.*

One point may amuse you. He said he thought the author was an older woman—"a woman of experience," as he put it. I said I was sure she was young. I must have been rather vehement for he looked up over his glasses and said, "Well, don't take it so hard, Phil. It won't ruin the book's chances if she is over forty-five." Then he told me that the manuscript merited a personal reply and for me to take charge of it from then on. So, that's the story. There is often a delay with reader's reports but it is exaggerated in the case of your book because the two Giles was most set on are both on vacation, one in California and the other in Europe; but they are due back this month. It may be necessary to omit two or three of the poems in the present group and wait until you have several new ones to add. But I am sure that eventually you will be published! Over that I shall be as thrilled as you, I can tell you!

As to my doings, there isn't much to report. I really work hard. Office all day, reading manuscripts at night. I have occasional dinners and theaters and of course many business luncheons, but in the main, as I've recently discovered, I'm pretty lonely. This evening about dusk I walked over to the ferry and rode to the Jersey side and back again. I often do this on a hot night, for a breath of air from the water but even more for the beauty of New York's lighted buildings. There is something ethereal in the millions of golden points against the gray blurred outlines of the rising stone and steel. And a mystery also. The way in which the hard realities of day can become transformed to loveliness by darkness! "And the moral of that is . . ." I don't quite know, but I think there may be one.

I was asked to have some photographs taken this spring for professional purposes so I'm enclosing one with my vital statistics on the back. Oh, I found a small frame in an antique shop a few days ago—Venetian mosaic of tiny flowers—which just suits your picture. Thank you again

185

*for it! And do write soon. I know I'm unreasonably greedy
—but there it is!*

Faithfully,
Philip

Violet held the photograph for a long time, while a wave of emotion stronger than anything she had ever known in her life swept over her. This was Philip's face, which until now had existed variously in her mind as that of a man of sixty, of fifty, of forty. She had never dared to think of any age below forty. But here from the card he looked back at her, *young*, and, beyond all her imagination, handsome. The eyes were straightforward, the nose good, the mouth kindly and a shade humorous, the chin strong. These attributes might pertain to any number of young men, but the sum of them, as she saw them here, represented a personality which spoke to her as though the lips themselves had moved in revelation.

"Oh Philip," she whispered, "is this really you!"

Then she remembered suddenly about the vital statistics, turned the photograph over and read:

> *Age—33*
> *Height—6 ft. 1 inch*
> *Weight—165 lbs.*
> *Eyes—gray; hair—brown*
> *Disposition—fairly good*
> *Talents—none to speak of*
> *General attitude—hopeful*

She smiled, but blushed also. The last underlined word she knew had not been written casually.

She sang a great deal during the next few days, and showed such a tendency to laugh over trifles that Katie attributed her high spirits to the large box of pickles which arrived with Mike's card. This latter gift met with the full approval of Josiah Hunt, who, after assisting at the opening, was presented with a jar to take home with him. Katie, with what she considered great subtlety, eyed her young mistress with sidewise glances as she spoke.

"There's nothing tastier than a good pickle, mind, an' these'll be enough to last us a year. An' the pickle-makin' business ain't to be sneezed at. Ninian says they've got this great big factory an' Mike's the only son. He's a pleasant, kindly chap an' all."

Violet's reply was somewhat vague, which Katie considered natural under the circumstances.

Violet's mind, as a matter of fact, when she could pin it down to Ladykirk, was busy pondering the idea of putting up a reward sign for the nightingale. For instead of approaching solution the mystery was growing greater with each passing week. There could hardly be any doubt that the nightingale was in the town. But who had it? Who had taken it? Even with the delicate new happiness lifting her heart she felt constantly the pangs of loss. As far as she knew—and certainly she *would* know—no other suspect had entered anyone's mind. Instead, the village seemed to be concentrating now upon their efforts to make up to Joe and Amanda Hicks for the former unwarranted mistrust.

"How much could we afford to offer for a reward?" Violet asked Katie one day.

They sat down at the kitchen table to consider, the blue sugar bowl between them.

"These last weeks have been good for transhens," said Katie, "an' nice, decent folk all of them. Not as fancy as Mr. Smith an' some of the others, but fair enough, an' every one of them takin' breakfast, which runs up the money. We must have enough now to bank." She counted the silver carefully and piled the pieces impressively before her on the table as Violet checked.

"Fourteen-fifty," she announced, "an' the six dollar bills in the desk left out of last month's money. Well, what think you? Would you offer ten?"

Violet was very sober.

"If we offer a reward at all I think it should be a big one—say twenty. Enough to make a little excitement and start people talking. Enough, you see, to make the person that has the nightingale really *want* to give it up. The question is, dare we take that much money?"

"I don't want this to run us into trouble about the orchard, mind," said Katie, "but our bills are all paid up an' the garden's just comin' in now. We won't need *too* much from the store. An' I could start givin' the transhens two pieces of flitch instead of three for their breakfasts an' make up with plenty biscuits an' jelly."

Violet sat, her chin on her hands, considering.

"I'll do it," she said suddenly, "and I'll tell you how. I meant to get a new winter coat this fall and . . ."

"An' it's yourself an' not your neighbor that needs it!" Katie put in.

"My old one will do another winter well enough with a fresh velvet collar. I'd rather have the nightingale back, if I can get it, than any amount of new clothes."

"Well, well," said Katie a shade grudgingly, "go ahead then an' see what comes of it. But it's my opeenion that nobody will ever come right out an' say, 'Here's your bird, give me the money,' they'll be too ashamed. They'll likely put up a story that they just happened to find it somewhere. As to your coat, you've got a nice air the way you wear it, anyhow. As the sayin' goes, 'It's the life of an auld hat to be weel cockit.' "

Violet laughed as she stood up. "Thanks for the compliment, Katie, and I think I'll go down and see the Newburt twins today about the signs. How many, I wonder, should I order?"

"Well, one for the Post Office an' one for the General. Would you want to ask Henry to put one up in the hardware?"

"I don't think so," Violet said.

"An' a good job if you don't. You ought to keep clear shot of him. What about one at the end of the bridge, or inside even?"

"I'll ask the Newburts about that. They should know."

It was an extremely hot afternoon, but armed with a white parasol Violet set forth at four o'clock to walk the length of Main Street to where the Newburt "boys," as they were still known, "kept bach" in a little house at the end of the bridge opposite the mill. They did shoe and harness repairing, and on the side painted the various *For Sale* and *Beware the Dog* signs for the community. Violet's progress down the street was punctuated by the inevitable and constant summer inquiry: "Warm enough for you?" "Hot enough for you, Vi'let?" "Warm enough for you today?"

When she reached the Newburt's open door the two

188

men spoke as one as they looked up, perspiring, from their work.

"Well, Miss Vi'let, is it hot enough for you?"

Violet laughed, which seemed to startle them. "Oh, I like warm weather," she said. Then as Bill, the one brother, pushed some harness off a chair and dusted it with his shirt sleeve, making a gesture to her, she sat down and explained her errand. To her surprise she found their interest in the mystery was intense. Bill questioned her again about each detail concerning it: where the nightingale had been kept; who knew of its hiding place; how long she and Katie had been absent the day of the tea.

"We've done a lot of thinkin', Ed an' me," Bill said finally; then, lowering his voice, he added, "an' we believe we know who might have took it."

Violet all but jumped. "You do?"

"That's right. Now we'll just sort of lead up to it. You ask her the rest, Ed."

"Well now," Ed said, "this is the way we thought it out. Most of the kids in town have seen the bird, haven't they?"

"Yes, they have."

"Now isn't there a boy you've had workin' for you once in a while, cuttin' the grass or mebbe cleanin' the stable special?"

Violet hesitated. "Well, yes. We've had Oliver Coates sometimes."

"An' he would know where you kep' the nightingale?"

"I suppose so. Yes, but so do . . ."

Ed raised a knotted finger. "Now, let's just go on. You mind two year ago at the U.P. Festival when Ben Losting come to it drunk with his gun an' raised a ruckus an' in the excitement Oliver Coates stole a ten-dollar bill from the cash box? Mind that?"

"Oh, Mr. Newburt, it's cruel even to mention that. He took it impulsively and then confessed and gave it back. He's a *good* boy! I'd never hold that against him, never!"

"Well now, just think a little furder. He wanted a bicycle *bad*, that's why he took the money. An' you know his pap. Old Oliver's the tightest man in this whole town, an' the strictest. An' they tell me he said he'd never get young Oliver a bicycle after that. So, you see."

"No," said Violet, "I don't see! The boy is perfectly

innocent. I would swear to that. And besides, what good could the nightingale possibly do him?"

Bill looked pleased. "Well, we just thought that one out too. You know Mrs. Coates's sister lives up in the city. Husband's got a big job. Policeman or something."

"Yes."

"An' young Oliver goes up just before school every summer to visit them. His pap makes him work hard enough the rest of the time but he always gets his week in the city, you know. I guess his mother sees to that."

"Yes," Violet admitted, "I know."

"Well then. Here's how we got it worked out. If he's got the bird he could take it along in his suitcase an' find a place up there to sell it. Oliver's smart an' he's been up in the city every year for his week for dear knows how long. Now you take Joe Hicks. Even if he'd had the nightingale I bet he couldn't have found a pawnshop or any place to sell it. He's so scared-like an' dumb. But Oliver's bright an' he wants a bicycle something fierce for he's talked about it in this very shop, hasn't he? So there it is."

"But this is dreadful!" Violet burst out. "You haven't a shred of evidence to go on. And even if all you've said were true—which it isn't—how would the boy explain where he got the money for the bicycle?"

A slight shadow fell upon the Newburt twins' faces. "That's the only thing we ain't quite worked out yet," Ed said, looking at Bill.

"And oh, I *hope* you haven't mentioned a word of this to anyone else!" Violet's voice was beseeching.

"Well, of course, we've only been workin' on this since the news got round that Joe Hicks was cleared. We both seen him that morning skitin' along over the bridge to the station with the little box under his arm, so of course we felt it was our duty to speak of *that*. But I suppose his story's true."

"It certainly is! And please don't say anything about young Oliver to anybody. I really beg you not to. And now I want to talk about the signs."

Their eyes opened wide as Violet mentioned the amount of the reward.

"By crickey!" Ed said. "That's enough to offer for a

190

horse, let alone a little singin' bird. You must set a powerful lot of store by it."

"I do," said Violet.

They worked out the wording, and the number of the bills—three, they decided upon: one for the Post Office, one for the General Store and one for the Mill.

"Want us to put them up for you?" Ed asked.

"Oh, if you would I'd be so grateful."

"Be ready by tomorrow," Bill said. "We're runnin' a little slack in other work just now, so I'll get right at these. Would fifty cents apiece be reasonable?"

"Perfectly. I'll pay you now and thank you very much. And . . ." as she turned to go, "you'll remember what I asked you?"

"Now don't you fret yourself," Ed said. "When these signs get up something's goin' to happen. You'll see. Somebody'll give himself away."

Violet felt ill at ease as she left. The Newburt twins were notorious gossips in a town where interest in other peoples' affairs was not only natural but inevitable. She feared desperately for the boy whose name was now in their minds. They had been careful not to promise to keep their suspicions to themselves, so young Oliver might wrongly suffer as Joe Hicks had done, from mistrust. She stopped in her tracks wishing she had never thought of the posters. And yet if, by means of them, the guilty one came forward to produce the nightingale and claim the reward, would that not be the surest way to clear the innocent? She drew a long, labored sigh and then crossed the road to look at the creek by the mill.

It was always a pleasant sight. The stream wound gracefully around a bend some little way above, with heavy greenery covering its banks. Here by the mill the water rushed in a smooth torrent over the dam and fell in foamy depths at the foot of Miller's Rock. Violet watched the opalescence of the spray in the late afternoon sun, the weathered gray of the bridge and the dull rosy lights on the old mill roof. She had always loved the mill and on an impulse now decided to go in and get some bran for Katie's muffins. It was usually made on Friday.

She stood for a moment inside, listening to the loud steady hum of the bands and grinders and smelling the

191

sweet, grainy air. When Mr. Harris appeared, his clothes coated with white, he waved a friendly hand.

"Want some bran?" he shouted above the noise. "Got some nice and fresh."

Violet signed that she did and took out her purse when, in a few minutes, he handed the brown paper bag to her.

"That's all right. No charge to you. Stoppin' in to see Seena?"

"Yes, I thought I would."

"Fine. Do her good. She's kinda restless."

"Thanks so much, Mr. Harris. I'd rather pay. . . ."

But with another wave he had disappeared and Violet started out and up the street to the Mill House, only the length of a lot away. Seena was rocking on the porch, her eyes fixed idly on the road in front of her. When she saw Violet she jumped up in pleasure.

"Come in, Vi! I saw you go into the Newburts' but I missed you someway when you came out."

"I went over to the mill to get some bran," Violet smiled.

"You and Henry!" Seena said in an odd voice. "I declare he's as regular as a clock. Every Friday after the store closes he comes for bran. I guess his mother bakes brown bread on Saturday. Sit down and tell me what's doing. Oh, but this town is dead! I suppose your Fourth of July party will have to last us the rest of the summer."

"I suppose so," Violet agreed, "or at least until time for the corn roasts to begin."

"That's right. It's August for them. I'd planned to have one out at the farm this year, a big one, and invite everybody. John liked the idea too. Well . . ."

"Oh, Seena, I am so truly sorry for you! I know how lonely and desolate you must feel. I wish I could do more for you. I have thought of one thing that might give us all a little diversion. You know we'll want to give Kitty a nice linen shower before her wedding. Why couldn't a few of us get together each week and embroider or crochet on our gifts? Wouldn't that be a good idea?"

"Be better than nothing," Seena said ungraciously, and then quickly changed her tone. "I didn't mean that the way it sounded, Vi. Yes, I'd like that. I'm pretty good at crocheting so I think I'll do a big centerpiece for her."

"I'll stick to embroidery," Violet said. "Either napkins
192

or pillow slips. I know Faith would join us and maybe Lucy and Peggy. You could always come to our house for it's on the back street and Kitty wouldn't see what we were up to. Besides, she's too excited and busy just now to pay much attention. I'll get in touch with the others and let you know. Would Tuesday of next week be all right for you?"

"Any day," Seena said. "Time hangs heavy enough. Not even much work to do compared with the farm. Vi?"

"Yes."

"I'm having trouble with that young donkey of a Jake. I've just about got to the end of my string. I'm going to put a stop to it, so I am."

"Seena! What does he do? What's the matter?"

"Do? He comes in here nearly every blessed night, that's what he does. Hitches that old rattletrap of a buckboard out there in front and comes up to the porch lookin' as if the devil himself was after him. I tell you I don't think the boy's *right*. He looks queer and he acts queer."

"But what does he want you to do?"

"What do you suppose?" Seena said bluntly. "He tries to kiss me and God knows what else if I didn't push him off. He's crazy. The idea of him thinking he could make up to *me*. But I'm going to get rid of him soon. I'll put it so he'll understand. I've just been too easy with him."

"Oh, Seena, I'm afraid you've led him on!"

"Fiddlesticks! I had to have him at the farm, didn't I? I'd have lost the crops if it hadn't been for him. So if I jollied him on a little, who could blame me? And he didn't act so crazy out there. It's since I sold the farm and came here that he's gone clear off his head. He keeps talking about *marrying* me! Can you imagine that? Says we could live in the tenant house on the farm and he'd go on helping Bob Halifax. I've got to put a stop to it."

"Couldn't your father talk to him?"

"That's the trouble. He won't. He's like you. He thinks I brought it on somehow and says if I got into the mess I'll have to get myself out. Well, one of these fine nights *I will*."

"Don't be too hard on him, Seena. The boy's desperately in love. You know that. He's so young and sort of innocent that he probably had the wild idea out at the farm that he and you would just stay on there. It seems so utterly absurd to us but to him it would seem real. So the sale of the farm and your coming here was a big jolt to him. Can't you talk kindly to him and explain that you couldn't ever love him or even think of marrying him? But be nice about it."

"Nice! I've told him all that a dozen times and he doesn't even seem to hear me. He just goes on and on and I won't stand it. If you hear that I chased him out the gate and threw a brick at him don't be surprised!"

"Be careful, Seena. I don't think either that the boy is quite himself, for he's desperate, wanting what he can't have."

"Lots of us want what we can't have," said Seena bitterly. "And we have to make the best of it. Don't worry," she added, "I'm not going to throw things at Jake but I *am* going to get rid of him soon."

Violet stood up to leave. "Will next Tuesday be all right then for our little fancy-work party?"

"Fine with me. I'm glad you stopped in, Vi. I always feel better for seeing you. I can talk to you, somehow."

"Come up any time," Violet said with quick warmth. "When you feel lonely or worried."

Then, as she walked up the street, she pondered on Seena's problems. For one thing it was incomprehensible to her how time could hang heavy on anyone's hands. For herself there was always in summer the cleaning of the big house, the garden work and the care of Prince. Then there were the happy hours of reading and the even more blissful ones of creation when a poem was coming into being. For she would soon have two more to add to the *book*, if such it ever was. She had finished "The Woods in the Spring," leaving the title unsettled until later when Philip would see it. And she was working upon another village ballad, this time the story of young Jake, which had touched her from the beginning.

She now gave Katie all the news she thought was wise and then, on second thought, returned to the kitchen and told what the Newburt twins had said about young Oliver Coates. It might be better to prepare her. To her surprise and relief Katie stormed in righteous wrath.

"That's wicked an' rideeculous, that! Yon's a good boy an' always a civil tongue in his head, which you can't say of many of them. Now we've got to stop this if we can.

194

The trouble is that if the Newburts have the idea in their heads, there's bound to be talk. Just you wait!"

They did not have long to wait. The signs were put up the following afternoon and at five o'clock Mary Jackson was over, her nose twitching with excitement.

"You didn't tell me you were puttin' up a *reward!*" she began.

"We only decided yesterday. An' how the Newburts got it up this soon beats me. You'd think the ink wouldn't be dry on it yet," said Katie.

"But here's what I wanted to tell you," Mary said, hitching her chair closer. "I was down in the Post Office an' Mr. Gordon just pointed at the window where the sign was. 'Look there!' he said. Well, if it wasn't young Oliver Coates just starin' at the sign as if he was bewitched. His eyes were nearly out of his head. Mr. Gordon said that when Bill Newburt had been in puttin' up the placard he'd told him *in the greatest confidence* that he an' Ed had just wondered a little about Oliver, considerin' what happened at the Festival that time two years ago. After all, he *did* take ten dollars then from the cash box. . . ."

"An' never spent a cent of it but confessed like a gentleman an' gave it back! Oh, if any suspicions like this get around it will be the wickedest thing ever happened!"

"But why would he stare at the sign as if he couldn't stop lookin' at it?"

"I'll tell you. It w's the *twenty dollars* he was lookin' at. He was likely thinkin', that's enough to buy a bicycle. An' I'd like to brain old Oliver for not gettin' the lad one. He's well able. The only tinner in the town an' plenty work all the time. He's an old skinflint an' walkin' up to church every Sunday with his Bible under his arm as if he was an apostle or something. Now listen!"

Katie stood militantly in front of her neighbor. "By the time them reward signs have been up two weeks we'll know, with all that money offered! If young Oliver took the bird, which he never did, you can be sure he'd come an' claim the money by that time, now can't you?"

"Y . . . yes, I suppose so," admitted Mary.

"Well then, what everybody's got to do is just hold their wheest an' pray the Lord to forgive them for imaginin'

195

things about their neighbors, especially a young boy like Oliver. An' Mary?"

"Yes."

"It's to be hoped you won't spread this."

"Oh no," she agreed at once, adding, "Of course I never keep anything from William."

Katie sighed audibly. "An' men the worst gossips by all odds when they get goin'! Oh well. Among them be it, but we'll hope for the best."

As she and Violet talked it over that night a depression settled upon them. They knew by all past experience that already there would be flowing through the town, like a still, small subterranean stream, the half-voiced suspicions concerning young Oliver. When they had said all they could to comfort each other, Katie settled in the rocker with Simon on her knee and her Bible in her hands, as Violet knew to read her *two* chapters.

"If it ain't wicked of me I'll be glad when I get as far as the Psalms," she said. "It'll make my evenings a bit freer-like."

Violet went to her room, as she often did now when darkness came on, for it was easier somehow to write her inmost thoughts to Philip by the soft shine of the lamp rather than in the full glare of the sun. The letters from New York were now coming almost daily and her own were winging as often back. Another change, and a still more subtle one than the altered signatures, was taking place within them. The half-humorous descriptions of life in Ladykirk or in the great city were growing shorter and shorter. Instead, a deeply subjective note was creeping in: their thoughts, their opinions, their most intimate feelings on many subjects. As Violet wrote of these she kept realizing with constant wonder how free the written word was from the normal inhibitions of speech.

So, now she wrote:

You asked how I feel about love, and whether my poem on the subject expressed my own convictions. Yes, it does. I know love may come in different ways to different people. For instance, I am now watching it come to my best friend—I've spoken to you of Faith. The new young farmer in the neighborhood (and a fine person) is seeing a great deal of her. She is very happy but

196

quietly so. I believe she would like to prolong the present stage of friendship indefinitely while love very gradually and decorously comes to them both. I know they will in the end be sure of each other's deep and lasting devotion, but I don't believe they'll know that sudden great burst of unspeakable joy I tried to describe. I wonder if I was over-imaginative about this? Or even—I hate to write the word—unmaidenly, to think of it?

Have I ever told you about the letter from the old great-uncle which came to my mother along with the singing bird as a wedding gift? He said he was giving it to her because he believed that when real love entered the heart it was as though a nightingale sang. I would like, if love ever comes to me, to hear this, and be swept away as by a flood.

His reply was immediate.

Nothing could have made me happier than your letter. Your feelings about love exactly coincide with my own. Indeed I'm going to make you a strange confession. All last winter and this spring I was seeing a good deal of a certain girl.

She's a niece of Giles whose family just moved to the city a year ago. I began taking her out for Giles's sake and then we just kept drifting along. But one night I sat down to think it all over. She's a very nice, attractive girl, but I knew that my fondness for her was merely liking and also, as you say, that I hoped eventually to feel the rushing torrent, and hear the song that never dies within the heart. I was in a bit of a spot because of Giles, but thank heaven I got out of it gracefully, I hope, and no-body hurt. The reason that I'm telling you all this, though, is that only a couple of weeks after the night that I communed with myself and clarified my own feelings your manuscript came to my desk! You can imagine, perhaps, how I felt as I read the particular poem we've been speaking of. It seemed to me that it was heaven-sent to support my own decision. I had wondered occasionally whether I was too romantic and unrealistic. But your words, as it were, supplied me with the viaticum for a wonderful emotional journey I might some day make. You can see why I was so eager to write to you and to learn more about

you. The editor, I fear, was lost even then in the man.
By the way, Giles said one of the poems suggested to
him that you had read Boccaccio. Have you?

To which Violet replied in part:

Yes. I read The Decameron *and* Tristram Shandy *and*
the Old Testament while still in my teens, thus gathering
a fairly good knowledge of the facts of life. But my
father agreed with Ruskin that the best thing for a young
girl was to turn her loose in a library and let her read
anything she pleased. She would eat a few thistles, of
course, but these would be easily digested because of the
excellence of the general fare. Right now, though, guess
what I'm reading, just a little each evening before I go to
bed? Tennyson's The Princess! *I reread it every summer*
because it seems to belong to the warm months. Tennyson
was certainly aware of "God's bright and infinite device
of days and reasons." I'm engaged, as I am each time I
read this, in trying to decide which of the "Songs" in it
is the most beautiful. If you think of it when you answer,
won't you tell me your favorite?

There was plenty to talk about in Ladykirk during the
next week. The reward signs, as Violet had hoped, shook
the town with interest. Twenty dollars was a large sum of
money. At every place of meeting men and women discussed again the theft of the nightingale, with a new and
poignant surmise to add to the original facts. For in
addition to the sly hints of the Newburt twins there was
the testimony of many eyes to add a semblance of validity
to them. Young Oliver Coates still stood transfixed before
the signs each time he passed them, mesmerized it seemed
by what he saw. What could this mean if it were not . . . ?
And yet, many argued, there had been a sight more evidence against Joe Hicks and *he* had been innocent. Of
course in the case of the boy he *had* been guilty once,
that time at the Festival. . . . But gave the money back,
others would hasten to put in. All the same . . . So it
was discussed pro and con while the underground stream
gathered momentum until it would eventually rise to the
surface. That is, until Oliver Coates, Senior, and Young

Oliver would hear of it. But other happenings were to post-pone this.

One hot evening when the air was heavy with a presage of thunder everyone along Main Street sat, fanning, on their porches, hoping for rain to relieve the oppression that would hold until the first lightning flash. Those at the lower end of town whose houses were immediately across from, or just above, the Mill House had been watching with keen interest the arrival, night after night, of Jake O'Dell in his old buckboard, and conjecturing freely upon its implications. Seena wouldn't be thinking of keeping company with anyone at all so soon after John Harvey's death! But *Jake O'Dell!* She was surely a pinch above *that*. But what was the meaning then of all these visits? Of course Seena would have made plenty of "sheep's eyes" at him when he was helping her out at the farm, and even the women grudgingly admitted her great physical attractions. As to the men, they all smiled a bit shame-facedly when the matter came up for there was not one of them who had not been at one time or another super-ficially moved by her beauty. So they said, with con-sidered judgment, that the poor boy was in the throes of calf's love.

It was before the storm broke that night that there was the sound of ungreased wheels, and the eyes on the porches, conditioned from peering into the dusk, discerned Jake tying his horse to the hitching post and going up the walk to the Mill House. Since he usually stayed for quite a while, the watchers settled in their chairs to endure the heat and await his leaving. William Jackson, having been on an errand to his brother Andrew's, near the bridge, was walking slowly up the opposite side of the street, com-menting upon the weather to all and sundry as he passed, trying to ask the inevitable question: *Is it hot enough for you*? before anyone asked it of him.

All at once there was the noise of hurrying feet across the way and an angry voice growing louder and more strident. Jake was half running down the Mill House walk with Seena's white dress in full pursuit. Her words when she reached the gate could be heard up and down the street.

"Now you get along home and never show yourself at this house again! I wouldn't marry you if you were the last

199

man on earth. *I wouldn't touch you with a dirty stick!*
That's what I think of you. Now you get away and leave
me alone. I never want to lay eyes on your face! And if
you ever come back here bothering me again, I'll have the
Squire at you. I'll have you arrested for disturbing the
peace. Now, *you go!*"

And suddenly the storm broke. In the first great flash
of lightning the watchers could see Jake's white face as he
climbed into the buckboard, but the thunder drowned the
sound of the wheels as he turned the horse and drove off
up the street.

It was late when the elements were finally appeased and
William Jackson got home. He went in first to apprize
Mary of all that had passed; then, since Violet's light was
still on in her livingroom, they both came over to tell her
the news. Katie, hearing the voices, came hurrying down
the back stairs in her wrapper.

"An' I'm tellin' you," said William, "I never heard such
a tongue-lashin' as Seena give that boy. I'm dead sure he'll
never go near her again."

"What did he say for himself?" Katie asked.

"Never a word. I guess he was just cowed, an' well he
might be. If you could have heard her! An' the worst
thing she said to him was, *'I wouldn't touch you with a
dirty stick!'* You know that's about the lowest thing you
could say to anybody."

"Tck! Tck!" said Katie. "That's no expression for a
woman!"

"Oh, she said *dirty*," William hastened to explain. "Nothing worse than that, but still an' all it was bad enough."

Violet broke in.

"I know Seena's been having trouble with Jake. She
really had to stop his visits. She told me she had tried to
tell him nicely that he mustn't come in and it did no
good. So I suppose she had to be harsh."

"Well, she was harsh all right, I'm tellin' you. I don't
think she'll see hide or hair of him again."

"An' a good job, I doubt," said Katie. "He's young. He'll
get over it, but Seena's what you might call a temptin'
female. It was no good business her havin' him out there
at the farm, the two of them. Ah, well, it's over an' done
with now. He'll find a young girl more his own stripe,
belike, an' settle down in the tenant house there. Young

200

Halifax says he's a good worker. I'll go put the kettle on now. We'll have a cup of tea before you go."

And the Sabbath dawned, serene and fair, with a pleasant stillness upon the town except for a light breeze that bore within it the scent of the garden flowers and the coolness of last night's rain. In the choir that morning Seena and Violet sat side by side. Before the service began Seena whispered, "I told him off last night."

"So I heard."

"Well, I had to."

"I suppose so."

Then they stood up to sing the doxology.

Robert Halifax drove off after church with Faith in his buggy beside him, and Violet surmised he had been invited to the manse for dinner. She herself had much to think about, far removed from the vicissitudes of Ladykirk. For the answer to her question as to which song in *The Princess* Philip liked best had come back quickly, and in a surprising form. When she drew the letter from its envelope she saw that it had no formal beginning or close. It was a typewritten sheet, headed: Now Sleeps the Crimson Petal.

> "Now sleeps the crimson petal, now the white;
> Nor waves the cypress in the palace walk;
> Nor winks the gold fin in the porphyry font.
> The firefly wakens. Waken thou with me.
> Now droops the milk-white peacock like a ghost,
> And like a ghost she glimmers on to me.
> Now lies the Earth all Danae to the stars,
> And all thy heart lies open unto me.
> Now slides the silent meteor on, and leaves
> A shining furrow, as thy thoughts in me.
> Now folds the lily all her sweetness up,
> and slips into the bosom of the lake;
> So fold thyself, my dearest, thou, and slip
> Into my bosom and be lost in me."

Below in his own handwriting was written: "But I think my favorite line in *The Princess* is this:

> "Ere seen I loved, and loved thee, seen."

His initials were the only signature.

As Violet sat through the bright afternoon rereading the sheet, pondering, shaken with emotion and then checking her wild dreaming, she tried to point out to herself that he had done only what she had asked of him. He had but copied down his favorite song from the poem, which, indeed, was usually the one she finally settled upon as her own choice. She had no reason to find a personal significance in it. But the line below! That was different.

Ere seen I loved, and loved thee, seen.

It was the thought of this line that sent the flame into her cheeks, that kept her from hearing Katie's call to supper and finally almost made her late to evening church. It rang in her mind as she walked across the street through the soft dusk and finally up the aisle to take her usual place in the choir. Her lips sang:

> *"Softly now the light of day*
> *Fades upon my sight away."*

But her heart as going over and over the words on Philip's enigmatic sheet of paper. But oh, *was* it enigmatic?

Seena was not there that night and Violet felt she understood why. The young widow, as she went out, would have had to pass through the group of young men at the church door and then pursue her way home accompanied by her father and mother, thus emphasizing her lonely estate. Faith and Bob Halifax had come in together so he must have been at the manse all afternoon. These considerations kept going through Violet's mind as the service proceeded in its time-honored fashion. But other thoughts, too, kept her from hearing the sermon.

> *Now folds the lily all her sweetness up,*
> *And slips into the bosom of the lake.*
> *So fold thyself, my dearest, thou, and slip*
> *Into my bosom and be lost in me.*

> *Ere seen I loved . . .*

After the benediction Faith caught Violet's arm: "We will walk over to the house with you," she said. Her eyes shone as she pronounced the *we*, and Violet's shone back at her, yet to each other the secrets of their hearts were still unspoken.

As the three went along the walk, Bob Halifax, who had been chatting with the other young men before the girls came out, said, "I hear Seena really lit into Jake last night. I'm sorry for the boy but I know he's been making a nuisance of himself. I tried my best to stop him but I could only go so far. I hope she hasn't scared him off for good though. I mean from these parts," he added laughing.

"Why do you say that?" Violet asked quickly.

"Oh, I meant I hope he hasn't run off and left me in the lurch at harvest time. It would be just like a young fellow his age to clear out, you know, if he was badly upset."

"What happened?" Faith asked anxiously.

Violet repeated in brief what she had heard from William Jackson and then turned to Bob.

"Did he seem all right this morning?"

"Well, that's the thing. He wasn't there. He didn't sleep at the farm last night. He had brought back the horse and the old buckboard he uses, but evidently he had gone on over home. I was in bed early and didn't hear him drive in. I'll check with the O'Dells if he doesn't turn up in the morning. I imagine he thought I'd soon hear about what happened and be embarrassed. But I'll try to be extra kind to him."

"Oh, that's good of you. He'll need a friend just now. Won't you come in?" Violet asked as they reached her gate.

"I believe not, thanks," Bob answered, looking at Faith. "I'll have to be getting back before it's too late. I'm an early riser, you know."

And deeper darkness fell upon the village as a few more hours passed and one by one the lamps were all extinguished. Within the homes, as on every night, some made love, some went instantly to sleep, some lay wakeful, brooding upon the problems of their lives. And over them all the stars shone down, golden, remote, indifferent. They shone upon the Mill House where Seena lay, restlessly tossing; upon the Carpenter home where Violet smiled as she touched the sheet of paper under her pillow;

203

upon the manse where Faith knelt, dreaming, by her bedroom window.

They shone over the calm countryside and the old Harvey farmhouse, now the abode of Robert Halifax. They shone, too, above his spreading barn which lay, on this night, in a deep and curious stillness. Not a breath of air stirred the freshly cut hay in the mows. Not a movement came from the sleeping beasts below in their stalls.

The next morning, as everyone was soon to learn, Bob Halifax rose as usual, grumbled to himself a little over his hasty breakfast as he found Jake was not yet back, then because his heart was essentially glad within him, had gone whistling out to the barn to do the early chores himself. There had been plenty of hay down for the animals over Sunday but now more was needed. He ran lightly up the stairs to the barn floor. At the top he stopped, reeled, and almost fell back. For from a coarse rope thrown over a rafter there hung a *tragic* shape!

CHAPTER NINE

AND darkness fell upon the villagers, a pall of the mind and of the spirit. It was not the fact of death itself. That, to them, as they lived close to each other and to the common round of earthy experience, was not quite the same as to those who dwelt in cities. Nature herself was near to them in seedtime and harvest and in the final fruitfulness of the dying year. So death, with all its sadness became ineluctably linked with the quiet processes of the laws by which their daily lives were governed. There was an acquiescence, as to lightning and blizzard and drought. There was also the comfort that came from their mutuality and the opening of heart to heart.

Even the sloping hillside behind the town with its white stones was a friendly place, for no strangers rested there; all were known, or known of, to the living and had a present immortality in this familiar remembrance. The village lay at the foot of the holy acre, and the smoke curling from the chimneys, the sound of the blacksmith's anvil, the plowman's call to his horse, the shouts of the children at play, were all pleasantly mingled in the summer air that moved among the grasses. They who lay there were close to all they had once known.

So, when death came naturally to the old or unnaturally to the young it was still accepted with a quiet sharing of the grief. Even the sudden taking off of John Harvey had at least been bound up within the common memory. The townsfolk could cite many examples over the years of a farmer's having been gored by a bull.

But the death of young Jake O'Dell was a thing apart from all they had known: a ghastly eerie, black thing, which made the women shiver in their beds and caused the voices of the men on store steps and in the barbershop to reach a lower tone and then sink into silence. For there was nothing in the mind even of the oldest with which to compare it. It stood alone, stark and desolate, against the backdrop of the years. The story of old Pappy Hawkes two generations before, who had been a general reprobate and, according to legend, the Parish Ram, so to speak, and who had taken poison because, as his residuary note stated, "there was no more fun livin'," had long since lost all its sinister quality and if referred to at all was done only as an amusing legend. But Jake! Poor young Jake! Ah, this was different.

After the first day's shock the thinking of the village began to penetrate the lives of those most intimately affected by the tragedy. Mr. Lyall, of course, had the hard part that first morning of going out to the farm along with Dr. Faraday and Mr. Hart, the undertaker. Of course there was nothing the doctor could do but there had to be a certificate. Someone had seen Bill Price, the coroner, drive out, but there wouldn't be much for him to do either. Mr. Lyall, though, had not only to go where there was trouble but *to stay with it*. What would the town ever do without him, people wondered. Some said a suicide wasn't supposed to have Christian burial, but Mr. Lyall had said firmly that Jake would have a funeral service like anyone else and it was to be at the O'Dell's the following Tuesday. He'd have to be buried in the Poor Ground, though, at the very top of the cemetery for the O'Dells couldn't afford to buy a lot. What that large and shiftless family felt about it all now, no one could conjecture.

But poor Mr. Halifax! They said he was taking it hard, and no wonder. Just new on his farm and John Harvey's accident hardly out of his mind yet likely—and now, this! They said he was staying over at Jeremy Lyall's at night. Oh, it must have been a terrible shock to him! There were those who wondered whether he might sell the farm and just get clear of it all, with such memories to rise up in him every time he went up to the barn floor!

But after these earliest considerations, placed around the circumference of the tragedy, were spoken from one end of the town to the other, there was a steady radial drawing in of opinion toward the very center of the darkness: the *cause*. And that cause was Seena.

Mary Jackson sat in the Carpenter kitchen on Tuesday morning with Katie and Violet, their faces all saddened and drawn.

"And they tell me," she said, "that Dr. Faraday's been to the Mill House *twice* and the neighbors got it from Mrs. Harris herself that he says Seena has to stay in bed and keep takin' these pills to quiet her down. They all say she's takin' this worse than John Harvey's death. She had hysterics then at the time, of course, but she soon got over them an' you know the day of his funeral how she marched out of the house, bold as brass with her widow's veil up, an' her face bare as your hand an' never a tear in her eye."

"Aye, she's a strange one, that," Katie sighed, "but this ought to bring her to her senses if anything will."

"I think I'll go down to see her tonight," Violet said soberly.

"You can save yourself the trouble," Mary Jackson said, "for the neighbors there all tell me Dr. Faraday says she's to see *no one* till he gives the word. I guess she's bad. Well, I pity her, sort of. It's a terrible thing to have on your conscience."

"Oh," Violet burst out ,"I hope everyone will pity her. She never thought of bringing on anything like this. Jake was just beside himself. Oh, it's all too horrible. I wish this day were over."

The tears ran down her cheeks and Katie spoke sharply. "Vi'let ain't fit to go to the funeral! Look at her! I can't thole it myself an' I'm old enough to bear up. I tell her there's no sense in thinkin' there must be a bit music. It won't do Jake any good now an' what'll those O'Dells care one way or the other? But there's no dealin' with her. She an' Faith Lyall, they're bound they'll go, but what they'll ever find to sing at a time like this beats me."

"I thought I'd told you," Violet said. "We're going to sing. 'There's a wideness in God's mercy, like the wideness of the sea.' That should include poor Jake."

"An' Mr. Hart says," Mary Jackson put in, "you'd be surprised how nice Jake looks. He says he drew his collar up real high. . . ."

"Oh, Mrs. Jackson, *don't!*" Violet said with a sob and abruptly left the kitchen.

By evening everything was over. Violet and Faith and several of the other women had taken garden flowers so the new grave in the Poor Ground was covered over with bloom when the first dew fell upon it. The girls, as they drove out to the O'Dell place, had come closer to sharing their new confidences than they had yet done. Faith spoke with such tenderness of Bob Halifax that her own feeling was plain, and Violet, in answer to a question, had said that she was not in love with Mike but was somewhat interested (what an understatement!) in the young editor who was handling her manuscript. They had merely exchanged letters, she added. But because of the tragedy that faced them they said no more about themselves and began to speak of Seena. Faith said her father had been to see her and he thought her condition was serious. She had spoken wildly of being a murderess and then had lapsed into a stony silence which he could not break. He had done his best and would go back again. No one else was allowed to see her.

"It's so very much harder to bear anything you bring upon yourself than something which just *happens* to you," Violet said musingly. "I feel so sorry for Seena for, while I know she was indiscreet in leading Jake on, it wouldn't be once in a million that anything like this could have come of it."

"I think," Faith said, "that there is something about Seena that almost sets a man crazy when he's in love with her. It was that way with John. Even the day when he talked to me out in the field, when he was so unhappy, I could see that he was still terribly in love with her and would do anything she asked. It's strange how sad life can be. And yet, how wonderful," she added half under her breath.

As the days passed, the town slowly recovered from the impact of the calamity, aided by the curative properties of constant conversation. Even this ghastly event which had taken place must gradually be made a part of the community pattern, in that it had happened to one of their number. Little by little the women ceased shuddering in their beds at night as they pictured it; the men in their groups spoke more matter-of-factly regarding it. Besides, when the subject of Jake had been drained dry, there were others to hold the public interest. There was Seena, first and foremost, and her strange withdrawal now into herself; there were the reward notices for the nightingale, which had yet elicited no response except to rivet suspicion upon the boy Oliver Coates, who had still kept stopping to stare at them until he began to notice the inquiring gaze of the townspeople upon him as he passed. Then he had colored to his hair roots and taken to traveling the back alleys. Something very strange, very questionable here, people said. And of course, as everyone knew, the boy had once . . . But if he *had* taken the nightingale why did he not manage to return it and get the reward? For one thing, the men said, his father would skin him alive if his guilt came out. Old Oliver was a hard man. Maybe the boy was just waiting until he had devised a way to return the bird without incriminating himself.

Violet went about her daily duties, charged with various emotions. So many, indeed, that she felt torn by them. Several letters had come from Mike, filled with optimism. He was finding he had a gift for salesmanship. He *liked* selling, and for the first time was taking a real interest in the pickle business. In his last he had mentioned that when he saw her next he hoped she would notice a change in him—and approve it. Poor, dear Mike! Violet thought. Which of course, were not the words which would rise to a girl's mind about the man she loved. Indeed, she was much more engrossed at the moment by the web that was weaving around the boy Oliver. One evening while she was up at the manse Mr. Lyall had

208

spoken to her of the situation. He was deeply concerned. It seemed that Oliver Senior had become aware of the suspicion in connection with his son and had been heard to say that he'd get the truth if he had to thrash it out of him. When Mr. Lyall heard this he took action. He went to old Oliver and told him that if he laid a hand on the boy for this reason the matter would be brought up in the church Session!

"I didn't know whether I dared do such a thing," Mr. Lyall confessed, "but I took a chance and it worked. Oliver is very proud of being an Elder and this seemed to give him pause. So he's promised now to restrain himself. But the boy! You don't believe he did it, do you, Violet?"

"Heavens, no! I'm fond of him and I really think he's fond of me. I *pity* him. I've been trying to think of something to do for him to offset all this. Oh, if only the nightingale could be found!"

"Yes, that would solve our problem. I've puzzled over every angle of the mystery and there seems no solution. It's absolutely baffling. If I hadn't been so close to young Oliver, over the last two years especially, I would be inclined to say this was *it*. The wonder is that it wasn't thought of before since he has helped you now and then. The boy could easily have been alone at some hour in your house; he knew where you kept the nightingale; he could have walked off with it in his pocket and hoped for a way to turn it into money, since he wants a bicycle with something close to desperation. You see? All the pieces seem to fit, combined of course with the memory of the poor boy's one understandable defection, for which he fully atoned. I can see how suspicion gathers and grows in the town. I've often felt like paraphrasing the Biblical statement and saying that here if you plant a *zephyr* you may reap a whirlwind!"

They both laughed and then grew grave again.

"I know that boy," Mr. Lyall went on. "I'm sure he's honest. And the trouble is this may all hang over him until the nightingale is found."

"If it ever is," Violet sighed.

"I'll try to keep the checkrein on old Oliver, and if you can think of any way to help me cheer up the boy I'll be very glad," Mr. Lyall concluded.

As Violet neared her own home that day she was

209

struck again by the shabby condition of the iron fence which ran around two sides of the square plot upon which the house stood. A fine, strong fence it was, having held up under the storms and sun of many years, but the black paint was now peeling, leaving reddish patches beneath it on the bare iron. She had planned to save enough money during the coming winter to add to the small fund she already had set aside for the painting of the house trim and the fence by next spring. Now another idea occurred to her. She went into the house and rang the Coates's number.

"Mrs. Coates?" she said. "This is Violet Carpenter." She could hear the older woman's intake of breath.

"Oh, Violet, this has about broke my heart. You know what they're layin' on young Oliver?"

"Nonsense!" Violet said matter-of-factly. "Don't listen to such talk. What I called for was to ask Oliver to stop by this evening after supper. I'd like him to help me with some work. Will you tell him?"

"You want *young* Oliver, Vi'let, even with all that's goin' round about him?"

"I certainly do!" She felt like adding that she wouldn't want *old* Oliver on a golden platter. "Just send him along—and, Mrs. Coates, don't pay any attention to any silly rumors. Look at what was said about Joe Hicks, and not a word of truth in it. Now, brace up. You surely trust your own son."

"I'll tell his father what you said, Vi'let, an' I hope it'll do him some good. The boy will be there tonight, I'll promise you. An' thanks, Vi'let."

It was strange, Violet thought, how certain she was that young Oliver was innocent. Even in the case of Joe Hicks she had had one or two fleeting doubts in view of all the circumstantial evidence against him. Now, as Mr. Lyall had said, there could be made a strong case against Oliver, and yet she could not believe it. There had always been something pathetic in the boy's attitude toward her.

"Do you mind?" he had asked her once, "that time I fell in the run right after school when I was a little kid an' I was scared to go home with my clothes all wet? I went back to you and you dried me out by the stove and then let me help you clean the blackboard. I never forgot that. You were always awful good to us kids, Miss Vi'let," he had added, shyly.

When Oliver arrived that evening he looked hunted.

"Miss Vi'let, you *know* . . ." he began.

"Of course I know, Oliver," she said briskly. "Now I want to talk to you about some work. Our iron fence needs painting badly. Do you suppose you could do it in the evenings? When are you finished with supper?"

" 'Bout six o'clock. We eat early. And I'd have nearly two hours before dark," he added eagerly.

"It's a big job for it will have to be well rubbed down first where the paint has been peeling and then the bare spots touched up before you start the real painting. And it's a long way round."

"I can do it, Miss Vi'let. Honest I can. I'd like to."

"Well, I think if you can it will be worth about fifteen dollars to me."

The boy's face shone. *"Fifteen!* Oh, Miss Vi'let! I've got eight saved up, little by little. And my mother might give me two. That would make enough for a . . . a bicycle! The reason I stared so at those reward signs was that I was thinking, oh if I somehow could find the nightingale and get that money. But now, it's going to be real, not just dreamin'."

Then suddenly a cloud crossed his sun. "It won't work," he said. "My father'll make me spend the money for clothes. He's done that before. I've saved up my eight dollars unbeknownst to him, and it's taken me a long time."

Violet patted his shoulder.

"Now listen," she said. "This is going to be our secret. I won't pay you anything until the work is finished. Then you and I will drive into Harrisville one day and do a little shopping! When we get back I'll go in home with you and tell your father that I planned the surprise, and take all the responsibility. You are going to work for me only in your normal free time, and I am the one who will be paying you, so I think we have a right between us to arrange for spending the money, don't you?"

For answer the boy turned aside, removed his glasses and ran his knuckles across his eyes.

"I'll start on the scrapin' right off," he said in a muffled voice and went out.

"There's an old stiff brush in the stable next to the currycombs," Violet called after him.

After that, each evening at six o'clock young Oliver could be seen working steadily at his task. It was ten days before the scraping was finished; then, the paint having been secured, he started in, painstakingly and with considerable skill, upon the job itself. Violet watched him with satisfaction. Coupled with her sympathetic interest in him was the delightful thought of ultimately getting the best of old Oliver, which few people had ever done. But if she had hoped that her hiring the boy to do this special work for her would allay the gossip concerning him she was mistaken. Mary Jackson put it concisely on one of her calls.

"As I just said to Mrs. Hummel, I said, if that ain't like Vi'let. Givin' that boy a job when he's likely the very one that took the bird! Just because she's got such a kind heart, I said."

"Aye, she has that an' all," Katie agreed. "If she was suppin' with the devil she'd give him the first bite!"

"Oh, come now," Violet laughed. "That's not true at all. I needed the fence painted and Oliver's doing a fine job. Who else could I have gotten to do it right now when Hal Strong's so busy working on barns and big jobs? Besides, Oliver's as innocent as any of us and I do hope people will soon stop talking."

"Well," Mary said with incontrovertible logic, "*somebody* stole the nightingale and if that boy doesn't look guilty I've never see anyone that did. He goes and comes in the alley whenever he can, and when he has to go on the street or into a store he turns red as a peony when anyone even looks at him."

"Can't you see why?" Violet asked with spirit. "He's heard now what people are thinking and he's embarrassed to death."

"And well he may be," said Mary. "I still think you'll find he's the one, an' William thinks so too. Who else could it have been? I've thought the town over an' so has William an' Oliver seems the likeliest. The Newburt boys are sure of it. William was in talkin' to them the other night, an' they said the boy had been in there once early this summer on an errand an' when he saw a bicycle they'd been fixin' he said he guessed he'd do *anything*

212

in the world to get one. They both remembered him sayin' it."

"What if he did?" Violet asked. "That means nothing. Any boy might say that about something he wanted badly! Oh, do stop blaming Oliver!"

"Well, well," Mary said, "I've got to go home but William wondered if you ought to have the Coates's house searched. Get a warrant from the Squire mebbe."

Violet turned away, knowing argument was useless. Only time and new evidence could stop the clamor of tongues. Eventually it would cease, she knew, in connection with Oliver, but then, oh, who next would fall under suspicion? She herself was caught up of necessity in the very center of this tangled web of circumstances. Would she ever be free of the distress, she wondered? Free to feel completely the warm and lovely emotion which like a tide was rising ever higher and higher in her heart.

It was ten days before Dr. Faraday said that Seena could see a few people, but only her closest friends at first. Mrs. Harris called Violet to suggest she come down that afternoon.

"You're the one she's asked for," she added.

As Violet went along the walk to the Mill House, the scene of her last call there rose to her mind with suffocating vividness. She could still hear Seena saying with determination, *"I'm going to get rid of him!"* And the other picture which the witnessing neighbors had drawn of Jake, being driven with hard and burning words to his buckboard on the fatal night itself, seemed now to her equally real. A feeling of actual faintness threatened her. She struggled to master it and rang the bell. Mrs. Harris came at once and seemed eager to talk to her.

"Sit down a minute, Violet. Seena's up in her room. She stays there most of the time. Oh, this last has just been too much for her. I know she made mistakes but we blame ourselves too. Harris has been terrible. He can't sleep either. You know Seena wanted him to talk to Jake, sort of man to man, and he wouldn't do it. He told her she had to run her own affairs. Now he feels if he'd only done it things might have been different. But then again you never know. . . ."

"Of course we don't, Mrs. Harris. And you mustn't

any of you keep on blaming yourselves. You must try to forget. Is Seena better?"

"I just don't know," her mother said. "She's eating some now, but not enough. She's still in a bad way. Go on up now if you want to. Maybe seeing you will brighten her up a little."

Violet went up the stairs and paused at the open door outside the big room which was Seena's. Seena herself was sitting, listless, in the rocking chair by the window. She looked up but she did not speak. Violet went toward her and took her hand.

"Seena, how are you? I've wanted for days to come to see you. Don't talk if you'd rather not. I'll tell you what little news I have."

She sat down and began recounting in detail the story of young Oliver and of her giving him the fence painting to show her trust in him. As she spoke she kept looking at Seena in wonder. The girl's beauty had always seemed due to the violence in her coloring and to her dynamic animation. Now she was white; she was still; and yet the beauty was stronger than ever. What strange power was latent in this girl which caused her personality to be projected upon others whether they would or not? Especially, Violet added in her mind, upon men. For as she watched her now, even she, another woman, could feel the force of the attraction of that pale face with the smouldering black eyes and frame of dark hair. Below her carelessly opened wrapper there was the hinted perfection of her full, rounded breasts.

When she had exhausted her news, Violet leaned toward her friend.

"Seena, are you . . . are you feeling better?"

"How can I?" Seena said heavily. "How can I ever feel better? I killed him. How can I forget that?"

"But you *didn't*, Seena. Even if you encouraged him when you were out at the farm. Even if you pretended you liked him and . . . and *flirted* with him a little, just think how many girls have done the same thing with men and with no such result as this with Jake. Can't you see that? Even admitting you did wrong, it was something in Jake himself that caused the gragedy. You *must* believe that."

"I can't," Seena said tonelessly. "I can only see the facts. You know what I think of when I go to bed? I see him

214

coming in from the field with his face and neck all tanned and warm. And he'd be laughing and wanting to kiss me. I let him once or twice then, God help me. His body was so strong and *alive*. And now I think of it lying up there in the Poor Ground and all that will happen to it. And I go crazy. I can't sleep. I don't think I ever will again. What right have I even to go on living when I've done that to him?"

"Seena, you must *try* to control your thoughts. You must think of other things. We all have sorrow, you know, and we have to bear it. If you will only go out a little it will help to put other normal things in your mind. Won't you come up some afternoon as I suggested before—maybe just you and Faith and I—and well, sew on something for Kitty's *shower?* We'll want to give her one before too long. Won't you come? Maybe on Thursday?"

But Seena shook her head.

"I'm too heartsick," she said. She paused a long moment and then added, "There was something I wanted more than anything in the world. Now, after this, I know I'll never get it. So, all in all, I don't care much whether I live or die."

Violet bent swiftly and kissed her friend.

"Please don't say that. As the days pass you'll feel differently. I'll come back soon."

"Yes," Seena said, "do. I can talk to you. That's something."

As Violet went home she wondered what it could be that Seena had wanted with such intensity. Had it been remarriage? Had she been thinking of leaving Ladykirk to find some sort of position elsewhere and now feared the sad story of Jake would pursue her and prevent her from carrying this out?

But it was not this question which kept recurring to Violet as the evening wore on. It was what Seena had said of Jake as he had been in the warmth of his vigorous young body, and as he lay now. . . .

The night advanced as usual. Katie read her two chapters in the kitchen, put Simon out and went up the back stairs. There were no "transhens" at the moment to be considered. Violet read for an hour in the living room; she sat for a time on the front porch, trying to feel at peace; then she put out the lights, went up to her room and prepared for bed. But once there she could not sleep. The

215

agonizing thoughts which she had been holding in abeyance now overcame her. The hours kept striking on the grandfather's clock at the foot of the stairs. At last she got up, lighted her lamp and got tablet and pencil.

Dear Philip (she wrote):
This is one of my dark, my blackest nights. I am sitting here by the window with the tears running down my cheeks, thinking that unless I can speak to another human being of the burden that lies on my heart I shall die of it. And you are the only one to whom I can speak. It is the terrible fact of mortality *which racks and tears me and will not let me rest. My beloved dead! I cannot endure the thought of the dissolution of the body! I cannot accept it. Oh, how can humanity bear this anguish and go on about the business of living! And yet I know that by tomorrow my own tears will be dry. I will see the sunlight and hear the mourning doves and gather the flowers in the garden. I may even sing a little and laugh. But once in a while, between the normal level of the days, come these black nights. My mother! With her bright smile and her soft hair curling about her face. My father! With his scholar's forehead, his quiet eyes and strong, tender hands. That these should become dust. . . . Oh, Omar was right. It will take much to drown the bitterness of this. As to my poem, "Oh Paradise," I tried to believe it when I wrote it. Tomorrow, perhaps, I will believe it again. But tonight I do not. It eases my heart a little to be honest and yet it leaves the essential pain greater than ever. For if I could only know, if I could only feel sure that the spirit itself survives. . . .*

Forgive me. I should not be burdening you with my private tortures. I wonder if, as an editor, you ever receive surprising confessions from authors to whom you are both friend and stranger? Whose lives you so profoundly touch because books represent so much of a writer's spiritual existence. Do you? I need not say that I am writing you now because I've grown to count upon your unfailing understanding.

Even as I have put this on paper, the blackness has lifted a little. I could lighten it still more if I dared go down to the piano and play some Schubert or the one thing of Bach which I know and love. But before I would more than strike a chord Katie would be upon me to see what was the matter.

"Playin' the piano at three in the morning! Get along back to bed now before you rouse the neighbors."

I don't know, as I've told you often before, what I would do without Katie. She is so dear and so necessary to me, and yet living with her only emphasizes my mental loneliness.

Perhaps I will not post this when morning comes. If I do I shall most certainly regret it. But if you ever receive it, oh, please answer! Tell me how you yourself feel.

The reply came as swiftly as was possible.

My heart aches (Philip wrote) to think of you alone and weeping in your despair. If only I could do something, say something to help you! At least—as you already know—I have suffered the same sorrow as you. And also, which you do not know, I have gone over the same road of anguish, of doubts and fears. As to the return of the body to the earth, there is no comfort except that which you yourself unconsciously mentioned: that we, the living, must continue to do our work in the light of the sun, as happily as may be, knowing that we and those we have lost are all bound up somehow together within the great framework of nature.

But as to the life after this one, here I have something I want to say to you. No one can prove the existence of the soul after death, but by the same token no one can prove that it does not so exist. Did it ever occur to you that the most difficult thing to prove is a negation? I remember hearing that once, and it has been of the greatest help to me. You could not, for example, prove that you never committed a murder, could you? A ridiculous example, but it illustrates the point. A negation of any kind slips through our fingers. There is nothing in it upon which we can catch and hold. So, I have reasoned this way: if the proof of the negative is as impossible as the proof of the positive in relation to immortality, why may we not with full intelligence rest our minds and hearts upon the latter? For my own part I have always had the greatest pull toward faith and believing. It is constructive; it is therapeutic; it

217

has vital force, and in the long run may get us nearer to the truth than doubt.

Did you ever hear of the old Scotch dominie who was asked his opinion in connection with the problem of immortality? He said he had an idea we would wake up after this life, look around and say, "Well, who'd 'a thought it!"

I wish I were with you that we could talk together. I long to be of even the slightest help to you. And this brings me to something I've been wanting desperately to ask you. I took part of my vacation at Easter but I have ten days left, and according to the office, the most convenient time for me to use it is the latter part of August. May I spend it in Ladykirk? You once mentioned an old hotel there. I feel I must see you before much longer. Perhaps you can guess why. In addition to my personal reasons I will have by then a full report and decision on your manuscript. I'm afraid I will be a bit nervous now until your answer comes.

It was Violet who was nervous as she penned it. Her hand trembled slightly as she wrote the few lines which she rushed to the Post Office.

Your letter brought me more comfort than I can ever tell you. Thank you, from my heart.

As to your coming to Ladykirk, I will be delighted to have you do so. But when I told Katie of your plan to stay at the hotel she was absolutely aghast.

"Stay at the hotel!" she said. "He'll do no such thing an' you can just tell him for me. Us with this big house to make him comfortable an' me to see he gets plenty to eat. He stays right here," she ended, "or he doesn't come at all!"

So you can see you have no choice. It will be fun having you join Mr. Herbert and me at breakfast! As to the proprieties, Katie is the most militant chaperon in the world. So, let's consider it settled, shall we?

With her heart singing within her, Violet entered upon August. In the small calendar in her own room she checked off the days. She knew her own feelings now beyond the possibility of a doubt. It would seem that Philip knew his, also. A radiance fell upon her which more

218

than one noticed, and Katie shrewdly decided that more had been going on between her charge and "this publisher fellow" than she had known. Her dreams of being linked to the great pickle factory receded.

"Ah, well," she sighed to herself, "that young Mike was a couthy chap an' all with a good business at his back, but we'll wait and see what this other one's like."

Violet herself still had disturbing thoughts concerning Mike. She decided at last to prepare him for her own state of heart. She phrased her letter gently but confessed that now there really *was* someone else. His reply was characteristic.

I knew it (he wrote) *after that last evening, but since "it is natural for man to indulge in the fond delusions of hope" (aren't you impressed with that quote? I had to commit it in college) I did keep on hoping. But what you have written me at least did not come as a complete shock. There is one thing which will ease my disappointment somewhat. I've found something I can do pretty well and I like doing it. My father wants me to take quite a swing around the states this fall so in seeing so many new places I may be able to forget Ladykirk a little (as if I ever could!). I would like to come out once more to say goodbye, if I may. I promise you I won't be mushy. Have some others in at the time if you prefer. I just want to see you again. I wish I had been made of different clay but I guess I'll be a pickle manufacturer to the end. Bless you always!*

Mike

Each evening young Oliver worked with steady, painstaking care upon the fence. Now that Philip was coming, Violet felt enormous satisfaction in the undertaking. The new paint would give the whole place a fresh and well-kept look. It was surprising what a difference it was making already.

As to Seena, the town was close to forgetting both Oliver and the nightingale for the time being in its steady concentration upon her. It was known that Dr. Faraday and Mr. Lyall were both alarmed and had consulted together; for Seena, instead of coming gradually back to normal living, seemed to sink deeper and deeper into her morbid remorse. She had told several people that she didn't care whether she lived or died, and once had even said something about "a life for a life." This was all serious enough, but as of last week a new and terrifying aspect had been added. Each day in the late afternoon Seena had taken to walking slowly down to the Mill and climbing to the top of Miller's Rock. Here she would sit for perhaps an hour, staring into the whirlpool below.

She always got up quietly after a time, and walked home, but everyone was frightened.

Mary Jackson added details. "The neighbors down there saw her father those first days try to hold her back but she just shook off his arm an' climbed up on the rock. Of course it's about the best place she could pick to get the sun, and heaven knows she needs it. She's still stone-white, I'm told. But for her to sit there lookin' into the deep-hole after all she's said about not wantin' to live . . . it certainly looks bad to me. You can see how Harris couldn't use *force* on her, for she's woman-grown an' everyone says they're afraid to cross her for fear she'll do the worst right off!"

"Aye, that's seerious, that," said Katie. "I don't like the looks of it."

Violet said nothing but decided to see Seena before another day went by. The early peaches were beginning to ripen, and she had promised Katie that she would drive up to the Four Points soon and get a bushel from one of the farmers there. She would leave, she thought, after an early lunch, and would stop at the Harris's as she returned in the later afternoon. She would try to reach Seena *before* she started down to the Rock.

She harnessed Prince and set off as planned. It was a mellow August day and as she jogged along she thought with an almost suffocating joy of the drives she and Philip would take when he came! She would show him all the loveliest views of the countryside. They would stop on the sunny hilltops, from which vantage points could be seen the wide harvest fields, now richly golden, with the far mountain ridges making a blue horizon to the east. They would drive slowly through her favorite woods, perhaps taking a picnic with them to eat beside the little stream there. Oh, she would show him every spot she loved! And all the while there would be the new physical closeness after the separation of the miles!

Then at home there would be the gay meals, for she knew they would laugh much together, and the evenings on the porch swing as they would sit looking into the soft darkness, speaking of grave and beautiful things. Her heart was one great burst of happiness as she contemplated all this!

Perhaps it was because her thoughts were so engaged that she did not urge Prince along faster; perhaps it was the delay at the farmhouse in getting the peaches; but in any case the afternoon shadows were slanting as Prince finally clattered again over the heavy planks of the covered bridge which led into the town. Violet looked at once to the right when she emerged into the sunlight and then swiftly turned the horse into the Mill yard. For there on the top of the Rock Seena was sitting, with bare feet hanging over the edge!

From the moment she saw this, everything happened so swiftly that Violet could recall it later only as a blur. For even as she got out of the buggy, determining to go up to the Rock, she saw Henry walking along the path which led to the back of the Mill. It went through her mind vaguely that this was Friday and Henry was coming as usual for fresh bran for his mother. Then, under her very eyes, and of course under Henry's, Seena suddenly stood up and jumped into the whirlpool below!

For one fraction of a second Violet and Henry both stood frozen. Then, throwing off some of his clothes as he ran, Henry tore toward the Rock, climbed it, kicked off his shoes and dived into the deep-hole, while Violet ran screaming into the Mill.

"Mr. Harris!" she called frantically, *"Mr. Harris! Get a rope! A rope!"*

The miller, his face as white as his coat, needed no explanation but rushed to the back of the Mill, with Violet behind him. On the platform there was a coiled rope. All ready, she remembered afterward. All too ready! He grasped it and started for the water.

"Henry saw her and dived in," Violet panted as she ran beside him. "He's a good swimmer. He'll save her."

"I'd had my eyes on her," Mr. Harris said through stiff lips. "I just went inside for a minute. . . ."

They had reached the water's edge beside the Rock and saw two heads raised with difficulty above the foam. Henry was battling toward the shore where the stream, while still deep, was reasonably calm. He was holding Seena up with one arm and striking out strongly with the other. Mr. Harris threw out the rope and Henry caught it; then the miller, bracing a foot against the base of the rock, pulled steadily, and slowly, slowly—it seemed an eternity to Violet—the two in the water neared the shore and managed, with the help of both Mr. Harris and herself, to climb out upon the grassy bank. Henry was breathing hard, and Seena, her eyes closed, her thin clothes sticking close to the contours of her body, leaned against him, her head on his shoulder, her long hair falling around her like a wet, dark cape. Henry's arm still held her to him.

"I . . . could have made it . . . myself," Henry said when he could speak, "but it's . . . tough going . . . there. Thanks . . . for the . . . rope."

Mr. Harris's eyes overflowed. "Thank you, Henry," he said simply. And then, "Are you all right, Seena?"

Seena opened her eyes and nodded to him and to Violet. Then she looked up into Henry's face with a smile of such sweetness that Violet involuntarily took a step back, as though she had witnessed something she should not have seen.

"She'll be fine in a little while," Henry answered for her. "We're both just . . . a little . . . winded yet." He drew her closer. "She's trembling. It was pretty cold down . . . there."

"I'll run up to the house and get a blanket," Violet said, glad for any action. "I'll only be a minute."

She ran to the Mill House and at sight of Mrs. Harris's anxious face burst out with the good news first.

"She's safe and sound. Henry dived in after her and Mr. Harris threw him a rope. Don't worry. I think now Seena may be different . . . better, you know. Maybe she felt she *had* to do this and now it's over. Just give me a blanket to put round her and maybe you could have some hot coffee ready for them when they get here. . . ."

Mrs. Harris was a practical woman. She didn't delay to ask questions. She got Violet a blanket and hurried to the kitchen, though her face twitched and her hands shook.

"It's a terrible shock to her just the same," Violet thought as she ran back again to the creek bank. Here a

222

group had now gathered: two men who were coming to the Mill on their own business, several women who had seen or heard the excitement from their porches, and some ubiquitous small boys. They were all standing about in a strange quiet as though there was nothing appropriate to say. Henry grasped the blanket and put it about Seena's shoulders after he had raised her to her feet.

"She'll be all right," he said, looking with grim distaste at the small crowd about them. "I'll take her up home."

"I'll help you," Mr. Harris said quickly.

But Henry shook his head. "No need," he said, "I'll see to her, and you have your work waiting you here."

Violet came close. "I'll go up along," she said quietly.

"Don't bother, Vi," Henry said. "The less fuss the better. I'll take care of her."

So the group parted in silence and Henry and Seena passed through. They moved slowly along the walk, Seena's head drooping against Henry's shoulder, his arm still holding her close. They reached the Mill House and entered the door before the watchers took their eyes from the strange sight.

There was plenty of conversation then in the Mill yard! Violet answered some of the questions and parried others while she went toward Prince, who, having tossed his head free of the checkrein, was calmly nibbling the grass near him.

"That's really all there is to tell," she concluded to the women still eagerly crowded around her. "Yes, I saw everything myself for I'd just driven into the yard here. But now it's all over. Safely over," she added as she got into the buggy and turned into the street.

But when she reached home, and had put Prince safely in his stall, she found her legs shaking beneath her as she went up the walk to the kitchen. She sank into a chair while the nervous tears poured down her cheeks. Katie flew to put the kettle forward, since to her mind tea was the panacea for all ills.

"What's wrong with you?" she kept repeating. "Tell a body, for heaven's sake, what's botherin' you!"

"It's the reaction," Violet managed to say at last. "I feel pretty shaken."

Then she told the story while Katie listened with her black eyes snapping.

"So she really did it!" Katie said when she had heard all. "Well, I doubt if she ever tries it again. This may have given her scare enough to quieten her down. I can see how she figured. She waited till Harris went into the Mill an' then she jumped! Never thinkin' that you an' Henry would be there. Aye, an' a good job it was you were. Specially Henry. Well, well, no wonder you're shook up. I feel sort of doncy myself. We'll have a cup of tea now to fettle us. I doubt Mary'll be over soon to get the *dee*tails."

She came about eight. William, it seemed had worked late and so Mary, for some strange reason, which she resented, had not heard the news until he got home. One new fact she had now to add to the others. Henry had stayed on at the Mill house.

"Of course," she said, "you can see how Mrs. Harris would keep him for supper after what he did. That would be the very least thanks she could give him. But they always eat at five o'clock. It seems funny he's there yet."

"There *yet!*" Katie exclaimed. "How do you know?"

"Well," Mary said with gentle cunning. "I called up the Martins just now and asked to speak to Henry. I told his mother I just wanted to say he'd done a brave deed an' she thanked me an' said he hadn't come home yet. So, that's how I know! William's gone downtown. He said a few of the men were sittin' on the store steps waitin' for Henry to congratulate him. They can see the Mill house from there," she added, "so he can't come out without their knowin' it. I'll be over if I hear anything further. I still can't figure why someone didn't tell me right away when it all happened." She looked reproachfully at her neighbors.

"I was so upset, Mrs. Jackson," Violet said, "and so was Katie when I told her. We couldn't talk about it at first." And with this Mary had to be content.

Violet went early to bed and fell almost at once to sleep. This last week had been tense with fears concerning Seena. Now the deed had been done, but with a safe issue. She thought of the smile on Seena's face as she had looked up at Henry. Perhaps the awful fear that must have gripped her when she was engulfed in the whirling water had given way, with her rescue, to thankfulness and a new acceptance of life. Violet drew a long breath of relaxation

224

and relief while the conscious world melted peacefully away.

The next morning, however, Mary Jackson was over before breakfast.

"I just had to tell you the latest," she said breathlessly. "You mind I said William was goin' to wait on the store steps last night till Henry come out of the Harris's. He said there was eight of them there waitin'. Well, it was *twelve o'clock midnight* when they saw him come out the door an' cross the street. When he got up to them old Nappy Newton—you know what kind of a tongue he's got —William says he just give a sort of cackle an' he said, 'Well Henry, I hope you've got paid for savin' Seena's life.' An' Henry just said, 'I have. In full,' he said, an' walked on lookin' neither to right or left of him like a man in a trance. William said they were all just struck dumb, kind of, an' nobody said a word of what they were all plannin' to say. Now *what* do you make of that?"

It was at this point that the telephone rang and Violet, thankful for the interruption, hurried into the living room to answer it. It was Faith on the wire.

"Vi," she said, "there's something I have to tell you right away. If I start down now along the back street, can you come to meet me?"

This was a system they had devised years back when they feared a special secret might be overheard beneath a roof.

"Of course. I'll start at once."

As she went, Violet wondered what could be on Faith's mind, for her voice had been quick and almost frightened. She was greatly disturbed, evidently, about something. Surely nothing had gone wrong with her friendship with Bob Halifax! Even so, she would hardly call up at this hour to discuss such a matter. No, it was something else, perhaps in a way connected with the dramatic events of yesterday. But what could it be? She went on, puzzled.

When they met, Faith still sounded agitated. "Let's walk along the creek bank," she said. "I want to be sure we're alone."

"What is it?" Violet asked. "Do tell me. I'm anxious."

"I didn't get home till late last night," Faith began, "for I was out at Jeremy's, so I didn't hear about Seena—and all—till then. But when I woke up this morning I suddenly remembered something I've got to tell. I haven't even spoken to Father yet. I thought I'd come first to you. Vi, *Seena can swim!*"

"Oh no!" Violet said, drawing back as though her friend had struck her. *"No!* How could you think such a thing?"

"It was soon after the Harrises moved here," Faith went on, more quietly. "She'd been up at our house and I walked back along, right here, to show her how pretty the creek is at the bend and she asked if anybody boated on it and I told her we never had an then she laughed and said, 'I suppose you've never gone swimming either,' and I was sort of shocked. I told her no girls ever did. And then she said she had learned up in Venango County where they used to live, She said her older brother taught her—the one who still lives there. Their mother made them wear clothes of some kind, but she and this brother practiced every summer when they were children and on into their teens until she was as good as he was. She said of course now she was grown up she'd never think of doing it, but she added, 'Of course when you once know how to swim, *you never forget.*'"

Faith stopped for breath and then went on. "I was interested just for the moment when she told me but that was all. It was like any story you hear about someone else's childhood. It didn't seem important to me, and I literally never thought of it again until this morning. Then it came back, and, Vi, it changes everything!"

Violet's normally gentle face had hardened.

"Then it was a trick! A low, cheap, deceitful trick! And she did it to try to catch Henry. If you could have seen her looking up at him and *leaning* on him as if she was half dead! And he was being taken in by it completely. I see it all now as plain as can be. Oh, I *hate* that girl! As if she hadn't done enough damage already! Now to try and snare Henry by such a nasty fraud, I won't *have* him deceived! He's too good for that. Something's got to be done about it."

"That's what I thought, Vi, and I felt you were the one to do it. Henry would listen to you when he wouldn't to most people."

"Oh," Violet cried as if in pain, "how could I possibly tell him? Just think what it would do to his pride alone.

Now he's a sort of hero. In the eyes of the whole town he saved Seena from drowning. Suppose he finds out the whole thing was a put-up job? I know Henry. He would be furious that he'd been made a fool of, but he'd be sort of crushed too. For of course, before long, somehow, the truth would leak out, and there would be plenty to poke fun at him."

The girls talked on while the creek in its quiet upper reaches flowed on below them as though there was no such thing as a whirling deep-hole farther down. At last they parted and Violet walked back home alone, her mind seething with uncertainty. This that she had heard had devastating implications. While she could not *love* Henry she had for him a real affection, dating from the days they had walked home from school together. She often wondered now, with something like a shudder of relief, how she had had the courage to refuse to marry him! But if that refusal had hurt his pride, how much more would this revelation which she felt must somehow be made!

Katie was full of conversation when Violet returned. Mrs. Hummel from the corner had run up for a few minutes, and Maggie Dunn also. Katie repeated delicately the gist of their words.

"Of course he might just have meant that Seena had *thanked* him . . ."

"But that wasn't what Nappy Newton was talking about an' Henry just seemed to agree. . . ."

"It wasn't like Henry at all, but after all he *did* save her life and . . ."

"Well, if he didn't mean it the way it sounded, what *did* he mean Payment *in full!* Now I ask you!"

Violet made small reply. Even when Katie said, "You know Henry as well as anybody. What do *you* think?" Violet did not answer but went on up to her room where she sat down to weigh possibilities. She had to make a decision and a prompt one. The easy way, of course, was to do nothing; to trust that future events would bring their own clarification. But time might work against Henry. She thought again of Seena's smile and of his close, protecting arm, and her anger against Seena surged within her. The truth, she finally thought, never did any harm; it was deception that was fraught with danger.

In the early afternoon she called the hardware store. It was Henry who answered.

"Hello," she said, her breath catching on the word. She hadn't expected this sudden fast beating of her heart.

"Why hello, Vi" Henry's voice came naturally but with unusual warmth. "Say, you were wonderful yesterday, getting the blanket and all. I should have called you up to thank you. Seena's pretty good today. I looked in around noon."

"Henry, I would like to see you, this evening if you can come up. It's important. There's something I want to talk to you about."

There was a noticeable pause as though Henry was startled and considering.

"Just for a few minutes," Violet added.

This seemed to reassure him, though his reply was a trifle stiff.

"All right. I'll come around seven. But not for very long," he added.

He was as good as his word. On the dot of the hour Violet heard his footsteps cross the porch as they had done so many times before. When she met him at the door she saw he was dressed in his Sunday best, even to his sailor hat. When she offered politely to take the latter, he declined.

"Don't bother," he said, "I won't be staying."

They entered the parlor and he sat down on the very spot from which he had, only last May, asked her to marry him. He laid his sailor primly on his knee and stared inquiringly and, it seemed, a little fearfully at Violet. *He looks as though he's afraid I've changed my mind,* Violet thought with an odd twinge of mirth. Then the seriousness of the occasion fell again upon her.

"Henry," she said slowly, "I don't know how to tell you this and yet I feel I must. As you once said to me, we were close friends for a long time, and we shall always, because of that, be interested in each other even though I . . . even though we . . . I could never, for instance, stand by and see you deceived or . . . or hoodwinked, and do nothing about it."

Henry's face was expressionless.

"So, there's really no point in trying to lead up to it.

228

I'll just give you the fact which I've found out. Henry, *Seena can swim!*"

His countenance did not change. "I know it," he said.

"You *know!* Who told you?"

"She did," he answered simply. And then for a long moment they sat staring at each other, Violet's eyes amazed, Henry's thoughtful.

"I'd sort of like to tell you all about it, Vi. What's past and gone between us does make us close in a way. I know you'll keep it to yourself, and I don't think Seena would mind. Well, it's like this." Henry leaned forward, twirling his sailor between his hands.

"When I took her home yesterday I carried her upstairs and then I sat down and we began to talk. And we talked till midnight. Mrs. Harris made us both eat a little and then we went right on. I never knew a man and a girl could tell each other everything they felt, everything they thought even, the way we did last night." He looked down, as though remembering, and then went on.

"This sounds like blowing my own horn or something but Seena said the first time she saw me after they moved here she knew I was the man she wanted to marry. But then you and I were as good as engaged, everybody thought, and so did I, and I didn't pay much attention to Seena one way or another. Then when John kept pressing her to marry him she thought mebbe that would get her mind off . . . off me and she took him. But it didn't work. She couldn't . . . stand it. When she asked me after he died to go out and take inventory for the sale I just went because I was sorry for her, and then . . ."

He paused and Violet waited.

"When we were there just ourselves all at once I was the one who sort of went crazy. And I fought like a steer against it. I hated myself. For one thing I'd just asked you to marry me, and then there was John, my friend, only a few weeks gone, and I knew I was in love with Seena. But Vi, you'll have to believe me it was all so different from anything I'd ever felt before. I . . . I don't know how to explain it. This just swept me clear off my feet. I'm ashamed to tell you, after . . ."

"Oh, Henry, I understand. Better than you can imagine!"

229

"You *do?*" he said in surprise. "I thought you'd feel hurt somehow after what had passed between us."

"Not at all. I know exactly what happened to you. The trouble with us was that neither of us was really in love."

"I know that now all right," said Henry, "but I'm sure relieved that you know it. Well, I've kept fighting it ever since, mostly from thinking about John. I was hardly even civil to Seena. And I couldn't sleep nights for thinking of her. It's been that bad with me. When the business of young Jake came and I heard how she was taking it, I felt I just had to go to see her but I still made myself hold back. Then she got this idea of jumping off the Rock just when she knew I'd be coming along. It didn't look as though she turned her head yesterday, but she saw me before she took the leap. And I tell you it *did* take courage even if . . ."

He stopped and eyed Violet sharply.

"How did *you* find out she can swim?"

"From Faith Lyall. Seena happened to mention it just after she first came here."

"She's forgot it then, for she thought nobody knew. Even her father and mother didn't realize how good she was. They used to think it wasn't quite decent, you know, for a girl to go swimming like that, so she usually slipped off and practiced on the Q.T. She said she'd swum clear across that creek up there and back many a time and they never knew. I wondered myself after we were out yesterday why she hadn't been more of a dead weight on me. It's a rough spot, that deep-hole, for even a good swimmer, and I was glad enough to see the rope. Well, anyway, that's the story."

"And you mean now you're . . . happy, Henry?"

"Vi, I never dreamed there was happiness like this in the world. You know we always said nobody could understand Seena. Well, I do now, for we talked our very hearts out last night. We're made for each other. Of course out of respect for John we won't be married till the year's up . . ." He looked off across the room as though forgetting Violet's presence. "That is," he added, "if we can wait."

Then he flushed and stood up.

"I've got to go," he said, "for I told Seena I'd be in

about seven-thirty. It's a relief to me that you don't hate me, Vi, even when you know how it is with me."

For answer she held out her hand and he took it in his strong clasp.

"I hope you'll be as happy some day as I am," he said.

"I think I will be," she answered, smiling.

"That Mike fellow?"

She shook her head, and knew by his expression that he was really incurious. "Tell Seena I'm *so* glad for both of you!"

"I'll do that," he said, his usual matter-of-fact countenance breaking into positive light. "And thanks, Vi."

She went with him to the porch, where he faced her suddenly. "You and Faith . . . you won't say anything about . . . the swimming? It would make it look sort of bad for Seena."

"Never a word," Violet said. "You know you can trust us."

"Good!" he answered and started off.

She watched him as he went down the back street—the quickest way to the Mill House. All at once he looked back, saw her, then waved his hat above his head exultantly.

When he was out of sight she still stood, reviewing all she had just been told. Then, although there was no one there to hear, or to have understood them if there had been, her words were audible on the evening air.

"I would never have thought it possible," she murmured, "but I believe *Henry* has heard the nightingale!"

CHAPTER TEN

As AUGUST advanced, a smiling peace descended upon the old town. After the stresses and strains of the last weeks the villagers relaxed to enjoy the normal accompaniments to summer's ending. It was the time of fruitfulness when trees and gardens yielded their bounty for skilled housewives to capture and store for the coming winter's use. Rich smells of pickling and preserving drifted upon the air. Women whose lives knew no outstanding fulfillments now surveyed rows of canned fruit and glasses of jelly with pride. Outside in the maple trees the cicadas kept up their rich, comfortable monotony of sound.

It was now known that Henry Martin was going regularly to see Seena! This would have been cause enough for conjecture and criticism if it had not been for his spectacular rescue of her, which the general public took at its face value. Men and women reminded each other that the old saying was that if a man saved a woman's life she ought to marry him if he wanted her—and of course if they were both free. Everyone felt sure there would be no talk of marriage yet awhile on account of John, but maybe as time went on this would really be a match, and the cure for Seena. For she was beginning to go about again, and there was a noticeable new gentleness in her face. Pretty as ever, indeed, but not in a *forward* way now. She was changed, that was sure, with all she had gone through, and for the better. As to Henry, everyone said he had never seemed in such high spirits, even before Violet turned him down.

"Well, well," Kate remarked one day, "among them be it, but it does begin to look as though those two would either make a spoon or spoil a horn!"

And while most of the town were unfamiliar with the Celtic proverb, they would have agreed with the substance of it.

Violet had quietly taken down the Reward signs. Time enough had elapsed for the test and nothing had come of it. With the placards no longer in evidence, the talk about young Oliver had died down a little, and conversation had settled into more pleasant channels. The most exciting of these was the spreading news, until now well kept, that Amanda and Joe Hicks were going to have a baby!

Katie flew through the house one morning to find Violet.

"What do you s'pose I just heard from Mrs. Hummel! Will wonders never cease! Amanda Hicks *is going to nurse!* An' them ten years married!"

Violet allowed her face to register proper surprise and Katie left her quickly to go over to Mary Jackson's.

Even the men discussed the marvel but in barbershop language.

"Well, I guess little Joe finally made it!" one citizen would say to the other, grinning.

"Yes, time an' perseverance an' the mouse ate the table," a townsman would reply with a guffaw.

But while their remarks savored of crudeness, in their hearts they rejoiced for Joe, and—without mentioning the matter to him while it was still women's business—they received him with extra cordiality to their midst when he joined them.

Yes, the warm calm days flowed on during these weeks as peacefully as the upper reaches of Ladykirk Creek. Squire Kendricks was heard to remark that he thought the millennium had hit the community for he hadn't had a shot-gun wedding nor a fence-line dispute now for nearly a year. Of course there was still the mystery of the nightingale but if it never *was* found, the incident would be woven into the fabric of the village as many another strange happening had been.

Violet herself was not merely content with the passing days (except for remembrance of her loss); she was so full of eager joy that she trembled a little for fear it was too great to know fulfillment. Then she chided herself as she recalled her father's remark once that the wickedest lines ever written were from the old hymn:

> *We should expect some danger nigh,*
> *When most we feel delight.*

At least she would never sink to that superstitious pessimism. But the wonder of the thought that Philip was actually coming, and coming, she was sure, as a lover, seemed almost incredible bliss. He had written that he had bought an auto!

"I've wanted one ever since I saw the first one years ago. I'm learning to drive the thing now and if I don't break an arm cranking it I really think I'm going to do pretty well. I'm outrageously proud of it and can't wait to take you for a ride, of course I'm going to use it to get to Ladykirk rather than the train. I've gotten goggles and a huge duster, and quite fancy myself as a regular speed demon. As a matter of fact I've once been up to thirty but am usually never over twenty-five per. I will

*have to take two days for the trip, but I'll extract a couple
of extras from the company to make up time. I think it
will be fun to have the auto there for our drives but
please tell Prince not to be hurt. I will want some trips
behind him too. I'm practically counting the hours. . . ."*

Another excited note came soon after, saying that the
last report on the book had just come in! It was highly
commendatory, suggesting only—as Giles had done at
the beginning—that the author would delay publication
until several poems of lesser significance had been replaced by others more in line with the general quality
of the work as a whole.

"We'll talk it over," he wrote, "when I come."

Violet was surprised at her reaction. She was happy,
delighted, of course with the news, but she found that
it now took second place. How strangely the heart could
redistribute its emphasis! But how could she bear such felicity
as Philip *and the book too?* She tried to control the wild
abandon of her thoughts.

There were a number of loose ends to be gathered up
before the time for the visit arrived. She carried out her
plan for the small sewing group to meet in the relative
seclusion of the Carpenter front porch to work on offerings
for Kitty's shower, which should take place, the girls decided, just before the wedding in September. When Violet
approached Seena once more about joining them she
found her only slightly hesitant.

"I guess I could come," she said slowly, "I think I'll
crochet a big centerpiece for her table. I'm quick at that."

"Wonderful!" Violet had answered, both surprised and
pleased. There was about Seena still a pale quiet which
contrasted sharply with her former vivacity, but with it
there was something like the rest of a spent but winning
runner, a contentment as of a long desired goal reached
at last. A line from Chaucer rose to Violet's mind as it
had often done before in connection with Seena. *Bold
was her face, and fair, and red of hue.* But only the fair-
ness could now apply.

The girls gossiped comfortably as they all sat with
their fancywork behind the screening honeysuckle one
afternoon. It was a gladsome little group, each with her
own private reason for happiness: Faith, Peggy, Lucy,

Violet—and Seena. For now, at least Violet knew, the latter, in spite of the burden of her memories, must also be accounted among those blest by love. Of course the news of Amanda and Joe Hicks was discussed at length. Old Becky Slade, it had been learned, was starting already to make a trundle-bed quilt that was to surpass all her formal needlework triumphs.

"Ten years before it happened!" Lucy said, though, Violet noticed, without envy. "Just imagine! I used to be afraid before I was married that I'd have a baby so soon all the old women would be counting on their fingers. Now I don't have to worry about that."

She smiled as she said it and Violet wondered. . . . But Lucy vouchsafed nothing more, and the remark seemed to pass unnoticed. Because of Seena's presence there was no reference to Bob Halifax and the farm. Indeed all the other girls were making a noticeable effort to avoid mention of anything that would disturb her, but rather to encircle her with kindness. She talked more as the hours went on, and a faint color came into her cheeks.

Violet had received a letter that morning from Mike. He asked if it would be convenient for him to come out Saturday evening of the following week. So now, after the lemonade and cake had been served and the girls were putting their crocheting and embroidery back into their work baskets, Violet broached the plan she had been considering all day.

"I want to ask you," she said, "if you can all come to a little party Saturday night of next week—the boys too. Mike is coming out."

There was a chorus of teasing cries but Violet spoke seriously.

"No, there's not a thing between Mike and me. Please, girls, believe me. But he doesn't know when he can get out to Ladykirk again for he's leaving next month on a long selling trip. He's met you all and likes you, and of course he's an old friend of Ninian's so I thought it would be pleasant for him if you could come when he's here. I'll ask Kitty and Howie, and Bob Halifax, and . . . Henry. What do you think?"

"I'm sure we can," Peggy said at once. Lucy agreed and Faith also. Seena hesitated.

"You'll come, Seena?" Violet asked.

"I'd like to but I don't know whether it would look right. After everything."

"It will just be a quiet party of our own crowd. Those of us who always go together. I'm sure it would do you good, and certainly all of us would think it was right."

Seena smiled shyly. "I'll let you know a little later, Vi."

When she's talked it over with Henry, Violet thought to herself after the girls had gone. Strange that her independent spirit should now be deferring to another.

Meanwhile Katie had begun upon a campaign of thorough cleaning though, as Violet told her, everything was in nice order already.

"I'll just give it a touch-up," Katie replied. Which consisted of polishing every exposed surface, washing all the windows and laundering all the curtains in the house.

"They were all clean in May," Violet protested, "when we first began to take tourists."

"Three months it's been. They need a bit freshenin' even if your publisher man wasn't comin'!"

"Mr. Haversham, Katie."

"Such a name to get your tongue round! What's his first one?"

"Philip."

"Aye, that's not too bad a one. I'll be usin' that."

So in the mornings, before the heat of the coal range grew unbearable, Violet and Katie took turns in the kitchen with the big flatirons, until there lay spread on the dining-room table and chairs great drifts of white scrim for all the upstairs windows. The lace curtains, of course, were carefully attached, scallop by scallop, to the pins of the wooden stretchers leaning now against the wall of the back porch.

"Well, it's been a big job an' all," Katie admitted, "an' I've been thinkin' we might get Mag to give us a hand for an extra day with the rest of the work. We've done pretty good with the transhens so far this month. Of course we can't take anyone in while your young man's here."

"Mr. Haversham, Katie."

"I never heard such a name! It wouldn't be *Irish,* think you?"

"Old English, more likely."

"Well, well, I 'spose he can't help it either way. The

236

first boy I see passin' I'll give him a flour sack for candy an' send him back to Mag's."

But the surprising reply came that Mag was sick in bed.

"That's a funny thing, now," Katie said. "She's always been strong as a horse an' never sick in her life as I know of. Of course she's not young, Mag. I doubt she'll be rubbin' seventy-five or so. Well, we'll just have to do our best. I *had* thought we'd wash down all the wood-work."

"Katie, that's ridiculous!"

"Well, well, it can go I guess. I don't want you all tired out when he comes. We'd better get to your dresses as soon as the curtains are up. I wonder what's wrong with her?"

The next afternoon, with a basket of eatables on her arm, Katie set off to find out, but when she came back she was sober.

"She looks poorly-lookin' to me, Mag. She's lyin' there with no list in her, an' she says she's just wore out. I think I'll slip back now an' again with a few vittles. We'll never miss them an' I doubt she doesn't cook much for herself. Ah, well, we'll just have to make out without her on the work."

Even as the house took on day by day a newly refreshed look on the inside so, with the painting of the fence, the outside steadily assumed a rejuvenated appearance. Oliver was now on the last lap of his job, and he and Violet discussed the details relating to the purchase of the bicycle in the evenings after his work was finished. The boy always looked carefully about him and lowered his voice even here on the Carpenter property as he spoke, and the sight of his hesitant fear made Violet more than ever jubilant that her plan would outwit old Oliver.

On a Friday evening the last brushstroke had been applied and Violet with her young workman walked slowly around the yard eyeing the fence from every angle.

"Excellent!" she said while he blushed under her praise. "I doubt if a real painter could have done it better. Now for the trip to Harrisville. What about going tomorrow?"

Oliver's eyes grew wide. *"Tomorrow!"* he echoed, as though the gates of heaven were opening too suddenly "As soon as that?"

"Why not?" said Violet. "Couldn't you tell your father that I need you? Aren't you off early sometimes on a Saturday?"

"I will be tomorrow for my father's goin' to do some work on the kitchen sink in the afternoon."

"Well then. You be up here by one o'clock and we'll be off. The only problem is how to get the bicycle home when we've bought it. Perhaps it could be tied to the back of the buggy."

"Oh, Miss Vi'let, I'll *ride* it back. I've learned for years now on the other fellahs' bikes. But it ain't like having one of your own," he put in earnestly. "If I ever have a bicycle I think I could ride it *round the world!* Honest I could!"

"There are a good many hills between here and Harrisville," Violet smiled.

"I can make them," he said. "I'll never know they ain't level ground if I have my bike."

"I believe you could," she said, "and Prince and I will keep alongside you as well as we can. All right, it's all settled. You come tomorrow with your money, and we'll go!"

But by eight o'clock that evening there was a knock at the side door. When Violet answered it, young Oliver stood there, his eyes red behind his glasses, his face white. He stammered his bad news.

"It's n-no use, Miss Vi'let. He's taken my eight dollars!"

"Oh, Oliver! What do you mean?"

"I was counting it again to put in my purse for tomorrow. I thought he was downtown. He come in and caught me. He was awful mad that I'd saved it up behind his back. He . . . he said I w-was *deceitful* and he took it all for to buy my school clothes."

He blinked back the tears. "And now my mother's scared to give me even the extra two dollars, and besides it wouldn't be enough."

Violet put an arm around his thin shoulders and he made no resistance. In fact for a moment he leaned against her in his despair, as though unable to stand up under it.

"Oliver," she said, her own voice not quite steady, "I'll have to think about this. But don't give up hope! Maybe we'll still find a way."

238

"I guess it was just too good to be true," the boy muttered, and then turned around as though he could trust himself to speak no further.

Violet went back to the kitchen, her anger seething within her, to pour it all out to Katie, who was now on her second chapter with Simon festooning her shoulder. When she heard the story her black eyes grew blacker.

"He's a *Beelzebub*, that's what he is, Oliver Coates. I wonder the Lord don't strike him down. An' him a church Elder. If they weren't in for life, he'd never get another vote from me, I'll tell you. It shows how a man can be mealy-mouthed on the outside and be black in his heart. Well, what's to be done now?"

"I was thinking like this," said Violet slowly. "I would have had to pay anyone fifteen dollars or more for painting the fence. And I am *so* glad to have it done just now. I really owe Oliver something extra for that. Then, if the signs had brought back the nightingale, I would have had to pay the twenty dollars reward. Of course I didn't get the bird but I am twenty dollars richer than if I had. I wondered if I dared take ten of that to put with the bicycle money. Oh, I can't bear that boy's disappointment."

"Take it!" said Katie promptly, "an' a good job too. We'll not let that old Pharisee get the best of us. An' if we can live *with* that ten dollars, we can live without it! So I say, go ahead!"

Violet stooped and kissed the old woman's cheek impulsively. "You're such a comfort, Katie. Now the trick will be to get the bicycle home."

"Why don't you try Josiah Hunt? He makes a trip to Harrisville now an' again. If he was goin' anyway I doubt he wouldn't charge anything, an' you could mebbe ride in with him."

"I'll call him this minute. Oh, if I can get this put through as a complete surprise to young Oliver himself, it may be much better than the other way. Now he'll not be an accomplice at all, so if old Oliver is wrathy it will be only toward me. I declare, I believe it's all going to work out for the best!"

"Aye, God moves in a mysteerious way. Get along now an' call Josiah!"

That worthy gentleman, eager for business and full of

curiosity as usual, appeared promptly and settled himself on the living-room sofa.

"Well now, Vi'let, what's on your mind that won't wait till mornin'?" he asked.

"Can you keep a secret?"

"I've kep' several in my day. You have to in my work. I've delivered some boxes that looked pretty funny comin' to a Temperance town an' I've just looked the other way and kep' my mouth shut. An' I've seen some folks takin' the train separate-like that I suspicioned would be gettin' together later on, an' . . ."

"I know you're very discreet, Mr. Hunt, and you're kind, too. That's why I want your help."

She told him then all the story of young Oliver and the bicycle, and of what she hoped to do about it. Josiah twisted his long dew-laps in consideration.

"I got an errant I have to do in Harrisville some day soon. Could go tomorrow as well as any time. An' I'll tell you what. I know a fellah that's got a bicycle shop down on Spring Street. He'd do well by you. Got all kinds."

"Oh, Mr. Hunt, that's wonderful news for I didn't know where to go without shopping round."

"Yep. I'll take you there. Tell you, Miss Vi'let, seems like I'm goin' to enjoy this here little jaunt. Old Oliver done me a mean turn once. Don't know whether he meant to or whether it was an accident, kind of, but I never forgot it. An' I've always liked the kid. I never thought he took your singin' bird. An' he ought to have his bicycle. So, sposin' I stop for you tomorrow forenoon after I get my last deliverin' done. Say, nine-thirty, thereabouts?"

"Fine, and I do thank you."

As Katie often remarked afterwards it seemed like a special *dees*pensation of Providence, the way things worked out the next day. Josiah came at the time appointed to pick Violet up. They reached Harrisville at eleven o'clock and drove straight to the shop. Here, in an incredibly short time, Violet purchased a second-hand bicycle, now repainted and shining, for *twenty dollars!*

"It wasn't used only six months," the proprietor explained. "The boy's family moved out west and he had to turn it in. Of course I have to make a reduction on it but I can promise you it's good as new."

Josiah, who had supervised the purchase with freely

vocal interest, then put the bike in the back of the hack and drove on about his *errant*. Violet, elated past all telling, hurried to Main Street and ran up the steep, tobacco-and-dust-flavored stairs to Mr. Huntley's office. She had not seen him since the day she and Katie had called in their first despair over the lost treasure.

"Why, Violet!" he exclaimed. "You look radiant! Have you come to tell me the nightingale's found at last?"

He held her slim hands in his own, and feasted on her young loveliness. "Sit down and tell me all about it."

He listened carefully as she recounted the details of the mistrust which had surrounded Joe Hicks, his proven innocence, and then the suspicion which had fastened itself on the boy Oliver.

"And you're sure he's not guilty?"

"Yes, I am. I can't quite explain. . . . My feeling wouldn't stand up in a court of law."

Mr. Huntley raised a finger.

"I've seen more *hunches* correct in my time than supposed facts. By the way," he asked, "do you know how we came by that odd word *hunch?*"

"I haven't an idea," Violet smiled.

"Well, I'll tell you. Long ago the gamblers had a superstition that it brought them luck if they touched the hump of a hunchback. Look in your Webster and you'll find it. The history of words is a hobby of mine."

"It was one of Father's, too."

"Yes, we used to swap queer ones now and then. But as to the nightingale, I have my own *hunch* about that."

"Oh, what, Mr. Huntley?"

"I still think it's in the town and will eventually come to light, and that in the simplest way possible. Knowing Ladykirk as I do, I don't believe it was what we might call a dramatic theft. Now this boy would seem to be the perfect solution of the mystery only you say he's *not*."

"No, I'm sure of it."

Mr. Huntley thoughtfully rubbed the side of his nose.

"That story of the bicycle touches me a little. I'm an old bachelor but I like boys. And I know what it is to have a father who holds the purse strings tight. I grew up on a farm, and my terrible longing was for a colt of my own. I never got it. So I'd like to make a contribution toward the bicycle. You say he's really earned fifteen dollars?"

"Yes."

"Well, it's a very small amount but I want to add the extra five. Don't refuse, Violet. It isn't for you. It's for the boy, and it will give me pleasure to have a little finger in the pie."

He opened his wallet, drew out the bill and handed it to her.

She hesitated a second and then took it.

"Since it's for Oliver," she said, "and thank you very much. I must go now for Josiah will be waiting for me soon in front of the Courthouse. He has to be back to meet the afternoon train. It's been wonderful to see you, Mr. Huntley! You've made me very happy."

"It looks to me," he said shrewdly, "as though something else is operating for your happiness. Am I right?"

"Maybe. If I ever have any news you'll be one of the first to know, and thanks again for everything."

She reached up impulsively and kissed his lined cheek.

"Thank *you*, my dear," he said. "That will warm my heart for a long time."

Violet found Josiah and his hack already at the appointed spot, and they were soon jogging along the familiar road back, eating the sandwiches Violet had provided and discussing the disposition of the bicycle once they reached the Coates's home.

"Tell you what," Josiah said, "when we get there, I'll unload the bike, wheel 'er up the walk an' lean 'er again' the house. You can go to the door if there's nobody outside an' I'll wait round too, an' see what happens."

Main Street looked deserted as they finally entered the town. Nappy Newton sat alone sunning himself, as was his wont, on the store steps; aside from that, porches and other steps were empty since it was too early for general relaxation. The Coates house had no signs of life about it as Josiah took the bicycle out and wheeled it into the yard. Violet, feeling suddenly more nervous than she had dreamed possible, crossed the front porch and rang the bell. Mrs. Coates came, wiping her hands on her apron.

"Is Mr. Coates in?" Violet asked hurriedly, "and young Oliver?"

"Why, yes," the woman answered, staring incredulously into Violet's smiling face. "They're in the kitchen, workin' on my sink."

242

"Could you tell them to come out? I have something to show you all together."

Mrs. Coates caught Violet's arm. *"The nightingale?"* she breathed.

"No, but something else nice. Will you call them?"

In a few minutes they were all on the porch. Violet felt her throat tighten. What if old Oliver became very angry? What if he even refused to let the boy accept the bicycle? She pulled herself together and began, drawing upon her brightest expression.

"Mr. Coates," she said, "you know Oliver here has finished painting my fence. It was a big job and he's done it splendidly. Haven't you noticed it as you passed?"

"I guess it ain't *too* bad," he admitted grudgingly.

"It looks wonderful and I'm delighted. Now I've noticed that young people are often more pleased over a gift than over money itself so that's what I've done to pay Oliver. I've bought him a present. Won't you all come down on the walk and see it?"

Her hands felt clammy and her heart was racing but something told her to play a winsome part.

"There!" she said gayly. "What do you think of it, Mr. Coates?"

Young Oliver was speechless and Mrs. Coates was babbling incoherently.

Old Oliver's brow was very dark indeed.

"Miss Vi'let," he began sternly, "I told Oliver I would never . . ."

Violet caught his arm as though they were conspirators.

"I know," she nodded meaningly at him, "I understand how you felt, but you see this is my gift, and I've tried so hard to keep it a surprise." She came closer and looked up at him with all the blandishments of Eve. "I want you to check it over now and see what you think of it. I do so want you to be pleased." Her tone implied it had been bought for his express delectation.

Now old Oliver was a man and human; and it might be added that Mrs. Coates, while an estimable woman, was not noted for her beauty. To see a young and pretty face raised so close to his own in trusting deference was a new and exhilarating experience, enough to cause an unaccustomed warmth in his glacial veins.

"Just look it over," Violet was coaxing. "You see," she

lowered her voice, "it's really a second-hand one, but it was only used six months and it's been all repainted. I think it's a bargain but I do want your opinion of it before I'm satisfied. What do you think?"

Old Oliver, impelled toward the bicycle by a delicate pressure on his arm, examined it gingerly.

"Seems O.K. to me," he pronounced at last.

Violet clapped her hands. Castenets, she felt, would have expressed her mood better. "Oh, then everything is all right. Get on it, Oliver," she said, turning to the boy, "and let's see you ride it."

"What have you got to say first?" his father asked gruffly.

"Thanks, Miss Vi'let! Thank you . . ."

"You're more than welcome. You earned it. Now just enjoy it."

They all stood watching as young Oliver wheeled the bicycle to the sidewalk, bestrode it and rode off into his Paradise.

"How well he does it!" Violet commented. Then, turning to old Oliver, she extended her hand. She wanted to get away now as fast as possible.

"I appreciate your being so kind and so understanding about my gift, Mr. Coates. You have a fine boy and it's been a pleasure to have him work for me."

"An' you don't hold all the talk again' him?"

"I certainly do not. It's ridiculous. Good-bye, Mrs. Coates." Her smile here was not forced. "Good luck to all of you!"

She fairly ran down the walk to where Josiah, in earshot of course, was waiting.

"Give you a lift home?" he asked.

"Oh, please," she said as she crawled hastily into the hack on the driver's seat as though afraid old Oliver might still change his mind and pursue her.

Josiah waited until they had passed up the street and then, throwing his head back, he laughed uproariously.

"By gum an' by golly," he said when he could speak. "If I hadn't seen that with my own eyes I wouldn't have believed it even if the Reverend himself had told me. To see you makin' eyes at Oliver Coates an' him just meltin' down like a piece of butter on a hot griddle! Wait till I tell the men in the livery stable about *that* tonight!

Yessir, that was the best piece of play-actin' I ever seen in my life, danged if it wasn't."

"Oh, Mr. Hunt," Violet cried in distress. "You said you'd keep the secret. Please don't say anything that would be embarrassing to me . . . or to Mr. Coates, either. *Please*."

"Now, don't you worry. I can say you got young Oliver a bicycle to pay for his work, can't I? An' that I took you in to get it? All right? Well, then, I'll say that, just as old Oliver was gettin' his back up about it when you told him, you looked at him so gol-durned purty an' beseechin'-like that he softened down. I can say that, can't I? I can say there's more ways of tamin' a wildcat than shootin' him. An' I may *wink*. I won't promise I won't *wink*, but furder than that I won't go. Well, here we are," as he drew rein at the Carpenter's house.

"You done a good day's work today, Miss Vi'let, an' no mistake!" he added.

"And you, Mr. Hunt! How can I ever thank you for your part?"

"No need," he said. "Sure enjoyed it all. Specially the last part!" And he drove off, still chuckling.

Violet went inside and sank wearily into a chair as Katie rushed to meet her and hear the news.

"I've been the world's biggest hypocrite," she said, "but it seemed the only way possible to get results, so I hope I'll be forgiven." Then she launched into the details of the trip.

"Well, well, the Lord was with you," Katie pronounced with satisfaction. "An' to think you only had to spend the fifteen dollars an' no more! Aye, that's a good job, that. An' I doubt Mr. Huntley'll never miss the five he give you. I've always heard he's well fixed. So, you got the best of old Oliver?"

"At least I think he's going to let the boy keep his bicycle. I don't believe it agrees with me to dissemble, though. I feel as tired as if I'd done a two weeks' wash!"

"An' speakin' of the wash," Katie said, "I took a runback to see Mag while you was gone. I think she's bad. She's got a poor look to me. I did what I could for her an' I'll be goin' soon again. Mebbe a rest will fettle her but I think either Mr. Lyall or Dr. Faraday ought to know about her, just in case."

245

"I want to see Mr. Lyall anyway to tell him about the bicycle. I can go up this evening and then I'll speak about Mag. Poor soul! We'll have to do what we can for her."

"Oh, I 'most forgot to tell you I saw Billy Wade sniffin' round the orchard this mornin', pacin' it off along the front as though he was measurin' it already. He didn't come to the house so I couldn't very well say anything but my blood was risin' I can tell you. The gall of him! You've got till September anyway before he comes after you again, haven't you?"

"Yes. September."

"Well, you know what you can tell him then," Katie said as she went back to the kitchen.

Violet walked over to the west window and stood looking out at the old fruit trees. In May the thought of losing them had been like a stab in her heart. Now, all in these last weeks, the orchard, like her precious book itself, had become less important than—something else.

At the manse that evening there was jubilation over the story of the bicycle. In the safe and congenial group Violet told it all.

"I'm ashamed to say it but I really sort of flirted with old Oliver," she confessed. "I simply *had* to get him on my side. It was probably wicked of me."

They all laughed delightedly, and Mr. Lyall said, "I absolve you. Entirely. My only regret is that I wasn't there to see it."

Then he grew serious for a moment.

"Oliver Coates is really a good man. I'm sure he would go unhesitatingly to the stake for his religion if necessary, and he's honest and upright as the daylight, but he lacks a kind heart, and in the long run that's more important than martyrdom, I guess. Well, I'm more pleased than I can say over your triumph, Violet, and I assure you," he added twinkling, "that the end quite justified the means!"

Violet and Faith withdrew later to the parlor to discuss the coming party on Saturday night. All the guests had accepted, and Faith said that Bob Halifax was stopping to pick her up.

"You do l-like him, Faith, don't you?" Violet asked.

"He's very nice," Faith answered primly, and then, as

246

though feeling the inadequacy of her tone at least, she repeated, *"very* nice!"

They discussed then the matter of entertainment and refreshments, and Violet explained that Mike would probably never be back again and she did want the evening to be pleasant for him, especially since he himself had suggested that she invite some guests.

"What about Seena? Will she come?" Faith asked.

"I haven't heard but I think she will."

"Vi, you've always evaded an answer and I didn't want to press you but I would so like to know whether you ever told Henry what I knew about Seena."

"Yes, I did."

"What did he say?"

"He knew it already. She had told him herself."

"Afterwards, of course?"

Violet nodded. "But Faith, this is one secret we really must keep always. Did you tell your father and mother?"

"No. I wasn't sure I should."

"I'm glad. Though of course they would never have told either. You know I have a—a feeling about Henry and Seena."

"So have I."

"And so long as the town believes he really saved her life they won't be too critical about his seeing her so often."

"That's true. I hadn't thought of it. Oh, Vi, hasn't it been a strange summer? Father has often said that in all the years he's lived in Ladykirk the one thing he has never suffered from is *monotony!*"

They smiled at this, and then grew serious as they recounted the dramatic events scattered through the summer days. When Violet rose to go she looked at her friend hesitatingly.

"Faith," she said, coloring a little, "Philip Haversham, the editor I've spoken of, is coming at the end of the month."

"Here, to Ladykirk! *To see you?*"

"It seems so."

"Oh, Vi! And you've kept this all to yourself!"

"Well, you've been pretty secretive too, haven't you?"

"I suppose so. It seems strange that we could always talk together so freely when we had nothing really to tell!

But I never *dreamed* things had gone so far with you. I thought it was all just a pleasant correspondence. Oh, I'm so surprised and excited! Do you know what he looks like?"

"Yes, I have his picture."

"Of all the romantic things! Why, you've taken my breath away!" She went over to Violet and put her arms about her.

"When there is something really settled you'll tell me, won't you?"

"You know I will."

"And so will I," Faith answered. "Do you remember when we talked about love that day in the orchard?"

"Yes."

"I still feel the same way about it."

"I too," said Violet.

Then, because they were young and full of the excitement of happiness and hope, they laughed together as they moved toward the front door. Mr. Lyall, seeing them, called to his wife.

"Come on, Mary. Let's all see Violet home."

So the four of them sauntered slowly along the quiet street under the stars. As they neared the Carpenter house Violet remembered about Mag and told the facts as Katie had reported them.

"Oh, that's too bad," Mr. Lyall said. "I'll go to see her the first thing in the morning. Poor old Mag!"

"And I'll go along," Mrs. Lyall added at once, "and take a few dainties to tempt her appetite. I don't suppose she's able to do much about meals."

"Katie has been taking food but I'm sure yours will be very welcome."

"I'll see Dr. Faraday too," Mr. Lyall said, "and get him to look in and check on her. And thanks, Violet, for telling me."

On the evening of the party the local guests were the first to arrive. As Violet had predicted, Seena came, with Henry, who made a noticeable point of sitting beside her. She was quiet, her eyes had ceased their roving, and the contentment, already noted, lay now upon her softened features. When Mike finally came his attitude was anything but loverlike on the surface.

"Hello, Violet," he said heartily. "Gee, it's nice to be

here again! How are you, Ninian, you old bum! Lucy, I declare you're prettier than ever!" He moved on around the circle making friendly comments as he went. And then, without seeming effort, he became the life of the occasion. Dressed in Katie's sunbonnet and apron he made the hit of the evening in "Charades"; he arranged the new trick of having the four smallest girls lift the heaviest man in a chair by their finger tips as they released and then held their breath to the count; and when the singing began he was the one who kept thinking of more and more songs as his tenor rose above the other voices.

All in all it was a very gay evening, and a late one as the guests seemed reluctant to go. When the last good-byes had been called from the gate, however, Mike turned in silence to the porch and sat down beside Violet in the familiar swing. When he did speak it was with a question.

"Who is he, Violet? The other man."

She told him.

"How did you meet?" he asked.

"We haven't—yet."

He turned quickly. "You mean you've never seen him? That all the—the courtship has been done by letter?"

"That's true, Mike."

He gave a low whistle, and then, "Violet, will you promise me something?"

"If I can."

"It's just this. When you meet this fellow, if he's not what you expected, will you let me know?"

"Yes. But please don't count on that. I think I know him very well indeed."

"Well, I hope you won't be disappointed. Or rather, of course, I hope you *will* be, only that's not nice. I'll try to be unselfish. Do you mind if we just sit quiet here for a while?"

"No, Mike."

"As I've told you, this is the most peaceful place I've ever been. Ladykirk!" he repeated. "I'll never forget it, just as I'll never forget you."

The swing moved gently beneath them and there was no sound but the crickets in the vines. At last he spoke again.

"You mustn't feel too badly about me. I want to be honest. If you could love me I'd ask nothing more in this

249

world, and I'm sure if we married I'd never even *see* another woman the rest of my life. But when you can't care for me, then I don't want you to feel I'll go broken-hearted forever. I'm a sort of happy-go-lucky fellow. I'll try to get over this, and some day I may meet another girl. . . ."

"But *of course* you will, Mike!"

"Well, we'll see. But one thing you must believe. I'll always have the memory of this summer and of you in my heart. It all came to me when I needed it, and I have sense enough to be grateful, no matter how it has turned out. Do you know the picture of you I'll think of oftenest?"

"No," Violet said, her throat full.

"That night at church when you stood up in the choir and sang the song that made everybody wipe their eyes. That's worth remembering. Well," he got up slowly, "I know it's late and I'd better be on my way. I promised you I wouldn't get mushy and I'd better leave while I can make it good."

Violet stood up. "Oh, Mike, it's been wonderful knowing you. I—I do like you so *very* much."

"Ah! Ah! Be careful now, or I may get out of bounds." He held out his hand. "Good-bye, and the best of everything to you!"

He laid his cheek for a moment on the back of her hand and she could feel his lips against it. Then he hurried down the walk. At the gate he turned.

"Thanks for a fine evening. Lots of fun," he called in his usual voice. Then he cranked the car and was gone.

Violet sat down again upon the swing, her cheeks wet. *Dear, dear Mike,* she kept repeating to herself. But after a long while her tears became dry. She looked off into the night, thinking of another young man who would soon be sitting here beside her. And this time—she smiled.

It was the next Thursday, as the little sewing group sat on the wide back porch of the manse with their crocheting and embroidery, that Faith came back from the telephone with a puzzled face.

"That was Father," she said. "I don't know where he was calling from but the message was for you, Vi. He wants you to go back to Mag Parks as quickly as you can."

"Wants *me?*" Violet echoed. "You're sure he didn't mean Katie?"

"No, it was you. He knew you were here, and he asked you to please hurry."

"Of course," Violet said, dropping her work. She bade farewell to the girls and started down the street as fast as she could walk. The message, though, surprised her. Perhaps Mr. Lyall had tried to reach Katie and she was out. But why herself? And why the need for haste? She hurried along Main Street, turned to the right and almost ran down the little hill which led to a small squatters' patch behind the town where the poorest citizens dwelt— Nappy Newton and his like. The farthest shanty was Mag's home. When she reached it, the door was open into the single room with its coal range on one end and the bed at the other. Then she saw Mr. Lyall beckoning to her as he sat close to where Mag lay, one of his hands holding her big, knotted one.

"Here she is, Mrs. Parks. Here is Violet. Now you can tell her what you want to say."

Violet came close, shocked at what she saw. Mag's head was raised on the pillows, a deadly pallor upon her face; her eyes were half closed and her sunken cheeks moved in and out with her quick, shallow breathing.

"Mag," Mr. Lyall called, as though the familiar name might rouse her, "here is Violet!"

Mag's eyes suddenly flew open.

"Vi'let," she said between the quick breaths, "I ain't got long . . . I had to tell you . . . it was me took the bird . . . that day Katie went over to . . . Mary Jackson's an' you went off in the buggy. . . ."

She stopped and seemed to slip back into the stupor, then she roused again. "I didn't *steal* it, Vi'let. I never stole nothin' . . . I just borrowed it for I liked it so well. . . . I meant to put it back . . ."

Her voice all at once grew a little stronger. "I did take it up three times . . . but I never could get shed of Katie to put it in the bookcase. Then I thought . . . I'd keep it through the fall for comp'ny . . . you know when it gets dark so soon an' the wind sounds lonesome in the chimley. . . . I never *stole* it, Vi'let. I just liked it so . . ."

Her eyes turned toward Mr. Lyall as she gripped his hand. "You think they'll understand . . . about that . . . Up There?"

"Everything is understood up there, Mag. Don't worry. Where *is* the nightingale?"

"In the . . . green . . . tea can," she said in a whisper.

Violet went quickly over to the shelves beside the stove where Mag's cracked dishes were ranged with her pots and pans and various shabby receptacles. She took down the tea canister and removed the lid. Inside was the leather box! She took it out with unsteady fingers and carried it over to the bed.

"It's all right, Mag. I have it now, and I'm glad you've enjoyed it."

Mag's breath was very faint, all but guttering out as a candle in the wind.

"You'd better go on, Violet," Mr. Lyall said in a low voice. "It won't be long now."

"I'll stay," she said.

They watched in silence. Then suddenly they saw Mag's lips move.

"Play . . . it."

Violet guessed rather than heard the words. She took the tortoise-shell box from the outer one, wound it quickly and pressed the spring, then held it near Mag's face.

In the instant the nightingale rose and began to sing. When it disappeared beneath the golden filagree, once more Violet touched the spring, and again the poor room was filled with melody. Mag's eyes suddenly opened wide in unnatural brightness, then closed. Before this song was ended, her breathing had ceased, and Mr. Lyall had bowed his head.

Violet could not see clearly as he came around from the other side of the bed.

"You're a brave girl," he said quietly. "I'm glad you stayed."

"Do you think she heard it?"

"I'm sure she did."

They walked to the door.

"You go on, now," he said. "I'll stay here till Dr. Faraday comes. He was in earlier and said there was nothing more he could do for her. She was really saved great suffering by going now as she did. Would you mind stopping at his office on your way home to tell him? He'll let Mr. Hart know.—And so the great mystery is solved at last!" he added.

"It couldn't have been in a better way," Violet said huskily.

"That's what I've been thinking. But who would ever have guessed the truth? I'm glad for you, my dear, and thanks again."

The pavement seemed indistinct to Violet as she reached Main Street. She stopped for a moment at Dr. Faraday's and then for a few brief words with Mrs. Coates. All the way back home the uneven flagstones moved as in a mist before her and her feet often stumbled. Once in her own house she went to the bookshelves and placed the leather box where it had always stood; then, thankful that Katie was apparently over at Mary Jackson's, she sat down in her mother's chair, trembling. It was a hard experience she had just been through and all the details of it were still vividly impressed upon her senses. The reality of death, whether it took place in a comfortable bed-chamber or in a one-roomed shack, was the same, she thought, and left the witnesses shaken. She leaned her head back and closed her eyes.

But after a time, during which her mind had tenderly, as it were, rung the passing bell for Mag, it began slowly to focus upon the return of the nightingale. Ever since its disappearance three months before, her heart, in spite of the new joy that filled it, had held, deep down, a poignant sense of loss. Now, with the restoration of her treasure, with all its actual beauty and its symbolic meaning for her, this hurt was healed. Great waves of relief and thankfulness broke over her. When at last she heard a step in the kitchen she was able to run out calling, "Katie! Katie! I've got it back!" before she told the other sober piece of news.

Oh, there was a feast of talk in the village that night! When all had first paid their respects to Mag in the time-honored, and in this case truthful, observation: "Ah, well, she's now *at rest*, poor soul!" they turned with zest to the solution of the mystery that had for so long baffled them. It was now natural and deliciously stimulating to review all the details in connection with the various suspects: Mr. Smith, Joe Hicks and young Oliver! Nothing was overlooked of all that had passed; nothing was omitted. Those who up to the end had still cherished doubts of the innocence of any one of them now gave way

253

gracefully before the truth. When all had been said, there was the same kindly, elegiac comment repeated again and again from one end of the village to another: "To think all the time it was Mag! Well, she's *at rest* now."

When the last caller had left the Carpenter house that night Violet wrote two letters, one to Mr. Smith and one to Mr. Huntley. She would not tell Philip until he came —next week.

It hardly seemed possible the time was so near. Preparations within and without the house went on apace. The flower beds were freshly weeded, and young Oliver, assured now and beaming behind his thick glasses, cut the grass, cleaned the stable, shined up the buggy and would take nothing for it! Violet had decided at the last minute to paint two of the porch chairs, while Katie, almost in a frenzy, was turning out all the kitchen cupboards—an activity Violet had declared foolish and useless but from which Katie would not be deterred.

"There's no tellin' about men. They're such a blunderin' lot, you never know what they'll be gettin' into."

The day before the guest was expected was fraught with tension. Katie was sure she had made a mistake in the measurement of her veal-loaf ingredients, Violet was afraid her chocolate cake was going to *fall*, both of which fears ultimately proved to be groundless. There was, however, a tiny scorched spot on Violet's best pink voile, freshly ironed! After some bad moments a slight re-allocation of the gathers was found to conceal it. Worst of all was the fact that the newly painted porch chairs did not seem entirely dry! Two hours in the afternoon sun at last "fettled them," as Katie put it. So the day wore on, with its small anxieties, to the shutting of the evening. Then, as Violet prepared to go upstairs to her room, Katie, with a strange expression on her face, came and stood before her.

"Something's just hit me," she said, "like a clap of thunder, an' the wonder is it didn't strike me long ago. Here I've been so throng gettin' things in order I never even give a thought . . ."

She wiped her eyes and Violet was startled.

"Why, Katie, what in the world is the matter?"

"Well," said Katie, "when Henry Martin was comin' round I never fashed myself about it at all for if you'd

254

taken him, and glad I am you didn't, but if you had, he'd just have hung up his hat here an' nothin' to it. An' even this Mike was from nearby as you might say. But this young editor fellah he's from away in *New York* an' that's where his work is, an' it just now struck me what if he's wantin' *to take you there?*"

"Katie, you mustn't talk about things like that. I don't know what Mr. Haversham may . . . He's just coming for a visit," she ended lamely.

"Tut!" said Katie. "I can add two an' two as well as the next one. If he's comin' all this length he means business. An' what I'm sayin' is I'm not leavin' you, mind. Wherever you go, I'm goin'. I've done all but born you. You're like my own child, an' . . ."

"Katie, Katie," Violet said gently, "I don't know whether I'll ever leave here or not, but if I do, surely you know I'd take you with me!"

"Well, well," said Katie, her emotion making her voice harsh, "it's just as good to have things settled aforehand. An' one more thing I've got to say to you. I'd never leave Simon behind me, the poor beast."

Violet laughed, which prevented tears. She went over to the old woman and put her arms about her.

"Simon too," she said. "The three of us belong together."

When Violet was at last in bed she lay relaxed, a vast contentment replacing the nervous excitement of the day. The house, from top to bottom, was immaculate, all the curtains hanging white, all the furniture polished to shining. More than this, she realized that there was in the old rooms a certain distinction, which Philip would appreciate. She pictured him looking eagerly over the book titles as they ranged against the long living-room wall. He was sure to find many friends there.

But wonderful above all else was the fact that now, resting on the faded envelope behind the guarding volumes, the nightingale was in its accustomed place. She thought deeply of the part it had played in the life of the town that summer. Perhaps no one else would be fully aware of the connection, but she herself knew that because of it Joe and Amanda Hicks were going to have their longed-for child, that young Oliver Coates had achieved his boyish heart's desire, and that poor, forlorn Mag Parks, the real culprit, had lived for a time with beauty and

255

died, as it were, on the wings of song! When this was all true who could wish that the circumstances of the treasure's disappearance had been otherwise? Not she, certainly. But oh, the joy of its return, and at this very time!

The night outside was full of stars, which boded well for a fair day tomorrow. A small breeze blew in the window along with the peaceful iterance of the crickets' song, as Violet at last fell asleep.

It was four o'clock the next afternoon when Katie, her hair marvelously crimped and a highly starched white apron over her best black calico, heard a firm step on the front porch and flew to the door. A tall young man stood smiling at her.

"You're Katie!" he exclaimed, "and you're just as I imagined you!"

And Katie, looking upon him, loved him.

"Well, well, come away in. Vi'let's in the back yard cuttin' sweet peas. She's got the house full enough but she would have a few more. I told her, mind, she ought to stay in for you might be comin' any minute."

"May I go on through and find her there?" Philip asked eagerly, setting down his bag.

"Come along, then," Katie said, leading the way to the kitchen.

Violet heard him as he came down the back steps and reached the garden. She turned, letting fall the shears and flowers. For a long second they stared at each other, and then, as on one impulse, rushed together. When they met, his arms enfolded her and his lips pressed hard upon hers. After all, they were not strangers.

Katie, watching misty-eyed, saw it all from the kitchen window; Mary Jackson, coming along the orchard path stopped transfixed at the spectacle; Mrs. Hummel and Mrs. Dunn were both witnesses from their back yards. But none of this mattered. For to Violet and Philip there was all at once around them the sound of mighty rushing waters, while high and clear above them—a nightingale sang!